ANGELS FROM CALDERA

HOW PEACE CAME TO PLANET EARTH

MALCOLM McFALL

outskirtspress

DENVER, COLORADO

Outskirts Press, Inc.
http://www.outskirtspress.com

ISBN: 978-1-4787-7431-0

Outskirts Press and the "OP" logo are trademarks belonging to Outskirts Press, Inc.

PRINTED IN THE UNITED STATES OF AMERICA

PROLOGUE

DECEMBER 12, 1910

Ernest Appleton always figured death would come suddenly in a crevasse or an avalanche—not like this. For thirty-three days and nights they'd been pounded by a storm unlike any he'd known. His previous Antarctic expedition had been a disappointment; this one would end with nine well-preserved corpses a hard day from the Pole.

He loosened the tent flap and stared out at the whirling whiteness while he made up his mind. At length he secured the flap, opened his journal to December 12, 1910 and wrote:

My dearest Abigail,

I'm proud of the men. Each has faced death with courage. I've decided to fight through the storm to the Pole. For ten years I've lived to attain that objective and refuse to die without fighting for it. I'll always love you.

Ernest

He stuck his journal back in his knapsack and dug out a leather pouch. Hoarded morsels tumbled into his glove liner. He chose hardtack first and saved the jerky and chocolate. The hard unsalted biscuits were plain, but substantial. They made him thirsty and he took several sips from the canteen next to his knee. While he ate the jerky, he prayed for the strength to wage one last fight. They'd finished off the food after weeks of short rations and were down to the last of the kerosene. Unremitting winds lashed their tent, pierced the canvas, and attacked the flame in their lamp, seemingly bent on snuffing out even that meager source of warmth. The last cache of food and fuel was so far behind them, Appleton knew a let-up now wouldn't help.

They'd fought their way to the threshold, but the laurels due them and the Royal Geographical Society would fall to a more fortunate group in the future. He headed a British expedition, but dual citizenship and his home in Boston made Appleton a Yank among Brits. He conjured an image of his wife reading in the parlor with their son playing nearby and he spoke to her in his thought: You were right, Abigail, a good safe structural engineering career in Boston sounds damned good right now. While I'm at it, I also admit this God-forsaken place has storms I couldn't imagine when I boasted that weather couldn't kill me.

He'd eaten nothing in days and for weeks only enough to ward off starvation. Across from him, Longwell muttered in delirium, "Louise . . . take Tommy home before . . ." Hildebrecht's moaning had deteriorated to a whimper. Edwards was dead. Before he died, Appleton had transcribed his touching farewell to his parents and brothers, unbuttoned his tunic, and inserted the note over their youngest member's heart. He'd stopped breathing hours later.

Appleton's feet didn't ache, unless he moved. Twice he'd lanced the lump on his right foot and the frostbitten toes on his left. Puss of numerous hues still oozed from the holes. The blister fluid on his right heel had frozen and ached like a bone chip lodged on the back of his foot.

Finally, he ate the last square of chocolate, rich dark chocolate, and gave into thoughts of his impending death. Better than dying in bed of old age, he thought. He knew in his soul he couldn't have done better or tried harder. Some things just don't work out. Grimly, he pulled on his facemask and goggles for the last time. With a deep groan he forced himself onto his hands and feet and wavered there until his head quit swimming. Moving with slow determination, he tightened the hood of his fur-lined parka, plunged his glove liners into fur-lined sealskin mittens, grabbed his ice axe, took a deep breath, and stepped out into the gale. The minus seventy-degree tempest stabbed him like thousands of steel needles hurled on the wind, piercing layers of hide, wool, and cotton. Staggering in the swirling chaos, he fought to stay upright, then a mighty blast slammed him backwards over the tent rope.

After considerable exertion he was upright again. Before setting out, he wiped off his goggles and strained through the whiteout to see the other two tents, but couldn't. Memories flashed. He saw his jovial crew loading the ship in Santiago nine weeks before, and pictured a warm joyful reunion in heaven. Uncovering the compass on his wrist he turned due south and staggered off toward the Pole.

His frozen sealskin mukluks were torture devices, but increasing numbness gradually anesthetized his feet. After trudging less than a mile, he tumbled headlong into a deep powder-filled depression. With nothing to push down on, the struggle to get out exhausted him. Finally, he rolled onto hard ice and lay there until his breathing stabilized. In his mind he looked down on himself, an ant-like being sprawled on the 13,000-foot-thick ice of the south polar plateau, gasping for breath in the thin air.

Back on his feet, he concentrated on movement. In time with each stride, he said the Ninety-first, then the Twenty-third Psalm, all the poems and hymns he knew, and began to establish a semblance of his old relentless Antarctic slog. Bent at the waist, eyes on his feet, he pushed on and on.

After five miles, starvation-induced lightheadedness caused him to stagger and fall repeatedly. He'd now lost all feeling in his extremities and was unable to keep his balance in the chaotic winds.

A mile further, he stumbled and fell into another snow pit and lay there, gasping. When he gathered himself to fight his way out, his body barely responded. With all the strength he could muster, he drove his knees under him and then attempted to lunge toward solid footing. But his maximum effort amounted to little more than a feeble jerk. He had nothing left and realized the long fight was over. It surprised him that the end of the ordeal brought a strange sense of relief. There was no fear and for the first time in months he wasn't cold.

Snow soon covered his body. Not long after, sleep settled over him and his consciousness conjured up a dream of Orville and Wilber Wright landing nearby, picking him up and flying him off to safety. Then, after his rescue, his dreams turned to fishing with his son off his dock at home. Suddenly, an aberrant light interrupted his dream. He roused himself from sleep and watched the light evolve into a sunny vision—a beach and a tropical lagoon. It was dreamlike, but much more vivid than any dream he'd ever had. A clear blue sky glistened overhead and a warm breeze caressed him.

A small female relaxed in a low chair on the sand next to the lagoon. She wasn't human, but strangely beautiful with short buff-colored fur, slanted eyes, and pointed ears set high on her head. She turned toward him and spoke, in English, words he heard inside his thought, "Allow me to introduce myself, Ernest. My name is Hamama. I understand you're a bridge engineer."

It made him smile to think this exotic creature knew that about him. "Yes," he responded mentally, "bridges are my specialty."

"Would you come and help us build an important bridge?"

He opened his eyes and stared at the crystals crushed against his goggles and said, "I have no more strength, Hamama. If you can find me and get me out of this storm, I'll help you build your bridge."

CHAPTER ONE

PRESIDENT DAVID ANDREWS
AUGUST 10, 2034

President David Andrews ignored the warnings of imminent meltdown. Instead, he watched a digital worm inching its way across the heart rate axis labeled 185 beats per minute on his stationary bike monitor. Sweat dripped from his chin like a slow leak. His lungs screamed for respite. Finally, his leg muscles approaching refusal, the digital worm reached the vertical sixty second axis.

With a gasp of relief his chin dropped to his chest and he brought his heart rate down to 120 beats per minute. Then he straightened up, toweled off, and re-started the morning briefing tape of world news in his headphones. A glance at his watch told him he had forty minutes until his heavily scheduled day would begin at seven.

Centered on a twelve-foot-tall arched window trimmed with heavy wood molding, his bright orange exercise bike overlooked a small formal garden with a fountain glowing in the dawn light. The president's workout room in the White House residence had deep green carpeting, pale yellow walls, crème colored trim, and crystal chandeliers. To the right of the arched window, a row of Nautilus machines stood ready for workouts on alternate mornings. To the left, white racks of chrome free weights lined the wall.

Of all the American presidents, Andrews was the tallest and most athletic. His All-American basketball career at Princeton was well-documented. His successes in international cross country skiing were less well known, but more satisfying to the president.

As with most of his news briefings, the volatile Islamist government in Islamabad dominated. In the years leading up to 2030, the U.S. was aware of the instability boiling under the surface in Pakistan. Why, he wondered, hadn't more been done to avert the coup? Andrews thought back over the four year religious brawl that had raged in Pakistan since the overthrow of the secular government, as mullahs with private armies fought for regional control.

Special Agent Adrian Archer sat near the door directly behind him. Andrews studied his stout frame reflected in the arched window. His immense strength strained the seams of his blue blazer. Adrian had come to his security detail from a twelve-year stint as offensive left tackle for the Dallas Cowboys. Now his strength and courage were dedicated to the protection of the nation's "quarterback."

Seated in the hall outside the exercise room was Chief Warrant Officer Clyde Davis, with the "football." The nuclear launch codes stayed near the president night and day.

Suddenly, his chief of staff's reflection appeared in the window, briskly approaching the glass door of the workout room. Special Agent Archer stood and unlocked the door. The party was over. Andrews pulled his headphones down around his neck and slowed the pedals.

Without turning he asked, "What's up, Hank?"

"The Brits bagged one of Ahmad's people boarding a flight out of Heathrow two hours ago, Mr. President. We're meeting in the Situation Room at seven."

"What do we know, so far?"

"Roger didn't have details when he called. See you downstairs."

"Call downstairs and let'em know I need some toast and coffee after I shower."

⋙ ⟨◉⟩ ⋘

At six-fifty, Andrews headed downstairs to the Situation Room under the West Wing. Once inside the door, he saw his six closest advisors seated around the mahogany conference table illumined by light from recessed fixtures overhead.

The six sat in stony silence—the kind of silence that usually accompanied bad news. Two wore uniforms—one a four-star general and the other a four-star admiral. The three in suits, were his head of intelligence, national security adviser, and secretary of defense. The sixth, Vice President Joe Vandenberg, attended meetings by satellite downlink and his image appeared on a large TV monitor at the far end of the table to the president's right angled toward the group. The down lights illumined the mahogany conference table and the fronts of the seated men. The rest of the room faded to semi-darkness. Andrews noticed his pulse quicken a bit in anticipation as he sat down. The faces were so grim.

The television monitor framed the larger-than-life image of a broad-shouldered man in a dark suit with angular features and a flattop haircut. Vice President Vandenberg joined them from his NORAD operations center inside Cheyenne Mountain near Colorado Springs. "Morning Joe," Andrews said to the two dimensional image. "Even earlier for you, isn't it?" While he spoke he studied the face of the vice president. He'd never known anyone more different than himself. Joe Vandenberg was a natural warrior who only saw one side of most issues, but the former major general had proven himself the world's most effective counter-terrorist.

"Time doesn't mean much when you live where there's no day or night, Mr. President."

As Vandenberg spoke, Andrews sadly acknowledged the level of peril abroad in the world that necessitated a shadow executive branch of government holed up inside a mountain. "We all appreciate the sacrifices you make to insure continuity, Joe."

"It's a strange life we lead in here, but I know it's important. I'm anxious to hear what Roger has for us."

"Okay, Roger," Andrews turned to his head of intelligence, "was that the hint of a grin I just detected?"

Roger Christianson was pleased he could report a break in the long drought of information. "The old man the British captured this morning confirmed that Rashid's son, Mahmoud Ahmad, has solidified his control of World Jihad and has gained access to the Ahmad family fortune."

"Any word of reprisal?" Andrews asked.

On a tip in early June, the Counter Terrorism Corps had killed Mahmoud's father, Rashid Raza Ahmad, the world's preeminent terrorist, in a raid on a World Jihad compound outside Alexandria, Egypt. Andrews had immediately ordered every U.S. embassy, base, and ship around the world to full alert. Executives and foreign service personnel who couldn't be sent home were kept under heavy guard. In their efforts to thwart the expected reprisal, they'd milked their Middle Eastern sources dry, but until today had uncovered nothing.

National Security Adviser Nicolas Moore answered Andrews' question, "The old terrorist the British captured this morning says they're targeting New York City, but they haven't been able to pry specifics out of him. He may not know details. This is one of Ahmad's inner-circle who thought their leader's son was too young and hot-headed to take over, so they fought him for control of the organization. When Mahmoud finally won out, the father's cronies fled and haven't been heard from since."

While Moore spoke, Andrews' mind flashed back to the Pakistani coup in 2030. In the aftermath, several fundamentalist factions cobbled together the world's first Islamist state with a nuclear arsenal. World Jihad, the unacknowledged terrorist arm of the government, was then headed by Rashid Raza Ahmad, the scion of a wealthy family of smugglers from Peshawar, with Saudi connections.

Through the years, Andrews had developed something akin to admiration for the skill and daring of the head terrorist. Until his recent death, Ahmad had proven highly effective at raising money across the Muslim world and in wreaking havoc against U.S. and European assets. For years he'd operated from the western tribal lands, the Hindu Kush, and the caves along the Afghan border, a refuge for terrorists since the days of Alexander the Great.

Andrews turned back to the television image of his vice president. Vandenberg's hard eyes stared back. He still looked like an army general in civvies. "What's your reaction to Mahmoud taking over, Joe? And how do we stop them from hitting New York?" Vandenberg always made Andrews feel wishy-washy. There were no gray areas with him. He was always sure what had to be done and his solutions usually involved high-explosives and dead bodies.

Vandenberg's big voice broke in on Andrews' thoughts, "The old man was a lot smarter than his turd-brained son. We should blast'em tonight, Mr. President. Put some heat on the skinny bastard. We'll derail this attack, but we should hit the bunkers targeted by our recon satellite last night and not wait for them to attack."

General "Shoop" Mitchell, Counter Terrorism Corps commander, sitting to Andrew's left registered strong disagreement with a deep gravelly voice, "We have no confirmation from Langley on those latest images. My Special Ops team on the ground in Afghanistan is urging no action against those Pashtun bunkers at this time, Mr. President."

Vandenberg's face turned from stern to angry as his nemesis

rebutted his suggestion. His growing antipathy toward Andrews had been triggered by his initial fury over Andrews' promotion of Mitchell to head the Counter Terrorism Corps, despite his strong objections.

Secretary of Defense Martin Schrader chimed in, "We can't risk enraging the Pashtuns without confirmation of a World Jihad presence in those bunkers."

Andrews observed the flare-up between the vice president, who had built the Counter Terrorism Corps, and his two key military appointments in the three years since Joe left the army for politics. Martin and Shoop were his guys. He almost enjoyed the sparks they caused with Vandenberg.

Joe's complexion deepened in color as Schrader agreed with Mitchell and he mumbled, "How far would we have gotten in our war against terrorism, if we'd had to wait for you bozos to green light anything?"

Mitchell whirled and glared at the televised image, but before he could growl his rejoinder, Andrews intervened, "Gentlemen, we're facing a serious threat this morning that demands focus and complete cooperation."

Andrews supported Vandenberg's ferocity, but felt the need to constantly restrain him, "We'll hit any target you can sell me on, Joe; but we're not attacking the Pashtun villagers who've taken refuge in those old Taliban bunkers." He noted the clenching jaw muscles and the glare that always accompanied any sense Vandenberg had of being thwarted.

The door opened and a tall Hispanic member of the kitchen staff rolled a cart in with coffee and pastries. While the white uniformed young man carefully served each seated figure, Andrews sensed the heat in the room subside. He laced his fingers together and studied the faces around the table. He deeply appreciated the dedication and talent each brought to his job. Since the death of Rashid Raza

Ahmad, they'd all worked themselves to exhaustion to intercept the anticipated retaliation.

As he sipped the rich aromatic coffee, Andrews thought back over the evolution of the Counter Terrorism Corps which had grown out of the Delta Strike Force as international terrorism expanded. One of the keys to the Counter Terrorism Corps' success was maintaining a worldwide network of highly paid informants. Solid leads were worth millions. Through informants, double agents, spy satellites, and with General "G.I. Joe" Vandenberg ramrodding the worldwide effort, terrorists had been driven deep underground.

With all our high-tech tools, we still can't stop drug shipments getting into the Big Apple, Andrews thought. What makes us think we can we prevent a terrorist strike? He decided to start the discussion with something they knew, "Run back through what we've got on Mahmoud Ahmad, Roger."

Roger Christianson opened the folder, "Twenty-nine years old. A blend of modern tastes: western women, nightlife, and gambling, stirred in with a thick blend of ancient Islamic dogma."

Andrews listened to his intelligence czar and thought of the hypocrisy he'd encountered in the Muslim world. He recalled a trip when he was in the Senate, boarding a private Saudi jet returning to Riyadh from a shopping junket in Paris and observing the transformation of the women on board from stunning avant garde stylishness to completely veiled non-entities.

Christianson continued, "The young man is highly intelligent, but has little formal education. Growing up, Mahmoud lived in bunkers watching his father lead a worldwide terrorist effort against the West. In recent years he's been the organization's point man, recruiting and keeping their far-flung organization on task. He considered his father overly conservative. Where his father was patient and thorough, the son tends to be brash and spontaneous. Where the father was a recluse who trusted a handful of close associates, the son has hundreds of close contacts throughout the terrorist world."

"Sounds like we were better off with the old man running things," Andrews remarked.

"The lucky little punk should be dead." Vandenberg scowled. "We had him dead in our sights on a dirt road over the Hindu Kush, but the damned drone misfired."

"Wonder what he's been doing for the last two months?" Shoop Mitchell asked. "We expected an immediate reprisal after we killed his old man."

"It must have taken time for him to take control of the organization," Christianson responded. "We know the father's inner circle fought hard for control and there's a lot of loyalty to those older guys."

Andrews interrupted, "What approach are we taking in New York City, Roger?"

"We're putting New York on a high state of alert. The FBI, state and local law enforcement, plus the National Guard will all be coordinated by the CTC. Nuclear Emergency Search Teams are expanding their radius of operation and have deployed their latest gamma ray and neutron flux detectors throughout the city."

"Any indication Mahmoud has gotten his hands on a nuclear device, Roger?" Vandenberg asked.

"Nothing specific," Christianson responded. "But we know World Jihad has been trying for years to buy or steal a warhead. Pakistan has at least fifty, but to date they've been unwilling to let loose of any."

Andrews closed his eyes momentarily and envisioned Manhattan Island in the aftermath of a nuclear attack. The picture in his mind, he realized, was a facsimile of the famous photo of Hiroshima in 1945.

He opened his eyes and glanced at Vandenberg. Completely safe inside his granite mountain, Joe was oblivious to the nuclear peril those in Washington D.C. dealt with subconsciously every day. Andrews didn't like him, but he knew his presidency was because of him. His election had become a foregone conclusion when Vandenberg accepted the second spot on his ticket three years before. The killings, kidnappings, and bombings had so diminished under G.I. Joe's watch that Americans were starting to travel again and do business abroad. It made people feel safer to have the top terrorist-fighter in the world standing next to their president.

Andrews stood to end the meeting and said, "We've got a much different situation this time around. Back in '01, the Bush administration had no credible advance warning of that attack on New York City. This time the enemy has tipped us off. Let's throw everything we've got into this. Give me hourly updates."

On the way back to his private office, Angie O'Leary, Andrews' personal assistant, strode rapidly beside him as his long legs ate up the long hall, "What's next, Angie?" he asked.

The top of Angie's rich auburn hair didn't reach Andrews' shoulder. Her glasses were pointed on each side and had a government-issue look about them. Her earth-toned sweater and skirt were plain, but fitted. "You're fully booked today, Mr. President. The schedule is on your desk. You leave on Marine One at four this afternoon for the Master Teachers' convention at the Waldorf in New York City."

Andrews walked in silence until they reached his private office. New York City of all places, he thought. Angie stopped beside her desk and finally Andrews responded, "We're mounting a major effort this morning to stop a potential attack on New York City, Angie. News of it will hit the networks by noon. We need people to stay calm in the Big Apple. My being there should help lessen their fear."

In Newark, New Jersey, Natasha Cheatam knocked on the principal's open door. "I got your message and came straight from work, Mrs. Clements."

Without looking up, Elizabeth Clements held up a finger signaling her to wait while she finished her phone call. Natasha studied a new photo collage of the previous year at Central High spread across the wall opposite the windows. Mrs. Clements and her digital camera had recorded hundreds of important moments in her worn-out school located in the toughest part of Newark. It was a wall covered with kids having fun. Natasha recognized two mud-soaked football players holding a trophy triumphantly aloft, a boy and girl mugging for the camera while they painted over graffiti on Clean-up Day, happy kids decorating for the prom, shots from a school play, three girls hanging a sign across the main hall during Class elections, and a cheerleader getting a sponge in the face at a spirit squad car wash.

An orderly stack of legal folders occupied the right side of the principal's desk. The rest was clean. Even for summer school, she dressed in chief executive style; her navy suit jacket hung behind her on a wooden hanger. Despite the institutional furnishings, Natasha considered the principal's office comfortable and inviting.

The slender middle-aged black woman seated at the desk finished her call and looked up, "Come in, Natasha, and meet Katherine Larson, a roommate from my undergraduate days at Rutgers." She directed her next words to a person Natasha couldn't see from the doorway. "Natasha's on her way to an appointment in the financial aid office at NYU."

As she entered, Natasha looked at Ms. Larson but responded to Mrs. Clements, "Mama made me cancel that appointment in New York until the terrorist threat is over." Natasha shook Ms. Larson's hand, "Pleased to meet you, Miss Larson. I'm grateful for the scholarship Rutgers offered me."

The black middle-aged visitor stood and looked calmly into Natasha's eyes as she took her hand. She seemed as together as Mrs. Clements. Her expressive eyes were full of life and her warm smile came easily. Natasha saw none of the insecurity and heartache ever present in her own mama's eyes. Ms. Larson's handshake was firm and evoked a woman completely comfortable inside her dark skin. Natasha liked meeting another confirmation, besides Mrs. Clements, that her life goal was attainable. Looking into Ms. Larson's confident eyes she thought, Someday I'll have the kind of easy confidence you exude. Ms. Larson said, "Elizabeth and I graduated together from Rutgers, Natasha, but for the past twenty years, I've worked in the Admissions Office at Princeton."

Natasha smiled and said, "The slave driver over there made me complete that monster application and the financial aid stuff, even though I told her I wasn't going to any rich white peoples' school. But I'll do anything to get her off my back."

Ms. Larson smiled, "I know what a relentless pain she can be. I drove up here today, Natasha, to ask you to reconsider your decision."

Natasha stared at her, stunned at her words, "You mean you really think I could be happy there?"

Ms. Larson nodded, "I had similar reservations before I accepted a position in their Admissions Office. Elizabeth says you had a bad experience on our campus."

Natasha averted her eyes and nodded. The memory returned of her first experience as a rank minority trying to live with hundreds of white girls at a summer basketball camp.

At length she said, "Those white girls totally ignored me. It was unbelievable. My roommate wouldn't look at me, much less talk to me. I wanted out of there and had a hard time sticking it out."

Ms. Larson said, "You know that camp wasn't Princeton, Natasha. It was a privately run camp just using our facilities."

"I know," Natasha said, staring at her shoes, "but it's not only that. I can survive being ignored, but I know I couldn't keep up. Academically, those prep school kids must be years ahead of me."

"Natasha, Elizabeth has shown me some of your work, your grades and scores. You write as well as any incoming Princeton freshman."

It pleased Natasha to hear that, but didn't overcome her doubts. Her whole life she'd assumed the disadvantages of growing up in Newark would severely limit her life, no matter how hard she tried.

"Yes, but . . ." Natasha teared up as she admitted, "I'm still afraid I'd fail."

Both older women looked at each other knowingly, then back at Natasha. At length Ms. Larson continued, "What does your mother think, Natasha?"

"She doesn't understand how I feel. She's just heard Princeton's the best."

"And you don't think you're ready for the best."

"I think Princeton would be too much for me to deal with. Going to Rutgers will be plenty challenging for me."

Ms. Clements interjected, "Your mama told me you'd probably have to work two jobs to go to Rutgers. Their scholarship only covers tuition and books."

Mrs. Larson added, "You've accomplished something special, Natasha. We accept about 2,200 out of 32,000 applicants—mostly valedictorians like you. And our financial aid people have awarded you what amounts to a full scholarship. When Elizabeth called me, and told me of your concerns, I shared them with my boss, the Dean of Admissions." She took a letter out of her thin leather briefcase. "This is a letter from Mr. Bowser asking you to give our school a chance to prove itself to you. He also agreed that I could be your freshman advisor."

Natasha fought back an upwelling of emotion and refused to cry, but felt amazed that one of the world's great universities would reach out to her in this way.

While she opened and read the letter, Mrs. Clements said, "You've succeeded at everything you've ever put your mind to, Natasha. You deserve the best and you can do the work."

Ms. Larson added, "Most black girls are programmed from birth to think they can't succeed in this society, Natasha. I'm here to tell you that's not true. I know you can succeed at Princeton."

———⊙———

In midtown Manhattan, Samir al Hammabi took his turn watching through a tripod-mounted telescope in their suite on the top floor of the Radisson. Breathlessly he gasped in clipped Arabic, "There it is, Omar! Come look! It's here!"

Omar pressed his eye to the eyepiece and watched a Peterbilt eighteen-wheeler turn into the Javits Convention Center loading dock. The bright yellow truck was hauling a long green Michelin shipping container.

"I can't believe it, Omar! Praise Allah! With His help we are finally going to punish the infidels."

As Omar passed the eyepiece to Ali, Samir thought back over the innumerable disappointments that had led to this moment. He'd worked for twelve years after the Kuwait War to assemble the scientists, technology and research facilities to develop Saddam Hussein's nuclear program. That effort had been both funded and thwarted by the U.N. The funds were diverted from the U.N. Oil for Food program, but the U.N. inspection teams kept them from making real progress. Then, after the U.S. invasion, he'd fled from Iraq to Pakistan to join Rashid Ahmad, who was laying the groundwork for World Jihad.

A number of times over the last three years they'd been close to prying a warhead loose from the Pakistani government, but every time they were about to take delivery, one of the Mullahs would get cold feet. Over the years he'd also gotten empty promises from the Chinese and the North Koreans. Two years ago, when he'd all but given up, his prayers were finally answered.

Standing in a squalid Parisian basement negotiating the purchase of a container of conventional weapons from a French arms dealer, he first learned of a Ukrainian colonel who'd stolen dozens of warheads during the collapse of the Soviet Union. Months later, with a blizzard raging outside a Kiev warehouse, he'd purchased five one hundred kiloton warheads for one billion dollars. One of them was in the container now arriving at the Jacob Javits Convention Center in New York City.

Samir took another long satisfied look through the eyepiece at the container they'd last seen in Marseilles a month before, when they switched a lead-lined crate containing one of the Ukrainian bombs for an identical crate containing a portion of the Michelin trade show exhibit.

Samir and Omar shared a long quiet embrace and Samir whispered, "The long frustrating years have finally been rewarded, Omar."

Samir thought back over the thirty-one years since the defeat of the Iraqi Army in '03 and the death of his wife and three sons in the bombing. In the intervening years he'd thought of little except getting revenge against the Great Satan. He never imagined it would take so long.

Omar Khaliff put his arm around Samir's shoulders and said, "That crate we substituted on the Michelin loading dock in Marseilles will cause quite a commotion tonight, General."

"This will be a trucking convention like no other, Omar. The Great Satan will weep tonight like I've wept these thirty years. Let's go."

"Remind me, General, what's the delay programmed into the timer?"

"At 10:45 tonight hellfire will envelope this city."

As the three men carried their bags to the elevator, Ali asked Samir, "Shouldn't we check out, General?"

"Why? This hotel won't exist tomorrow."

They took the elevator down to their rental car in the hotel garage. Samir drove out of the garage and parked within two hundred feet of the green container a block and a half from the hotel.

At 6:45PM Samir turned to Omar sitting in the passenger seat next to him, nodded at the chrome box in his lap and said, "Now, Lieutenant."

Omar put his thumbs on the two vertical levers and pressed both forward. The amber light between the levers flashed, confirming receipt of the transmission.

Samir whispered, "Allah Akbar!"

CHAPTER TWO

From the podium Andrews scanned hundreds of Master Teachers gathered in the Waldorf Astoria ballroom, glanced at the teleprompter, but didn't read it. He knew how he wanted to end this speech. "I don't think it would be possible to gather a more important group of Americans than I'm looking at right now. The goal of recognizing and rewarding our greatest teachers is one I've supported for decades. Getting the program through Congress last year and signed into law was an important breakthrough for my administration and for me personally." The room erupted in sustained applause.

At length he continued, "We've been able to identify over thirty thousand of you teaching in kindergarten through twelfth grade in rural towns, suburbs, and inner city schools. The taxpayers of America overwhelmingly support the bonus pay you receive each month, and some of your school districts are beginning to restructure local pay levels to acknowledge your valuable contributions to your communities. This trend needs to be continued until your pay, retirement benefits, and your stature in communities across the country is equal to all other American professions."

Again their applause interrupted him. When he felt it ebbing he continued, "I'm curious. How many of you use the initials, M.T. after your name?"

Many in the ballroom raised their hands.

"And those boxes of Master Teacher Certificates I signed, how many of you have one hanging in your classroom back home?"

At that, every hand went up.

"Great teachers are beginning to be recognized, recompensed, and acknowledged across our country, and as a result, more of our top students are making the decision to become teachers." Again he was interrupted by enthusiastic applause. "And this is just the beginning. America is waking up to the fact that throwing money at schools doesn't work. Great teachers make educational programs work."

At that, the room erupted into a prolonged standing ovation.

"Thank you and God bless every one of you. I'm speaking for a grateful nation in thanking you for the work you're doing for the children of America. Goodnight and God bless you."

Andrews left the podium slowly, waving and smiling to the mostly middle-aged female crowd who were clapping and shouting their appreciation. He shook some hands that were thrust toward him. One young woman with large glasses and long hair wiped away tears with one hand as he shook the other.

Finally, he turned and followed his security detail through the kitchen to his limo. At 10:35PM he boarded Marine One, lifted off, and headed southwest. At his request, their route took them over the Freedom Tower and the World Trade Center memorial, where they flew between two vertical light beams that symbolized the twin towers.

"That morning in September of 2001 will stay with me my whole life, Angie," Andrews said, without turning from the window. "Life changed in America that day. And for me personally, it was an unforgettable morning."

"You've never told me, Mr. President."

"Hank and I were scheduled at a Republican fund raiser on the 101st floor of the World Trade Center. Can you imagine! I would have been near the top of the South Tower. On the way there I got the call that Diane had been diagnosed with cancer. So, I cancelled and went to the hospital to be with her.

"No one at that meeting survived. These light beams remind me of the thousands of brilliant lives we lost that morning, and the strange blessing I received from Diane's diagnosis."

Andrews had the pilot fly around the lighted Statue of Liberty, and then turned his gaze across the blackness to the lights along the Jersey shore. He closed his eyes and had been resting for several moments when the helicopter was suddenly filled with a blast of light so intense he could see it before he got his eyes open. Secret Service Agent Archer sitting across from him instinctively drew his sidearm. Then the shockwave hit them.

Natasha watched Newark slide by outside the bus window. She'd seen Lisa, her sister, and Julian, her brother, get thoroughly messed up on these mean streets. Both were still living, but Lisa had been stolen from her by crack cocaine and Julian by gang warfare.

After her night job at the public library and an hour curled up on a sofa at Starbucks studying French, she was headed home at 10:30PM, an hour later than usual. The dean's letter lay open on her lap. She read it again, "Ms. Larson tells me you've decided not to attend Princeton."

The bus slowed and Troy Jackson was illuminated by the streetlight as he emerged from a graffiti-covered metal shelter on the far corner. Troy was one of Julian's friends who'd graduated from Newark

Central the previous year after breaking most of the school's football rushing records. This season he'd played for a struggling community college team. He smiled at her, making his way up the aisle, then he swung in beside her.

"Long time, Tosh. How've you been?"

"Good. I followed your season in the sports section."

"Yeah, followed me to the hospital twice. I told that fool coach, if he don't get me some blockin, he can forget about next season. After what I've been through in my life, I ain't gonna die on no football field. It was pitiful, Natasha, big dudes hittin me untouched every play."

His expression changed from the harsh memories of football season to the wide grin she'd enjoyed since kindergarten, "My auntie showed me the article in the paper about your scholarship to Rutgers. That's my goal too, Natasha. My grades are comin up and I'll get one too, if I have the kind of season I need next year."

Natasha gazed into the small old stores they were passing with apartments upstairs and debated sharing her news. She noticed the corner store was vacant. Torn asphalt imitation brick siding revealed diagonal heavily weathered wood sheathing underneath. She handed him the letter she'd folded over when he sat down.

"Princeton!" he exclaimed in surprise. "Now you're gettin in way over your head, Natasha."

Hearing him say that elicited two responses in her. She was sorry she'd showed him the letter because his response was so predictable. And she hated the fact that he automatically sold her short, as she did herself.

"Why do you say that?" she asked, turning to meet his eyes.

"How many super rich white people do you hang with, Girl?"

"None."

"I didn't think so. They ain't nothin like you and me."

She wiped away a tear working its way around the outside of her cheek, "Bad idea, right?"

He nodded, and handed back the letter, "But congratulations for gettin accepted. You amaze the hell out of me, Natasha. Never knew no one works as hard as you in school."

"Remember me as a freshman? How skinny and scared I was? I couldn't stand the teasing. Going to school was like going to hell, until I discovered that pouring myself into the work actually made high school bearable. Then, the other kids tried to make me feel bad for doing good work."

"Sounds about right," he sneered, slouching down in the seat, crossing his arms and sticking his left leg into the aisle, "Damn fools. And that made you mad, didn't it."

She remembered at first being surprised at the reaction of the kids around her when she knew the answers, or handed in assignments. Especially the huge guy next to her in freshman English who coined the nickname that stuck with her that whole year. Finally, she realized, they resented her putting their poor efforts to shame.

"Nope. You know what? It made them seem smaller. Like maybe Skinny Minnie actually had the upper hand on them."

He laughed, "I'd forgotten that nickname. And you just kept workin, didn't you?"

"I need to get off here." She reached up and pulled the buzzer cord.

As though triggered by the cord, the entire eastern horizon suddenly erupted in a massive arcing light.

Natasha shielded her eyes with her hand and exclaimed, "Oh my God! What's that?"

Distracted by the immense flash, the driver sideswiped the parked cars next to the bus. When he jerked the wheel to the left away from the cars, Natasha was slammed against the sidewall and fell between the seats. The bus careened out of control across the median, turned over, and slid on its side into the oncoming traffic.

Henry Holt sat on the side of his bed holding the phone receiver to his right ear, so stunned he couldn't think or speak. General Mitchell on the other end of the line waited for his response.

The president's chief of staff fought to rally his thought, and finally asked, "To this point, General, you say the search has turned up no sign of Marine One?"

"That's correct, Mr. Holt. We know they were crossing the East River when the bomb detonated. At that point their transmissions ceased. We haven't been able to find any evidence of the crash."

Holt's mind was numb, but he heard himself ask, "Has the vice president been alerted?" He glanced at his bedside clock. It was 11:15PM.

"Yes sir. General Vandenberg has decided to stay at NORAD. The chief justice is on her way to Colorado in case the vice president needs to be sworn in as president."

Holt put the receiver in his lap and covered the mouthpiece to muffle sobs welling up that he couldn't stifle. Why hadn't he voiced his opposition to the trip to New York? Images from their years of friendship swirled in his thought; Andrews' delight after winning that first election for the County Board of Supervisors in Illinois. They'd waged two successful campaigns for Congress and four in the Senate. Andrews was the older brother he'd never had, his closest friend, and the man America needed now more than ever. The thought of Vandenberg taking over terrified him. How many million innocent Muslims will die in the coming days?

At length he said, "Set up the Security Council meeting at 12:30 so the vice president can preside by downlink. I'll be there early to work with you, General."

"Yes sir. I'm sure you know how hard the Joint Chiefs are taking this loss, but we assure you we're equal to job ahead of us."

"I know that, General. We'll get through it."

Holt felt useless and alone. For so long his sole function had been to help and support his oversized friend. His immediate reaction was to hurry upstairs to help and support. He couldn't fathom the thought that his great friend and America's leader was gone.

Henry Holt dialed the vice president's private line, skirting Colonel Jim Braxton, his chief of staff.

Vandenberg's canned authoritative voice answered, "Yes, Mr. Holt."

"This was a tough call to make, Mr. Vice President."

"Sorry about your boss, Hank. Any sign of Marine One?"

"No. No sign whatever."

"You can rest assured, Mr. Holt, the bastards who did this are going to find out what happens when you piss off a superpower."

Holt clenched his eyes shut and his jaws together, and saw in his mind missiles emerging from dozens of silos and submarines. "We'll be ready for you to head up the Security Council meeting at 12:30, sir. Also, I want you to know, I'll stay as long as you and Colonel Braxton feel you need my help."

"Thanks, Hank. We'll count on you while we're getting saddled up."

"See you in a little more than an hour. Call if you need anything before the meeting."

Vandenberg slowly replaced the receiver on his phone, took off his reading glasses, closed his eyes, and was swept by a wave of adrenaline. *This is what I've lived my life for. Andrews is toast. No one in a chopper survives a hit like that.* He grinned. *Yep, from this point on things are going to be real different. We're going to make those bastards wish they'd never been born! Now we use our big stuff.*

Wonder how long they'll have to look for Andrews' body before

I take the oath? I'll work from here while we incinerate their asses.

He spent the rest of the hour considering the immediate ramifications. How many major companies are now headless? He knew it was in the hundreds. How large will the mass exodus be from the major cities? After some thought he came up with an estimate of 20% to 30%. So, for instance, from the LA metroplex we're talking over a million people fleeing this week. The economy's going to tank, big time. After the exodus we'll have massive looting to deal with. And how do we find these World Jihad sons of bitches before they hit us again?

The TV was muted on the far wall. He hit the button, listened to the talking heads, and watched the footage of the devastation in New York City. The major networks had lost their headquarters and news studios. A few news crews had been issued radiation suits with breathing apparatus and were able to get into the blast zone. Predictably, the next shots showed gridlocked freeways as millions of Americans fled major cities. Vandenberg finished getting dressed and started preparing for the meeting.

⸺⸺ ((◦)) ⸺⸺

Andrews' first thought as he regained consciousness was, God I'm so cold! Slowly he became aware that he was lying on damp concrete with his head propped up on a low curb. What a stench! Terrible smoke and a toxic smell, so vile it was like inhaling fumes of smoldering plastic. And there was no escaping it. He couldn't move! He had no feeling in his arms or legs. Staring at his feet, he willed himself to tap them together, but couldn't. Pain blasted him at the slightest movement of his head, which forced him to lie absolutely still.

Looking between his feet, beyond a low wall he saw the smoking wreckage of the helicopter and remembered the intense flash before the chopper was slammed. By what? It had to be a shockwave. New York City must have been hit by an atomic bomb just after I left. What about the others? Angie and Archer? He couldn't imagine anyone, including himself, surviving such a crash. The famous photo image of Hiroshima flashed in his thought again. His mind reeled at the thought of Manhattan in smoldering ruins. Sobs welled up. Tears ran into his ears then dripped onto the curb. A vision of that crowd of master teachers burned to nothing made him cry out in grief. And how many others!

He felt at that moment like he'd been through enough. The thought came, Hell, others can take it from here. I should be dead anyway. How ironic, to survive that crash and then die of exposure. He envisioned himself trying to lead America as a quadriplegic. FDR managed to be president from a wheelchair, but that was before television. With a concerted effort he shut out the pain and the grief for a moment and focused on the scene around him.

High above he saw the hole the chopper made in the metal roof when it crashed into this deserted warehouse. The tail section of Marine One hung from a steel truss below the hole. Through the shattered windows above the brick wall opposite, he could see flames reflected on the clouds, like the primitive special effects over Atlanta in Gone With The Wind. To his right he caught a glimpse of Agent Archer's thick lower leg in grey flannel slacks.

"Adrian!" he shouted, but got no response. Then, he noticed he was wrapped in Adrian's navy blue topcoat. Forgetting the consequences, he tried to turn toward the agent's body. The attempt caused an explosion of pain inside him, as though he'd grabbed a 1,000-volt power line. He blacked out again.

In the hall outside the National Security Council meeting, Holt stopped at a large framed photograph and stared into the sad eyes of Abraham Lincoln. The 16ᵗʰ president stared back. In his thought Holt addressed the Great Emancipator, We found out tonight, Mr. Lincoln, how terrible this job can be. The Civil War exploded on your watch and nuclear terrorism on ours. Tonight we lost more people in a few minutes, than you lost in our worst war. It looks like another great president . . . has been taken from us . . . my best friend. He sighed, turned, and trudged down the hall toward the meeting.

At half an hour past midnight, the National Security Council sat with fixed stares around the long table. In Holts' mind, he again imagined the million-degree blast sweeping through Times Square burning the crowd to nothing.

Holt sat down in his usual place at the president's left. The large flat-screen on a stand had taken President Andrews' place at the head of the table. Vice President Vandenberg opened the meeting, "To use Roosevelt's words, August 10, 2034 is another day 'that will live in infamy.' We've got a joint session of Congress at ten hundred hours, gentlemen, and with their blessing, we're going to hit Pakistan with multiple warheads. The countries of the world will soon know that supporting nuclear terrorism has terrible consequences."

Holt, who normally said little at these meetings, responded, "What about our policy of proportionate response, Mr. Vice President? It would seem proportionate to hit Islamabad."

Vandenberg's huge fist slammed the table in front of him and made everyone jump. "After today, terrorist sympathizers will know there's a hell of a price to pay for nuking a U.S. city. You lose half your god damned country!"

Holt looked from face to face around the table. They seemed too intimidated to respond, so he replied, trying to keep his voice level, "I urge you to give this more thought, Mr. Vice President. People understand 'an eye for an eye.' They won't accept massive obliteration. The whole Muslim world would unite against us."

Vandenberg's larger than life face glared from the screen, as he looked for support for his fury. The blank expressions and dead silence seemed to increase his anger. But to Holt's surprise, he moderated his position and said, "I'm not yet resolved on the scale of our retaliation, but it's clear, either we strike hard or we crawl on our knees. Those are our choices and I assure you, gentlemen, we're not going to crawl. Mr. Holt, run the digital recording that was delivered to the <u>L.A. Times</u> last night."

The lights dimmed and the image of a dark-haired male in a ski mask appeared on a large screen opposite Vandenberg's monitor. In a heavy Middle Eastern accent he began to speak slowly in English, "Finally the infidel has received a mighty death blow in partial repayment for the murder of Rashid Ahmad and countless other crimes against Muslims. We now have nuclear warheads planted in dozens of your cities which will soon be detonated. The end of your world domination is finally at hand. Allahu Akbar!"

Holt's eyes went from face to face around the table. They looked like cadavers. As the terrorist spoke, Holt felt the balance of world power shifting. Certainly one of their bombs was planted near where they now sat and would probably be detonated next. He imagined himself briefly as a Roman watching Alaric's Visigoths scaling the walls of Rome in the fifth century and bringing with them the Dark Ages.

When the lights came back up, Vandenberg continued, "The publisher of the <u>L.A. Times</u> has agreed to release nothing until after the joint session. What's the damage report, Nicolas?"

Holt was impressed. As opposed to his own reaction of deep shock and the bewildered expressions around the table, Vandenberg was unfazed by the threatening tirade. In fact, he was in his element. He was obviously born to lead and to fight. Also, he was inside a granite mountain.

National Security Advisor, Nicolas Moore, sat up and regained his normal crispness, "We're estimating 2.4 million fatalities."

Holt felt the blow of that number like a ball bat to his chest. While he regained his equilibrium, he stared at Vandenberg's agonized reaction to such a horrible number, much more than they'd been told earlier. Vandenberg's lips drew taut across his gritted teeth and his eyes bulged with rage. At length the vice president's face recovered to the fierce glare they'd seen so often, then he slowly repeated, "2.4 million ..."

Mr. Moore continued, "Of the four or five million injured, we're losing about twenty thousand an hour, mostly burn and radiation cases."

"How would you describe our emergency response to this point?" Vandenberg asked.

"Chaotic. By mid-morning we'll have fifty thousand reasonably coordinated people in radiation suits involved directly in the rescue effort, but we're completely unprepared for this number of burn cases. In the whole country we're able to handle something like ten thousand serious burn patients. Tonight, a million New Yorkers are dying from third-degree burns."

Nicolas Moore went on, "The wind is moving the radioactive fallout into upstate New York and the National Guard is handling that evacuation effort. You've seen the news footage. With first light, we'll have aerial shots."

Holt studied Vandenberg glaring at his hands clasped on the table in front of him. At length, he cleared his throat and demanded, "Roger, how do we find the bastards?"

Roger Christianson, Director of Intelligence, answered, "One of the scenarios we worked last evening put the terrorists in New York yesterday to trigger the bomb. We went through the databases of hotels, rental car companies, and all the airlines with flights out of J.F.K., La Guardia, and Newark."

"And?" Vandenberg prodded.

"This was just confirmed. On a United flight from J.F.K. to Houston at 8:40PM, there were three males traveling on what we've just confirmed were falsified Moroccan passports. The Air France agent in Marseilles who issued the tickets went through a photo file and identified two Pakistani operatives and an Iraqi general, Samir al Hammabi, with known ties to World Jihad."

Vandenberg cleared his voice and said, "I knew they'd eventually get warheads from the Pakistanis. General Mitchell, get multiple warheads targeted to take out their ten largest cities. Call the congressional leadership, Holt, and tell them what we're bringing to the joint session. Roger, coordinate your people with the FBI and the Houston Police. I want that Iraqi and the two Pakistanis. And evacuate Houston."

"I'll have a hundred agents in Houston by the end of the day, Mr. Vice President," Christianson responded.

Vandenberg continued, "By the start of the joint session of Congress, we need a plan for a land, air and sea blockade that'll stop them from getting any more bombs into the country. No trucks, planes, or containers get in that haven't been inspected and cleared by the Counter Terrorism Corps. I want confirmation of the source of that bomb and what it'll take to track down any others they've smuggled in. Prepare whatever legislation we need to authorize the armed forces and the National Guard to join law enforcement in a nationwide search effort, even if it takes Martial Law. And have our allies send us all the burn specialists they can round up."

"Yes, Mr. Vice President," Holt said.

Vandenberg stood and left. The screen went blank. Holt had never missed David Andrews more in his life.

Andrews awoke from a dream of his father standing over him on the basketball court in front of the high school student body, demanding that he get up and shake off his injury. Awaking to reality was even worse. The fumes given off by the smoldering helicopter made him nauseous. As foul an acrid smell as he could imagine.

In addition to the numbness of his arms and legs, now there was an intense disembodied fiery pain in the region of his lower back. He opened his eyes and saw what looked like the light of dawn coming through the dirty broken windows on the high wall opposite. Then he realized it was the light from the fires across the river. He couldn't quit shivering which caused even more pain, like lying on a live wire.

Ghastly images of the carnage across the river filled his imagination, generating a stream of anger, grief, and hatred. That roomful of master teachers again came to mind and grief washed over him. He pictured the earnest expression of the young long-haired teacher weeping at his appreciation of her excellence. At length, he realized that that room of teachers was just the tip of the iceberg. Last night much of the cream of the nation had been destroyed. He knew he should be at the center of the storm of activity, directing the rescue effort and planning the retaliation. Instead, the world's most powerful man lay helpless in a cold dank abandoned warehouse.

Then at the left limit of his peripheral vision he glimpsed Angie's profile. She was also laid with her head on the curb, several yards away. Unable to move, he called out, "Angie!" But got no response. Then, he heard the wump wump wump of a helicopter drawing nearer and getting louder, then it faded into the distance.

The cold from the damp floor was building in his body and he tried to suppress violent bouts of shivering. "God!" he shouted into the vastness above him, "I can't stand this much longer!" At that he was hit by another wave of despair. The staggering carnage across the river slammed him anew. Sobs again racked his breathing and caused bursts of incendiary pain that made him scream. Screaming made the pain worse. Once fear got its foot in the door of his thought, it immediately began laying out the facts of his situation.

How many more hours of this could he survive? He'd never experienced pain this intense. He imagined the enormous effort being waged to fight the fires and rescue the injured in the smoldering shell of Manhattan. Tears again dripped from his ear lobes. Through his sobs he felt himself fading and realized that could be a way out of this misery and he considered allowing himself to slip away.

When that dark suggestion came he stopped everything: stopped sobbing, stopped the collapse of his thinking, stopped envisioning the death and destruction, even stopped shivering. There was something he could do. He closed his eyes and prayed with all his heart.

Growing up, his mother had proven to him that it's possible to make contact with the Being who creates and operates the universe. If petitioned with the right motives, he knew from experience, this creative Being would actually provide specific answers to problems.

During his presidency, the steady barrage of tough problems had taught him to pray more and more effectively. As in most things, practice helped. He shunted his anger, grief, and pain aside, shut out preconceived answers, cleared his thought to listen, and asked from the bottom of his heart for help.

Again there was a flash of light inside his closed eyes. When he opened them his heart leaped, adrenaline raced through his system, and he gasped at the sight of her.

CHAPTER THREE

A GLOWING APPARITION
AUGUST 11, 2034

A glowing apparition sitting on the low concrete wall between Andrews and the helicopter wreckage said, "Good morning, David."

"What the hell?" he stammered, heart pounding, eyes wide, "Who are you?"

She seemed to be made of condensed light, about half his size with calm upturned eyes. They examined each other for a moment before she spoke again, "I've come to help you."

Andrews stared at her in silence, then muttered, "You have?"

"You asked for help, didn't you?"

He figured she was probably a pain induced hallucination, but he answered anyway, "Yes. Yes, I did. Maybe . . . maybe you could contact the people who are looking for me."

"David, you're going to have to break the human cycle of violence breeding more violence."

Andrews stared at her, dumbfounded. That was the most far-fetched suggestion he could imagine, offered in all seriousness. He almost laughed. "Lady, you may not have noticed, but I'm paralyzed here. All I can move are my mouth and eyes."

She continued as though she hadn't heard, "David, if your chain-reaction weapons are released in retaliation for this attack, it will be the beginning of the end of human life."

"HOLY JESUS!" he exclaimed, his words echoing down the cavernous building.

His outburst obviously surprised her. After a moment she said, "Just keep praying. The answers will come."

"You'll come back?"

"Probably not, but you'll get the ideas you need." She smiled at him and grew fainter. She was leaving!

"Wait! Please wait!"

Her form lingered, though with lessened illumination.

"Can you contact the people who are looking for me and let them know where I am?"

"Your body should work now."

At that instant he realized the numbness was gone. Still afraid of the pain, he made some tiny movements with various body parts and then some more normal ones. Amazing! Everything worked! He sat up and started to thank her, but now she was almost invisible.

"Wait! Please!"

She smiled at him, seeming to enjoy his importunity. She increased her visible presence slightly and asked, "What is it, David?"

"How did you do that? How'd you heal my body?"

"Your messenger taught his followers to heal. You can learn it from his teachings."

"Okay, I'll try. But give me something specific I can use, to deal with these nuclear terrorists."

She considered his request for a moment. Then said, "Study what your messenger taught about enemies in his Sermon on the Mount. That's how you access the power."

Then, smiling at him, she faded to nothing.

In the distance a male voice called out, "Natasha." Then it exclaimed, "Nurse, come here! Her eyelids moved!"

Natasha heard a female voice now and felt squeezing. Her left hand was definitely being squeezed. The man tried again, "Natasha!"

She managed a feeble return squeeze, then she opened her left eyelid a slit.

A blurry male figure said, "I'm here with you, Natasha. You're going to be all right."

She tried to respond, but her mouth wouldn't work. She placed the voice and the face.

Reverend Pettis said, "Don't try to talk. Just rest."

She wondered what the Reverend had been through. She'd never seen him look so haggard.

"When the bomb went off, your bus driver lost control."

The memory flooded back. She opened her swollen lips and made a barely recognizable sound, "Bomb?"

He nodded, "Terrorists destroyed New York City."

"New York?" she whispered, wondering how a bomb thirty-five miles away could make such a flash.

He answered the unasked question, "They exploded an atomic bomb downtown."

The thought of an atomic bomb in downtown New York hit her like the sidewall of the bus.

"The doctor says in a week or so, we can take you home."

She became aware of the noise in the ward, "Many?" she mouthed and motioned with her eyes beyond the cloth partition.

"We're swamped. All the hospitals within five hundred miles are crammed. By the way," he smiled, "Troy Jackson's been asking about you. He pulled you out of that burning bus, and helped in here all night."

She nodded again, and took inventory: right eye swollen shut, right side of her face extremely painful, her mouth and jaw obviously messed up. Everything ached.

He continued, "I need to see some other people, but I wanted you to know something. Sitting here, praying beside you last night, a voice spoke to me inside my thought."

Not far away a nurse called to him, "Reverend Pettis, you're needed, right now, please!"

He turned away from Natasha and said with an uncharacteristic edge to his voice, "Nurse, I said I'd be with you shortly." He turned back to Natasha and continued, "The voice came to me clear as a bell. It said you're going to help bring God's message to the world."

Sitting on the clammy slab of the abandoned factory, Andrews couldn't take his eyes from the spot where the small glowing figure had been sitting seconds before. His body felt remarkably normal, as though she'd awakened him from a terrible dream of being paralyzed. He massaged the back of his neck and both legs. The numbness and pain were gone. He was just stiff. He checked his watch. It was 4:45AM.

Questions tumbled over one another. Was she an angel? Why so alien looking? He'd always pictured angels with human forms. She seemed a magnificently wise little being, made of . . . what? Where had she come from? Where did she go?

For the first time in a long time he felt grateful to be president. His job made him the one to receive her and her remarkable message. Meeting her had lifted his spirits enormously. His grief and sadness had vanished, along with the paralysis and pain. The worst day of his life had suddenly turned into a day of fantastic possibilities. Since beings like her existed and were willing to help, there was no telling what the future could hold.

He stood up, pulled Archer's overcoat around his shoulders and checked his Special Agent for a pulse. There was none. A compound fracture had mangled Adrian's right arm and bloodied the back of his slightly deformed head. Next, he pressed his fingertips to Angie's neck. Her body was startlingly cold, but he detected a barely discernible pulse. Her nose and right cheekbone were smashed, and he hoped all the dried blood made her injuries look worse than they were. He slipped off Archer's ample overcoat and carefully wrapped her small body in it.

After a walk around the wreckage, he knew the crew, the chief warrant officer with the "football," and the rest of his security detail, had perished. Staring at the twisted aluminum and charred cockpit, it seemed more miraculous than ever that he'd survived. Typical of Archer, this amazing man's last act was saving his president in spite of his own terrible injuries.

If Angie was going to survive, she needed help immediately. Andrews checked Archer's belt for his combination phone/walkie-talkie, but came up empty. With effort he rolled Adrian's heavy body onto its side, but found nothing underneath. Sitting back on his heels, wondering what would be the most effective thing to do, he heard the thumping sounds of an approaching chopper. It lingered above the hole in the roof and illumined the crash scene with its floodlight. Andrews ran into the circle of light and waved both arms. The crew turned off the light and descended on the waterfront side of the building.

Andrews ran across the cavernous old factory, amazed at how well his body now worked. After he'd run two-thirds of the way, the double doors on the far wall banged open and six soldiers jogged in rolling three gurneys. As they approached, he directed them to Adrian and Angie beyond the wreckage.

Approaching the open doors he wondered if he would get another chance to thank his angel messenger. How had she given them his location, he wondered? Outside the building, he stopped and stared at the fires. The world's mightiest skyline had been reduced to shattered smoking stumps of buildings.

When he reached the helicopter, a Marine medic approached with a syringe half full of clear liquid, "How about something to ease your pain, Mr. President?"

"No thanks, Doc."

The medic stared at him confused. "Are you sure, sir? You fell several hundred feet onto concrete, and you're not in terrible pain?"

"I'm okay."

The Marine medic stared in disbelief, tempted to insist. Finally, he turned away muttering, "This isn't possible!"

Andrews sat down on a seat near the side door and the co-pilot handed him a telephone. "A secure call from Henry Holt, Mr. President. He asked us to call him as soon as we knew anything."

"Hello, Hank."

"Mr. President?" Holt said, his voice cracking.

"Hank, you must be in the eye of some storm over there."

"I've been keeping myself together to this point, but the sound of your voice is . . ." There was a long labored intake of breath and a pause, "I . . . didn't think I'd ever hear it again."

"Hank, you have no idea how important you are to me right now. There's no one else I can tell what I've been through. It's too . . ."

After a long pause Holt asked, "It's too what, Mr. President? Miraculous?"

"We'll need to be alone before I can tell you what happened, but that's what it was."

As they talked, Andrews took in the scene across the river. The world famous skyline was gone. The bridges were gone. "I'm looking at the fires across the river. Have you seen this? Manhattan is just burning wreckage. I've never seen anything like it. Seems impossible that one explosive device could do this."

The medic handed him a steaming cup, and wrapped him in a dark blanket. Coffee never tasted better.

Holt was hesitant responding, "I know, sir. I promised the medic I wouldn't get into current events with you. He said you've come through a terrible crash, are probably in deep shock, and need solid rest for several days."

"We both know that's not going to happen. You need to assure me we've done nothing to retaliate."

"The vice president asked the House to pass a Declaration of War on Pakistan. The Senate is expected to pass it soon after the House approval. He's also requested a joint session of Congress at ten this morning. He's going to ask their blessing to send Pakistan back to the Stone Age."

"Cancel and re-schedule, Holt. I'll meet with both houses this evening."

"Are you up to that, Mr. President?"

"I'm okay. I've got a lot to tell you. We lost Adrian and the others. Angie's barely hanging on. I'll fill you in after I sleep for a while." He disconnected and watched the gurneys with Adrian's body and Angie's unconscious form being stowed. Then the chopper lifted off.

Struggling to breathe, because of his anger and disappointment, Vandenberg covered the phone with his hand. He filled his chest and fought for control of his furious thoughts, "That's amazing, Holt!" he managed to say. As he exhaled, he struggled to relax and transmit nothing of his true feelings over the phone. His thoughts raged, IMPOSSIBLE! You don't walk away from a chopper that's been slammed to the ground by a nuclear blast wave! This screws up everything!

Holt could tell that Vandenberg had already assumed the presidency and was being demoted during this conversation,

"Everyone else died in the crash except Miss O'Leary and she's in critical condition."

"But he came through without a scratch! Isn't that unbelievable, Holt." The vice president spoke as naturally as he could manage, while his right fist almost crushed the receiver. The veins of his neck and forehead bulged.

"The Marine captain I spoke to at the crash site said it was the most amazing case of survival he's seen in twenty years of air rescue work. The president has re-scheduled the joint session for seven this evening."

"What great news! Great news! Of course. Sure. I'll look forward to hearing his speech to the joint session. We're still gonna blast'em, aren't we, Holt?"

"I honestly don't know. We'll both find out this evening. He's probably sound asleep in the Marine chopper on his way home."

"Okay. That's good. Well, ask him to call after he gets some rest. Yeah, the chief justice will soon leave for home. It's great she wasn't needed here."

Vandenberg hung up and stared at the knob on the door of his nightstand, opened it and took out a heavy tumbler and a fifth of Jack Daniels. Pouring himself about four fingers, he said aloud to reassure himself, "Calm down. You'll get your shot at running the big show soon enough."

As the chopper gained altitude, Andrews sipped the hot coffee and stared at the devastation that had been Manhattan. He could tell from his reaction to the burning wreckage, that his encounter with the "angel" had impacted him profoundly. The scene below saddened him, but there was no overwhelming grief or anger. Laying his head back and closing his eyes, he focused on his small ethereal visitor, and tried to grasp her message.

She didn't say how human life would end, but I'm sure she could foresee a horrible cycle of retaliation. If we send those missiles, we're headed for extinction. "Keep praying," she said. "Answers will come."

From the cockpit he heard radio chatter from a rescue crew urgently calling for help to reach trapped survivors in a subway tunnel. Someone yelled to the crew down in the tunnel that the president had been found alive. Cheers came through the static that made Andrews smile.

Then his thought returned to his small feline-looking benefactor. When I pressed her for some specific action, I expected steps I could take to stop the terrorists. But instead of their whereabouts, she said, "Study what your messenger taught about enemies in his Sermon on the Mount. That's how you access the power."

And she wasn't just blowing smoke. She meant it. While she spoke of accessing power, the busted stuff in my body was being mended. The power she could access was mending my spinal cord perfectly. She didn't even ask me what was wrong or check out the damage. The medical profession, with all its technology, is still unable to repair severed spinal cords.

I needed information to stop a crew of mass murderers and she referred me to Jesus' Sermon on the Mount. Why? Why wasn't she willing to get involved and lead me to them? Lady, if I can't strike back, I need names and addresses, not the Golden Rule! And love your enemies. That could only seem like practical advice to an angel. She's probably never had to deal with terrorists.

Carefully he raised his head from the seatback, sipped the strong coffee, and saw they were now over some dark rural area. He glanced at his watch, it was 5:20. The face of the crewman across from him was illumined by the pale green lights of the instrument panel in front of him. Andrews laid his head back, closed his eyes, and could see the angel's small face in his thought. He said to her, You have no idea what I'll be up against trying to sell this idea of yours. Love nuclear terrorists. Where's the power in that? I'll get run out of D.C. on a rail.

Most of the Sunday mornings of his youth were spent in a Methodist Sunday School, where he got his early grounding in The Bible. In Junior High he was already six-foot-four and played center for their church team in addition to the school team. His dad was non-religious, but went along with his wife's efforts to bring up their son in her religion. When they couldn't make it to church, she conducted the class, which usually focused on the Sermon on the Mount. She told him if he had Matthew 5, 6, and 7 engraved on his heart, he wouldn't need anything else to be a true Christian. Andrews could recite much of it by heart.

He went over and over the passages regarding how to deal with enemies and how those ideas could provide an access to power. What a message for the leader of the world's most powerful country, immediately following a nuclear attack. Do good to them that hate you, and pray for them which despitefully use you and persecute you—the absolute opposite of every use of power he was aware of. Blessed are the humble! They will inherit the earth.

Explain that to World Jihad! Or Congress for that matter. Blessed are the merciful! They will find mercy. Blessed are the peacemakers! And Jesus' most familiar teaching, You have heard the saying, An eye for an eye and a tooth for a tooth. But I tell you, whoever strikes you on the right cheek, turn the other to him as well.

Craziness! he thought. We've just suffered the most devastating terrorist attack in history, and she suggests there's actual power in turning the other cheek. My whole life I've wrestled with that concept. I know it worked for him, but it couldn't seem less relevant to this situation.

He'd always considered the Sermon on the Mount a guidebook for the way God wants us to live, never as a manual for accessing His power. He pondered the dubious concept that power could flow from loving your enemies. How could love trump nuclear warheads?

The Marine helicopter landed on the roof of a Newark hospital and orderlies quickly wheeled Angie to a waiting elevator. Before liftoff, the crew chief asked him, "Pardon me, Mr. President, but how did you manage to come through that crash unhurt?"

Andrews managed a small smile, "Lucky, I guess."

The Marine shook his head, "No. No sir. That had to be way more than luck. That had to be God's doing. Yes sir, you must of had a real honest-ta-God miracle."

"How'd you find us, Captain?"

"Part of the miracle, sir. A red pulsating light suddenly appeared on our GPS map of the waterfront showing us exactly where you'd crashed. We thought at first we'd homed in on a tracking device from Marine One, until we saw what was left of it. None of us understand the source of that signal. Do you, sir?"

Andrews stared back at him, while gratitude swelled in his heart. Finally, he mumbled, "No, son, I sure don't."

Then he realized one of the big changes since his angel encounter was a lessening of his normal mental overload of job-related details. He wasn't focused on the myriad details the bombing would normally trigger and the lists of prioritized tasks. Instead, he focused on her. She seemed like a being from another dimension or from the distant future, with knowledge that made human life seem primitive. He sensed her urging him to make a quantum leap out of his present paradigm into a higher concept of life and power.

Suddenly he felt extremely tired, closed his eyes and laid his seat back. As sleep closed in, he conjured up the angel's smiling face and said to her in his thought, I'll never forget what you did for me tonight. And I'll do my best to access the power.

When he woke up, he was in his own bed. He had no recollection of landing or walking into the White House. That coffee! The Medic drugged my coffee! Infuriated, he reached for his bedside phone and dialed Holt.

"Drugging me is not acceptable, Hank! You know I hate drugs. You're supposed to protect me from that kind of stuff!"

"Sorry, Mr. President. The Marine medic did that on his own, without my knowledge. I think everyone involved in that scene last night was in total disbelief that you could walk away from such a crash. Each person I talked to was incredulous. The medic couldn't accept the fact that you weren't in terrible pain. When you wouldn't let him give you an injection, he put a sedative in your coffee. Believe me, when I found out, I let him know the enormity of the mistake he'd made. He asked me to give you his apology and let you know he was beside himself over your complete defiance of every known law of physics. He'd even calculated the foot/pounds of impact you experienced when you hit that concrete slab. How are you feeling after your sleep?"

"Better. Any word on Angie?"

"Touch and go, is all they'll say."

"What time is it?"

"It's two o'clock. We've got a joint session in five hours. I've got writers standing by."

"No thanks, Hank. I know what I need to say."

"Hold on now, Mr. President. This is a critical point in our history. If you've ever had to say something exactly right, this is it! This speech will be the chapter heading on your presidency in a hundred years."

Andrews was surprised that he couldn't share his angel experience over the phone, even with his oldest and closest friend. "I know our normal approach would be to work together to define the main ideas and then get professional wordsmiths to frame it, but this is different."

"It's bigger and more important is all. How else is this different, Mr. President?"

"It's different because I was told what I have to say. Come about an hour early and I'll explain it to you."

When Ernest Appleton walked into the boulder-strewn clearing, the other members of the Calderan Council were discussing the attack on New York City. The clearing had almost the feeling of a room enclosed by dense tropical foliage. A small stream wound its way through the boulders and back into the lush jungle.

The other six members of the Council barely acknowledged his arrival. Appleton, hesitant to break into their discussion, pulled his shoulder-length hair back and watched a fish caught in a small eddy next to the boulder he'd chosen.

The others in the clearing, he knew, could readily discern the feelings he was wrestling with. He actually agreed with their harsh assessment of the human world. What an unholy stew of emotion they are, he thought, angry children venting their hatred of each other with chain-reaction weapons.

He rarely felt the burden of his human heritage any longer, but studying the small wise beings around him in the clearing, his human roots seemed extremely obvious.

"My wife was encouraged by her meeting with the president this morning," Appleton began.

The slight jet black female across from him turned, peered at him with pale yellow eyes and said, "Humans have launched the opening salvo of their final death throes."

A male to Appleton's left addressed him, "It would be wise, Lord Appleton, if you could set aside your sympathetic feelings. You've moved far beyond your kind."

A female on Appleton's right chimed in, "Anyone who's witnessed the nuclear devastation of a hospitable planet can appreciate the building consensus among Calderans that we should step in before the humans destroy the planet we also call home."

Appleton decided to make his proposal before the case against his request became any stronger, "Hamama discerned a genuinely prayerful heart in President Andrews and feels his surprising receptivity to the message may exist in more human hearts than we thought. We ask that the Council approve a mission to the human world by our daughter in an attempt to measure this latent receptivity among humans."

The request was greeted by a long silence. At length the female on Appleton's right said, "We know your daughter is waiting nearby. Ask the princess to join us and tell us of her proposed mission."

A tall beautiful human-looking girl entered the clearing and sat down next to Lord Appleton. Her blonde hair was braided and the braids were tied behind her head. She wore a long loose-fitting burnt-sienna gown made of an airy material. After a pause she said, "Good morning, Council members. As father has told you, my mother was deeply moved by the genuine prayerfulness she discerned in the American president. She asked if I'd be willing to go to my father's homeland to measure the current level of receptivity among his people to the message."

The Calderan Council member who had invited her to join them asked, "And how do you intend to measure their receptiveness, Your Highness?"

Liza Jane answered, "Father thinks it will be possible for me to move into his college school near New York and live among the students and get to know them. From that base, I plan to branch out and get to know a wider cross-section of the president's people. My mother will stay in close contact with me."

The female to Lord Appleton's right responded, "We acknowledge the importance of Queen Hamama's oversight of the project, and ask for a few moments as the Council takes the matter under advisement."

After several minutes, but with no outward sign of their intercommunication, the female on Appleton's right delivered their decision, "We've reached accord, Lord Appleton. Queen Hamama must have found a substantial reason for optimism in this president, or she wouldn't be willing to put your daughter at such risk."

Ernest Appleton responded, "This is a very special moment for me, as you can imagine. It is my great desire that we reach out to my species at this crucial moment."

The female Council member continued, "Several of us suspect humans are actually more immersed in hatred now than they were when the message was originally given them. Some among us doubt your daughter is adequately advanced in the Way to undertake such a mission.

"But we're willing to set aside our doubts and support your request. We understand how important it is for you to help your species and we recognize that by the progress you've made in demonstrating the Way, you've proven what's possible for humans.

"At the same time we remind you, it's not the Calderan mission in the universe to protect errant life forms from the consequences of rejecting the message."

At 5:30PM Holt walked into the sitting room of the president's bedroom, "Okay. I'm dying to know. Who told you what to say, Mr. President, and what is it?"

Andrews tossed his reading glasses on the thin stack of yellow lined tablet pages of notes on the writing table in front of him and stared at his friend. "Have a seat, Hank."

When Holt was seated on one of the two facing small sofas by the fireplace, Andrews came around the table and sat down opposite. They stared at each other for a moment before Andrews said, "I've just been through a life-changing experience."

Holt started to say something, but Andrews put up his hand, "This is hard to actually say out loud, even to my oldest friend, but I'll try. I was unconscious in that burning wreckage. Somehow, Adrian got Angie and me out before he died. When I came to, I was lying in excruciating pain, completely paralyzed."

Again, Holt opened his mouth and Andrews stopped him, "After being tortured by pain and exposure for about four or five hours, losing consciousness once or twice, I finally realized there was something I could do for myself."

Holt tried to wait through the long pause, but couldn't, "What could you do?"

"I started praying for help with my whole heart."

"Your prayer was obviously answered, but how?"

"You're the only person I could say this to, Hank, and for now it has to stay between us."

He paused, leaned forward and began, "Suddenly, there was a small glowing female sitting on the low wall across from me, like you're sitting across from me now."

Hank's mouth was half open as though forming a sound, but wasn't. His head was cocked to one side and his stare was strange, almost pained, with his brow deeply furrowed. Finally, he mumbled, "Who was she?"

"She introduced herself and seemed to be made of condensed light or something—quite beautiful, but more sort of feline, than human. She called me David and said she'd come to help me."

Holt asked, "Was she an angel?"

"Well, she wasn't a figment of my imagination. I'm positive of that. Then she told me, 'If you retaliate with chain reaction weapons, human life will end.'"

"Whoa! What a thing to say!"

"She was dead certain, Hank. And I believe her. She said it was up to me to break this 'violence breeds more violence' cycle before it's too late, and I intend to give it my best shot. She said I could access the power that can save us, if I focus completely on that effort."

"Is she going to help you? God knows you'll need help. Refusing to retaliate is not going to go over well at all, I can assure you."

"I hope she'll help me. I haven't been able to think about anything but our visit since I met her. She was trying to push me to access the same power she was using to heal my injuries."

"What power is that?"

"Spiritual power, Hank. The same power Jesus used to heal leprosy. I had no sensation that my spinal cord was being spliced together perfectly until it was done. It felt like there was nothing to it, but I'll never get over the mental mending she was doing as we talked."

"What was she like? Condescending and impatient—or kind and upbeat? I've never met an angel."

"I had the feeling she knew things I couldn't possibly understand. That she was trying to relate to me in terms I could grasp—like you'd talk to a two-year-old. The key thing I got from her was that long ago we were given access to the power that could save us from nuclear terrorism, but we lost it. She urged me to regain access to that power."

"What's it going to take to access that power, Mr. President?"

"That leads me to what I wanted to talk to you about. This next chapter of my life is probably going to get ugly, Holt. We both know that what she gave me to do is probably beyond my capacity to lead the nation, but I've got to try. You've mentioned retiring recently and I thought this might be a good time. You don't need to go through this seemingly hopeless battle with me."

"You'd have to see your face to know what I'm thinking right now. It's remarkable. I've worked beside you for three decades, watched you lose Diane, and saw how terribly that hurt you."

Andrews stood and said, "I need to get dressed. Come with me and finish that thought while I dress. Sounds like you're going to stay."

"Since Diane passed, I've been hoping you'd somehow be able to recover some of your old spirit. Now finally, just look at you! Your eyes are full of life . . . you're glowing like the David Andrews I watched give his first campaign speech thirty years ago."

"Thanks for staying. I'm obviously going to need all the help I can get."

Holt looked at him a while, and then Andrews saw the corners of his mouth curl into a small smile, "I wouldn't miss this for anything. An angel! What next, Mr. President?"

CHAPTER FOUR

THE JOINT SESSION
AUGUST 11, 2034

Angry voices from the House chambers reverberated in the corridor as Andrews approached the door with Holt.

"No notes?" Holt asked.

"Nope. This one's off the cuff."

"How do you figure it'll play in Peoria?"

"Badly, at first I think. But after the initial reaction dies down, I hope people will start to see it's the way to go."

The sergeant-at-arms walked into the mouth of the House Chamber and announced in as strident a voice as he could, "Mr. Speaker, the President of the United States!", but his words were swallowed in the din.

Andrews walked through the doorway and went unnoticed except by those who had to be moved aside by his security detail. Once inside, he saw the floor of the enormous room was a cauldron of emotion. Faces inches apart shouted at each other to be heard. Above, the gallery was brimming with the same unanimity of anger and hatred. What they wanted was for the last sound heard in much of Pakistan to be the scream of an incoming ICBM.

As Andrews mounted the podium, the Speaker of the House

pounded his gavel to no avail. Finally, he moved the framed block he was pounding over next to his microphone which greatly increased the volume of his pounding until the lawmakers began to quiet and find their seats.

When Andrews stepped to the podium the room quieted, "I come to you on the darkest day in our history, to tell you what I plan to do."

Before he could go on, shouted demands for the massive retaliation Vandenberg had promised drowned him out. Andrews listened and waited, then yielded to the Speaker, whose gavel finally quieted the room.

"I've been thinking about the right response and have made a decision."

Another uproar began, but this time he was able to quell it by raising his hands and could at length finish his sentence, "There will be no nuclear retaliation."

After a shocked silence, the legislators erupted in furious disagreement. People stood on chairs shaking their fists and screaming at him. Abe Wasserman, a congressman from New York City, pushed and shoved his way down the aisle toward Andrews with such vile invective that he had to be stopped by the president's security people, who removed him from the chamber. With his big hands gripping both sides of the podium, Andrews bowed his head and prayed silently: Help me turn their anger, God. I know how justified they feel in their hearts.

One by one, they lessened their bombast.

"Of course . . ." he attempted to continue and gave up.

"Of course we're . . ." He stopped again and waited until finally the noise level diminished enough to be heard, "Of course we're outraged. Our natural reaction is to put on war paint and go slaughter millions of them in return."

The shouting became intermittent, the protests were less lengthy, and people began taking their seats.

"'Two roads diverged in a wood.' In his famous poem, Robert Frost decided to take the road less traveled and 'it has made all the difference.'" Andrews spoke without looking away from his hearers and this seemed to help engage the crowd in what he was saying. His eyes went from one face to another, legislators he'd known for years. His years in the Congress and the Senate seemed to be gaining him the courtesy and decorum American lawmakers accord each other.

"The 'road' we're all tempted to take is the heavily traveled road of vengeance that leads to more and more nuclear horror. The other 'road' is overgrown from lack of use. It's the less traveled road to world peace and it's the road I've decided to take."

Emotions again began to flare. Abe Wasserman of New York, who'd been readmitted to the chamber, stood and shouted, "If we show weakness, they'll hit us again. They just murdered over a million New Yorkers!"

Hundreds stood as one, shouting their support for the congressman from Manhattan.

"Earlier this morning, working with your leaders, Vice President Vandenberg ordered multiple thermonuclear warheads to be prepared for launch after this joint session. By midnight those warheads would have killed tens of millions of innocent Pakistanis. The blasts would maim, burn, and inflict radiation sickness on countless others. Would that have ended terrorism? Of course not. It would have multiplied it a hundred fold."

"But what if they've planted more bombs?" someone in the balcony shouted. Dozens chimed in with the questioner. The room rumbled with a heavy murmur of agreement. Heads nodded as congressmen and senators acknowledged the intolerable prospect of more bombings.

"They may have planted more. We're going to work as hard as we can to capture those responsible and stop them from destroying any more cities. I'm praying we can convince the terrorists to work out their grievances without resorting to another nuclear weapon, but we may fail."

The crowd reacted angrily. A small highly animated congresswoman down front shot to her feet and shouted, "Mr. President, you can't be suggesting we do nothing . . . in response to the worst attack in our nation's history!"

"We're not going to do nothing, Congresswoman Richardson. We're going to do everything humanly possible to find the terrorists and stop them. But, what we're not going to do is murder millions of innocent people in response." Andrews felt his complexion reddening, so he took a long breath, looked away from his challenger, and took a drink of cold water. His gaze panned the crowd and he put himself in their place. How Pollyannaish he must sound to them. How could one person, even a president, stand alone against such unanimity? He sensed that not one person in that whole crowd agreed with him. What would they do with him? Overthrow his administration? Impeach him? Lynch him? Then he heard the angel's clear voice again inside his thought, ". . . human life will end."

He took another deep breath and continued, "Turning the other cheek is terribly hard at a time like this, but whether we strike back or not, we could get bombed again."

He went on as they protested, "In fact, we may all die on the road to peace. Regardless, I will not be provoked to nuclear attack. We'll do our best to stop them, but there are no guarantees. I'm committed to work toward peace, no matter what the consequences, so help me God."

At that, he stood quietly and made eye contact with many in the crowd, then turned and looked at the others on the podium. Their faces were stone-like and no hands were extended to him. While the chamber filled with negative murmuring, Andrews made his way up the center aisle. No one reached out to shake his hand.

As he exited, a TV camera lingered on the furious countenance of Joe Vandenberg, glaring from a large screen beside the podium.

When the president and his retinue had cleared the chamber, CNN switched to their studio. A panel of five political commentators, four male and one female, looked at the camera with blank expressions. Not only had they not received an advanced copy of the president's speech, they'd been totally blindsided by his message.

At his producer's urging, Ted Kaufman, the moderator, broke the awkward dead air, "I think we're all shocked by what we just heard. Bryan Van Vleck, what was your reaction to the president's speech?"

"Hell, Ted, I'm completely flummoxed. This is not what the American people wanted to hear. I'm sure it's impossible for most people to consider turning the other cheek, after millions of Americans have been killed in a nuclear attack."

Carla Simpson interrupted, "Can you imagine FDR making that speech after Pearl Harbor, or George W. after the World Trade Center? I'm already getting reports of impeachment talk on the floor of the House."

Walter Boone chimed in, "It sounded like Neville Chamberlain trying to appease Hitler, espousing peace at any price just before World War II swept through Europe."

Bernie Salzburg continued, "This wasn't the President Andrews we all know. Makes me wonder if the trauma of the crash has affected his mind."

Ted Kaufman asked, "You suspect he's ..."

Salzberg continued, "Andrews sounded totally out of character. Like a different person. It's possible to have a mental short circuit when you're dealing with something as horrific as the crash he went through last night."

Kaufman paused, then wondered aloud, "Or, could he be right? Have we come to the fork in the path he spoke about? Have we entered a new paradigm, where the knee-jerk reactions of the past are no longer relevant? If we kill millions of innocent Pakistanis what will we have gained?"

The other correspondents all spoke at once, Bernie Salzberg pointed out, "Unilateral surrender to a terrorist country would be suicidal."

Carla Simpson overrode Salzberg's soft voice, "Americans have no intention of committing mass suicide."

Kaufman listened to the others, then turned to the camera, "I agree with the president. Obviously my four colleagues do not. No one on the panel knows that last night I lost my wife and three children in the terrorists' attack. This morning I forced myself to come to work buoyed by the expectation of massive retaliation. But as I listened to the president's speech, I realized . . . incinerating millions of innocent Pakistani men, women, and children wouldn't heal my grief. It would deepen it."

Kaufman's revelation silenced the panel. The network switched to Capitol Hill, where an interviewer asked a congressional leader why he had joined the group pushing for immediate impeachment.

***

Natasha woke in a sweat, lingering in the aftermath of her nightmare in which her bus rolled over and over. The sky in her dream was a mass of crimson flames. The screams and moans she woke to seemed like a continuation of her nightmare. Laying still, every joint and muscle of her body ached. Then, someone said her name.

She cracked open her left eye and saw Troy Jackson frowning at her from the end of the linen screen beside her bed. She regretted having him see her so banged up; but managed a messed-up smile.

"Knock knock," he said smiling faintly.

"Come in," she whispered through swollen lips.

"How you doin?" he asked. He wore a hospital gown, his bare muscular arms hanging on a pair of crutches, and his left leg encased in a cast to the knee.

"Some better. You?"

"Won't need to worry about getting a scholarship to Rutgers for a while," he grinned. Then, more seriously, "These people in here are messed up bad, Natasha."

"I know."

"Manhattan's history."

"Reverend Pettis told me. Said you pulled me out that bus."

"Yeah. I had help. You're heavier than you look."

"Thanks, Troy." Looking deep into his dark eyes she was able to extinguish the mental image of being burned to death. "I'll never forget what you did. No one's ever saved my life before. He said the bus was burning."

"You'd have done the same for me," he said, looking down from her intense eyes.

Interesting, she thought. How handsome he was when he felt sheepish, caught doing a good deed. She'd seen him in terrible fights through the years. He fought like a wild animal. During football games when he wasn't playing, he paced the sideline like a ferocious warrior. Right now, he was the kind boy his granny raised, "He also said you helped in here all night."

"Yeah, couldn't sleep. My leg hurts and they need the pain-killers for people a lot worse off than me. Working keeps my mind off my leg."

"Sounds like hundreds packed in here."

Their conversation was punctuated by anguished cries from beyond the cloth divider. It sounded like the aftermath of a battle with hundreds lying wounded on the field.

"They're bringing 'em in by the truck load, Tosh. Last night I saw the director trying to tell a driver there was no more room, just as another truck drove in, then another."

"Oh my."

"Toughest night I've ever had," he said. She could feel his agony as he looked at the floor while he quelled his emotion. One big tear fell. After a ragged intake of breath and an effort to clear his throat he continued, "Folks dyin' right and left. We unload injured people from the trucks, then load up our dead to make more room in here."

Suddenly, a female several beds away screamed in agony, "Help me! God, help me! I can't stand this pain!"

After staring at him in silence for a moment, Natasha responded, "That's so awful, Troy. How could you work like that with your leg in a cast?"

"I'm just resting on these crutches. I've put miles on this cast. My pain is nothing, Natasha. These people are all burned and blown up."

As he spoke, Natasha heard a helicopter landing on the roof and sirens approaching in the distance.

"Wish I could help," she said, trying to raise herself.

"No. No. You need to stay put. You can pray for all of us. Ask God to ease this suffering. He'll listen to you. Their burns are too painful for many of these folks."

He picked up the free-standing cloth-covered divider to her left and put it against the wall on her right. The scene down the length of the ward shocked her, crammed with beds crowded together and cots lined the aisle between the beds. Troy leaned down and spoke to the white girl next to Natasha. Her head was completely bandaged leaving openings for her right eye, nose and mouth. The bandages were stained on the left side of her head and her left eye and ear were missing.

"This here's Alexandra. Calls herself Alex. She told me last night she wants to die." He winked and left, swinging his legs down the aisle. Beyond the girl, Reverend Pettis knelt beside a black woman.

Natasha asked the girl, "Alexandra, have you met Reverend Pettis? He's talking to the lady next to you."

The girl was lying on her right side facing Natasha, and moved her head enough to stare unblinking at Natasha with her right eye. The left side of her mouth had been burned and she sucked saliva as she said in a husky whisper, "Told him not to bother . . . I'll be dead soon."

Natasha's injuries suddenly seemed minor and fleeting. She knew she'd be up and around in a few weeks, long before this girl could even begin the long painful process of rehabilitation. She tried to think of something to say to get her past the present, "I can see you telling your grandkids all about this, decades from now."

"If tonight's anything like last night, I'll end it myself, somehow or get Troy to help me."

"Were you near the bomb blast?"

"My family was on Fifth Avenue. They were the lucky ones," she said without emotion. "I was visiting a friend in Brooklyn." Alexandra got quiet and they both listened to Robert Pettis praying aloud to God to embrace the soul of this good woman. He closed the woman's eyes and laid her hand down.

Alexandra asked, "You think she's gone on to another place?"

"I think family and friends who passed before will be there to meet her and she'll go on with them."

"But without a burned body?"

"Um hum. What do you think?" Natasha prayed for her new friend and asked God to give her the courage to go on. She tried to imagine her feelings of loss and hopelessness.

"No idea. Probably just lights out. Want to hear something funny?"

"I'm ready for something funny."

The girl made sort of a twisted smile and said, "My left leg's plaid. The heat burned the pattern of my skirt on it."

Both girls giggled at the thought and Natasha joked, "I've heard of permanent cosmetics, but plaid legs! That'll never catch on."

They were quiet for a moment looking at each other. Alex didn't blink and Natasha wondered if she could. "Where do you go to school?" Natasha asked, wanting to change the subject.

Alex's mouth twisted and she sobbed painfully, "My Dad was so . . . proud."

"He was?"

"Next month I was starting at Princeton, his beloved old school."

Troy had returned without his crutches and was joined by another man to carry the black woman's body away.

Natasha responded, "You should tough this out, Alexandra, and go to Princeton, for him."

"Natasha's going to Rutgers, aren't you" Troy said from the end of her bed.

Natasha wondered if she could recover in the weeks before school started in September, "I haven't decided yet" she replied. "I'll probably go to Princeton with Alex."

Natasha saw Troy's exasperated expression, his hands forming fists, and waited for his predictable response; "You should listen to me, Natasha. They'll hurt you down there."

"You don't know me that way, Troy. I can deal with rich white people."

"I don't think so. You're better off with your own."

Natasha recalled some of the worst moments of her basketball camp experience the summer before her Junior year at Princeton. How mean those young white girls could be. "If it gets too bad, I can always transfer to Rutgers."

Troy turned away with a snort and returned to his work. He and the other man carefully moved the dead woman's body from the bed onto a stretcher and carried it away. Just before clearing the doorway to Natasha's right, he looked back at her and frowned.

The two girls didn't speak for a while, then Alex broke the silence, "If I get to Princeton, I'll be your friend, Natasha."

"You're going to make it, Alex . . . and we'll be great friends."

Natasha smiled at her and prayed to herself, please help her, God. Give her the courage to live.

Alone in his private quarters inside Cheyenne Mountain near Colorado Springs, Vandenberg stared at CSPAN on a large TV screen. Congressmen and women milled about on the floor of the House of Representatives discussing the president's speech.

If I were there, I'd have been tempted to kill the bastard. I can't be associated with a gutless traitor. How do I take over and get us back on track? I know fifty operatives who could take him out tonight, a dozen generals who would back me in a coup. He knew he shouldn't talk to anyone until he got complete control of his anger. If a hint of what he was thinking got out, it would blow his chances of ever becoming president.

He listened to the CNN talking heads and swore at Ted Kaufman's cowardice. Finally, he calmed himself and decided to take no action immediately. I'll wait and see how this plays out. The country won't go for this crap. He drained his glass. In the meantime, I'll run some ideas by a few close friends.

Andrews sat with Holt in his office scanning the TV news shows. Public reaction was overwhelmingly negative. "The people seem as unified as their representatives on Capitol Hill, Hank."

"Americans want to hit 'em hard," Holt replied.

The latest caller to a cable talk show practically screamed into his cell phone; "We lose millions in a nuclear attack and do nothing! We've got thousands of nukes we've sworn we'd use if someone hit us. Now 'Android' chickens out. He's got to step down and hand the keys to Vandenberg."

"Wonder how he really feels," Andrews joked.

"I'm not surprised," Holt said. "In a Washington Post poll earlier today just under 90% of Americans were in favor of nuclear retaliation."

"What would satisfy that last caller, besides sending the missiles, Hank?"

"Holt leaned back in the deep sofa and thought, "At the very least, we'd have to nail all the people involved, then locate and disarm all the bombs they have left."

As Holt spoke, Andrews thought to himself, We're talking about a needle in a hell of a haystack.

Holt continued, "Take a look at this. My secretary recorded it while we were still up on the hill." He ran video of Ted Kaufman's change of heart comments, after Andrews' speech.

Andrews got a bit choked up as he listened, "Jesus, Holt, a voice of reason in the damned wilderness. Do you figure there may be more Ted Kaufmans out there than we think?"

Holt excused himself and walked toward the door, "I hope so. We'll do some polling to find out."

CHAPTER FIVE

NEWARK HOSPITAL
AUGUST 12, 2034

At 11AM on August 12th the House of Representatives voted unanimously in favor of a Declaration of War on Pakistan.

———※《◎》※———

General Samir al Hammabi looked and felt like his new alias, Hector Rivera, dressed in dark linen slacks and a pleated white dress shirt. His mustache and hair now sported an upper class Latin cut. He liked the hand-tooled boots and his thin cigars. During their training, he, Ali, and Omar had become fluent in Mexican Spanish.

Lieutenant Omar Khaliff had just returned to Houston from off-loading a crate from a Libyan freighter in Vera Cruz, Mexico and stowing it in the hold of his forty-foot cabin cruiser now moored in Galveston Bay. Driving south on Highway 45 toward Galveston at 7:30AM, the three savored their triumph.

Samir assured them, "When we finish destroying five cities, the U.S. will be a severely weakened nation that will be forced to retreat from the Middle East."

"General, what were your thoughts during Andrews' speech last night?" Omar asked.

"I thought it was a great lie. An effort designed to make us think twice about hitting our next target," Samir responded.

After some reflection Omar admitted, "I was shocked by what he said. I think we all expected hate and anger followed by a massive nuclear retaliation. If he keeps his generals from striking back, it could make us look bad in the eyes of Muslims, if we destroy more of their cities."

As Omar spoke, Samir read the sign at the entrance to the L.B.J. Space Center. When finished he replied, "I agree. It was a wise strategy. I too was surprised, as I am whenever Western leaders show any wisdom. Your reaction is obviously the reaction they were hoping to achieve, but after they lose another city, their massive retaliation will show the world that his peace mutterings were lies."

Omar nodded, "Yes. I am sure you are right."

Samir added, "Our leadership is safe in Somalia. We will soon have the rest of our bombs in place. After the infidels destroy Pakistan, a river of money will flow to World Jihad from throughout the Muslim world. Then we will purchase the rest of the Ukrainian colonel's bombs and destroy this whole corrupt country."

⸺⸺◈⸺⸺

Andrews sat alone in the sitting area of his bedroom, framing the questions for which he needed answers. A yellow tablet on his lap had pages of notes and questions. He'd shut off all but emergency interruptions and stayed focused. How could she mend my spinal cord metaphysically? What power did the mending? What did that mending say about spinal cords? What was the nature of her healing power? What was her part in the healing? To whom can I turn to find answers to these and other questions?

She seemed sure I could access the power needed to stop the terrorists. What has to change in my thought to get in touch with the Being that knows who and where they are? I suspect I may have to break down my whole thought process and rebuild it. All the busyness, the noise, the junk thoughts, and the thousands of job-related diversions have to go. Is it possible for me to become a powerful spiritually-minded thinker? Can I drop my material-mindedness?

Elisha, one of his biblical heroes, came to mind. The king of Syria was enraged because an ambush he'd set to capture a unit of the Israelite army had come to naught. They'd obviously been tipped off. He asked his advisers to tell him who among them was a spy for the king of Israel? His chief adviser answered, "None O King, but Elisha, the man of God, tells the King of Israel what you say in your bedchamber."

I know if Elisha was sitting here next to me he could tell me where the terrorists and the bombs are hidden. Could he teach me how to know such things? Could he explain how he healed Naaman, the Syrian general, of leprosy? Is there anyone alive today who could clearly explain how spiritual healing is done?

An idea came and he reached for the phone on the coffee table in front of him and he rang Holt. "Hank, I read an article recently by a Princeton Nobel laureate in their Alumni magazine, a Dr. Kramer, physics professor. I need you to contact him and ask him if we could pick him up for a meeting with me. Maybe he can help me answer some questions I'm wrestling with."

———— ◈ ————

Later that morning the three jihadis walked from their car to the Galveston Yacht Harbor and boarded the cabin cruiser. Omar fired up the twin diesels and headed slowly up the Houston Ship

Channel riding low because of the hundred-kiloton warhead stowed in a lead-lined compartment below the waterline.

Over the sound of the diesels Samir asked Omar, "Did you have any problems with the Coast Guard on your journey from Vera Cruz?"

"No. As you ordered, I kept the radio on their frequency band. Their ships that normally inspect boats arriving from Mexico were in Corpus Christi for a hastily called training session. The officers are being trained to use newly issued scanning devices that detect radioactivity on ships entering U.S. waters."

"It is perfectly clear, Omar. Allah is opening the way for us."

Two hours after entering the Houston Ship Channel, Omar's powerboat passed under the Sam Houston Parkway and the East Loop Freeway and docked in a leased berth in the Port of Houston. Their boat and their bomb were moored less than a mile from the city center.

That evening in Omar's dockside condo, Samir forced himself to watch American television. It was even more revolting than he remembered. Women acted like harlots. Teenagers respected nothing. Men were depicted as buffoons or amoral trash. It angered him to think of the power this serpent's spell cast over much of the Muslim youth of the world. He studied Ali's expressions and reactions. He appeared to be mesmerized by what they were watching and it obviously jolted him when Samir turned off the TV.

Samir's father, a well-known muezzin, called the faithful to prayer five times each day in Baghdad. Now his son led this small group kneeling on prayer rugs in the condo living room.

Allahu Akbar (God is most great.)
God is the Supreme Being over all things.
I bear witness that there is no deity except God.

I bear witness that Muhammad is the messenger of God.
Come to prayer.
Come to salvation.
Allahu Akbar.

After their washing ritual, the three faced Mecca and repeated the sacred phrases standing, bowing, prostrating themselves and sitting. At the end of their prayer, they wished each other peace and the blessings of God.

That night Samir watched the TV coverage of trucks and cars jamming the Gulf Freeway piled with furniture and boxes and learned they had been traced to Houston. Evacuation information preempted radio and television programming. Lists of housing alternatives in Texas were updated hourly. Later, grim-faced anchors showed video of bumper-to-bumper traffic as panic-stricken people fled from all the major cities of America.

Samir had a second cassette delivered to NBC in Los Angeles announcing that the murder of Rashid Raza Ahmad had not yet been fully avenged, and millions more must die.

Frantic callers besieged legislative offices and White House operators demanding that the president and congress do something, before the terrorists destroyed another city.

————)((O)) ————

Andrews sat in on portions of the all-day meetings at the Pentagon on the 12th that set in motion the nationwide search effort of all cargo flights, commercial vans, box trucks, eighteen-wheelers, shipping containers, and box cars. Under the command of the Counter Terrorism Corps, the Army Reserve would man inspection points along all the interstate highways, air and sea cargo shipments. The National Guard would handle the state highway systems and rail cars. A lead seal system was developed to allow previously inspected and sealed cargo spaces to pass through.

Andrews and General Mitchell, head of the CTC, worked patiently with the Reserve and Guard officers to move them toward the realization that it was not only possible for them to implement this massive search effort by September 1st, it was imperative. When he was confident that the hundreds of officers involved were mentally yielding to the possibility of meeting the deadline, he left.

Dressing for a state dinner for the prime minister of England at 7PM, Andrews felt more single than usual. He couldn't get Diane off his mind. He imagined her talking to him from the dressing room, as she did her make-up. What a difference it would make to have her support right now. She never had to say anything. Her strength just flowed into him when he needed it. As he put on his clip-on black bow tie, he imagined her arms around his shoulders and her breasts pressed against his back as she tied his bow tie, looking over his shoulder in the mirror. He'd tried putting up with a valet right after his election, but didn't like having a personal servant.

He appreciated John Noble coming to show England's support. Diplomats were fleeing Washington in droves and here he was, arriving at once to stand beside his friends. There had been hundreds of calls of support, but Andrews admired this courageous gesture, made in spite of the media outcry in England opposing the trip. So, he'd hastily ordered a full state dinner, with all the flourishes. Holt and others had resisted, but Andrews felt they could all use a jolt of normalcy.

Out in the foyer he heard Holt, Clyde Alexander and their wives talking. Feeling painfully solitary, he slipped on his coat and walked out to join them. Striding down the stairs he walked behind the color guard and nodded to acknowledge the musical announcement of his arrival. After a dinner featuring prime rib and Yorkshire pudding, Andrews walked to the podium and looked at the hundred or so beautiful people.

"Thanks for coming on short notice. I was remembering during dessert that Abigail Adams hung out their laundry to dry in this room. The White House wasn't finished when they lived here and soon after they left, a foreign power burned it to the ground." For a moment he paused as if thinking hard, "I can't remember which one."

Stifled laughter rippled through the crowd at the reference to the War of 1812, and the British torching of the Executive Mansion. John Noble blushed a bit as he laughed.

"I don't need to rehash the list of ties we have with our Mother country, or who's always first to stand at our side, or we at theirs, when the going gets tough. It's moments like these when we're reminded who our best friends are." Andrews turned to his left and gestured toward the guest of honor, "Please join me in welcoming John Noble, Prime Minister of Great Britain."

People finally took their seats after a lengthy standing ovation. Noble and Andrews shook hands and the prime minister asked him to stay at the podium.

"Thank you for your warm American welcome. I know it's late in coming, but I apologize for that incident involving the White House in 1812. But when you see what you naughty colonists have become, you can hardly blame us for trying so desperately to hang onto you." After the laughter died down, his joyful expression turned serious and he continued, "We all knew we'd have to deal with nuclear terrorism one day, didn't we?"

Many nodded in acknowledgement. He made eye contact around the room, and then continued, "And none of us had any idea how we would deal with it, did we? Well, it's come. You have to deal with it, and you've got the right man for the job. Yes, I know, there's a firestorm of disagreement with President Andrews in our press, too. At first I couldn't understand his reasoning myself. If Islamic terrorists wiped out London and several million of our people, and I had a thousand nukes at the ready, I'm sure much of the Muslim world would lie in ashes right now."

Andrews glanced around the room and took in the heavy expressions and the absolute stillness. He hadn't been able to meet the prime minister's jet or have tea with him, as was their usual custom. So he was as interested as everyone else to hear what he was going to say.

"I was positively stunned listening to your president, who I thought I knew quite well, talking about turning the other cheek at a moment like this. I expected America, and its leader, to unleash its power on the homeland of the perpetrators. 'Turn the other cheek.' I'd liked to have seen my face when he said that. I'm sure you could have knocked me down with a feather. So, I sat down and thought for a long while about his approach to the problem. I was determined to understand, because I knew the depth of thought he'd brought to bear before he would utter such a thing."

Turning to the president he said, "I had to fly over to tell you, I finally got it; and that you're a godsend to us all for the stand you're taking."

Amazing, Andrews thought, as he took in the surprised looks on many faces. A world leader who gets it!

"Hopefully, this will be a turning point for all humanity. The most powerful man in the world is standing at the crossroads pointing down the road to peace, when the rest of us are demanding Armageddon."

To a great ovation, the two men stood with their hands clasped and cameras flashing. Finally, Andrews sat down and Mr. Noble continued, "While I sat there trying to grasp this radical stand he'd taken, I remembered a story from my childhood about another singular American who made a great difference. Suddenly everything the president said made perfect sense.

"My grandfather was an Oxford professor of anthropology who specialized in the Native American tribes of the Northeastern United States. My friends in those days and I played a bit of cowboys and Indians and I loved his tales. They were often true, as this one is. Allow me to draw a bit on your own history to explain what I grasped about the stand your president is taking."

Quietly the kitchen staff cleared the dessert dishes from the tables and refilled coffee cups and water glasses. While Andrews sipped the dark roast coffee, he surveyed the room. Every face wore an expression of complete attentiveness. Holt winked at him from the next table and smiled.

"About 1550AD there were numerous Iroquois tribes of American Indians living in what is now New York state. They hated each other passionately and were constantly at war. The Mohawk Chief, Dekanawida, tried in vain for years to convince his tribe that they and the neighboring tribes came from the same source, spoke dialects of the same language, and should be allies.

"Finally, after another terrible atrocity perpetrated by his own warriors, the chief gave in to his discouragement and left. He walked for many miles to the west. Exhausted at length, he sat down by a lake to rest and think about what he should do. He thought into the night. Another lone Indian pulled his canoe up onto the bank and started a fire. Dekanawida walked out from hiding and introduced himself.

"They shared dinner by the fire and the Mohawk chief explained his frustration with his tribe who wouldn't listen to his hopes for unity and peace among the Iroquois tribes, but went on killing and being killed by their neighbors. The other Indian told him his name was Hiawatha and that he had been driven from his Onondaga homeland after all his brothers were murdered and he alone escaped. He said he had come to this lake to learn the secrets of life and good government. He showed Dekanawida the wampum belts he had woven with white and black shells that taught his philosophy of good and evil, of peace and war, and of life and death."

Andrews was surprised that he didn't know this important piece of history. He remembered reading Henry Wadsworth Longfellow's poem in his youth, but didn't recall these details.

"Dekanawida knew it was the philosophy he himself was seeking and recognized in his new friend the charisma he lacked. So, he got Hiawatha to return with him and explain his new philosophy to the Mohicans. Eventually, with Dekanawida leading the way, the Mohawk, Cayuga, Oneida, Onondaga, and Seneca tribes formed the Iroquois Confederacy. The Five Nations lived in peace for many generations under Hiawatha's laws. Dekanawida was ever after known as the Great Peacemaker. If any outside tribe considered attacking one, they knew they were attacking all of the Five Nations and usually thought better of it.

"President Andrews is saying to the whole world, enough is enough. Everyone knows we have the power to destroy the entire planet, but we've decided to bury the tomahawk and strive for a lasting peace free of nuclear holocaust. Your president is making an unprecedented stand for world peace."

Picking up his glass he concluded, "I've come across a rather large pond today to drink a toast to you, President Andrews. I pray your efforts for peace succeed and you also become known as the Great Peacemaker."

◦◦◦◦◦◦

Vandenberg knew the kind of drivel to expect from the prime

minister and refused to be tied in by downlink. Instead he studied the eyes and expressions of the men seated around his conference table, looking for signs of weakness. He'd handpicked the cabinet members of his shadow government for their loyalty. Most were ex-military, and Andrews' refusal to retaliate was anathema to them all.

"Colonel Braxton, I'm reassigning you to the White House. Teleconferencing and low-level representation is no longer adequate. You're to monitor everything and report daily to me personally."

Jim Braxton had been Vandenberg's adjutant for fifteen years and their thinking was almost always in synch.

Vandenberg continued, "I won't undertake any drastic steps if the impeachment process is begun in short order and prosecuted expeditiously. Andrews must be gone soon or this country will begin to crack. Eighty-five percent of Americans are demanding nuclear retaliation and seventy-five percent are in favor of impeachment."

⸻ ◈ ⸻

In the night, Natasha prayed for Alexandra. Earlier their nurse had told her that Alex was fading. She asked God with all her heart to save her new friend. As she reached out, her own pain lessened. Medical teams and supplies had begun arriving from other areas of the country, and the doctors had sedated Alexandra. Going through each of Peter's and Paul's healings in the Book of Acts, Natasha tried to understand how they'd performed them. Unconsciously, she put her hands behind her head and brought her knees up to support her Bible as she read.

Alexandra whispered, "Looks like you're feeling better."

"I didn't know you were awake. I've been praying for you, but I seem to be the one who's improving."

"I had the strangest dream," Alexandra said.

"Tell me."

"In Junior High, after an overnight, I went to my friend's Sunday School. It's the only church service I can remember. It was a strange dream with no people, just the podium in that Sunday School with a sign over it. More like a vision."

"What did the sign say?"

"God is Love."

Natasha closed her eyes tight and said silently, Thank you!

"When I woke up just now . . . I knew."

Natasha waited for her to continue, heard her crying softly and asked, "What, Alex? What did you know?"

"It was Him, Natasha. The God you pray to wanted me to know what He is. He gave me a sign—literally. And if He's Love, I definitely want to get to know Him."

"Love, huh," Natasha responded. "Not what most folks think about it."

After a while Alex said, "Yesterday I had a body that made boys, even grown men, gawk at me embarrassingly. Sometimes I mistook male attraction for love."

Natasha chuckled, "I know how that goes. I can't get over the fact that God gave you a sign to let you know who He is."

————))•((————

At quarter past three in the morning of the 13th, Andrews was wide awake sitting up in bed praying for Angie. The hourly updates of her condition were not encouraging. She hadn't regained consciousness and her vital signs were weakening.

Hell, he said to himself, I can be there for an early breakfast and check on her myself. I should go thank the doctors and nurses for all they're doing anyway. And while I'm at it, I can let them know how important that young woman is to me.

He got up, walked to the door, and said to the Marine guard in the hall, "Let the Duty Officer know I need Marine Two, my security detail, and Mr. Holt ready to go to the Newark hospital in thirty minutes."

———— ◦《◉》◦ ————

When Natasha woke up it was morning and Alexandra's body had been taken away. An older comatose black woman had taken her place. Shocked by the loss of her new friend, she stared at the ceiling, crying from grief, heartsick that her prayers had been brushed aside. Finally, she whispered, "Safe journey, Alex."

Before dawn a tall well-dressed man came in with a crowd and a TV crew. His security people stayed ahead of and behind the president and his chief of staff, Mr. Holt, a slightly rotund balding middle-aged man, who barely came up to the president's shoulder, had the look of someone who would rather be someplace else.

Natasha marveled at the president's kindness as he moved from bed to bed, every expression and gesture was genuine. His concern for each patient was understated, but heartfelt. On the other side of the aisle he lingered a long while, seated next to the bed of his personal assistant. Troy had told Natasha that Miss O'Leary was badly injured in the crash of the president's helicopter leaving New York City on the 10th.

When the president got to Natasha's bed, he smiled and said, "Troy over there tells me you've been praying for some of the patients in the ward, Natasha."

"Yes sir. Troy knows all these people and lets them know I'll pray for them if they ask, and several have."

"Are you able to help them?"

"He says I'm helping them. Would you like me to pray for you?"

"Yes," he said smiling. "But more importantly, I need you to pray for my personal assistant over there." He pointed at Angie's bed across the aisle. "She's in a coma and not doing well. I need her. The country needs her, Natasha."

"I'll start praying for her right away, Mr. President."

"Thank you," he said starting to leave, then he turned back, "I almost forgot. Troy asked me to convince you to go to Rutgers, instead of Princeton, Natasha. He thinks you're making a big mistake, attending a rich white school."

"Is that what you think?" she asked.

"Did you know Princeton's my alma mater?"

"Yes, sir."

"If I hear you went to Rutgers . . . "

Natasha smiled, "What?"

"I'll send soldiers to pack you up and move you to Princeton."

Natasha laughed, "Okay then, I'll go to your school, Mr. President. But if they're mean to this poor black girl down there, like Troy says, what'll you do about it?"

"I'll send soldiers to find the culprits and move them to Rutgers."

"I'll take names."

"Good. I'll stop by this fall and look you up."

He left smiling and waving to everyone. How on earth could the man be so charming, kidding like that, Natasha wondered in amazement, with the weight of all this bearing down on him?

She felt honored to be asked to pray for his personal assistant. It helped her set aside the intense disappointment she felt at the loss of Alexandra. Reading in the Book of Acts, she focused on trying to understand how Peter healed so many.

Reverend Pettis walked by and saw her studying The Bible. "That's quite a book you're reading, Miss Cheatam. An all-time best seller, I'm told."

"How did Peter do his healing work, Reverend?"

"I've been thinking about that for years, Natasha. A lot of folks say Jesus must have given him special powers, but I think that's a cop out."

"So you think it's something he learned from Jesus. Then, it must be possible for us to learn, as well."

"Yep. That's what I think. I've done some healing along the way and want very much to do more."

Natasha was quiet for a moment, then said, "I've read and re-read all of Jesus' healings and I think it has to do with how he saw people. Seems to me, Jesus saw the spiritual man God made—and his seeing and knowing somehow changed things. The president asked me to pray for Miss O'Leary. Would you pray with me? He needs her."

Reverend Pettis brought over a folding chair and whispered, "Okay, let's pray together quietly until we can see her as God made her and knows her."

<hr>

Andrews was quiet on the way back to D.C. He tossed and turned night after night, but refused to take sleep medication. The sleep he did manage was often filled with dreams he hated. So, as the big blue helicopter took him home, he laid his seat back and drifted in and out of sleep. His dream this night was not of death and chaos, but an old familiar basketball memory of his dad pushing him to play harder. How could he play harder? Already 6'-4" in the seventh grade, he could score at will. These were his friends and the last thing he wanted to do was embarrass them. The message his father drummed into him that season centered on his lack of a "killer instinct."

The chopper hit some bad air that woke him up, but he continued thinking about the reoccurring dreams he had about his dad. The maddest he ever made him was in his sophomore year of high school. On a long holiday weekend he discovered cross-country skiing and decided to quit basketball. It was well worth his Dad's tirades. At first, it was the fantastic quiet he enjoyed the most. He also loved being alone in the unblemished snow on trails through evergreen forests near his hometown of Hibbing, Minnesota. At 6'-8" in high school he wasn't competitive downhill, but discovered he could be quite a force cross-country. He met Diane at a national qualifier in Colorado and was dazzled by her beauty, her spirit, and her downhill racing. But, in his senior year he gave in to his dad and returned to basketball to insure his admission to Princeton. At Princeton his father began pressuring him to go to law school and join his law firm. The dreams always ended suddenly with his dad's fatal heart attack just before his graduation from law school.

—◦◦◦—

Staring at the wall of video monitors that kept him up to the minute on the world outside his granite mountain, Vandenberg sensed the nation turning to him for leadership. At pivotal points in his career, he'd always felt alone. He'd split with his pacifist parents over his decision to accept an appointment to West Point, and then choosing a military career. Army life drove off his wife and kids. Then, years of complete focus on the task at hand in a dozen foreign posts had removed him far from all of them. Surrounded by staff and the officer corps he rarely spent time alone, but in moments like this, his lack of a real family closed in on him.

Outside the mahogany doors of his office, his staff worked to keep pace with the flood of support pouring in from the media and top political figures, as a vote to conduct impeachment hearings approached in the House of Representatives.

Already this morning they'd fielded numerous requests for statements and interviews from media spokespeople who quoted numerous polls showing that millions wanted him to lead them out of this catastrophe. Computer screens behind him updated the storm of controversy created by the president's speech that raged throughout the capitol, the nation and the world.

Vandenberg knew that never in history had a vice president prepared so thoroughly to assume the presidency. For two years Vandenberg had carefully chosen his shadow government, and prepared them to take over at a moment's notice. He'd disciplined himself to learn the political, economic, diplomatic, and social aspects of the job. He could debate fiscal and monetary policy with the best of them. He'd assembled a stronger team than Andrews', but their answers and solutions to the nation's problems were routinely ignored. Vandenberg prepared for his meeting with his National Security Adviser filled with renewed energy. His time was coming. He could feel it.

Leading up to the president's address to the world at 9PM on the 13th, all the networks ran tape of the devastation, toured an overcrowded New Jersey hospital, and panned across rows of body bags in a Brooklyn gymnasium.

A woman described being blasted out the window of a building that exploded in flames a second later. A burly truck driver told of being blown off the road into the Hudson River. He breathed air trapped in the cab, until he realized no rescuers were coming to pull him out and he'd have to swim to the surface as best he could. The mushroom cloud, hundreds of burning vehicles, and the charred trees and grass along the riverbank told him what had happened.

Andrews looked up from the notes on his desk in the Oval Office and spoke, "In the past, when a man hated his neighbor, he sometimes killed him. On August 10th a few hate-filled men killed millions of Americans in New York City with a single nuclear bomb.

"We've created weapons powerful enough to destroy our planet. Anger, hatred, and ignorance tempt us to use them. Most Americans are demanding the destruction of Pakistan, the homeland of the terrorists. On television we've seen millions fleeing our anticipated counterattack. Innocent Pakistanis will not be slaughtered to avenge our great loss. We will not strike back against them—they're innocent.

"I keep this picture on my desk to remind me." He picked up a front page of a recent Christian Science Monitor. "Zoom in on this, would you?" A color photo filled the screen of an attractive dark-skinned Pakistani girl in a colorful head scarf, her deeply soulful eyes looked calmly at the camera. "To me, this young girl in Islamabad, represents all Pakistanis. What a terrible crime it would be to kill her and millions like her in retaliation for the evil act of a few hate-filled men."

"In one of Abraham Lincoln's darkest hours, he said something that applies to our situation today. He said, 'The dogmas of the quiet past are inadequate to the stormy present. The occasion is piled high with difficulty and we must rise with the occasion. As our case is new, so must we think anew and act anew. We must disenthrall ourselves and then we shall save our country. It is the eternal struggle between two principles, right and wrong, throughout the world.'

"I would only change one of President Lincoln's words, 'We must disenthrall ourselves and then we shall save our . . . planet.' I looked up the word 'disenthrall.' It means to break a spell. The spell I'm talking about causes many of us to believe that peace can be gained by killing millions.

"In the past, striking back has often shown man's courage to stand up for what is right. With nuclear weapons, honor and bravery lose their meaning. Mankind has come to a turning point." He paused a moment, looked into the camera lens and added, "Quite a word, isn't it—man . . . kind.

"We must change our approach to settling disputes. The United Nations was one of our great loses on the 10th. We must re-build the UN and give it an important role to play in building peace. I urge the terrorists to give up their nuclear weapons, and work with me to right the wrongs done them.

"As you know, millions of Americans are demanding a massive nuclear retaliation against the homeland of the terrorists who destroyed New York City. If we killed millions of Pakistanis, can you imagine what would follow? Millions more would die on both continents in counterattack after counterattack. And there would be no turning back. I am committed to avoiding this global catastrophe. We must work together and build a lasting world peace. That's what I'm committed to doing. The future of humanity is at stake. Thank you and God bless the United States of America."

CHAPTER SIX

HOUSTON
AUGUST 14, 2034

Andrews and Holt sat at opposite ends of a yellow goose down sofa with a floral pattern, in the rustic living room of the Lodge at Camp David. It was 10AM on August 14th and Andrews was watching the CSpan coverage of the Judicial Committee hearings. Holt was going through a pile of correspondence on the coffee table.

Holt tried to interrupt the president, "They're almost to a stopping point before they vote, Mr. President. Maybe you could spend some time on requests we've received from congressmen who need help raising money for their midterm elections. I've got a list of the Republican candidates for Congress who have been supportive of your refusal to retaliate. Warner in the 5th District of Nebraska has been with us all along, Mr. President. Mr. President . . ."

Andrews responded without looking away from the television, "Hank, we've got a committee talking about impeaching me, and you want me to think about an election that may take place after I'm gone."

"Should I call Doug Warner's people and tell them we can't schedule their fund-raiser because we're too busy getting impeached?"

"Back off a hair, Mr. Holt. Right now I'm interested in this Judiciary Committee hearing. We'll think about helping Mr. Warner when I'm better able to focus on his request. So far, in the second hour of this hearing I've heard three members who might be opposed to my impeachment. Three!"

Wilber Samuels, congressman from New York, was speaking to the thirty-nine-person committee, "Mr. Chairman, let's get this matter to the floor of the House! If my count is correct, I'm the twenty-eighth member of the committee who feels strongly that the president's refusal to act on our Declaration of War is an impeachable offense."

The Chairman, Henry Seek, summed up the morning session of the committee, "Ladies and gentlemen, it appears after only three hours of debate and discussion that we're ready for a vote. Congressman Simpson of California has called for the question. All those in favor say aye." The "ayes" were clearly a majority. "Those opposed. The ayes have it. So, we'll proceed to a vote. A 'Yes' vote is a vote to send the matter to the House of Representatives for a vote on whether or not to authorize this committee to draft an Article or Articles of Impeachment."

Andrews looked at Holt, "The first step was mighty quick, Hank. You'd better get moving with my legal team. At this rate, it won't be long before they're needed."

Hank nodded, "I can see that. The vote is coming up now. Thirty-one 'Yes' votes and eight 'No's.' I'll meet tonight with Frankhauser and get the AG's office moving. By the way, Dr. Kramer will meet with you at 7PM here at Camp David on the 18th."

⸻ ◉ ⸻

Samir al Hammabi glanced at his watch as the second hand swept past noon on August 14th. His United flight was over New Mexico en route to San Diego. The first-class flight attendant leaned down and asked what he would like to drink, as Houston was incinerated.

He didn't meet her gaze, just shook his head, closed his eyes, and imagined the blast.

Moments later the passengers heard the electronic click of the plane's public address system, then a momentary pause with muffled background noises, "This is the captain." Then, another pause with audible heavy breathing and several throat-clearings, "God have mercy ladies and gentlemen . . . I've just received the worst news of . . . my life. Houston has just been . . . destroyed."

The blood drained from the flight attendant's face, she dropped the tray she was carrying, staggered, and collapsed in the aisle. A chorus of wailing and weeping erupted from the passengers. Samir turned to the window and studied the cloud formations.

In his thought he saw his wife Sabeen's face smiling at him. The most wonderful woman Allah ever made had been taken from him the first night of the bombardment of Baghdad in 2003, along with his three sons, and their home. He knew well how the passengers from Houston felt right now, but it surprised him that these mighty blows against the Great Satan weren't lessening his own sense of loss.

For two hundred million dollars he'd purchased a device that had just destroyed a city of over a million people. And beyond the actual destruction, fear was paralyzing the entire country. Now, on to Los Angeles for the next blow. I'll always love you Sabeen, he said in his thought.

He knew what he was doing was for a great cause, but all this death and destruction wasn't lessening the void he felt inside, as he thought it would.

Soon after the attack on Houston, at 2PM Eastern Daylight Time on August 14th, the Senate passed unanimously the Declaration of War on Pakistan, initiated by the House of Representatives two days before. An hour later, the House voted overwhelmingly to proceed with the impeachment inquiry recommended by the Judiciary Committee, and referred the matter back to the committee to draft Articles of Impeachment.

The summer recess for both the House and the Senate, scheduled from August 14th to September 8th was delayed a week. House members were adamant about limiting the delay to one week before getting back to their home districts to prepare for their upcoming election campaigns. The Judiciary Committee members agreed to stay in Washington and take staggered trips home to handle their campaign business, while still fulfilling their committee responsibilities.

On Wednesday morning August 16th, President Andrews stood at the podium in the National Cathedral and looked out at a sea of grief-stricken faces. Andrews chose not to break the silence for a while. Finally, sensing the moment was right he said, "We decided not to postpone this service despite the terrible blow we experienced on Monday. The loss of life in Houston, while horrific, was far less than it would have been if we hadn't picked up the trail of the terrorists leading from New York to Houston. We were able to evacuate over a half million people, but it was still the second worst attack in our history."

Andrews was quiet for a moment and recollected several of the ideas put forward by the clerical speakers who had preceded him. They'd called for steadfastness and courage in the hardest time in the history of the nation.

"It's good to be together in this cathedral which symbolizes the spiritual foundation of our nation. I've loved the soulfulness of the music this morning and the wisdom shared by our four inspired clerical speakers: Catholic, Protestant, Jewish, and Muslim. I'll keep my remarks brief because little needs to be added to what they said.

"I ask for your prayers . . ."

Andrews stopped as a stout man with a buzz cut in the seventh row rose slowly from the pew to a standing position–his head bowed. Slowly he raised his face, which was wet from tears and he said in a low voice, "I can't sit here and listen to this without speaking, Mr. President."

Andrews looked from side to side and raised his hands to stop Secret Service agents who had started moving toward the man interrupting the service.

Andrews said, "Please continue, sir."

"On Monday I lost my wife, my two girls and their families, Mr. President. All the people I love most . . . in the world," he stopped and put both hands on the pew in front of him, bowed his head again and sobbed quietly. His thick wide shoulders shook with the sobs.

Andrews waited.

After a moment the man regained control, wiped his face on his coat sleeve, and continued, "I'm a retired Marine, Mr. President. I know how to fight, and kill, and die; but I have no idea how to pray. I have no training in praying. I believe in God. I believe my people are with Him in heaven, but I'll be damned if I believe we should sit here praying, while these murdering bastards kill our people. I'm sorry, sir, but I couldn't sit here and not let you know that. We should let'um have it, Mr. President. Blow'em all to hell."

He was quiet for a moment, as though searching for more words, then said, "That's it. Thank you for letting me speak." He slowly sat back down.

Andrews was quiet, his head bowed, and his hands on the podium. Finally, he looked at the man in the seventh row and said, "Thank you for your service to our country. I'm so sorry for your terrible loss. You may know, I too lost a wife I loved very much . . . and have never gotten over it. This is a terrible time for most Americans. Many more of our countrymen agree with you, I'm told, than with me regarding the destruction of Pakistan."

He stopped for a moment and made eye contact among the pews, then continued, "We all feel the same way—angry, sad, grief-stricken, vengeful . . . all of us, but this nation stands for ideals greater than those feelings. We stand for goodness and mercy, as well as for strength. We're a nation of good people—not mass-murderers. We're the people who must stop the killing—not escalate it. How could we think it right to kill millions of completely innocent Pakistani men, women, and children—wonderful people like this Marine's family, and somehow figure we're even. We would be as evil as the terrorists. And they would strike back at us ten-fold. And then we would strike back at them a hundred-fold. When would it stop? It would stop when they were all dead—or we were all dead.

"Somehow we've got to get it through our heads that we can't kill our way out of this problem. Exploding nuclear bombs in defenseless cities doesn't lead to peace, it leads to total death and destruction."

He was quiet for a moment, then went on, "Once again, I ask for your prayers. Sincerely. All of you here with me this morning and those watching throughout the country. These blows threaten the foundations of our nation, our democracy, and our freedom. Right now, tens of millions are fleeing our cities. Our economy is in free-fall. We've reached a critical point in our history. We must stop these terrorists and recover from this destruction. And we must do it without resorting to mass murder ourselves.

"I know the power of prayer. We can find these terrorists and bring them to justice. Fight your fears. These are times that demand courage and determination. Our nation will survive. God bless the United States of America."

On the afternoon of the 16th Henry Seek, congressman from Alabama, made the opening statement on the first day of impeachment hearings in the Judiciary Committee with all thirty-nine members present. Andrews watched the NBC television broadcast in his private office.

Congressman Seek's unmistakable southern drawl began, "Committee members are urged to be brief and well-prepared throughout these hearings. The five-minute rule for questions and answers from experts and witnesses appearing before the committee will be strictly enforced. The first panel to come before us is a group of constitutional lawyers prepared to answer questions regarding the constitutional standards for impeachment of a president. They will also take questions on the president's oath, his responsibility to protect and defend the Constitution, and his responsibilities as commander in chief."

Andrews listened and took notes. Holt brought in a new poll that showed some movement, especially among women and young people, supporting his stand for not retaliating against Pakistan. Reading through the polls he felt encouragement—a rare feeling of late.

On the morning of the 17th, the committee met in a closed hearing and got a detailed presentation by the administration's legal team of the nationwide truck and van search being implemented September 1st to find and stop the terrorists. In the afternoon, the White House Chief Counsel, Charles Frankhauser, laid out their position that there was no proven linkage between the government of Pakistan and World Jihad, nor was there proof that the nuclear bombs detonated in New York and Houston by World Jihad were obtained from the government of Pakistan.

—◦—

Andrews prayed at Camp David to know if he should step down as almost every news source was advocating, to save the nation more bitterness and division. A vote to remove still seemed a certainty in the Senate.

While he was deep in thought, Holt knocked on his door and showed Dr. Kramer into his private study, then left the two men alone. Andrews came around the desk shook his hand and invited Kramer to sit down in a plaid wing-backed chair by the rustic stone fireplace.

The elderly physicist wore a tan corduroy sport coat with dark elbow patches and brown slacks. His full beard hid his mouth, but his eyes were youthful beneath a pair of upswept eyebrows that gave his face a wistful expression.

"Thank you for coming Dr. Kramer. I trust you were well taken care of on the trip here."

"Yes. I was Mr. President. Your helicopter is quiet and comfortable. I got some good thinking done."

"I read your article in the Princeton Alumni publication with great interest and wanted to talk to you about your work on the Zero Point Field."

"You do? That's surprising. What is your interest in that work?"

"My answer to your question, Doctor, in fact this entire discussion needs to stay between the two of us. Is that agreeable?"

"Of course."

A kitchen attendant rolled a cart in and served a light supper of seafood chowder and Caesar salad.

"You may know that my helicopter crashed when New York was bombed. After lying paralyzed in terrible pain for hours I was healed of complete paralysis by a mysterious visitor. Since then I've been trying to understand how that could be possible. I don't talk about it because it seems too strange to most people. When I read your article in the Princeton Alumni magazine I wondered if you could provide any insight into the possibility of that kind of healing."

Dr. Kramer turned his gaze to the fire and was quiet for some time. At length without looking away from the flames he said, "I can see a possible connection. Physics shows us that on the subatomic scale, the building blocks of matter are not at all what we experience with our physical senses."

"You mean E = MC squared."

"As I explained in that article you read, Dr. Einstein was telling us, in his famous equation, that mass is a concentration of energy. My research partners and I agree that mass, or matter, is a form of energy, in a similar way that ice is a form of water."

"So, Doctor, where do you see a connection to my healing?"

"I think it's commonly known that stress can cause disease in the body. Mainstream physicians agree, I think, that there is a definite connection between thought and the body. So, if thought can cause disease, it seems logical that thought can cure disease. After all, my research leads me to think the body must be a mental construction."

"So the person who healed my spinal cord . . . could have learned how to erase an injury that actually took place in a purely mental realm."

Dr. Kramer sat smiling at the president, then turned back to the burning logs. "Or perhaps he or she worked from the basis that no crash actually took place in that mental realm."

After a period of thought, Andrews said, "You lost me."

"You asked me to extrapolate from my research and attempt to explain how your spinal cord could be metaphysically repaired.

Obviously, I'm theorizing in an area outside my field, but rather than beg off, I'm willing to take a shot at answering your question. Say that you're made of ideas—your hands, hips, spinal cord are all constructed of complex ideas that have evolved over many millennia, and give them their form and function."

"Are you saying the only thing real about my spinal cord is its function?"

"In this scenario we're discussing, flesh and bones are hypothetical—they're energy concentrations."

After thinking that through Andrews asked, "What happens to your hand if you pick up a hot pan?"

"The person who healed your spinal cord would not be burned by the pan and could heal your hand if you picked up the pan."

The two men went on for another hour until Dr. Kramer remembered an early morning meeting back at school.

Andrews stared at the fire for a long while, thinking about Dr. Kramer's answers and began to see the possibilities. If a body is a construct of thought, then it must be possible for a body to be changed by changed thought.

Natasha held Angie's right hand and said, "I'm going home now, Miss O'Leary, but I'll continue to pray for you, if you want me to."

Angie couldn't reply because of her breathing apparatus, but she looked into Natasha's eyes, squeezed her hand, and nodded.

"The nurses report you're doing better and I'll check back with them every day. Troy tells me he'll take special care of you."

Natasha squeezed Angie's hand back then patted her shoulder.

She and Troy turned and walked down the narrow aisle lined with cots on both sides. Her smile felt almost normal as she greeted several patients who made eye contact with her. She no longer gasped inwardly at damaged faces or bodies. Her days and nights of prayer had lifted her thought and helped her see through the material picture of burned flesh and hideous wounds, to behold the spiritual perfect individuals God created. She had never felt such a deep sense of peace, yet she was surrounded by the most terrible matter pictures she could imagine.

She got some brave smiles back along the way. Several people reached out and took her hand as she passed. A badly burned gentleman who had lost his legs gestured to her to bend down to him, "This is a great day, Miss. Someone's leaving here alive on their own two feet."

An older white lady took her hand as she passed and stopped her, "Troy told us you were praying for us day and night, Miss Cheatam. God bless you. Don't stop. We need your prayers."

Natasha heard Troy's whispered reminder of the lady's name and replied, "I won't stop, Wilma. God bless you and help you come out of this a better stronger person."

With Troy supporting her left arm, Natasha walked slowly to the nurses' station in the hall outside her ward to say goodbye to Reverend Pettis, who was having coffee with the head nurse, "You're looking more like yourself, Reverend Pettis," she said then embraced him and kissed his freshly shaved cheek.

"And look at you!" After just one week I can already recognize your exquisite face again."

⟞⟝●⟞⟝

On the third day of Judicial Committee hearings, the panel addressing the committee was made up of specialists from the CIA and the CTC on the relationship between the government of Pakistan and World Jihad.

Mr. Seek, the committee chairman, asked Mike Ritter, the Deputy Director of the CIA, "Mr. Ritter, I'm looking at seven captured communications from Rashid Raza Ahmad of World Jihad to agents of the Pakistani military seeking to obtain nuclear warheads. They were submitted to this committee from your agency. All the committee members have copies. Would you address those communications, sir?"

"Yes, Mr. Chairman. The seven intercepted communications you refer to were sent in various encrypted formats to Pakistani military officials in 2032 and 2033."

"Another intercepted communication appears to be a reply from a Pakistani military official agreeing to the release of nuclear warheads. Is that true?"

"Yes, sir ..." The hearing was suddenly interrupted by an eruption of commotion throughout the hearing room. News people rushed from the room to quiet locations where they could use cell phones to file their reports.

Mr. Seek had to use his gavel repeatedly, before he could bring the room back to order. "I won't issue this warning twice. If our committee is disrupted like this again, I'll clear the room and we'll conduct the rest of our business in private. Now, Mr. Ritter, would you continue?"

"Yes, sir. The official who is named in that communication has since sworn he never sent such a message and that Pakistan has never and will never release a nuclear weapon to World Jihad or any other terrorist organization."

"Has your agency been able to verify the communication in one way or another?"

"We know it was sent from the Pakistani Army general staff offices, Mr. Chairman, but we have no way of knowing who sent it. Its validity was investigated for three months last year with Pakistan's full cooperation. It involved our agency and the CTC going through weapon lists and inventories released before and after the date of the communication. Both of our agencies reached the conclusion that no nuclear weapons were released from Pakistan to World Jihad."

On August 19ᵗʰ, the fourth day of committee hearings, Mr. Frankhauser provided an affidavit signed by the Pakistani official noted as agreeing to the release of nuclear warheads, swearing that no warheads had ever been released to World Jihad. In the afternoon session the committee members went again into a closed hearing and debated the newly released secret intelligence documents linking World Jihad and the government of Pakistan.

A majority of the committee clearly believed that the terrorists' request for nuclear warheads and Pakistan's agreement to supply them, constituted the smoking gun they needed—despite the affidavits and the president's attorney's protestations to the contrary. Mr. Samuelson of Colorado summed up the majority position, "Mr. Chairman, we have a decoded message issued from the Pakistani general staff offices agreeing to supply nuclear warheads to World Jihad. Millions of our citizens and two of our cities have been destroyed by known World Jihad terrorists using nuclear warheads. I move that we draft a resolution containing an Article of Impeachment." His motion passed 34 to 5.

On Sunday August 20ᵗʰ, the Judiciary Committee drafted the resolution and voted again 34 to 5 to send to the House of Representatives an Article of Impeachment charging President David Andrews with refusing to carry out the duly constituted Declaration of War on Pakistan, failure to defend the Constitution, and failure to defend the nation as commander in chief. That afternoon the House of Representatives voted 399 to 36 to send the matter to the Senate for trial. The next morning the members of both houses of Congress left for their home districts to begin campaigning for the fall elections.

Ted Kaufman turned from Bernie Salzberg and spoke to the CNN camera, "The impeachment hearings in the House of Representatives concluded today, and lasted only six days. David Andrews became the third president to be impeached by the House of Representatives. Only 36 representatives out of 435 voted against moving ahead with impeachment proceedings.

"Bernie, how would you describe the debate we witnessed in the House, besides being surprisingly brief?"

Over Salzberg's right shoulder, the wall-sized TV screen still showed the members of Congress milling about the House chamber discussing the historic vote.

"The bomb that destroyed Houston sealed his fate, Ted. The president's refusal to retaliate has a modest level of support around the country, but the overwhelming majority of Americans want Andrews removed from office and a massive nuclear retaliation against the terrorists' nation."

"How do you see this playing out in the Senate? Are the votes there to remove the president from office?"

"Yes. The Senate is strongly behind the vice president's stand for nuclear retaliation."

"Do you expect a lengthy trial?"

"No. Less than a month."

"Thanks for your good work during the House hearings, Bernie. The case for impeachment seemed to hinge on the validity of that intercepted message from the Pakistani military headquarters to release warheads to World Jihad. The CTC inspectors testified that their warhead inventory before and after that communication never changed. Did that testimony carry any weight among the members of Congress?"

"Ted, neither the members of Congress nor the American people really care about those easily doctored inventory lists. The mere fact that the head of World Jihad and the Pakistani military discussed the release of warheads for two years was enough."

"Thanks for talking with us, Bernie. You've helped millions follow this historic debate. It sounds like you agree with the final vote."

"Yes I do. Our enemies must know we will respond powerfully, if attacked."

"This is Ted Kaufman bidding you good night. My boss told me to be sure I don't give you the impression that this news organization comes down on one side or the other in this debate. But speaking for myself personally and for the Americans who support the president's position, a growing minority feel we must do everything we can to end the cycle of violence breeding more violence."

Outside the entrance to the Emergency Room, Troy helped Natasha into the front passenger seat of a new black Cadillac sedan.

"Where'd you get this?" she asked.

"The director loaned it to me. Said it had never served a better purpose. You're our first patient to get well enough to leave."

"You know, Troy, it seemed like the more I prayed for the people you referred me to, the faster my own recovery went."

"I know two of those people have made dramatic progress since you began praying for them."

"I'm so glad. Who besides Miss O'Leary? I've been able to watch her progress."

"When I asked you to include Mrs. Wright in your prayers, all she could do was cry and scream, day and night. That was her that grabbed your hand as we went by."

"Oh, Wilma. She seems to be doing much better."

"As soon as you took up her case, she started getting a grip on herself, and now she's praying for other people. Have you always been able to pray like this, Tosh? The results have been obvious, and not only to me. The morning you and Reverend Pettis began praying for Miss O'Leary, her vital signs started moving up the clipboard. The next day she came out of her coma. Now, every day she's making steady progress."

"Thanks for your encouragement, Troy. I sure wasn't able to help Alexandra, in spite of my best efforts, and I suspect Reverend Pettis had a lot to do with Miss O'Leary's improvement."

It felt good to be in such a nice car and she could tell Troy was taking it real easy for her. It surprised her how empty the streets and sidewalks were.

"Where is everybody?" she asked.

"Those who could, have flown the coop. All over the country, the big cities are emptying out from fear of the terrorists. Any word on your mama?"

"Thanks for asking. She's doing better. I think I mentioned to you, she kind of collapsed after the bombing and my injuries. She was in bed for three or four days at the Lutheran Care Center where she works. Now she's home and doing better."

"That's good. I've been wanting to tell you, Tosh. I've had a change of heart."

"How's that?"

"I think you should definitely go to Princeton and blow the doors off that place."

"What changed your mind?"

"All these days and nights I've been thinkin about a lot of things as I worked."

"Like what?" She enjoyed watching his expression when he was deeply thoughtful. His face got especially kind and vulnerable.

"Well," he said turning toward her, "I'm headin in a whole new direction, Natasha. No more football, for one thing."

"But you're so good at it."

"Nah. Not really. Not fast enough for Division One. And I love what I've been doin this past week. I've never been in a position to help people like this before. Dr. Lambertson, the Director, says I can work at the hospital as much as I want while I go to college . . . and listen to this, Tosh. He told me last night he'd get me into Rutgers with a full scholarship. Turns out he's on the Board of Trustees."

"That's the best news I've heard in a long time, Troy. I think we should both go blow some doors off."

"Amen to that, Sis," he said, using her family nickname. "Dr. Lambertson says I should look into becoming a physical therapist, and he's writing a letter of recommendation for me to the dean of that department."

"So, this terrible disaster has given you a whole new direction."

"The doctor thinks I'll be good at it and he says the need is huge. I've never known how good it feels to help people. It makes me feel like I matter. At the end of the day I look in the mirror and know I made life better for some people."

"That sounds like a great way to live, Troy."

＊＊＊

On September 4th the predawn glow revealed the savageness of the desert landscape southeast of San Diego. When the sun breached the ridge, the temperature jumped twenty degrees and reminded Samir of the day in June when he first met the Tijuana drug lords. He'd always thought of the U.S. as a land of mild weather and soft people. That afternoon surprised him. Heat equal to anything he'd felt in the Middle East had sweat running down his body for hours. He didn't anticipate the seriousness of the problem the malfunctioning air-conditioning unit in their van represented that afternoon. He would not soon forget those hours they spent exploring every Jeep track, arroyo, and livestock trail along the Mexican border to chart a route their heavily loaded van could negotiate from this remote drop site.

In the three weeks since Houston, he'd transported the third warhead up through Mexico, and made a deal with the Alcaldo brothers to smuggle the weapon across the border. The Alcaldos had built an underground hanger and warehouse under a desert hill west of Tecate, Mexico, across the border from Potrero, California. On rare occasions, usually around midnight, a large earth-covered steeply angled door would slide open and a camouflage-painted C-23 Sherpa cargo plane would emerge. Bought from military surplus in the 20's, this bumble bee-looking craft with stubby wings, bloated body, and twin tails would take off from an unmarked dirt strip for the short hop across the border and back. It operated at such a low altitude it had never been detected by DEA radar units.

The billionaire drug-running brothers figured the more disruption they could generate in the States, the more profitable their business would become. More importantly, though, they needed cash. Their business was suffering. Never had moving product into the U.S. been so difficult.

The Mexican beside him said, "He's coming."

Samir strained, but could hear nothing. Seconds later he picked up the distant drone, then he saw a dark shape hugging the rough terrain coming toward them. The nearly invisible two-engine guppy-shaped plane brushed the cactus as it touched down and wheeled around at the end of the dirt clearing. The engines were kept running.

Samir smiled. They'd gotten the third warhead into the U.S., and he expected word later in the day confirming the arrival of the fourth. In his thought he saw two more massive mushroom clouds. After all these years, we're finally bringing this evil monster to its knees, he thought.

The rear of the plane between the two tail-sections was lowered hydraulically to form a ramp and three pallets of cocaine stacked in five kilo packets rolled down the ramp into the Mexican's truck. Next, the plane's cargo crew set up a roller extension on the lowered ramp and offloaded the bomb crate into the van. Samir handed Luis Alcaldo a suitcase containing the second half of his million-dollar fee. The pilot revved the engines and rumbled and bumped across the sagebrush dotted landscape, lifted off, and headed back across the border.

Samir drove slowly and carefully on a dirt road through the rock-pile hills. Near El Cajon, his satellite phone rang.

"Yes, Arturo."

"I'm back in Kansas City, General."

"Good. Have you located the Hyundai transmissions?"

"Si, senior. Emery Air Freight is storing them for us."

"Good. After L.A. we'll deal with Kansas City. What's happening in Atlanta?"

"The lathe cannot be found, General. Roberto is working with the Lufthansa agents, tracking it in their computer, and going through air freight warehouses. So far, there's no sign of the Biesse crate. Their paperwork indicates it was never loaded on that flight."

Samir subdued his anger and replied calmly, "The Biesse rep traced it through Frankfurt to Atlanta on that flight. I'm looking at his paperwork."

The five-axis computer-controlled woodworking lathe he'd purchased in the U.S., from a German distributor had been replaced with a warhead in a lead-lined container en route to the air freight warehouse in Frankfurt.

"You must find it, Arturo."

"I will, General."

CHAPTER SEVEN

**LOS ANGELES
SEPTEMBER 4, 2034**

Andrews steeled himself on the way to the Domestic Policy meeting. He would have cancelled, but Holt told him the Secret Service had picked up some leads that a coup was being considered by some of Vandenberg's supporters, if the trial didn't go their way. His staff busied themselves sending out resumes. Most felt they were a Senate vote away from being unemployed. When he walked into the meeting, his Domestic Policy staff was gathered in the sitting area of his office.

"What's first?" he asked, as if he didn't know.

Owen Spelling, his Senior Domestic Policy Advisor, asked, "Don't we owe it to the American people to take out Islamabad, Mr. President? Every polling organization we know of shows a huge majority favors such a strike."

"No Owen. We're not going to murder millions of innocent people. We're going to find and stop the terrorists."

"Your approval rating is at a historic low, sir. Are we actually going to get thrown out of here without a fight?"

"In order to raise my approval rating, are you recommending that we unleash a million-degree fireball on hundreds of thousands of children, like your girls, Owen. I won't do it. The possibility of peace would be lost forever."

"With all due respect, Mr. President, to most Americans you seem more concerned about Pakistani children, than you are about the American children who have been murdered."

"Owen, you need to show me some data to back up that statement. The American people know me better than that." Andrews' hours of preparation kept his anger in check. "I know Colonel Braxton is ill. Is the vice president joining us by video hook-up this morning?"

"Before we change the subject, Mr. President," Owen continued, "I take issue with your comment regarding your approval rating. The people who put you in this job do matter, and it seems to them that as long as our enemies use nuclear weapons, they're safe from American power."

As Owen spoke, Andrews recalled a Tolstoy quote from <u>War and Peace,</u> something to the effect that leaders appear effective, as long as they lead where the people want to go. Tolstoy compared Napoleon to a tugboat maneuvering an ocean liner toward a pier. The tugboat appeared effective and powerful, as long as those piloting the liner wanted their ship docked at the pier. He envisioned himself as a tug getting run over by an angry liner. If only there was a way, he thought, to convince the American people that nuclear retaliation was not an option, period.

"Of course the voters matter, Owen. But if they insist on vaporizing millions of innocent people, they'll have to find someone else to push that button."

"Speaking of the man who'll succeed you, if the Senate votes to remove, the vice president cancelled again this morning. Said he had too much on his plate. We all know he's gearing up to take over. One of the plans I hear they're considering is to target the capitols of all Muslim nations and announce to the world that they will all be destroyed if another American city is bombed."

Roger Christianson, the CIA director, said, "Mr. President, our people have picked up rumors of a coup. If the Senate votes to acquit, some of the top military brass are determined to move Vice President Vandenberg into the White House."

The thought crossed Andrews' mind to bring up the angel's warning, but he decided it would be counter-productive in this group. Some of them obviously felt sure his cause was lost. Talk of an angel would probably raise concerns for his sanity.

"Owen and Roger, by the end of the day, I need the names of the officers suspected of supporting a coup, and the steps and legislation required to establish Martial Law. Sounds like we may need it."

"Yes, sir," Owen replied.

Gordon Bowser quieted the alarm so it wouldn't wake his wife and stared at the green characters, 5:25AM, on Monday September 4th. Slowly it sank in. This week the Princeton Class of 2038 begin arriving for orientation. He fought off the temptation to slip back to sleep and threw off the covers.

In a steaming shower he wondered how many of the new class would actually show up. The nuclear nightmare dominated life at Princeton, as it did the rest of the country. Gordon still didn't know how many students would attend a university in the megalopolis between Philadelphia and Boston, from which millions were still fleeing.

His network of alumni contacts had polled the new students and reported the class would probably be eight hundred or less, instead of the normal fifteen hundred. A shocking number had perished, and many were badly injured. The dean's office estimated over a thousand no-shows among returning students and several hundred professors had taken leaves of absence. Class schedules were in chaos. The terrorists had wreaked havoc at Princeton, too.

Gordon saw the envelope when he opened his office door. He slid his letter opener under the seal and took out an elegant, but masculine, handwritten note:

Dear Mr. Bowser:

My daughter, Liza Jane Appleton, has decided, rather late I'm afraid, to attend Princeton and plans to arrive Thursday, September 7. Please deposit the balance of the enclosed check, over the amount of her tuition, room and board, in the endowment fund.

Ernest Appleton, Class of '98

What an attitude! No application, no letters of reference, and no transcripts—just a short note from her dad three days before orientation. He flipped the note over and looked at a certified check for one hundred million dollars.

⊷⊶《●》⊷⊶

On Highway 5 near San Onofre the traffic slowed to a crawl. When they stopped, Samir got out and saw a mile up ahead the back-up was caused by a roadblock at a converted truck inspection station. The highway was divided making it impossible to make a U-turn to avoid the inspection station.

Omar uttered an uncharacteristic profanity.

"Set the timer," Samir said. During the weeks it had taken them to get the third and fourth bombs into the country, the Americans had mounted the search operation he'd read about, that apparently covered all the highways of America. It seemed like an impossible task within that time frame.

Omar reached down and got the transmitter from the canvas bag between the seats, then asked, "Same delay?"

"Yes. Four hours. I wanted to be able to set the timers manually, but the munitions guys told me if they could be set, they could be unset."

"So, now that the timer's triggered?"

"There's no stopping it. How many clips are loaded?"

"Two for each of us," Omar answered, reaching into the canvas case between the seats, he handed two twelve-inch clips to Ali, who sat behind the front seats. A young National Guardsman wearing a helmet and fatigues directed them to a vast holding area where soldiers searched hundreds of trucks and vans.

After they'd parked, an army officer checked their passports and Samir's Mexican driver's license, then told them to open the back. Samir slid out casually. Using his relaxed Mexican accent he asked, "What's the problem, Lieutenant?"

The young officer gave no answer. The green glass in the observation booth behind him was obviously bulletproof. Next to them, an irate trucker roared profanity about the hour he'd lost while they searched his eighteen-wheeler.

Samir studied the layout of the inspection holding area. The officer they were dealing with had only a sidearm. The real problem was an armored personnel carrier guarding the exit to the holding area with a 50 caliber machine gun mounted on top. To get their van out that exit they would have to disable that gun.

<hr />

For a while, Gordon just stared at the check. Through the years he'd had wealthy parents hint that a substantial contribution was tied to the admission of their underachieving son or daughter. One Fortune 500 CEO had even promised a library or an athletic facility; but in his twelve years as dean of admissions, this enormous check took the cake.

He punched the intercom and asked, "Margaret, where'd this envelope come from?"

The door opened and his assistant, a short plump fortyish woman, walked in smiling, "Something interesting?"

"To say the least. Do you have any time to help with this? I've got a full plate today."

"Later this morning I've got some time. When I came in this morning everything was locked and that envelope was lying there."

As Gordon listened he wondered, what kind of person are we dealing with here? The corridors of their building had a new state-of-the-art security alarm system. The locks on the doors between the corridors and the offices were the latest high-tech electronic combination locks, supposedly foolproof. How did Appleton get through all that security?

Margaret continued, "I called housekeeping and they checked with the lady who cleans in here. She said she cleaned your desktop just before she left about eight last night and the envelope was not there. What's in it?"

"Princeton's most interesting applicant ever. I'll need your help with it later this morning."

"An applicant for this class?"

He nodded, "She's arriving on Thursday."

———— ⊰((◍))⊱ ————

"Pull the boxes out of there," the soldier ordered.

"You think we're smuggling bombs in cardboard boxes, Senor?"

The soldier repeated, "Tell your friends to help you and get those boxes out of there, Mister."

"Miguel," he called to Ali, "Come. Give me a hand."

"What about the other guy?" the man asked.

"He's so sick, he can hardly sit up. Must be the water," he chuckled, but got no reaction.

Ali and Samir unloaded the boxes of horse supplements they'd bought at a tack store near the race track in Del Mar to cover the crate.

"What's in the crate?"

"My wife's relatives," Samir smirked.

The officer glared at him.

"Look for yourself. It's a truck engine."

"Open it." He went over to his Humvee and got a portable neutron flux detector from the back.

Omar tossed Ali an Uzi and reached behind the passenger seat for the rocket launcher. Then, he blasted the turret on top of the personnel carrier and put the machine gun out of commission. Reloaded he blew out the observation booth window. The walls and doors of that building were so heavy, the explosion only came out the windows. Ali got down behind the bomb crate and kept his Uzi firing in short bursts. Sirens sounded as Samir drove out of the holding area. The guardsmen took cover and tried to return the fire, taking care not to hit the scattering non-combatants. Samir smirked to himself that they were able to escape because the soldiers were concerned about collateral damage.

The National Guard commander decided against pitting his unarmored vehicles against the rocket launcher. He figured these Mexicans were probably heavily-armed drug smugglers, but there was a strong possibility they were nuclear terrorists. He contacted the security office at Camp Pendleton, the adjacent Marine base. After describing the van, he warned them about the rocket launcher and automatic weapons.

"Why aren't they coming after us?" Omar wondered.

"Their Humvees can't deal with our rockets. They must be calling in an air strike further up this highway."

Samir kept the accelerator floored and weaved through the moderate traffic, horn blaring.

"We should leave this big highway and use the back roads," Omar suggested.

"No. They will close every route between here and L.A. We will drive as far north as we can. Every mile the population density increases. Are you two ready to die with me?"

Both nodded.

———◦((◦))◦———

As he worked, Gordon Bowser couldn't keep his mind off E.A. Appleton. His call to the alumni office had turned up nothing on an Appleton in the class of 1998, but they faxed the names of several living alumni or surviving spouses named Appleton from 1969 and 1981.

As Gordon printed out a draft of his speech for the opening session, Margaret buzzed him, "I've got Louise Appleton of Chicago on the line, Mr. Bowser. She's the widow of Winston Appleton, Class of '69. E.A. Appleton would have been her husband's great uncle, if he hadn't died in 1910."

"Mrs. Appleton, Gordon Bowser from Princeton, we're looking among the living for an E.A. Appleton."

A crackly voice answered, "I know of one Appleton with those initials, Gordon. He's my only famous relative, but he died in 1910."

"What can you tell me about him?"

"Winnie kept a scrapbook on his career in the library."

After several minutes, she came back on the line a bit winded, "There now, I can talk without taxing my memory. Let's see, Sir

Ernest was born in London in 1876 and moved to Boston at age five. He graduated from Princeton in 1898, in structural engineering."

Gordon was jolted by the date. This isn't possible! While she spoke, he did the math. Could the note and the check possibly have been sent by a 158-year-old knight of the British Empire!

"So, he became a famous engineer?"

"Young man, what do they teach at that school these days? Educated people should know that Sir Ernest Appleton was one of our greatest explorers."

"Sorry, Mrs. Appleton. Would you please fill me in?"

"My bridge group's arriving, Mr. Bowser, so I need to go. You're welcome to come and look at this book, or I could send it to you."

"Thanks. That won't be necessary. Glad someone's living normally in Chicago."

"Terrorists don't scare me, Gordon. Not at my age."

Gordon buzzed Margaret, "Ask your friend over in the archives if they have anything on Sir Ernest Appleton, Class of 1898."

"1898! Mr. Bowser, you can't be serious!"

"See what you can find. Someone using his name and claiming to be from the Class of '98 just gave us a very large check."

⸺ ◈ ⸺

Pulling into Princeton, Ary Hussein smiled at his step-brother's lack of understanding. First of all, he'd talked himself hoarse trying to make him understand why he needed to leave Amman, go to Princeton, and get involved in the peace movement. Then, he'd tried to explain why he wanted to arrive by himself with a few of his things, and fit in like an ordinary American student.

Instead, here he was arriving in an entourage of four Mercedes limos and a Ryder truck loaded with more stuff than he could ever use.

Ary was glad for the early start. The campus was almost deserted at 7:30AM. A re-match of a World Cup game between Jordan and Italy was on cable television at 3:30PM and the twelve embassy staff people manning the limos were determined to be back in D.C. by then.

When the four gray cars pulled up in front of Rockefeller dorm, Ary got out and went to work. Of the twelve embassy guys, three worked almost as hard as Ary, making dozens of trips up to his second-floor room.

It had been a month since the New York City bombing, but to Andrews it seemed much longer. He felt frustrated with the rate of his progress, but he was determined to make the breakthrough the angel had challenged him to make. His days began at 4AM with two hours in prayer and Bible study. The weeks since his angel encounter and his meeting with Dr. Kramer had been the most intense of his life and he could tell his mental standpoint was definitely changing.

He worked to remove matter from his concept of life. His brain had nothing to do with his intelligence. His heart and blood he now understood were devoid of life. His stomach and digestive system were not the source of energy. He was not the sum of his matter parts. His life was spiritual and came from God. In fact, he was one hundred percent a spiritual being. He was made of ideas and qualities, and each of these ideas and qualities were perfectible. He knew it was possible to move beyond material existence. He'd met living proof.

That's what she was doing, coaxing me to drop my mortal concept of myself and become truly powerful. Her thought was based on spiritual laws which enabled her to operate on a higher plane than he could. He wondered sometimes in the night what her life was like. What could she do? How much power did she have at her disposal?

She was able to splice his severed spinal cord. Why did it respond to her thought? Why didn't she fix Angie and Adrian? What could she see in me? He knew it had little to do with her words. She was enormously more than her words.

Henry Holt barged in on President Andrews, who was deep in thought in the sitting area of his office, "We've got a gunfight . . . "

Andrews' eyes were closed tight and his head rested on his right fist as he thought deeply, seated in a beige upholstered chair. He raised his left hand without opening his eyes and asked, "Can this wait? I feel like I'm on the verge of understanding something I've been wrestling with."

"No sir. This is too good to wait. Some Army Reserve troops are in a gun battle and hot pursuit of suspected terrorists at an inspection facility south of Los Angeles."

Andrews was quiet for a moment while he worked his way out of his deep concentration. Finally, he sat up and opened his eyes and took a deep breath. "They got through our roadblock?"

"Yes sir. Actually, we aren't sure yet if they're terrorists or drug smugglers, but I wanted you to know what's going on."

"Thanks, Hank. Shoop promised me we'd have our nationwide dragnet set up on the 1st. It sounds like we may have flushed out some terrorists on the 4th."

Holt continued, "The suspects are fleeing north on an interstate highway that runs through the middle of Camp Pendleton in a van with a bomb-sized crate in the back."

"Call Shoop and tell him I'm very pleased with his efforts. Hopefully, this is the break we've been looking for. Keep me informed. I'm going to stay with this. Feels like I'm making real progress."

At 4:15PM the ringing of his phone broke Gordon's concentration. After years of practice, he had trained himself to memorize the names and faces of the entire freshman class. The application on his desk included the picture of a great-looking African American girl from Newark. Back in February he'd written next to her picture with heavy red pencil "MUST ADMIT!"

He glanced through the items highlighted by the other readers in his department: junior class president, student council president, 4.0 GPA, 2060 SAT score, number one in her class, varsity basketball, and valedictorian. He recalled Mrs. Larson's efforts and the letter he'd written to convince Miss Cheatam that she would have a good experience at Princeton.

He smiled back at her picture and whispered, as he had to each photograph that afternoon, "Well done, Natasha Cheatam! Welcome to Princeton." Then, he picked up the receiver and said, "Sorry to keep you Margaret, what've you found?"

"Mr. Bowser, this has to be the most unbelievable set of circumstances we've ever dealt with."

"Tell me."

"I've been hoping for something to take my mind off of current events and this has done it. Without the check I'd think someone was pulling an elaborate prank, but Sir Ernest and his daughter must be as real as the check. The archives document the loss of his Antarctic expedition near the Pole in 1910. The catch is, they found everyone's body but his. He left a farewell note behind to his wife explaining that he was going to fight his way through the storm that had pinned them down for over a month and reach the South Pole."

"Did you call First Boston Bank?"

"Yes sir. As you suggested, I looked in the alumni directory and found a number for Sam Mitchell, the president of the bank, and asked him if he was aware of the check we received. He said it was the only check ever issued from an account opened in the early

1930's by, you guessed it, Ernest Appleton. And get this—it just gets better and better—Appleton showed up at the bank in the depths of the Great Depression with five armored cars loaded with ten tons of gold bullion."

Gordon reached over to his calculator and punched in the numbers. "Wow, that's 320,000 ounces! So a hundred years ago he was not only alive, he was already loaded. I wonder where he came across all that gold."

"I hadn't done the math, but Mr. Mitchell said that deposit is one of the great legends in their history. In fact, it helped the bank survive the Great Depression."

"And you said this was the first check ever written against that account?"

"Yes sir. Mr. Mitchell said they never heard again from Mr. Appleton and were never contacted by an executor or his heirs to claim the gold. They built a special vault in the 30's for his gold and named it the Appleton vault. When he deposited the gold it was worth $35 an ounce. Today it's worth over thirty times more."

"What triggered the check?"

"Almost a year ago they received a wire instructing them to sell $150 million dollars-worth of the gold and put the proceeds in a trust account. Our check was the first ever written from that account."

"Thanks for the good work, Margaret. Fantastic stuff, isn't it? You read mysteries. Have you got this one figured out? Sounds like Appleton discovered the fountain of youth, then tunneled into Fort Knox."

Gordon set the rest of the folders aside and called his friend Neal Thompson in Princeton's Administrative office and told him, in confidence, about the note and the check. Neal replied that it was a welcome possibility after the constant diet of bad news they'd dealt with for the past month. The university was faced with a multi-million-dollar deficit for the year. Their investment portfolio was in shambles, as were their New York real estate holdings. Thompson invited Gordon to come to a special trustees' meeting Wednesday evening.

—⊃«◊»⊂—

To Natasha, the small town seemed immaculate. Everything looked antique, but freshly painted with no litter or graffiti. She felt a million miles from home. Newark was little more than an hour away, but it couldn't have seemed more remote. She'd spent the night at Ms. Larson's small lovely home off campus and was deeply impressed. Everything was perfect. They had dinner in a screened-in porch looking into a grove of birch trees, and breakfast in a small nook Natasha thought could be in a magazine. On the short cab ride, she marveled at the order and beauty of the town, as she had two years before when she arrived for the basketball camp.

When the cab turned into the campus she imagined it was like driving into an ancient European university. Huge trees and lawns surrounded stone buildings with slate roofs, dormer windows and covered walkways. She quieted the voice inside asking what in the world she was doing in such a place. A chubby squirrel bounded across the lawn. Birds were singing.

The gray-suited bodyguards were leaning against the limos arguing about Jordan's soccer prospects when Ary came down for the last boxes, his sweat-soaked silk shirt stuck to his back. On the far side of the street an attractive black girl in white shorts, a tank top, and sandals got out of a cab. The driver pulled three old suitcases and a cardboard box from the trunk.

Ary had seen black people in England, but he'd never actually met one. It surprised him that the first Princeton student he saw was black. He walked over, stuck out his hand, and said with his best American accent, "Hi, my name's Ary. Can I give you a hand with your stuff?"

She turned and looked at him with almond-shaped eyes, then flashed a great smile, "Oh, thank you, I'm Natasha."

"Your last name isn't Cheatam is it?"

"How did you know?"

"You're my next-door neighbor. I saw your name on the door and figured there couldn't be too many Natashas running loose around here."

Ary picked up the suitcases and she managed the box. Squeezing between two limos, Natasha said from behind him, "Somebody's sure arriving in style this morning." She was pleased she didn't feel self-conscious about her modest arrival and few belongings.

Approaching the entry door, a massive bodyguard came out mopping his face and neck with a handkerchief, "That's the last of it, Your High—" but was cut off by Ary's exasperated expression. The big man glanced furtively at Natasha, then back at Ary, "Call, if you need anything."

Ary put the suitcases down and shook his hand, "Thanks Ahmad, I'll tell my brother how much I appreciated your help this morning."

Natasha watched as the gray suits climbed into the long cars and headed down the quiet tree-lined lane. Natasha turned to Ary and asked, "Your Highness?"

"They call me that in Jordan. My step-brother's the king."

"So, why were all those guys standing around, while you and Ahmad did the work?"

"The truth is, Natasha, being a prince isn't what it once was, I can tell you for a fact."

Natasha filled the stairwell with laughter and said, "I can't believe it. The first student I meet in prince town is a prince."

"Where do you come from, Miss Cheatam?"

"I come from the roughest toughest part of Newark, New Jersey, Prince Hussein."

"How'd you know my last name?"

"You're surprised I know the name of Jordan's royal family? Your grandmother is American and went to Princeton."

"I am surprised you know such things. Most Americans don't."

Ary put down the bags and opened the door to No. 208. Natasha walked in and stood quietly in her new home. It was nothing like her plain vanilla room at the basketball camp. It was a spacious corner room with a high angled ceiling and leaded casement windows that opened into massive trees. When she turned back to him, tear tracks lined her cheeks. She tried to smile, then turned away unable to quell her emotions.

Ary turned her toward him, handed her a handkerchief and hugged her tenderly.

She wiped her tears and said, "Sorry to lose it, Ary. This is a bigger day in my life than it is in yours, isn't it?"

"I envy you."

"Why is that?"

"Those are such great feelings when something's so fantastic you feel like you're going to burst. To me, it's a fine place, like many I've been sent off to."

Natasha smiled, "I've never lived any place this wonderful. Actually, I've hardly ever been out of Newark."

Her ingenuousness was refreshing. His English and Swiss prep school friends had gone to such boring lengths to create images of sophistication. He liked her candid humility.

"What do you know about your roommate?" he asked.

"She's foreign too, I think. Her name's Liza Jane Appleton."

"Sounds American," he said, "maybe British. Look, why don't you relax and get settled. I'll go downstairs and see if I can find another ravishing freshman to help move into Rockefeller."

"Thanks again, Your Highness. It meant a lot to have you walk over and introduce yourself. It wasn't easy arriving here by myself, not knowing anyone."

"Maybe you can cut the "Highness" stuff. Can I take you to dinner?"

"Sure."

She made her bed, laid down, and stared into the light filtering through the branches, fighting off the strong attraction she felt for her neighbor. She worked to be satisfied with sharing friendship. Black males sometimes dated non-black women, but non-black men with black women—very rare. She wasn't about to let anything spoil this morning. "Thank you, Father," she whispered, closed her eyes, and smiled, "You've given me so much to be thankful for."

— ◦((◉))◦ —

Approaching Mission Viejo, Samir spotted the helicopters in his side mirror flying just above the traffic. Several flew a few miles ahead, landed and blocked the southbound traffic. Two landed on the highway behind them and held up the northbound flow. The lead chopper had something suspended below the nose. He couldn't make out what it was, but suddenly the van engine started missing badly, then died. Samir put it in neutral and tried to re-start it. As the van rolled to a stop, he realized the suspended device was an electromagnetic pulse generator that had scrambled the microprocessor chip that controlled the injection system of their engine.

Behind the EPG scrambler unit were a dozen helicopters full of combat-ready Marines who'd been engaged in a tactical exercise nearby. They'd reloaded their weapons en route with live ammo. They touched down in the rugged terrain above and below the van. San

Diego and Orange County radio and television stations interrupted their programming to flash emergency evacuation instructions.

Samir showed Omar on his map the huge adjacent marine base. As he pointed, a concussion shell slammed through the sidewall of their van and exploded in a blinding flash and deafening blast. In the thick smoke, the three lay unconscious, blackened and bloody. Minutes later, they were manacled and on the way to the infirmary at the base detention center. Two of them died en route.

Captain Jack Sullivan climbed into the back of the van and used a tire iron to pry off the lid of the wooden crate. Inside the crate there was a metal container with a lid too heavy for him to lift. Six Marines lifted and slid it off the crate.

Captain Sullivan let out a low whistle. The Marines behind him looked at each other with fear-filled eyes, but said nothing. They knew what they were looking at in that crate. Sullivan turned to them and with calm voice told them, "We don't appear to be in immediate danger. Assuming this timer is accurate, we've got three hours and twenty-one minutes until this baby blows.

"Get some more guys and carefully lift this wood cradle and the warhead out of this crate and set it on the road. The warhead should weigh about five hundred pounds. Take it slow and be sure you've got enough people to do the job. I'm going to get a cargo chopper from the base to lift it out of here. If the wood cradle isn't strong enough to support the weight of the warhead when you lift it, leave it in the crate and let me know."

Sullivan walked up the slope to his mobile command post so he could patch through to his secure landline. After ordering a cargo chopper from the base, he reached his mentor at the Pentagon, "Colonel James, this is Captain Jack Sullivan calling from Camp Pendleton just north of San Diego. I need some help."

"Yes Jack. What can I do?"

"We just captured three terrorists on Highway 5 next to Camp

Pendleton with what looks like a Soviet era 100 kiloton warhead in the back of their van. It's got an integral timer that shows less than three and a half hours until detonation."

"I assume the timer has no access keys or controls."

"Right. They must have triggered it electronically."

"Well," Colonel James said, "thank goodness we've got some time. If you had tried to destroy the timing mechanism it would have automatically detonated. Have you got a cargo chopper nearby?"

"Yes sir. A Chinook with a lift mechanism will be here in fifteen minutes."

"Good. You go ahead and handle the loading and securing of the warhead and I'll make arrangements to clear a detonation site with a fifteen-mile radius. Take the device north across the San Bernardino Mountains to Cadiz dry lake, east of the Twenty-nine Palms Marine base in the desert. They'll be ready for you in two hours." The colonel phoned base security at Twenty-nine Palms and had them evacuate the Cadiz dry lake area. Civilian and military flight controllers were ordered to re-route flight paths, and roadblocks were established on all roads within fifteen miles on all sides.

Three hours and twenty-seven minutes later, a blast equal to a hundred thousand tons of TNT rocked the desert of southeastern California. There were no casualties.

⸺ ◦◉◦ ⸺

During the afternoon, Ary organized his room and said his prayers. He prayed five times a day, mostly for a more loving heart, and for a change of heart within the extremist Muslims killing in the name of Allah. Recently his prayers had become more urgent and focused. He asked Allah to help him find an effective role to play in the elimination of nuclear terrorism. The idea of attending

Princeton had come during deep prayer, to be closer to the peace movement and more able to help. His prayers today were to become an instrument for peace.

His whole life he'd watched and admired his grandmother as she worked for nuclear disarmament. Her founding and leadership role in Global Zero over the last twenty-five years had made nuclear disarmament a priority for the great powers. Global Zero's goal of complete disarmament by 2030 had not been achieved, but their efforts had provoked a lot of progress. The advent of nuclear terrorism had set her organization's effort back at least a decade.

He e-mailed his grandmother and thanked her again for helping him get admitted to Princeton after the New York City bombing and for standing up for him in his efforts to convince the rest of the family that this was where he needed to be. He told her he felt completely at home here, that it must be her DNA passed on to him that made everything feel so right. He wrote that he'd decided within hours of arriving in the U.S. that this would be his home for the rest of his life.

Then he wrote for an hour in his journal. Being here, he realized how much freedom his grandmother had sacrificed to marry his grandfather, and how deeply she must have loved him. From being a liberated well-educated American woman, she was willing to subjugate herself, lower her profile, and marry a Muslim. Still she'd been able to help millions of women around the world.

His stepbrother had no way of understanding these feelings that filled him. He was completely at home in Jordan and looked at the U.S. as an alien culture filled with decadence. Ary sat back, closed his eyes, filled his lungs, and smiled. It was as though he'd been living abroad his whole life and had finally come home. Here he was, far from judgmental eyes, from the reach of ancient customs, and free from the cultural restrictions he felt were obsolete.

The Jordanian women who'd been introduced to him as potential wives were bound up with customs that made women lesser beings. The women his prep school friends in England and Switzerland set him up with were too fast and worldly for his taste. In his heart, he knew he was looking for an American girl like his grandmother, modest but full of important ideas, chaste but brimming with confidence and self-worth. From birth he'd been told he could have any woman he wanted, as long as she was Sunni, from an excellent family, and well-educated. He wanted a wider choice.

He wrote several paragraphs about Natasha, his first American acquaintance. Rare, he wrote, a rare representative of her race. He smiled at the thought of the two of them carrying all her worldly possessions up the stairs in one trip. She must be an exceptional combination of qualities to have been admitted to this world-class university from an American ghetto high school. He noted her beauty and self-sufficiency; there was no guile and no grasping. He'd gone through life being painfully desired, his status sorely coveted. For years he'd longed to become a fully independent man without family baggage. At the bottom of the page about Natasha in his journal he drew a rose growing from a crack in a concrete sidewalk and named it Natasha.

He wrote an affirmation of his life goal to become a successful international businessman, independent of family connections. Finally, he closed his journal, hauled a load of extra stuff down to storage, then walked down the hall to meet some of his classmates.

He stuck his head into Brad Spear's open door and introduced himself. Brad invited him in and served English Breakfast tea in handmade stoneware cups and Oreo cookies on an antique pewter plate. Oscar Peterson's piano filled the room softly from small speakers in each corner.

"You sure are organized," Ary commented.

"Yeah. The football team's been here for two weeks. You the Jordanian prince?"

"I thought it might not be that obvious."

Two other football players came in and Brad introduced Harvey and Tim. Tim was the size of the other two combined. He put his thick arm around Brad's shoulders and mimicking his drawl said, "You're looking at Princeton's new starting quarterback."

"Wow!" Ary exclaimed, "A freshman quarterback. That's unusual, isn't it?"

"Unheard of!" Harvey drawled. "This here Okie walked in here and put on quite a show, for sure."

"Okie?" Ary asked.

"I'm from Tulsa, Oklahoma," Brad said, "so they call me that."

Tim and Harvey helped Ary carry his last loads to storage in the basement on their way to practice and they said they'd look for him at dinner. He liked these American kids with their lack of pretense and easy way of sharing. His grandmother had told him it would be special and, as usual, she was right.

———※《◉》※———

At 6PM on September 4th Muhammad, Samir's man in Missouri, heard the news of his commander's capture, drove to the Emery Air Freight warehouse, and pressed the levers of his remote radio transmitter forward until the amber light flashed. Four hours later, a 40,000-foot mushroom-shaped cloud erupted over Kansas City, after hundreds of thousands had been incinerated at ground level.

CHAPTER EIGHT

AMAZING GRACE
SEPTEMBER 6, 2034

Ary urgently knocked on Natasha's door. When she opened it he said, "You need to see what's happening on the news."

They hurried next door to his room and stared in horror as an eight-mile-high mushroom cloud rose above the remains of Kansas City.

"Oh my God! Not again!" she exclaimed. "This is so horrible! I hoped we'd captured them all in California."

The network coverage switched from the nuclear blast to the gates at the entrance to the Pentagon. A crowd of five hundred had exploded in violence at word of the Kansas City bombing. A dozen Marine guards, unable to restrain the mob, were trapped against the fence and had to shoot into the rioters in self-defense. Seven protestors were killed and a dozen wounded. Heavily armed replacements now stood guard in armored assault vehicles with water cannons.

Andrews sat at his desk with his face in his hands, praying for relief from the anger and depression that gripped him. It had been such an encouragement to find and stop the terrorists before they could hit L.A. Andrews made himself acknowledge and focus on that positive development. He tried for over an hour to shed his overwhelming grief and reach a mental place where he could receive inspiration, but he couldn't. Terrorists were still destroying American cities, seemingly at will.

The month spent developing a more spiritually-minded thought seemed wasted. How could he bear this job another day? He now prayed to be lifted out of this ordeal he felt helpless to resolve. No sooner had the military captured one group of terrorists than another struck. He tried to envision the angel's radiant face, and the utter peace in her eyes. Holding her close in his mind, he felt his thought moving toward prayerfulness.

Samir regained consciousness with terrible pain in his head and roaring in his ears. He opened his eyes, but could see nothing. When he tried to inspect the bandages covering his eyes, he discovered the shackles.

Lying helpless in excruciating pain was unbearable at first. With work, he was able to block out enough of the pain to think clearly. He had to give the Marines credit. If they'd had a week to prepare, he couldn't imagine a more effective response.

He felt a hand on his arm and a distant voice, as though coming through a wall. Listening as hard as he could, he caught a few words "blind" and "deaf" were two of them.

That'll make it tough for you sons-of-jackals to interrogate me, he thought and wondered what drugs and devices were being used on Omar and Ali.

He allowed a few thoughts of his life and his hopes for the future, but no sniveling. He'd always known he would die in the line of duty and this amounted to the same.

He shouted, "Allah Akbar!" but heard nothing, just sensed the vibrations.

Again, he felt the hand on his arm and voices like mice tittering in the distance. He knew they would execute him when they realized he was no use to them. That was fine. He could be of no further service to his country, and he'd exacted revenge for the loss of his family, his career, and his way of life along with tens of thousands of elite Republican Guards under his command in Iraq.

The roaring and pain in his head suddenly ceased and his thought filled with light. The image of a small alien female formed in the light.

She looked at him kindly and said, "I can help you out of your darkness, if you'll let me, General."

He was surprised he could hear her perfectly, then realized she was speaking inside his thought. He decided to try to speak to her the same way, "How did you find your way into my thinking, small elegant one?"

"It's my job to do God's bidding, General, and sometimes He bids me to speak consciousness to consciousness, as we are right now."

"It's strange to have another being inside my thought."

"Consciousness is actually all that's real about either of us, Samir."

———— ((O)) ————

At dinner Ary and Natasha sat with Brad, Tim, and Harvey. Brad looked up from the front page of the Princeton Daily and asked, "What do you guys know about the 'Hundred Million Dollar Coed?'" He tossed the paper in the middle of the table. A bold headline read, "Mystery Coed's Father Sends a Check for a Hundred Million With Her Last Minute Application!"

Natasha said, "I heard someone talking about that article while I was waiting to see my advisor. Some old guy wrote a huge check trying to get his daughter admitted this week."

Brad smiled, "It says the check came from the ghost of an alum who died over a hundred years ago in Antarctica."

Harvey laughed, "The guys at the <u>Daily</u> are just screwing around. Ghosts don't use checking accounts."

***

Casual banter around the large walnut table in Nassau Hall preceded the meeting. This routine dated back to a time before Washington's presidency. Portraits of the general, and other Revolutionary War heroes lined the yellowed walls. Robert Troster, the chairman, rapped his gavel softly for the group to come to order, "Gordon Bowser says he has an item that could have a major impact on our deficit."

Gordon stood and said, "Ladies and gentlemen, you may have read about this in today's Princeton Daily. A student reporter who works in the archives picked up the story from the research my assistant was doing earlier this week. On Monday we received a note from our oldest and one of our most renowned alumni, who wants his daughter to attend Princeton. Sir Ernest Appleton disappeared on his second attempt to reach the South Pole in 1910. No one's heard from him in a hundred and twenty-four years, until this morning."

Robert Troster interrupted, "I think most of us know of Ernest Appleton's career, but it seems impossible that he could be alive today. How old would that make him?"

"He was born in 1876, so if the note is actually from him, he's a hundred and fifty-eight."

"Good heavens, man!" Troster exclaimed. "That's unbelievable! It's biblical! Are you sure?"

Gordon smiled and replied, "No, sir. At this point I'm only sure of one thing."

"And what's that?" Mr. Troster asked.

"His check's good."

"What check?"

Gordon didn't answer, but started passing out a package of information he'd put together from the material Margaret copied in the archives, "I'll let you see for yourselves."

Bob Troster asked, "Do you mean to say Sir Ernest had a baby girl when he was over a hundred and thirty?"

Gordon answered as he passed out the packets, "We don't know how old Liza Jane Appleton is, yet."

The trustees each registered the same dumbfounded expression as, one by one; they turned to the photocopy of the check.

A Churchillian gentleman next to Bob Troster boomed, "A hundred million!"

Gordon continued, "As you can see, Sir Ernest sent no application, no return address, and no phone number. His daughter is simply going to show up for orientation tomorrow."

"Are you suggesting," Bob Troster asked, "that we ignore our admission requirements?"

"When my assistant was researching the archives on Monday, she came across the position of Scholar in Residence, which was not uncommon in the late 1800s. Gifted artists and scholars, who didn't meet the requirements for admission, were sometimes welcomed into undergraduate life on that basis. Apparently they added a good deal to the university community. I propose we offer Scholar in Residency status to Sir Ernest's daughter, while she fulfills the requirements for admission.

"I also propose we ask Appleton's approval to deposit at least twenty-five million into the general account, instead of having to put it all in the endowment fund."

Troster took a deep breath and asked the trustees, "Well ladies and gentlemen, how do you want to handle this?"

The treasurer, a thin pallid man at the far end of the table chimed in, "The future is so uncertain, Bob, I'd like to get the use of the entire balance. We have no idea how long all this will last or how bad it will get."

Mr. Troster asked, "What do you think, Gordon?"

"I'll ask."

The Board quickly approved Gordon's request. As he gathered his papers and got up to leave, Bob Troster asked, "How will you communicate with him?"

"The same way he did with me, I guess. Leave the answer on my desk tonight."

When Gordon got back to his office, there was already another note on his desk in the same handwriting:

Thanks, Gordon. Use the balance as you see fit. Urge President Andrews to meet with my daughter as soon as possible.

EA

Walking back to the dorm from dinner it surprised Natasha that she and Ary talked so easily. She asked about his life in Jordan and questions she'd always had about Islam.

"Where'd you get your knowledge of my part of the world, Natasha?"

"It's my high school principal's fault. There was a box in her office with my name on it. Every Friday on my way home, I'd stop and pick up a stack of books, papers, and magazines to read. There's a prayer vigil tonight in the square near the Nassau Inn, would you like to come with me?"

"Sure. Do you think a Muslim will be welcome?"

"I don't know. We don't want to confuse God, do we?"

Ary chuckled, "He can probably sort it out."

The destruction of Kansas City felt to many like a terrible shot to the heart of the nation. Millions were so numbed by the thought of a third city destroyed they could barely talk about it. Where would they strike next? What could be done to end this horror?

The leadership of both houses of Congress called their members back into session. On Thursday September 7th millions watched the first day of the Senate trial carried by all the networks. "Hear ye! Hear ye! Hear ye!" the sergeant at arms called out, "All persons are commanded to keep silent on pain of imprisonment, while the House of Representatives is exhibiting to the Senate the Article of Impeachment against David William Andrews, President of the United States."

The trial opened before all 100 senators with the reading of the charge against the president and the swearing in of the presiding officer, Chief Justice of the Supreme Court, Constance Evelyn Ames. During the afternoon the Senate met in closed session to hammer out a bipartisan plan for procedural rules to govern the trial. Each side would get 24 hours to present its case without witnesses. The Senate would then have two days for a question and answer session. Only after that would the Senate vote on motions to dismiss the case or to proceed with the trial and request a list of witnesses.

The nation was riveted to the coverage of the historic proceedings. The two-thirds majority vote required for removal seemed assured. Chief Justice Ames gaveled the trial to order. The twelve managers from the House of Representatives presented the evidence against the president. They built a solid case showing clear and substantial evidence linking World Jihad with the government of Pakistan. They also showed a recently obtained video confession, shot in a British prison, by a trusted associate of Rashid Raza Ahmad, the deceased leader of World Jihad, swearing that Pakistan was indeed the source of nuclear warheads to the terrorist organization.

The president's lawyers in the Senate advanced the idea that humans had reached a crucial turning point. They argued that no matter how hard it was to leave our missiles in the silos, we must. To save the world from an ever escalating nuclear horror the United States must stand fast for world peace.

Speculation was rampant among the media—which senators would vote for and which against the president's removal from office? Media estimates were 67 solid votes to remove and 12 probable. Polls indicated that the percentage of Americans demanding immediate nuclear retaliation against Pakistan had increased after the Kansas City bombing to 87%.

Talk shows were dominated by furious voices rattling nuclear "sabers" and pouring out fury for Andrews and his cowardice. Christian churches were divided. Some clergy preached the path to peace lay in wiping out the murderous Muslims. Others focused on reducing hate and anger. A few in the clergy taught that the terrorists could be redeemed and forgiven, even though their terrible deeds were unforgiveable. Workshops and seminars everywhere were crammed with people trying to break the grip of the emotions overwhelming them. Road rage had become rampant. Domestic violence was epidemic.

Andrews had reconciled himself to being the first president removed from office, but felt a deep disappointment that he'd been unable to adequately champion the cause of non-violence. After a month spent trying to learn how to access the power of love, he didn't feel significant progress, but the effort was obviously helping him cope. He'd overcome most of his anger and grief, but he couldn't access any real power. He wondered from time to time why she hadn't been more willing to help.

He figured the old adage 'good eventually prevails' was no longer true. How could good prevail when a single act of evil could be so horrendous? A few now had the power to kill millions in minutes. He knew nuclear retaliation was not the answer, but this awful feeling of impotence was also unacceptable. She said he would get answers if he prayed. Obviously, he didn't pray effectively enough, or he would know where the terrorists were hiding and where the bombs were planted. He had prayed his absolute best and received no specific answers.

Andrews was actually looking forward to the Senate's decision and planned to be packed and ready to mount the stairs of Air Force One for the last time. His great desire was to be as far away from this job and this city as possible and spend weeks alone with no phones, no Secret Service, no press corps . . . no one.

For years, pushing himself on cross-country training runs through silent forests, he'd contemplated the ultimate cross-country skiing challenge, a solo expedition to the South Pole. Antarctica was on his mind again. The stack of books beside his bed described every aspect of the untamed continent at the bottom of the planet. Of course there was danger, but also incredible beauty and complete solitude. Whatever the challenge, he felt sure it would be a pleasure compared to this impossible job.

Every day he budgeted time to plan his expedition. Just thinking about it was a tonic for his battered psyche. His morning and evening workouts increased in intensity. Despite a heavy heart, he pushed his body to new levels of performance, imagining the challenges he would face at the bottom of the world.

Andrews was emotionally exhausted. The destruction of New York and Houston were the worst gut punches of his life. When Los Angeles was saved, his spirits soared, and then they were blasted anew by the devastation of Kansas City. Even with a prayerful heart, sadness cloaked his thought. He forced down small meals. Sleep had become a stranger.

Natasha was moved by the depth of feeling in Palmer Square outside the Nassau Inn as she and Ary moved through the crowd toward the stage. Hundreds around them were holding hands with their heads bowed in earnest prayer, while a local priest asked God to save the world. Ary took her hand in his and they both took a seat on a stone wall circling a large tree to the left of the stage.

The priest was followed by a black boys' choir in burgundy robes. Their small faces were softly illumined in the candlelight. The choir director, a powerfully built black man with a full beard, looked enormous standing in front of his small choir members.

At his signal, their high clear voices began the opening line of "Amazing Grace." Natasha looked at the faces around them, glowing in the light of hundreds of candles. Moved by the music, many were tear-streaked as they reached out to their Creator and listened to the crystalline voices filling the night. What a shame, she thought, that it had taken nuclear holocaust to bring all these people to this evening of prayer together.

After several more local clergy and another less inspiring choir, Ary and Natasha strolled in silence away from the crowd onto Nassau Street. At his invitation they stopped in a small coffee house and sat down at a table by the front window.

"Thanks for taking me with you tonight," Ary said. "I can't get those voices out of my head. What was the hymn those boys were singing?"

"Amazing Grace is one of my favorites. Since the bombings

began, it's become almost a national hymn. Millions of Americans are praying for the first time. It spans all the Christian denominations and means a lot to people."

"How do Christians define grace?"

"God's gift of unmerited pardon. An eighteenth-century priest who was a reformed slave ship captain wrote that hymn. He felt he'd been given an amazing gift of forgiveness."

"What does it mean," he asked, "'T'was grace that taught my heart to fear,' when we're all working to keep from being fearful?"

"And grace my fear relieved," she added.

"That's good. But why do we need to learn to fear?"

She was quiet for a moment, gazing into his dark eyes and sipping the rich coffee. "Maybe Mr. Newton felt most of us wouldn't pray wholeheartedly for forgiveness without a stiff dose of fear."

Ary sensed a reservoir of wisdom where that response came from. "If these bombs don't turn us to prayer, I guess nothing will."

Natasha nodded, "That's the good coming out of all this, millions are turning."

Back at their dorm, Ary took her key, unlocked the door, and then knocked before he opened it. "Anybody home?" There was no answer.

"Guess my roommate's going to miss the start of orientation. Thanks for going with me tonight, Ary."

"It was my pleasure," he said as he unlocked his own door. "I'll never forget those small black angels singing Amazing Grace. See you in the morning, Natasha."

Natasha tried for hours to get him off her mind, but couldn't. She'd never known such a warm gentle man.

Andrews prayed his way through the evening next to the fire in the living room of the lodge at Camp David. He prayed for the removal of self and ego from his thought, he prayed for the courage and steadfastness of the people. He prayed that the Senators weighing the course of history would express wisdom and he prayed for the redemption of the captured terrorist.

Since Kansas City he'd been having headaches that started early in the day and got progressively worse. After toughing them out for several days he decided to try to heal himself. After a late dinner he read chapters 15, 16 and 17 in the gospel of John. As he read, he imagined himself one of the disciples listening to Jesus explain how they were to proceed after his exit from human life. Normally the headaches ruled out reading, but he read through the discomfort. He loved the part where Jesus promised he'd always be with them and his spirit would help them when they prayed. He read that part several times before he realized his headache was gone. He was grateful and allowed himself to drift into a sound sleep.

When he woke up, the fire had died out and he was covered by a warm blanket. Instead of getting up, he buzzed his Marine guard for some hot chocolate and spent another hour praying. The guard re-kindled the fire. In the absolute stillness of the night his prayer felt more effective than usual as he asked God for direction.

In an instant the angel being slipped into his thinking and smiled at him, "Remember David, if your nuclear weapons are unleashed, it will mark the beginning of the end of human life." He sat bolt upright and responded inside his thought, "Where have you been? I'm presiding over a disaster here, praying my butt off and getting nowhere."

She smiled at him with such utter kindness, his anger melted away. Then she said, "Your prayers are too passive, David. You need to pray with more urgency and greater expectancy."

"Okay," he acknowledged, "I need a major breakthrough right now!"

"Better. Why don't you go meet with General al Hammabi?"

"What good could that do?" he asked, but she was gone.

Now he felt wide awake and encouraged by the angel's visit. His Marine attendant filled his cup and turned on the television. The twenty-four-hour cable news shows all recited the litany of terrors facing the nation. As he watched, he remembered FDR's famous quote, 'The only thing we have to fear—is fear itself.' Never had those words seemed more true. Fear had the nation by the throat. Normally optimistic energetic Americans by the millions felt displaced and depressed. No one talked about anything but the bombings. Liquor stores were stripped bare daily, even though distilleries and breweries worked around the clock. Drug dealers were screaming for product. Hospitals were inundated with the myriad maladies induced by extreme fear and grief. Looting was epidemic in abandoned inner cities. Almost no American was unaffected.

The Dow Jones Industrials had plummeted over 60% and were still being sold off. Companies were failing by the hundreds. Unemployment had hit thirty-four percent, an all-time high. Consumers weren't buying anything but necessities. Millions had lost family members. Tens of millions were fleeing big cities. Scores of millions lived in constant terror. Church services were crowded at all hours. Hundreds of thousands who'd never been religious were making their first attempt at prayer in a neighborhood church.

Every day, chanting crowds outside the Pentagon demanded the destruction of Pakistan. Riots erupted when the badly outnumbered "Give Peace a Chance" demonstrators dared to show up. News programs, editorial pages, and talk shows attacked Andrews and the "peace nerds" relentlessly.

Andrews turned off the television and worked to develop his spiritual consciousness. He read from the stack of books on the end table next to him, trying to understand how Jesus healed and how he taught his students and others to heal. He discovered that healing was a strong current in Christianity for over three hundred years after Jesus' departure. He read the writings of modern healers in charismatic movements within mainline churches, and those in smaller healing disciplines.

Vandenberg was elated. There was a feeling abroad in the country that he would soon take control and lead them to safety. Millions anxiously awaited the end of the Senate trial. The talk on the street was that if G.I. Joe had been in charge, none of this would have happened. As the tide of support grew, he became ever more bold in his public statements, acknowledging the need for stronger leadership at this pivotal point in history. Cloaking his ambition in a sense of duty, he assured the nation he was ready to lead, if called upon.

His shadow government worked harder than ever, now that it appeared certain they would soon be taking over. Vandenberg drove them. He was adamant that they be completely ready with action plans, detailed to the minute, covering every conceivable contingency. On the third day after taking over they would strike Pakistan with the most devastating attack the world had ever known.

Every morning and evening news show got a well-crafted sound bite from Vandenberg's press secretary. Twenty-four hours a day cable channels re-lived the bombings, speculated on the terrorists' next target, and debated how a Vandenberg administration would respond. Most predicted he'd send missiles within days of assuming power. News anchors and correspondents now referred to his presidency as a "when" and not an "if."

Andrews welcomed Barclay Tullis, his contact with Adventure Network, into his private office and asked Angie to hold his calls. Angie had recovered enough to work two or three short days a week.

"How was your flight from Wellington, Mr. Tullis? I hope you got my message that I thought you should wait until I get to New Zealand to go through your package."

"The flight was long, but pleasant enough." He handed Andrews a binder and said, "Adventure Network is proud to be working with you on this expedition, Mr. President. You can probably appreciate that you're the highest profile client in our company's history and we want to get you outfitted correctly. It's important that your clothing fit properly, and because of your height, some of it will have to be custom made. I have the president of Gore-Tex outside, in case you have time for a fitting."

Andrews leaned back in his chair and smiled. The binder was titled Andrews' Antarctic Expedition—2034. After years of dreaming, this was the closest he'd felt to making this dream a reality. He thumbed through it and admired its thoroughness. There were eight dividers marked "Time Schedule", "Route", "Maps", "Clothing", "Equipment", "Cache Locations", "Cache Contents", and "Emergency Provisions." It was hard, but he closed it and laid it on his desk.

"Let's take some quick measurements so you can start the long lead time items. Otherwise, we'll need to put off our meeting until Saturday."

Mr. Tullis nodded. "We'll be back."

CHAPTER NINE

LIZA JANE APPLETON
SEPTEMBER 7, 2034

On Thursday at 6PM Andrews dialed his chief of staff's extension, "Hank, I need you to cancel my appointments for tomorrow and Saturday and set me up with a ride in an F-35. I want to take a look at Kansas City in a two-seater that can hover, and I need to make arrangements to move out of Washington and put everything into storage in Springfield. From there I'll go on to the west coast and meet with General al Hammabi."

"Mr. President, the man can't. . ."

"I know. He can't see or hear. I'm going on the instructions of my angel friend I told you about."

"You don't want to take Air Force One?"

"No. I'll be at Andrews Air Force Base at 7AM and you need to meet me out west in the big jet."

———⊷(◉)⊷———

In the early morning hours on Friday when the Class of 2038 was asleep, but in plain sight of a few freshmen who saw it out of their windows in Rockefeller, a glistening blue-green shape descended at a steep angle from the high clouds over Princeton, New Jersey. It streaked across the treetops and slate roofs and stopped behind the Institute for Advanced Studies. Its polished metallic exterior glistened in the moonlight. There were no visible jets or motors, and it made no sound. About the size of a small house, the ship seemed locked in place above the terraced lawn, then it descended slowly and came to rest. Two figures inside the ship walked past one of the oval windows.

A window slid open and a girl's voice with an American accent broke the stillness, "Yes, I remember, Rockefeller, Room 208." A tall feminine form in a black bodysuit stepped out of the window, put a bare foot on the glistening base and said, "Thanks Father, I'll stay in touch. Oh, you said you had some money for me."

After a pause, a hand protruding from a full brown sleeve gave her some folded bills.

"Goodbye. Love you, too," she said as they embraced. She kissed his cheek, smiled at him, slung a light pack onto her back, walked off the edge of the ship, and headed toward the undergraduate campus. The back-lighted male figure watched her for several minutes then left the window. Seconds later the ship rose abruptly, streaked south, and disappeared into the clouds. The girl was nearly invisible, except when she walked beneath the lamps along the deserted walk.

⸻))(((⸻

Andrews grinned when he saw the F-35 from his helicopter. It looked like a toy plane parked in front of the enormous doors of the Air Force One hanger. He climbed down the steps, saluted his Marine guard, and walked toward the fighter jet. The diminutive pilot in a royal blue flight suit was talking with a ground crewman who was first to see and salute the approaching president. The pilot did a crisp about-face and saluted.

"Climb aboard, Mr. President. I'm Captain Beth LaBoe and I've got orders to deliver you to Camp Pendleton, after a stop at Scott Air Force Base in Missouri this morning. This gentleman has us fueled up, so if you're ready, let's rock and roll."

Andrews climbed awkwardly into the rear cockpit that had been hurriedly modified to accommodate his length. Captain Laboe helped him get strapped in, showed him his oxygen equipment and communication controls. Then, she climbed in and went to work.

Andrews listened in his headphones to Captain LaBoe getting clearance. In seconds they ascended vertically to a hundred feet, then she hit it. He was unprepared for the power. An invisible fist punched his upper body into the seat back and took his breath away.

They hurtled into the early morning light, climbing twenty thousand feet per minute. He closed his eyes and smiled at the vision of his pilot, a modern day damsel with her spurs dug deep in the flanks of a fire-breathing dragon, roaring westward.

—————————=((O))=—————————

In the middle of Natasha's dream the people in her hospital ward quit screaming. She slept peacefully the rest of the night. Near dawn on Friday, she woke feeling truly refreshed for the first time in a month. She sat up and smiled when she realized where she was, stretched and leaned back against the headboard in the stillness. The white lace-trimmed nightgown her mother made glowed in the moonlight. Mama, she thought, you were right, we do deserve the best.

Newark seemed light years away from the great trees moving against her window. She felt rich and happy sitting in this scene of quiet order, years of striving rewarded. She turned on the lamp, reached for her Bible, and screamed at the sight of a form in black spandex laying on the bed six feet away. Her scream woke the form. It slowly turned over and looked at her, a white face framed in a black hood.

"You startled me!" Natasha exclaimed breathlessly. "When did you get in? How did you get in? I locked the door."

The girl smiled and pushed the hood off her head. Thick blond hair fell around her face on the pillow, "You're wonderful to look at," she said. "I've never seen a dark-skinned person before."

While she thought about that shocking statement, Natasha asked again, "How did you get in?"

"My name's Liza Jane, what's yours?"

"You're not going to tell me, are you?"

"Do you mind?"

"Not really," Natasha replied. Then she noticed the curtain move at the far end of her bed and the screen leaning against the wall. "You climbed in the window?" There was no response so she continued, "My name is Natasha and this is the best morning of my life so far."

"Why is that, Natasha?"

"In a while, I'm going to breakfast that someone else is cooking. After breakfast it'll be time for our orientation assembly in the most glorious chapel I've ever seen. At noon, the freshman chorus I'm in will sing for the class picnic, and then I have an appointment with my advisor, a wonderful lady I adore. Before dinner I plan to come back to our beautiful room, rest, read my Bible, and then go to my choral practice. That's a day in heaven for me."

Liza Jane smiled broadly; "Do you figure it can get even better than this, Natasha?" She glanced sideways to catch the response.

The almond eyes were closed and Natasha's face now glowed in the warm dawn light. "I hope so," she said peacefully, "but, if it doesn't, this is plenty good enough."

"I'm surprised you read the Bible."

"Why is that?"

"I thought Americans didn't."

"Most don't, but I do."

Liza Jane was quiet for a while then said, "I need to borrow something to wear."

Natasha looked around, "Where's your stuff?"

"I didn't bring anything. I'll get some things here, but I do need to borrow something to wear this morning."

"What's that you've got on, some kind of ninja suit? Say, listen, I met a girl at dinner last night who was your size. I'll ask her."

The altimeter hit 57,000 feet over western Virginia with the air speed steady at Mach 1.3. He heard a cheerful voice in his headphones, "How's it going back there?"

"Great!" After he answered, Andrews realized how long it'd been since he'd felt anything close to "great." He felt like his old self at that moment.

"There's hot coffee in that thermos by your knee."

"Thanks. We're rattling windows down there aren't we, Captain." He looked down and pictured sleeping families being jolted awake as the F-35's sonic wake slammed their houses.

"At this airspeed we go through our fuel at quite a clip. Over Ohio we'll rendezvous with a tanker. Until then, I'll leave you to your thoughts. I can imagine you've got a lot on your mind, sir."

"Can we take a look at Kansas City before we land at Scott? I'd like to see it."

"We'll be there in forty minutes. Mr. Holt told me. I'll let you know."

Near Columbus, Ohio the F-35 dropped down to 15,000 feet and slowed to 400 miles per hour. Andrews listened as Beth made contact with the tanker. He wished he had a daughter this able and confident, then he spotted the big slow-moving tanker. Beth cocked the wings and quickly closed the gap, then as deftly as a hummingbird, she brought the nimble craft up slowly, disturbingly close to the underside of the tanker's tail section. From it trailed a long metal boom. To the right of their cockpit Beth positioned a receiving "basket" and moved close enough to insert the trailing boom.

Filled up, she pulled away, thanked the tanker crew and accelerated west. An hour later they slowed again and descended below the cloud cover to 1000 feet.

"K.C.'s coming up, Mr. President. We're fifty miles from ground zero."

The endless fields of Missouri looked normal enough. Outlying homes and out-buildings were damaged, but standing. One of the highway bridge sections across the Missouri River was in place, the others were gone. The train bridge next to it looked usable.

As they approached the city, the damage worsened rapidly. Large buildings showed extensive damage. Homes were obliterated. Debris covered the ground and filled the streets like a scene after the worst hurricane.

They passed over a highway that disappeared and reappeared in jagged strips from the reddish-tan coloring of the blast zone. A meandering brown stream cut through the highway where a bridge should have been.

Then he saw it. The burned rubble—miles of it in all directions. Here and there something resembling a structure midst endless debris. Captain LaBoe slowed and hovered here and there as the president requested. There were recognizable features, a swimming pool, orderly patches that had been a subdivision, a cul de sac, walls of a concrete building, gray tree trunks lying in a row, a brown pond.

At ground zero there was nothing. The point of the inconceivable blast was a crater about two thousand feet in diameter and three hundred feet deep. His emotions were boiling below the surface of his thought, but he held them in check. He was determined to focus on what he was seeing. The pattern of devastation reversed beyond the crater from total to minor damage.

Andrews laid his helmet back and closed his eyes. Nuclear chain reaction was so merciless. Temperatures hotter than the sun unleashed on innocent people, on children. His face contorted as sobs racked his chest. Tears fogged up his visor. He raised the visor and gave in to his grief. The scene below was like a preview of the apocalypse.

Trembling, he sensed another wave of tears and let go again. This time, he could think while he wept and slowly regained his composure. If all Americans could see what I just saw, I think they'd change their minds about doing that to innocent strangers. Andrews struggled to regain his composure and wiped the tears from his face. Somehow the American people must keep their government from going through with Vandenberg's mass murder.

Captain LaBoe's voice broke in, "You okay back there?"

He tried to respond, but couldn't. In a moment an unnatural voice said, "I'm getting it back together."

"Good," she said. "More people every day are supporting your efforts to stop the nuclear insanity your opponents are planning."

"I appreciate your support. Unfortunately, you and I are in the minority and I'm about to get fired."

"You've done the best you could do, Mr. President."

Beth accelerated and climbed back to fifteen thousand feet. He grinned at the power, closed his eyes and turned his thought to the task at hand. He needed to re-activate his personal checking account, re-activate his credit cards, and arrange for his favorite Mayflower crew to move him out of Washington into storage in Springfield.

He sensed the start of their descent, opened his eyes, and listened to Captain LaBoe getting clearance from the tower at Scott Air Force Base.

They dropped like a rock on their approach. Beth spoke evenly with the air traffic controller, as they plummeted. Andrews flinched from the jolt of the landing gears locking into place and realized he wasn't breathing. He forced himself to relax and breathe. Beth's voice was calmly monitoring a routine landing and he was scared stiff by their rate of fall. He closed his eyes and continued to breathe deeply until they descended vertically and touched down a hundred feet from an olive green helicopter. The ground crew rolled a stair platform over to the side of the plane and climbed up to help Andrews out. Standing on the wing he said, "Thanks for the ride, Captain. That sight back there brings life into crisp focus, doesn't it? We'd better do our best living today."

"I suspect you're doing it, Mr. President," the bright-eyed pilot responded. "The Air Force is proud to be at your service this morning. I'll be on call here when you're ready to go on to the west coast."

"I should be ready by early afternoon."

"Yes sir. Mr. Holt told me."

He shook her small strong hand, smiled, climbed down the stairs and walked toward the helicopter.

Outside Camp Pendleton the president's motorcade passed through huge crowds of protestors chanting "Nuke Pakistan!" as it approached the gate. A pulsating forest of signs demanded death for the captured terrorist and removal of the do-nothing president. Execute the Terrorist! Remember NYC! Houston Lives in our Hearts! KC—Murder in the Heartland! Riot-garbed Marine MP's strained to hold them back. Looking at the twisted expression of one especially hostile protestor, the angel's instructions came back, "Study what your messenger taught about enemies. That's how you access the power." It had become increasingly obvious to Andrews that the standard definitions of military power were inadequate to deal with the problems now facing humanity. New answers are required and he thought the angel was trying to show him the kind of power needed. What he wasn't sure of was whether he had what it took to access that power.

Since his second encounter with the angel, he'd begun delegating more of his work. His cabinet and staff members were stretched, but hadn't buckled. He didn't answer questions about what he did alone in his office as he prayed for days on end. The media suggested he was hiding.

His thought was more in alignment with Jesus' teachings than he'd ever imagined possible. His heart had grown more peaceful. He was able for longer periods to control the thoughts he entertained. The suggestions of failure and weakness sooner fell away. He more effectively intercepted thoughts that came to discourage or condemn. His consciousness was more focused than ever.

Besides studying what Jesus taught about enemies and trying to understand how those teachings could give access to power, Andrews' new mission was to pray continuously. He now thought of the source of ideas to be like a radio broadcast, able to communicate all ideas constantly, and man as able to receive the specific ideas needed. Reaching out periodically in prayer was no longer enough.

He was past hating the terrorists. He knew the Iraqi general had been hypnotized by hatred and revenge, as were millions of others who had lost so much. His weapons were all that made him different from any other angry violent man.

Holt had strongly advised against this trip, and his arguments made sense: what good could it possibly do trying to communicate with a deaf and blind terrorist? The Senate was poised to vote on his removal and this cross-country junket, that seemed pointless, could affect some votes.

While he waited, Andrews prayed in the base chapel to be able to see the Iraqi general as a perfect spiritual creation. The media was having a field day characterizing this Don Quixotesque foray as symbolic of his entire presidency. None of this mattered to him. His prayers quenched his doubts; he was where he was supposed to be.

An hour after the president's arrival, Samir was led into the base chapel. At Andrews' request, he was unshackled and dressed in civilian clothes. His head was fully bandaged. The guards seated the general across from the president, saluted, and left.

In Samir's thought, the glowing female said, "Why don't you tell the president what we've been discussing, General?"

In a low hesitant voice Samir said, "Blindness, Mr. President, has given me a new kind of vision."

"Explain what you mean, General."

"An angel inside my thought has taught me to see with new eyes."

Andrews realized how ridiculous that would have sounded a month ago and asked, "Can you hear me, General?"

"No I can't, but the angel relayed your question. She'll help us speak to each other."

"You said 'she.' Ask her if I've met her."

The question made the glowing form inside Samir's thought giggle, which made Samir smile, "She says she counseled you to spare Pakistan."

"I wish she'd convinced you to spare my country."

Samir's countenance fell and he replied sadly, "I've learned a great deal from her. I'm a different person than the one who did those terrible things."

"Tell me what you've learned, General al Hammabi."

"In the years since the U.S. invasion of Iraq, I've thought of almost nothing but finding a way to strike back at your nation. My wife and sons were killed in the bombing. My home, my career and my life were destroyed. I was consumed with hatred. But the angel has taught me that messengers throughout history have received instructions from angels like her to turn people away from their tribal gods and prepare their thought for Allah's ultimate message that 'we must love one another'."

Andrews said nothing. His amazement at Samir's statement caused an upwelling of emotion. At length he said, "We've never really gotten that message, have we."

"No. It seems like weakness to us, but she's convinced me, Mr. President, it's the source of real power and it's essential for humanity's survival."

"Will you work with me to stop the bombing?" Andrews asked.

"Yes, I will. As a Muslim, I've always considered ours as the only true messenger, but now I know it's Allah's great message of loving one another that's all-important. Many messengers have tried to bring that crucial message to mankind."

Suddenly, the angel appeared in Andrews' thought and Samir was left in darkness. The glowing female asked Andrews to pray with her to heal Samir's hearing and sight.

He closed his eyes and prayed with all the love he could muster, to see the reformed terrorist as a spiritual being, perfect and whole. As he prayed, the angel smiled at him and a glowing sense of well-being pervaded his thought, then she was gone.

Samir sensed his sight and hearing being restored. It was the most sublime sensation he'd ever felt. A palpable sense of goodness filled his consciousness. Finally, he unwound his bandages and looked at the president.

"The angel healed you," Andrews said. "Can you hear?"

"Yes, I hear you perfectly."

"Are there more bombs planted?"

Samir told him about Muhammad and Kareem and the lost bomb in Atlanta. He drew detailed maps that pinpointed the locations of some smaller dirty nuclear bombs hidden in sealed caves along the Afghan border. Also, he gave Andrews the name and location of the Ukrainian colonel who had agreed to sell them up to a dozen more 100-kiloton bombs for $200 million dollars apiece.

"Muhammad and Kareem are working independently, Mr. President. I'll order them to stop, but they may not obey. Is it possible, after all this, for you to forgive me?"

The two stared at each other for a while before Andrews answered, "That's the message, isn't it, General? I'll never pardon the person who destroyed so much and killed so many, even if that person no longer exists. Unfortunately, General, you'll have to pay for those terrible deeds. I'll do everything I can to spare your life, but I won't pardon you."

The evening newscasts and morning headlines proclaiming the president's remarkable success in dealing with the captured terrorist shocked and amazed the nation. In the Senate, the president's team of attorneys requested and were granted a recess in the trial, before the start of closing arguments. Although many of their constituents were demanding a quick resolution to the trial, the senators agreed that the president's amazing success in dealing with the surviving terrorist had to be given due consideration.

⟫●⟪

On the way to breakfast, Natasha knocked on Ary's door. After several knocks he called out, "Come in."

She opened his door and found him kneeling with his back to

the door facing the windows and the rising sun. The two girls waited quietly while he finished his silent prayer. The floor was covered with overlapping Persian rugs. The walls were painted a rich terra cotta and the ceiling a pale sky blue. The furnishings were tan leather and dark walnut.

When he stood and turned to them, Natasha said, "Ary Hussein this is my roommate, Liza Jane Appleton."

They shook hands and Ary said, "You must have gotten in pretty late. Natasha and I thought you were going to miss orientation today."

The three talked casually on the way to the dining hall. It was a warm morning and Liza Jane wore a pair of borrowed white shorts, a black Princeton tank top, and deck shoes that were a bit tight. Natasha asked, "Ary, what's been happening since Kansas City was bombed? I feel out of touch."

"Amazing things have been happening, Natasha. On the news last night they ran tape of the president coming out of a meeting with the Iraqi general captured in California on his way to nuke L.A."

"Really?" Natasha exclaimed. "I read that the only terrorist who survived the capture was blind and deaf."

"That's one of the reasons the meeting was amazing. When the prisoner came out of their meeting he could see and hear."

Natasha stared at Ary intently then said, "How can we be talking about removing this president from office? To me he's the answer, not the problem."

"That's not all. The Iraqi general apparently renounced terrorism and volunteered to help the president find the remaining terrorists and their bombs."

"Wow! What a fantastic turnaround!"

Ary nodded, "The senators have backed away from a vote on removal, because of the president's surprising success at Camp Pendleton. A lot more people are getting behind him."

When they walked into the dining hall, the din grew quieter. Most of the male heads turned and stared at the two coeds. Princeton males thought such great-looking girls went to Florida State or UCLA. Ary picked up a paper on the way in. The headline of the <u>Princeton Daily</u> read "Hundred Million Dollar Coed Watch Continues."

When they got to the food, Liza Jane casually chose the same things Natasha took.

The three found a table and sat down together. Ary read from the <u>Daily</u>, "In separate sightings two freshmen claim they saw a blue-green ship descend from the sky over Princeton last night after midnight. They both described the same classic flying saucer shape and said it stopped over near the graduate school campus, then headed south at high speed."

"Do you guys believe those things exist?" Natasha asked.

"They've got to be real," Ary said. "How could so many sightings all be illusions?"

Liza Jane duplicated Natasha's preparation of her food, cream in the coffee, sugar on the grapefruit, milk and sugar on the hot cereal, all with as casual an air as she could manage.

Ary watched her and could tell everything was new to her. When she winced sampling the grapefruit, their eyes met and Ary smiled, "Not sweet enough for you?"

"More tart than I'm used to."

——◦((◦))◦——

Andrews made a series of secure calls from Air Force One at 37,000 feet as they crossed the Rockies. Hundreds of FBI agents had been dispatched to Atlanta along with six CTC rapid deployment units and the Georgia National Guard. The evacuation of Atlanta was underway and proceeding in an orderly way. All lanes of the roads leading out of Atlanta were filled with outgoing traffic.

In the meantime, one of the largest domestic manhunts in American history was under way for two Pakistanis traveling on Mexican passports. Lufthansa Air Freight was conducting a worldwide search of their air cargo system for the missing Biesse crate containing a 100 kiloton warhead in a lead-lined crate supposedly sent from Frankfurt to Atlanta. Those manning the roadblocks around Atlanta had poster-sized artist sketches of the two terrorists.

Holt worked quietly across from the president for the first leg of the flight while Andrews mobilized the manhunt and the search for the missing bomb. Finally, he asked, "Mr. President, what happened back there? And what's with that grin you can't get off your face?"

Andrews paused between calls and looked at his old friend. "I witnessed the power, Hank."

"What power?"

"The power that transcends atomic power. I don't know how it works on a global scale, but it sure works great up close and personal."

Holt responded, "The terrorist comes out of your powwow hearing and seeing, and the two of you are like long-lost buddies. Then, you go to work to stop his accomplices in Georgia using information from the general. How did it happen? The whole turnaround seems amazing!"

"I've always known the truth of what Jesus taught, Hank, but I've never experienced the power like this."

"The press corps up front is speechless. They're sitting with fixed stares and no idea what to write. When they ask me what happened, I just shrug and smile. What should I tell them? What happened? Give me the story."

"Hank, remember what I told you after my first encounter with the angel, what she said about accessing God's power?"

"I remember. She told you to study what Jesus taught about enemies, but what has that got to do with this?"

"She took one of the angriest mass murderers in history and completely changed his nature with her pure love. He's no longer the same man who killed those millions."

"How'd she do it?"

"How can I help you understand? In the book of Acts in the Bible . . ."

"Whoa! Mr. President. Please. Don't go biblical on me."

"Just listen for a moment, Hank. It won't hurt you. You want to understand how God's power operates and the best examples I know of are in the Bible."

"Okay. But remember, I don't know the Bible like you."

"Saul of Tarsus was an angry Jewish zealot on his way to Damascus to terrorize Christians. On the way, Jesus appeared to him in his thought, transformed his heart, and turned him into Paul the great teacher of Christianity across the Roman Empire."

"Is that what happened to the Iraqi general?"

"Something similar. The angel appeared in his thinking and transformed him into a reasonable loving man."

"She did this to help you?"

Andrews nodded. "I wasn't getting it on my own, so she stepped in to show me the power."

"And the general is on our side now?"

"Tonight he's going on television to order the two remaining terrorists to stop the bombing and give themselves up. We'll have to see if they obey."

Holt studied Andrews for a while, then smiled, "You need to keep praying, Mr. President. It's working. Oh, before I forget, Ted Kaufman asked for a private interview when we get back. For the most part he's hung in there with us and deserves a favor."

About the same time that Air Force One touched down at Andrews AFB, Special Forces helicopters landed in the rugged mountains along the Afghanistan/Pakistan border with heavily armed troops equipped to blast open sealed caves containing the remainder of World Jihad's nuclear arsenal.

———————

On the way back to the dorm after breakfast, Ary remarked to Liza Jane, "Our food's new to you, isn't it?"

"Yes. This is my first trip to America."

"You're her, aren't you?"

"I'm whom, Ary?"

He pulled the <u>Daily</u> from under his arm and pointed at the headline.

"Didn't take you long to figure me out, did it?"

"Where are you from?"

"I'm from a small country you've never heard of."

"You can tell us, can't she Natasha. We won't tell."

Liza Jane was quiet for a while as they walked, then said, "After orientation, come back to our room and we'll talk."

"About what?" Ary asked.

"I'm going to ask you both to help me."

Natasha figured they could help her put together a wardrobe and get her bearings and said, "We'll be glad to help you."

"After you get back from the chapel we'll talk. Then, you can decide."

Natasha asked, "You're not going?"

"No, I have an important appointment."

They were almost to the dorm when Natasha asked her again, "Help you with what, Liza Jane?"

"My mission is to see if it's possible for people to give up violence."

CHAPTER TEN

NATASHA AND ARY SIGN UP
SEPTEMBER 9, 2034

Andrews' private office was covered with maps and aerial photos of Antarctica laying out topography, glacial conditions and proposed supply drop locations along his route to the Pole. As Andrews put on silk-like long underwear, a silver Gore-tex outer suit, and a thick navy blue parka, Dave Best from the W.L. Gore Company explained the clothing system, "You're headed into the toughest conditions our planet has to offer, Mr. President. Our clothing system is good, but there are no guarantees."

"Everything's lighter and less bulky than I expected."

"This layered system will keep you alive down to minus fifty degrees Fahrenheit, with winds up to thirty or forty miles per hour. If conditions get worse than that, you'll have to wait it out under cover."

"I've been reading about the storm that pinned down Appleton's expedition in 1910. How unusual was it?"

"The information we've gotten from Sir Ernest's journal describes one of the worst storms on record. You can count on that place throwing powerful weather at you."

At the end of the hour he'd allowed for the meeting, they'd

discussed everything from Velcro closures to two-way zippers, Houdini draw cords, sock and glove liners, facemasks, crampons and gaiters.

Barclay explained, "This clothing system is designed to seal your body heat in, wick perspiration away from your skin, and allow it to evaporate."

"To wrap it up for this evening," Dave said, "let's focus on the equipment for your hands and feet. They're the hardest to protect with body heat. In extreme cold, your mind can alter your circulation to horde warmth around your vital organs. It's willing to sacrifice your fingers and toes to protect your heart and lungs, if it gets cold enough."

Andrews put on what looked like astronaut gloves and thick mukluk boots and was pleased they weren't as heavy as they looked.

When Barclay started spreading out information about the camping gear, Andrews said, "Sorry, Mr. Tullis, I've run out of time. You'll need to leave the rest for me to read. I was just wondering, standing here in this state-of-the-art equipment, could Sir Ernest have made it to the Pole if he'd had this stuff?"

"We're not sure he didn't make it, Mr. President, but you're right, his equipment was half as efficient and twice as heavy. It certainly would have helped. Oh, by the way, the National Science Foundation application is included in your binder and we need to submit as soon as possible. They've gotten quite selective about which expeditions to Antarctica get approved."

"Yes. I've gone through it with the Director, who is an old friend I appointed to that job last year. He thought I would probably be approved."

Natasha and Ary walked in silence toward the chapel.

Natasha was stunned by her roommate's mission statement. What kind of a person would say something like that? This is one of the most important mornings of my life, not a time to get distracted. She was determined to make the most of her first day at Princeton and enjoy being with Ary.

She turned to Ary and asked, "What do you make of her?"

"I'm not sure. What she said was shocking enough, but the way she said it was even more so."

"I know," Natasha agreed. "The look in her eyes. She wasn't messing with us."

"No, she was serious," Ary responded. "I don't think she's a nut case, either. Interesting timing isn't it, with your country about to remove Andrews and turn to a warrior president."

"Yeah. She's about to see how violent this country can get. Her words keep ringing in my head, 'My mission is to see if it's possible for people to give up violence.' God, that's a weird thing to say."

Andrews was reading in bed when his phone rang. "Henry Holt, Mr. President. I just found out that three days ago Clyde Alexander in the State Department got an important call from Bob Troster at Princeton."

"About what?"

Holt relayed the bizarre message about the check from the ancient, supposedly deceased, alum urging Andrews to contact his daughter. "He told one of his people to relay the message to me, but for some reason it didn't reach me until this evening."

"What's the old alum's name, Hank?"

"Ernest Appleton."

Andrews responded, "You're kidding, right."

"Nope. That's the name. Heard of him?"

"Heard of him? One of the books on my nightstand is about him—his last attempt on the South Pole. They found the other eight bodies of the expedition members, but never found Sir Ernest's body."

"No wonder. Doesn't sound like he's dead."

"That's not really possible, Hank."

"Bob Troster thinks it is. They got a First Boston cashier's check for a hundred million dollars from him with a note saying he was in the Princeton Class of 1898."

"Sounds like Ernest has learned some amazing secrets from whoever it was that rescued him on the South Polar Plateau."

"When was his last expedition?" Holt asked.

"1910."

"Unbelievable, isn't it? No wonder the guys in Clyde's office didn't take it seriously. The strangest part is that he has a freshman daughter who moved into Rockefeller dorm today."

"Holt, call Troster and find out if he can put me in touch with E.A. Appleton. It's not every day you get to meet one of your boyhood heroes."

"That's the point of my call. Appleton's note requests that you meet with his daughter as soon as possible."

"Contact the daughter and get me a meeting with her father. I can't see the benefit of meeting with the daughter."

Natasha walked back to Rockefeller alone. Ary had been waylaid by three aggressive freshmen girls on the way out of the chapel. She'd been ignored, predictably. She didn't feel jealous. Her thought was reconciled to her race and color and what they meant in this mostly white community. She cared for Ary deeply, felt grateful for his friendship, but wouldn't allow herself to consider romantic possibilities.

But what a morning! Dr. Troster had inspired her and made her re-think her roommate's mission. He said the future of humanity lies in the balance. That it's up to all Americans to stop our country from resorting to mass murder. He said it's up to our generation to find ways to overcome global injustice, jealousy, distrust, and hatred—before it's too late.

Just sitting in the chapel was inspiring. Mr. Bowser, the Dean of Admissions, made the welcoming speech and put on a show of his incredible memory. He asked people who wanted to, to stand; then he introduced each one to the assembly, told where they were from, and gave interesting details about each.

Walking up the path she still felt like an outsider, passing herself off as a Princeton student. The other students seemed to feel at home—like they belonged. Ary obviously did. Why didn't she?

When she opened the door to her room it was dark. The blinds were closed. She flipped the light switch, but nothing happened. "Lock the door," a muffled voice said.

The unnatural voice gave her goosebumps. Gradually, as her eyes grew accustomed to the darkness, Liza Jane became visible, curled up on her desk chair, her feet on the desk, arms around her legs, and her face against her thighs.

"Lock the door," she repeated. It was an older voice and distant.

Natasha locked the door and asked, "What are you doing in here in the dark?"

"Sorry, Natasha, it's hard for me to disengage from communals with my mother."

Natasha wanted to leave, go to the administration, and request a normal roommate. All the inspiration from the orientation assembly drained away, replaced by anxiety she hated. She stood there in the dark and finally said, "We decided against a phone, Liza Jane. How were you talking to her?"

Liza Jane stood up, stretched, groaned, walked unsteadily to her bed and sat down. "Is Ary going to join us?"

Natasha asked, "Mind if I open the blinds? You never answer my questions."

"Open them. Have a seat. I'm ready to answer questions."

"I don't know when Ary's coming back. I left him surrounded by a bunch of girls on the steps of the chapel."

There was a knock on the door and Ary asked, "Can I come in?"

Natasha unlocked the door and let him in, then locked it again. "Liza Jane says she's ready to answer questions."

"I turned around and you were gone," he said to Natasha.

"Next time I'll take a number," she said feigning anger. "When I came in, my roommate said she was speaking with her mother. My first question was 'how' since we have no phone."

Ary sat down next to Natasha on her bed facing a weary-looking Liza Jane who, at length, responded, "My mother and I speak to each other in our thought."

That response, delivered offhandedly, was followed by a period of silence.

Natasha looked at her, took a deep breath and said, "You're no run-of-the-mill Princeton freshman, are you."

Before she could respond, Ary said, "You came on that ship those guys saw last night, didn't you?"

With the trace of a smile, some of the energy returned to Liza Jane's eyes. "That was my father's ship. Sorry, I'm trying to get myself going again. Communing takes a lot out of me."

Ary was shocked that he'd guessed right about her father's ship and felt confused by her talk of telepathic communication.

Natasha wanted out more than ever, but sat staring at her, "You're from some other world?"

"Sort of."

"Oh my God!" she gasped. Both Natasha and Ary drew back involuntarily from the human-looking alien.

"I didn't mean to startle you. I'm from this planet."

Ary asked, "From what country?"

"I'm from Caldera."

Natasha studied her face to see if she was serious, "You're from a country no one's ever heard of."

"I think I get it," Ary said. "You've come because of the bombings."

She nodded, "I told my mother about both of you. She agreed that the hardest part of the mission will be getting people to grasp the possibility of giving up violence."

Natasha collapsed backwards on her bed and stared at the ceiling. "Weird as it seems—I believe this stuff you're saying."

"Will you both help me?"

"I don't know," Natasha whispered. "What makes you think you can do such a thing?"

Ary said, "I want to help. Come on Natasha, you heard Dr. Troster. Let's be part of her mission."

Natasha sat up and looked from one to the other, "I have a great desire to be a run-of-the-mill Princeton freshman. I hate it that just when my life is coming together, the rest of the world is falling apart."

Liza Jane said, "What if the possibilities of your life are richer than you can imagine, Natasha?"

As Liza Jane said that, Reverend Pettis' words in the hospital came back to her, "My pastor was told while he prayed for me in the hospital after the first bomb that I was going to help bring God's message to the world."

Liza Jane smiled and her eyes shone. After a moment of reflection she said, "I'd like to meet him sometime."

"Anyway," Natasha said, "I'll help. What do we have to do?"

Liza Jane said, "Good. We'll be Princeton freshmen for the time being. First, I should tell you I'm the daughter of the king and queen of the most powerful people on our planet."

Natasha looked dazed, "Royalty on all sides. Caldera is more powerful than the U.S.?"

"Yes. Believe me, you two. I wouldn't have come if I couldn't help."

Ary said, "I can't imagine what we can do, but we're willing to try, aren't we, Natasha."

"Yes. But I need to go. I can just make it. Our chorus sings in the quad at the freshman picnic in twenty minutes." She hopped up, brushed her hair, slipped on her shoes and hustled out.

Then Ary remembered, "We should go buy some clothes for you. Why don't we skip the picnic, get some lunch, and shop?"

They climbed into Ary's burgundy Corvette convertible and headed off campus.

"Great car, Ary."

"Would you like to drive it?"

"I don't know how. Let me watch you, then I'll try."

"What's Caldera like?" he asked.

"Come home with me and I'll show you."

"I'd love to!" Ary exclaimed. "Where is it?"

She smiled and said, "Let's have that be a surprise. I'm going home in a few weeks. Why don't you come with me and I'll show you. It'll seem pretty primitive to you."

"Yeah, right, like your dad's ship. Wait a minute. He's not picking us up is he?"

Liza Jane nodded.

"Oh my God!"

"Don't mention it to Natasha. I want her to come too, but let's keep my father's ship a surprise for her."

Ted Kaufman sat with President Andrews in his private study and spoke to the television camera framing them both. "First, I'd like to thank President Andrews for granting this private interview. Last week, Mr. President, I wrote an editorial that took you to task for what seemed like a waste of your time, flying to the west coast to meet with the surviving terrorist of the three captured on their way to destroy Los Angeles. I wrote what many were thinking, that such a meeting was doomed to failure because the doctors at Camp Pendleton had confirmed that the Iraqi general was permanently blind and deaf.

"I think the whole nation was shocked when you walked out of that meeting with a hearing and seeing General al Hammabi, who agreed to try to stop the other members of his terrorist cell from doing any more bombing, and was cooperating, you said, in other ways as well. Would you please tell us what happened during that meeting and how all this came to pass?"

"The general's hearing and sight were healed spiritually, Ted, but his most remarkable healing was his heart."

"He had a heart problem, too?"

"Yes. His heart was filled with hate that had to be healed, as well. Many in your audience are familiar with spiritual healing. It won't be difficult for them to understand."

"What about the rest of us, Mr. President? I spoke with the doctor who had examined the general and said his hearing and sight were permanently damaged. He had no idea how they could have been restored. Please explain how you were able to do such a thing."

"I didn't do the healing, Ted. In order to get that answer you'll need to interview General al Hammabi, and if you want to, I'll make those arrangements."

"Thank you. I would like to get that story. What should we tell the people who are coming to Washington hoping you can heal them, as well?"

"Tell them I'm working to be able to heal metaphysically, but am not yet able to do so. Right now we're facing the most serious problem in human history and it must be healed."

"You mean nuclear terrorism."

"Yes. I'm convinced that it will only be eliminated when we learn to love one another. There's no easier answer. Sending missiles would only compound the problem. When you meet Samir al Hammabi, ask him what he's learned about the power of love."

Ary and Liza Jane pulled into an enclosed mall and parked outside a seafood restaurant.

Sitting in a corner booth, Ary started making a list of the clothes she'd need, but finally stopped writing and said, "I think we need to do the whole mall."

"Thanks for the help, I wouldn't have any idea what to buy or where to find it."

"I'll enjoy this. I've been on some intense shopping trips with my sisters in London, getting them ready for school. How are you going to pay?"

"What do you mean?"

"You know, credit cards? Cash? Checks?"

"Oh yes of course, I have some money."

"How much? That'll determine how much shopping we do."

She opened her backpack, found the folded bills her father had given her, and tossed them on the table.

"Oh my God!" Ary gasped, covering the stack.

"Why'd you do that?"

"Damn, girl!" he whispered, looking both ways, "You can't carry this kind of cash around with you!"

"Robbers?"

"Or worse." Under the table Ary fingered through the stack and confirmed they were all thousand dollar bills, rolled them in his hand and handed them back, glancing at a passing busboy to see if he noticed. "We've got to get that deposited, get you some plastic, and a checking account."

"How much is there?"

"At least a hundred thousand. That's been lying on the floor in your room since you got here?"

"People want this paper money very much, don't they?"

"There are people who would kill for that wad of cash."

Liza Jane was visibly shaken by Ary's statement, "How could pieces of printed paper be that important to someone?"

"At our age, that money represents years of work."

"What do you mean—work?"

"Like these people," Ary pointed at the uniformed employees of the restaurant. "They make ten or fifteen dollars an hour. That pile of bills represents years of paychecks to them."

"I see. People trade time for money. How would someone rationalize taking my money for themselves?"

Ary chuckled, "He or she would figure that life would be a hell of a lot easier with your money in their account."

"They would be willing to make my life harder to make their life easier?"

"A lot of people would."

Liza Jane was quiet, considering that idea.

"That surprises you? Now, maybe you can see why peace is such a tough proposition."

"It's hard to come to grips with such an idea."

"You don't have greed or theft in Caldera?"

Liza Jane decided to let the discussion drop. She could tell Ary was also convinced of the importance of money. "They're just forms of self-defeating ignorance," she said.

Ary stared at her, fascinated by his new friend's perspective, "We'd better get moving."

Walking toward the cashier, Liza Jane felt discouraged for the first time, face-to-face with one of the fundamental fallacies of the human world—that good can be gained by doing evil. Suddenly, she understood the rationale people used to justify terrorism. She handed one of her bills to the cashier, who just stared at it.

At length, the young girl looked up and said, "I've never even seen one of these. We can't change it. Have you got anything smaller?"

"No I don't. Please keep the change," Liza Jane said walking away, still reeling from the thought of someone being willing to forfeit their access to power by stealing a handful of ornate paper.

"No. No. No," Ary stepped in, handed the girl his Visa card, and gave Liza Jane back the thousand-dollar bill.

The cashier took his card, still staring blankly at Liza Jane.

"She's foreign." Ary said, "Doesn't know our money yet."

"I guess not."

Ary laughed as they walked to the car, "I've never known anyone less interested in money than you. Those bills mean nothing to you, do they."

"You mentioned time, Ary. That it would take a lot of time to get that much money."

"It's actually a popular expression 'time is money.'"

"So, the person stealing my money would actually be trying to get more time—more life. That's it, isn't it. Money represents life to many people."

"It's sad, but I think you're right."

"The human belief that life is getting shorter with the passage of time, makes them desperate to get more of it."

"You don't think that way about time?"

"No."

They went into Midland Marine bank, where Liza Jane met with the new accounts manager to open a money market account with a Visa card.

Ida Mae Bianchi's eyes got wide as she thumbed through the bills. She asked Liza Jane, "Do you know how valuable these bills are?"

Liza Jane turned to Ary with a confused look, "What does she mean? It's printed right on them."

Ary asked Mrs. Bianchi, "Are they rare?"

She handed the bills back and left her desk. In a few moments she returned with a currency book and showed them a picture of the $1,000 bill with Grover Cleveland's picture, and explained, "These bills are quite rare. Thousand dollar bills were last printed in 1934, not many were printed, and yours are in perfect condition. They're worth over $2,000 apiece."

Before they left, they met with the bank manager who agreed to keep the bills in his safe, until Ary found collectors willing to buy the bills. They opened her account for $100,000, gave her a receipt for the bills in his safe, and issued a Visa card.

Afterward, they headed for the mall. In a few hours they'd put together a dozen outfits. Working skillfully with the sales clerks, Ary set her up for fall and winter with boots, hats and coats. Liza Jane went along with everything Ary and the clerks suggested. After making arrangements to ship everything to school, they headed back to the car.

Ary chuckled, "My sisters couldn't have done what we just did in a week."

"Clothes don't mean so much to me. What you and the clerks picked out will do fine."

In an empty part of the parking lot, they switched places so Liza

Jane could drive. In minutes the Corvette was whirling left and right in controlled power spins like waltzing in and around the concrete bases of the light standards.

Both howled with delight as she used the engine, gears, brakes, tires and suspension like a grand prix driver. To Ary it was like a fabulous theme park thrill ride. He could tell she intuitively stayed just inside the cars potential, without causing damage.

"Man!" he shrieked, "You go from novice to advanced in five minutes. What you're doing is supposed to take tons of practice. You sure you've never driven before?"

"I'm sure. Using fire for power is exciting, isn't it? Our machinery isn't this much fun, but, I guess you know these engines are fouling our planet."

"The emissions?"

"Millions of these fires rolling around put a lot of carbon monoxide in the atmosphere. But, I must admit, I'm enjoying this."

The afternoon was warming up, so Ary put the top down, slipped a Vivaldi capsule in the player and Liza Jane headed out of town on a small country road. They drove without speaking, taking in the intense greens of the early fall, a cloudless sky and the undulating road that wound its way past small farms and through rural villages.

After a while, Liza Jane said, "Feels like I'm touching the soul of my father's homeland out here."

Ary turned down the music and said, "I've been trying to imagine a land without money or greed."

"And I've been trying to grasp the idea that some people believe they'll be better off by stealing."

Ary looked at her for a while then asked, "Time doesn't concern you?"

"It doesn't measure anything. There's just now and now."

"But, sooner or later, you come to the last 'now.'"

Liza Jane let it drop.

Bob Troster's phone rang at 9:45PM. He was surprised when the caller introduced himself, "This is Henry Holt, Dr. Troster, President Andrews' chief of staff."

The Princeton president told Holt about the check and the note they'd received, and the little they knew about E.A. Appleton.

"So, you've never actually spoken to him."

"No, but earlier today his daughter moved into her dorm."

"So we understand. Dr. Troster, the president would like to speak with her by telephone in the morning."

"I'll get in touch with her and ask her to call you."

He wrote down Holt's direct line, called Gordon Bowser, who lived near the campus, and asked him to go talk to Miss Appleton as soon as possible.

Gordon's car pulled into the parking lot across from Rockefeller. He climbed the stairs, turned down the hall and found No. 208. It opened before he knocked. One of the most sriking faces he'd ever seen, peered out and said, "I've been expecting you, Gordon."

She came out into the dimly lit hall, dressed in a man's oversized dress shirt over a black body suit. Barefooted, she was still four inches taller. "We need to meet downstairs, so we don't wake my roommate."

She collapsed girlishly at the end of a sofa and said, "When can we arrange the meeting."

"Meeting? You already know?"

"Your president wants to meet with me."

Gordon stared at her in surprise, then said, "He wants to speak with you tomorrow morning."

"I'll be glad to speak with him."

Gordon dug Holt's number from his pocket and said, "They'll

want you standing by on the telephone. This is Mr. Holt's number at the White House."

She didn't take the note, "Let the president know I'll meet him in my room at 10AM on Tuesday the 12th."

"You mean by telephone."

"No. We need to meet in person."

"Miss Appleton, I'm sure he's too busy to drop everything and come up here to talk with you."

"Give him the message, Gordon. He'll come."

At their cavernous home that night, Ida Mae Bianchi told her husband, Larry, about the amazing young Princeton student she'd opened an account for that morning.

Larry, preoccupied as usual during their dinners together, tried to sound interested, "Rich eh? What's so unusual about that? You've opened hundreds of accounts through the years for rich students."

"Never anything like this. You remember that story in the paper about that old alum that got his daughter admitted a week before freshman orientation by sending the school a check for a hundred million dollars?"

"You think this was the girl?"

"I think so. For one thing, she opened her account with a hundred thousand dollar bills."

"Hell, Ida Mae, they don't print thousands anymore."

"These were perfect 1934 issued bills, worth at least $2,000 apiece."

Larry was fully engaged in the discussion at this point, "That's damned interesting, Ida Mae. You said 'for one thing.' What else tipped you off?"

"Wait'll you hear this. At the end of the day we got a call from a

Senior VP at First Boston Bank informing us that they were setting up an automatic wire transfer agreement, backed by her father's account, to maintain the daughter's balance at $100,000 and pay her Visa charges each month."

Larry's mind was in gear now, "Fantastic! So, no matter what she spends . . ."

"That's right," Ida Mae interjected. "And that's not all. Almost as an afterthought, she added her roommate's name to the account and got her a Visa card too!"

"Mama mia! So her roomy has an unlimited expense account too!" After a long pause during which they looked deep into each other's eyes, he asked, "You thinking what I'm thinking, Ida Mae?"

⸺◉⸺

Andrews couldn't sleep. He stared into the darkness above his bed and thought about his future. How should a fired president spend the rest of his life? Today he'd given Vandenberg's advance people permission to start the transition process. They exuded contempt. You could cut the gloom among his people downstairs with a knife.

Holt had told him that morning he'd walked past a supply room door, heard something strange, opened the door and there were three female staff people inside hugging each other and crying. Andrews had always had such respect for the American people, for democracy, for the wisdom of the common man. How could it be right to turn the reins of government over to a professional killer at this point? They say they want it, but do they really want the biggest bloodbath in history? How could he explain the angel's message to the people?

He'd thought through a dozen plans of how to go forward, but none seemed right. He reminded himself that there would be plenty of time to think about the future in Antarctica. And when I get back, if Vandenberg and World Jihad haven't wiped everything out, maybe there'll be a peace movement I can join. When he finished that thought he realized how long and hard he'd worked to get to the place where he could wait comfortably for direction and answers to prayer.

The Senate vote was scheduled for Wednesday the 13th. Joe Vandenberg was preparing to unleash the greatest mass murder in human history soon after. Andrews was working to prepare himself for the complete life change he was about to experience. De-personalize, he reminded himself. This nation can get along fine without me as president, and I'm so ready to become a private citizen.

His bedside phone rang, "Henry Holt, Mr. President."

"Any luck reaching Sir Ernest?"

"No sir. Just the daughter."

"Have we tried everything? My intuition tells me he could be a critical player in my life going forward. I was so hoping to meet him."

"He's completely unreachable. We've tried everything."

"Have you got her standing by for my call in the morning?"

"No, sir. She said she needs to meet with you, in her dorm room at 10AM on Tuesday, in person."

"Does that make any sense, Hank?"

"Your call, Mr. President. Given the circumstances surrounding her father, she may be someone you want to meet. Especially since her father requested the meeting."

"Have we got the Tuesday evening banquets under control?"

"Yes sir. Do I set up the meeting?"

Andrews sighed, "Yeah, I guess."

Just after 9 AM on Monday, Liza Jane waited outside Dr. Dan Kramer's office in the Institute for Advanced Studies. While she waited, she re-read an article by him and his research associates entitled "Beyond E=mc squared. A First Glimpse of a Universe Without Mass." The article began: "The most famous of all equations must surely be E=mc squared. In popular culture, that relation between energy and mass is virtually synonymous with relativity, and Einstein, its originator, has become a symbol of modern physics. The usual interpretation of the equation is that one kind of fundamental physical thing, mass (m in the equation), can be converted into a quite different kind of fundamental physical thing, energy (E in the equation), and vice versa; the two quantities are inextricably intertwined, related by the factor c squared, the square of the velocity of light.

"Recent work by this research team and others now appears to offer a radically different insight into the relation E=mc squared, as well as into the very idea of mass itself. To put it simply, the concept of mass may be neither fundamental nor necessary in physics. In the view we will present, Einstein's formula is even more significant than physicists have realized. It is actually a statement about how much energy is required to give the appearance of a certain amount of mass, rather than about the conversion of one fundamental thing, energy, into another fundamental thing, mass.

"Indeed, if that view is correct, there is no such thing as mass, only electric charge and energy, which together create the illusion of mass. The physical universe is made up of massless electric charges immersed in a vast, energetic, all-pervasive electromagnetic field. It is the interaction of those charges and the electromagnetic field that creates the appearance of mass."

She looked up when a lanky bearded older man turned the corner from the hall, his wrinkled plaid sport shirt tucked carelessly into brown slacks. His mouth was invisible down in his beard, thin lips tightly closed. His most distinctive features were heavy eyebrows that pointed upward at opposite angles. His movements were almost sprightly, those of a man half his age.

"Dr. Kramer?"

"Yes."

"I was hoping to spend a few minutes with you."

"I'm pressed for time right now. What is it you need?"

"I've come to ask you to be my advisor. The people in the dean's office told me I needed to ask you personally."

"You're an undergraduate?"

"Yes, sir."

"They could've saved you the trouble. They know I only work with doctoral candidates in my department."

"My father gave me your paper on the zero point field and suggested I meet you. Take some classes, if possible."

"Have you had much physics?"

"My studies haven't been so narrowly defined, but I know 'physics', as you call it."

"Interesting, Miss . . ."

"Appleton. Liza Jane Appleton."

"Hmm . . . where have I heard that name. You're aware of my work on the zero point field?"

"Yes. I'm excited about it."

"You are?" His eyes gave away the thin smile down in his beard. "Well, come in and let's discuss it."

He opened the door to a cluttered office. The wall opposite the door was an overflowing floor to ceiling bookcase. His desk was buried under folders, papers and open books. One small bare spot harbored the remains of a day-old Chinese lunch. On the wall were four haphazardly arranged degree certificates and a photo of a young Dan Kramer being awarded the Albert Einstein Award as Princeton's most promising graduate from the physics department.

He sat down and motioned awkwardly to the only other chair. His stutter recurred and he had trouble saying, "My first thought is that you need four years of college physics before my classes would mean much to you."

"They gave me this envelope to give to you," she said. She couldn't help but adore this brilliant, awkward man.

He opened the envelope and looked at a blank advisor's file card. A handwritten post-it asked him to fill in the blanks, if he agreed to be her advisor.

"I wouldn't take much of your time."

"I'm working with five doctoral candidates, teaching three graduate classes and chairing the department again. My own research is suffering."

"Your research is going to change human history."

Dr. Kramer was still mulling his dilemma, "I need more time to work. What? What did you say?"

"You and your research associates have found the path that leads to the underlying reality."

"We have?" he said blankly, staring at the young girl. It was her tone that got him. She seemed sure of what she'd just said.

"I'd like to help, if you'd let me."

"You want to help? With the ZPF work?"

"Yes, sir."

"And how do you propose to do that?"

"You're on the verge of a breakthrough that will change everything."

"We are? How do you know this?"

"It's a secret I'll share with you at some point. I come from a culture that's further down this road than you are. Will you be my advisor?"

"Of course."

"The ideas you're working with lead to the unification principle that human scientists have searched for."

He stared as his mind raced. Finally, he stammered, "Our work leads to the Unified Field Theory?"

"It's more than a theory, Doctor. Your zero point field is actually the reflex image of the universal field."

He caught himself before he reacted angrily, "And what field are you saying the ZPF is the reflex image of?"

"The universal field is consciousness. If you focus on the principle that underlies energy formations, you'll lead the way out of the mirage."

He suddenly remembered his 10AM meeting of department heads and said, "I need to go now, but look forward to hearing more about this field of consciousness."

He had dozens of questions buzzing in his thought, but he resisted getting into them and making his colleagues wait. "Let me see," he said picking up her card. "I guess we should fill this out. Home address?"

"I don't have a home address, Dr. Kramer."

"I'll fill in my home address. I assume you don't have a phone number either."

"No sir."

"Never mind, I'll fill this out."

Kramer sat transfixed, bearded chin in his thin hand, "So, energy is a manifestation of . . . of consciousness?"

"Not really. The electromagnetic universe appears to be a mixture of energy and consciousness, but the two don't actually mix. Penetrate the energy mirage and surprising things start to happen. The consciousness field is actually an intelligent creative force. In fact, we're made of the consciousness of that force."

Kramer sat in stunned silence, trying to calmly assimilate this remarkable stream of revolutionary concepts. He hadn't thought of the connection between God and physics since his late night debates with graduate student friends while he wrote his dissertation. His inspirational role model, Dr. Einstein, was sure that physics proved the existence of God. At length he asked, "Are you saying that God is what's real behind the energy forms?"

"The road you're on leads out of the illusion, to life and peace."

Kramer was staring at her, but not seeing her.

"You've found the answer to the bomb Dr. Einstein felt so terrible about." Liza Jane stood and stuck out her hand to say goodbye, but he was gone, lost in thoughts of Dr. Einstein, his lifelong inspiration. A tear worked its way into his beard.

She put down her hand, waved tentatively, opened the door and said, "I'll look forward to working with you."

He didn't hear. So, she closed the door and walked out.

Walking up the sidewalk to Rockefeller on her way back from the graduate school campus, Liza Jane passed a red plumbing truck without noticing the two men studying her.

"That's her, Ian," Larry Bianchi said, while he took her picture with his cell phone, then added, "The answer to all my problems."

CHAPTER ELEVEN

THE PRINCETON MEETING
SEPTEMBER 11, 2034

Sitting at her desk, Natasha thumbed through a binder she'd been given by her choral director, of the music she needed to learn. Several songs were marked for their first practice that evening.

A knock came at the door. When she opened it, a student asked her name and then handed her a sealed envelope from the front desk. In the envelope was a phone message from her uncle Derek. Her mother had fainted after lunch and been taken to a nearby hospital.

Natasha lay down on her bed. Thoughts started flowing about her mother's poor health, the sadness she carried in her heart because of her drunk absent husband, and the terrible problems her two oldest children piled on her. As usual, with these thoughts of her mother came tears and feelings of discouragement. Natasha had never felt she could help her dear mother, who was loaded down with unsolvable problems she hadn't caused.

Liza Jane walked in and stood looking at Natasha, then sat down next to her and stroked her hair, "Problems?"

"Yeah, my uncle had to rush my mama to the hospital."

"What's wrong?"

"Her heart's weak. She fainted after lunch."

"Let's go see her. Ary will loan us his car."

"There's a train in two hours. We can't take his car to Newark."

"I have a feeling your mother needs us, Natasha. There's no time to worry about what we drive."

A half hour later they were headed northeast on the New Jersey Turnpike. Natasha drove in silence, praying for her mother.

Liza Jane sensed her efforts and asked, "Can you heal?"

Natasha was slow answering, "I've had prayers answered. I was able to help some patients when I was in the hospital, but I don't have the gift of healing—like Peter and Paul. I couldn't heal a burned girl in the bed next to me."

"She died?"

Natasha nodded, "I tried so hard. She would have been a Princeton freshman. I think about her all the time."

"The Bible doesn't tell you how to heal?"

"I've tried, but have never gotten it. This morning I was reading about a Roman army officer whose servant was sick and he asked Jesus to heal him."

"Strange thing for a pagan soldier to ask."

"He said he understood that Jesus had authority over sickness."

Liza Jane smiled, "Of course. A military man would understand that."

"He said his men had to obey his orders because Roman law gave him authority."

"That's it, exactly, Natasha. You don't have to 'try' to heal. The power isn't yours; it's the operation of law."

"I wanted to help her. I just couldn't."

They were quiet for several miles before Liza Jane said, "I have some of that authority, Natasha."

"You can heal?"

"If your messenger taught a bunch of fishermen, why not us?"

"I've always thought he must have bestowed some special power on them, so they could help him, but my pastor says that's a cop out."

"What does it mean 'cop out'?"

"A phony reason why they could do it, but I can't."

"Didn't he tell his students to teach others?"

They drove on in the drone of the powerful engine. At length Natasha said, "He did say that and I would love to learn."

Past Edison and Menlo Park the countryside gave way to the sprawl near Staten Island. The birthplace of America's industrial might was now a shadow of its original significance. Natasha summoned her courage as she prepared to drive the glistening burgundy sports car into one of Newark's crumbling industrial neighborhoods, enjoying their discussion about spiritual healing.

Natasha asked, "Did Jesus come to your people, too?"

"Our messenger came long ago, born as one of us. Calderans aren't human, Natasha."

After thinking about that for a while, Natasha smiled and said, "I never thought of another species having its own Christmas."

The outskirts of Newark were dismal miles of urban decay. Natasha fought her fear as they turned off the turnpike into the oldest part of town and parked in front of a dilapidated red brick hospital. The brightly-lit entry was an island of light on the lifeless street. The few working street lights illumined decrepit buildings, scattered debris and broken glass. Two car skeletons lay stripped on the sidewalk. Natasha rolled to a stop in the heavily-lighted no parking zone in front of the entrance.

"We may get towed, but this is probably the safest place to leave Ary's car."

The Emergency Room desk was unattended. The staff was down at the end of the hall taking charge of four injured people being rolled in the side door on gurneys, paramedics walked beside them holding bags of fluid aloft. The staff's urgent communications were crisp and clear, obviously those of experienced professionals. The girls waited and listened to the chorus of voices getting help for the injured.

Finally, a large Latino male nurse with a ponytail walked over and asked pleasantly, "What can I do for you?"

Natasha answered, "We came to see my mother in E97."

He walked over to the desk and picked up a clipboard, "Dr. Whitcomb is the man. I saw him walk through here a while ago. Have a seat and I'll find him for you."

A few minutes later, he returned and said, "Dr. Whitcomb would like to see you in his office. E61 down that hall."

They filed quietly into Dr. Whitcomb's small orderly office. He looked up from a stack of computer printouts, walked around his desk with a kind, but concerned expression and shook hands with both girls. He was a tall slender middle-aged black man in pale green scrubs.

"Please have a seat," he said, perching on the front of his desk.

"How's my mama, Doctor?" Natasha asked calmly.

Liza Jane put her hand on Natasha's on the chair arm.

"We're not able to help her a great deal, I'm afraid. Her heart's barely functioning."

Natasha's hand gripped Liza Jane's, "We're not losing her, are we?"

"I'm afraid so."

"There must be something that can be done, Doctor!" she said raising her voice and wiping away tears. She turned to Liza Jane who was looking at their interlaced black and white fingers.

"We're doing all we can," he said. "I'm afraid it's not enough."

"Can we see her?" Natasha asked.

"She's not conscious, Natasha."

Liza Jane said firmly, "It's important that we see her."

He looked from one to the other, then said, "Okay, let's walk down and look in."

He opened the door and they stood at the end of the bed. Mrs. Cheatam had tubes and electrodes attached to her and a breathing apparatus covering her mouth and nose. She appeared to be sleeping, but her expression showed the strain of constricted breathing. Two machines with digital read-outs stood guard beside the inclined bed. Mrs. Cheatam's sweet face reminded Liza Jane of her daughter's.

Natasha lost her composure and leaned against Liza Jane's shoulder, crying softly.

Liza Jane asked, "Doctor, would you mind leaving us with her for a while?"

"That'll be alright," he said, scanning the digital monitors. "She's actually doing a bit better, now."

When he was gone, Liza Jane said, "They've given up."

"He said they're doing everything they can."

"If we don't step in, she'll die tonight."

Natasha's tears were clogging her voice, but she forced herself to ask, "Can you help her?"

"These machines only monitor bodily functions. Your mother's problem is beyond their reach."

Natasha cleared her throat, "Do what you can, please."

"I have. Her heart's working better now."

"It is?"

"You were right. It was all clogged up with worry and sadness."

Natasha looked at her mother's face. The distress was gone. She was sleeping peacefully, her breathing relaxed and easy. Natasha leaned over and gave her a kiss on the forehead.

Her mother's eyes opened. She tried to hug her daughter, but the breathing apparatus covering much of her face got in the way. She pulled it away from her face and asked, "What's all this?"

"You had one of your fainting spells. Derek brought you to the hospital."

"Of all the foolish things to do. I feel fine."

"This is Liza Jane, my roommate from school."

"Natasha, you said your roommate was pretty. That's not half of what this child is. Liza Jane's a beauty. Come give me a hug, Roommate."

Liza Jane and Natasha both managed to hug her, sitting on each side of the bed, when the door opened and Dr. Whitcomb looked in, "What's going on in here?" he asked sternly. Then he saw Margaret Cheatam's smiling face.

"Life, Doc," Natasha said, her head nestled on her mother's shoulder.

Dr. Whitcomb looked confused and busied himself with the digital monitors. Then, he looked again at his patient's smiling face and said, "Well I'll be . . ."

He left and came back with a nurse. Together they ran tests, while their patient talked happily with her visitors. After a while, he stopped analyzing and just stood smiling at Mrs. Cheatam. "It's wonderful. I don't understand it, but it appears to be true."

"She's well, isn't she, Doc?" Natasha asked.

"Pump, valves, pipes, lungs, everything seems to be working fine."

"Can we take her home?"

"No, no. If this miracle holds, maybe tomorrow. You two go on now, and let her get a good night's sleep."

"Goodnight, Mama. I'd like to invite Liza Jane to our house, if that's okay. She wants to meet Reverend Pettis."

"What do you think? Of course, it's alright. Now, run along, like the man said. I've got to get my rest."

The two held hands walking down the brightly-lit hall in step. Natasha turned to Liza Jane with a glowing smile and said, "I'll be forever grateful to you, for saving her."

Andrews and Holt stood on the south-facing portico outside the residence in the White House, staring in amazement at the largest gathering in the history of the American capitol. From the White House to the tidal basin and from the Capitol Building to the Lincoln Memorial, the National Mall was a sea of humanity numbering in millions. Most had come to support the presidency of David Andrews.

"Astounding isn't it Hank! At the eleventh hour our cause is gaining some traction. Will this change any votes?"

Holt was so absorbed in the scene as he panned across the sea of people through binoculars, he didn't answer.

"What's the latest count on the vote?"

Holt finally lowered the binoculars, "A few more names have moved into the undecided column, but more than enough votes still appear solid for removal."

The two old friends looked at each other for a moment before Andrews said, "We've had some great years together, haven't we, Hank?"

After an emotional silence Holt replied, "We did the best we could."

Andrews sighed, "Yeah. But we couldn't be leaving a bigger mess behind."

The impending vote in the Senate to acquit or remove President Andrews would be held against the backdrop of the deepest and widest rift between Americans since the Civil War. The minority, in favor of a peaceful resolution, were no less vehement than the majority. Families were divided with powerful emotions on both sides of the issue. Husbands and wives were bitterly split on the subject. Fights broke out among brothers and friends. Violence often flared on campuses and within companies when discussion turned to the Andrews vote.

The nation faced what many felt was a point of no return. Once the missiles were sent the world would enter a state of nuclear violence from which it might not recover.

In spite of the masses of people already in Washington and constant pleas from government officials to stop coming, tens of thousands more were on their way. Many felt they had to try to prevent another nuclear holocaust. Others, when they heard of the hoards demonstrating in the capitol in support of the president, packed up and headed out to show their support for Vice President Vandenberg. This vote in the Senate would determine the future direction of the country and they wanted to be there to express their viewpoint.

Ted Kaufman spoke directly to the camera in front of him, "Bernie Salzberg is in the Senate chambers tonight as both sides prepare to make their closing statements in the trial. So, we won't get our nightly update from him.

"Instead, I want to share a story with you that, even though I know it's true, I still have a hard time believing. With President Andrews' help, last night I spent an hour with General al Hammabi, the Iraqi terrorist responsible for the destruction of New York City, Houston and Kansas City, and was captured on his way to destroy Los Angeles.

"Let me preface the story by saying, I left the Jewish faith in Columbia's School of Journalism and haven't had what you could call a religious thought since. These are not the ramblings of a religious extremist, but the reporting of well-documented facts."

As the camera rolled and millions listened, Ted Kaufman carefully documented the transformation of General Samir al Hammabi. Then, he explained that President Andrews was well-acquainted with the angel that appeared to the Iraqi general, as he prepared himself to die.

"General al Hammabi calmly explained to me that the angel is trying to show humanity God's ultimate message to mankind. We must love one another. It's not optional. The rejection of the message ends in extinction and he said that's the road we're going down, and we're gaining speed.

"The general gave me a detailed account of how the angel worked with President Andrews to heal his sight and hearing. He expressed deep regret for his terrible deeds.

"Fellow Americans, I'm just a television journalist, but I urge you to think about what I've just reported. These are extraordinary times we're living in and our president is an extraordinary leader. He knows we can't kill our way out of this problem, so he's trying to show us how to love our way out."

※

When Liza Jane and Natasha emerged from the hospital, Ary's car was covered by a brightly-lighted bunch of raucous black men sitting in and on the Corvette, passing a half-empty bottle of something strong and cheap. The street resounded with their crude banter and play-fighting.

Natasha grabbed Liza Jane's arm and tried to pull her back, whispering urgently, "We need to go call for help."

Liza Jane resisted her tugging, looked at her, then at the eight men. One sitting on the trunk shoved the smaller man next to him, who tumbled off backwards onto the asphalt, amid gales of laughter. "I can handle this," she said.

"No, you don't know this kind of man."

Liza Jane pulled away and started down the steps. Natasha ran inside to call for help.

Liza Jane approached the group to a chorus of whistles and lecherous slurs. Heedless, she focused on the quiet thin man in the middle, eyeing her calmly. He wore a tattered overcoat with the collar up and a long scarf, despite the warm evening. Sitting on the hood, he leaned against the windshield, resting a bearded chin on his forearm.

The others got their bravado from the group and the liquor; the thin one had his own. His left eye stared obliquely. The white of his right eye was discolored, its cloudy iris ticked slightly as it looked at her. The others obviously deferred to him, their leader they called Duke.

When she reached the sidewalk, Duke said with a raspy voice, "We're gonna take the car, but we need the key. We haven't been able to hotwire it."

"You're trying to steal my friend's car?"

"What's it look like, ya stupid bitch?" someone muttered to loud laughter.

Two of them moved in behind her and waited for a signal from Duke. One made lewd gestures to the others' amusement. Duke stopped him with a glance. He kept his smile to himself, but was amazed at the white girl's calm in a situation that would unnerve most women.

"My friend and I need to get back to school. Is there some kind of ransom I can pay you to free the car?"

That ignited lurid ranting from all but Duke.

"I could make it worth your while," she added.

The seven howled in raucous delight at the prospect of ravaging her. Even Duke cracked a smile at her naiveté. The stocky sullen one sitting on the passenger door next to Duke mumbled, "Let's grab the bitch and split."

"What kind of ransom?" Duke asked to more vulgarity. He studied her and wondered: how could a young girl, surrounded by lust-filled drunks, stand there with no fear or anger? He couldn't even detect any scorn.

"Your good eye's going bad on you, isn't it, Duke."

He stiffened from his slouch. His expression hardened, "You a doctor?"

"You could say that," she smiled. "Tell your friends to get off the car, send someone inside to tell my friend, Natasha, there's no problem out here, and I'll work on your eyes."

Duke stared at her while he thought. She was obviously messing with him, trying to throw him off balance. But her tone, for a second he'd believed her. As he thought of a suitable response, her face came into clear focus.

"Oh!" he exclaimed, putting his hand to his right eye. He bent over, took his hand away and blinked repeatedly, looked at her again and exclaimed, "Holy Shit!"

"What's wrong, Duke?" the stocky one asked.

"Eddie! What you sittin' there for? Get your fat butt up those steps and find the black bitch that went back inside, and tell her there ain't no problem out here."

Eddie started to protest, but Duke glared at him and pointed emphatically. Reluctantly, with plaintive hand gestures, Eddie slid off the door and started up the steps.

"And the rest of you niggers," Duke scowled, "what you doin messin with this young girl's car? Get off!"

Slowly, his confused cronies abandoned the Corvette.

"That's more like it!" he snarled.

When Natasha and Eddie appeared at the top of the steps, sirens sounded in the distance. Natasha surveyed the scene trying to figure it out, still frightened.

"That any better?" Liza Jane asked.

"Ain't seen this good since the Iraq War," he smiled. He was now standing straighter with a hint of his former master sergeant's bearing. "Thank you, kindly, young lady," he said, offering her his hand.

She took it, smiled at him and watched his left eye come to life, realign itself and look at her.

His lips quivered and a tear rolled down his face. He lifted her hand and kissed it, leaving teardrops glistening on the back of her hand in the overhead light. "Will you be driving home, Miss?"

"No. Natasha's driving."

He turned with a courtly gesture and opened the passenger door for her.

Kneeling on the sidewalk to talk to her he said, "Please forgive our rudeness, young lady. I'll never forget what you done for me, tonight. If I can ever do anything for you, just call. Everyone on the south side knows Duke Sims."

"I'll bet they do, Mr. Sims. Actually, I'll need some help in a couple of weeks. I'll contact you."

"I'll await your call, Miss . . ."

"Liza Jane," she said.

"Goodnight, Little Liza Jane," he said with a musical turn. "And God bless you." He smiled and patted her arm.

Eddie escorted Natasha through the somber group and opened the driver's door.

She half smiled and asked, "What've you been doing out here?"

"Duke and I have been seeing each other more clearly, haven't we, Mr. Sims."

"Indeed we have, Liza Jane. Drive careful, Natasha."

Natasha started the car and moved away from the curb, shifting deliberately. She made a careful U-turn at the intersection with the tires crunching broken glass. As they drove by, Duke Sims came to attention and gave the Corvette a crisp salute.

On the way to the onramp they passed two speeding police cars headed for the hospital. On the turnpike, Natasha gave her a sideways look and a sly smile, "Healing again, weren't you?"

"He's a good man under all that toughness. It just takes clear seeing."

They rode in silence for half an hour as the powerful dark red machine made its way back to the country. Natasha couldn't get over the power her roommate had to fully repair her mama's failing heart. How could prayer alter an interior organ like that? She made a commitment to achieve that level of prayer power down the road. She realized there was nothing in life she would rather achieve.

"Sorry you missed your choral practice tonight. Would you sing something?"

Natasha put her head against the headrest and started humming, then sang with a low soulfulness.

Amazing grace, how sweet the sound
That saved a wretch like me.
I once was lost, but now I'm found
Was blind, but now I see.

T'was grace that taught my heart to fear
And grace my fears relieved.
How precious did that grace appear
The hour I first believed.

She glanced over. The oncoming headlights made her friend's eyes glisten, "Are those tears, Liza Jane?"

"Some of the sweetest sounds I've ever heard. You make me proud to be half human."

Natasha smiled, "Half human. I never thought of that. Is that a problem for your people?"

"They've always loved me. It was my father who was hard for them to accept."

"I'm real familiar with non-acceptance. How did he make his breakthrough?"

"The Calderans were devoted to my mother and she was in love with the lion-hearted human she'd rescued from the ice. It's taken time, but they've grown to love my father."

"Do you get homesick?"

"Sure. But, I'm glad to be here. Can you come to Caldera with me? I'm going home in a week or two."

"I would love to come," she smiled and sang,

Through many dangers, toils, and snares
I have already come.
Tis grace hath brought me safe thus far
And grace will lead me home.

At 9:30 on Tuesday morning, the presidential helicopter settled on a remote Princeton ball field. Clyde Alexander, Holt, Andrews and six Secret Service agents climbed into two waiting limousines for the short trip to Rockefeller.

Ary answered his phone for the tenth time in an hour. Henry Holt introduced himself then said, "I was given this number to speak with Miss Appleton."

"She's next door, Mr. Holt. She doesn't want to talk with anyone on the telephone."

Holt relayed the message to the president.

The lead Secret Service agent said, "Mr. President, you should re-think this meeting. A dozen agents have found nothing on the identity of this girl. Nothing! That's not plausible for a real person. She could be a contract killer for all we know."

Andrews took the phone, "This is President Andrews, to whom am I speaking, please?"

"This is Crown Prince Ary Hussein of Jordan, Mr. President, Liza Jane Appleton's next-door neighbor. What can I do for you, sir?"

"Prince Hussein, the secretary of state, my chief of staff and some security people are with me. Can they stay in your room while I meet with your neighbor?"

"Sure. The princess invited me to be part of your meeting next door in her room."

A crowd had gathered outside Rockefeller. A rumor had spread that the president was meeting with Crown Prince Hussein about a Middle Eastern crisis. The president waved to the students, walked upstairs and knocked on Liza Jane's door.

The door opened and he was surprised to be greeted by an attractive black girl, "Welcome, Mr. President. My name is Natasha Cheatam. We met last month in Newark Hospital."

"Of course, Natasha. I didn't recognize you."

"No wonder. I was a beat up mess back then."

"So, you came to Princeton, after all."

Natasha flashed her big smile at him, "You didn't leave me much choice, did you. Let me introduce my roommate, Princess Liza Jane Appleton of Caldera and our neighbor Crown Prince Ary Hussein of Jordan."

"I'm so pleased to meet you both. Before we start, I wanted to make sure you all understand I'm about to be voted out of office. Most of the people on the planet know, but I wanted to be sure you understand I'm meeting with you as someone soon to be a private citizen."

"Yes we know," Liza Jane acknowledged. "My mother told me we should go ahead with our meeting."

"Where is Caldera, Your Highness?" As Andrews asked the question, he was struck by her beauty and poise. Her eyes were like none he'd seen. They were greenish-yellow. And the way she looked at him. How could an eighteen-year-old girl have such confidence? He rarely felt awe, but that was definitely the feeling he had. Everything about her seemed based on deep-seated knowledge.

Liza Jane said, "Mr. President, before we begin, your aides need to remove all their listening devices."

"They're nervous. They haven't been able to find any information on you and they're concerned for my safety."

"I can sense everything they're doing. If they attempt to eavesdrop in any way, this meeting won't take place."

As Andrews left the room to tell Holt to unplug all the surveillance equipment, he stopped in the hall, put his hand on the wall, lowered his head and tried to calm himself, surprised his heart was pounding.

Holt came out of Ary's room with a worried expression, "You alright, Mr. President? You don't look so good."

"This is rich stuff, Holt." He ordered all the listening devices turned off and returned to Liza Jane's room.

When he walked back in, the blinds had been closed and the room was lit only by Natasha's desk lamp, "Why so dark?" he asked.

"I've got a surprise for you," Liza Jane said, "but first, why don't you let me know why you wanted to meet with me."

"I asked about your country. Where is Caldera?"

"Let's start with the reason you came."

"Okay," he said, a bit taken aback by her manner. He was used to leading discussions. "Recently your father, one of my heroes by the way, sent me a message asking me to meet with you. Are you aware of that?"

"Yes sir. My father has agreed to join us and help you understand more about our people, who may be willing to help you."

"Your father's here? I was told he wouldn't be."

"We'll meet with him by transponder."

"What's that?"

"It's like a telephone, but better for important communication."

"I see," the president said, nonplussed. She spoke with total conviction. "First, how about some info on you and your father before he joins us?"

"He's always loved this country, David. Do you mind if I call you David?"

"No," he said hesitantly, again taken aback. He hadn't been called by his first name by anyone, but the angel, since his wife died. Hearing her use it was pleasing, but threw him off balance a bit.

"Good. Call me Liza Jane. Father told me this morning the only president he's met was Theodore Roosevelt, before his second expedition. He likes what he knows about you, especially your prayerfulness."

"How could he know that? I don't let it out."

"Frankly, David, the depth of your prayer is why we're talking, and why my father is willing to meet you."

"Really? But, how does he know?"

"My mother told him."

"How could she know?"

"When you get to know her you'll understand." Turning to Ary she asked, "What should we tell the president, Ary? Maybe you'd fill him in."

Ary told him of E.A.'s rescue and marriage to the Calderan queen, and his appointment to their Council.

"No wonder you didn't want anyone listening! Your father was adopted by a completely secret community."

"I want you to know," Liza Jane explained, "the Calderans didn't evolve from primates. We're not related to humans."

"You're not?" Andrews gasped in shocked amazement.

"I got my outward appearance from my father, but Calderans evolved from a different mammal."

"Wow! Somewhere the earth harbors an advanced species humans know nothing about, who may be willing to help us."

"Let's get my father to fill you in on the Calderan people. Shall I invite him to join us?"

"By all means," the president agreed taking a deep breath and shifting his weight in the unpadded desk chair.

Liza Jane went to her backpack and pulled out a black cube about four inches on all sides, hinged in the middle. She opened it to an eight-inch by four-inch shape and laid it on her desk top. They watched a dim light under the glass that formed the top of both halves grow brighter.

A small figure began forming in the light above the box. Liza Jane said, "Good morning, Father."

The image was startling to Natasha, like a dead person appearing in a séance. She stared at the small handsome face coming into focus. An eighteen-inch tall male figure with thick shoulder-length grey hair in a black bodysuit and riding boots now stood suspended in the light.

Andrews figured it must be some sort of advanced hologram.

"Father, let me introduce David Andrews, the President of the United States, my roommate, Natasha Cheatam of Newark, New Jersey, and Ary Hussein, the Crown Prince of Jordon, my father, Lord Ernest Appleton of Caldera."

The small bearded figure bowed and said, "I'm honored to meet you all."

Andrews was shocked that the hologram image could see, hear and speak and stared for a long moment in wonderment.

After an awkward silence, E.A. continued, "Transponders take a bit of getting used to, don't they?"

"Yes," Andrews managed, "I'll be candid, Your Lordship. I think your daughter has put me in a mild state of shock, telling me about people we had no idea existed. Then, you appear out of thin air. Let me catch my breath for a moment. Why don't you get things started for us?"

"Jane loves what I've told her of her human heritage and has long wanted to visit your world. Recently she received permission from our Council to come and appraise the level of receptivity among humans to the ideas required for their survival."

Andrews said, "I need to know what help she needs from us. But first let me reiterate that in the next few days I'll probably be removed from office. The new president plans to use massive force and a majority of the American people are behind him. I did my best to turn our people away from nuclear retaliation, but was unable to do so."

E.A. responded, "The stand you took was tremendously important. None of us knows what will come of it, but millions now support peace. You should never underestimate the power of a right idea."

"I don't. And I'm grateful to hear there's a possibility that your people may be willing to help us."

Liza Jane asked, "What about you, David? Can you join our peace campaign?"

"No. Definitely not. You probably don't understand that I would be a huge negative influence. Millions hate me and they're sick and tired of hearing about peace from me. Besides, I'm exhausted and need to take a few months off to re-charge. Then, I'll see if there's some low profile way I can help. Anyway, back to what kind of help your daughter needs for her campaign."

"You don't need to be burdened with logistics. The Calderan people are already producing all we'll need. After you've finished recharging, perhaps you'll join our effort."

David smiled at Lord Appleton's tactfulness. "I forget I'm letting go of the levers of power in our nation and won't be able to help much. Perhaps you'd explain to me where Calderans get their power."

"Our power comes from our relationship with the Giver of Life."

"You mean . . . like Abraham's covenant with God?"

E.A. smiled and nodded, "The same. When a life form anywhere in the universe reaches Abraham's capacity to receive spiritual ideas from the Creator, they're invited to enter the covenant. If they're true to it, the Creator protects and guides them."

"How do you feel humans have kept the covenant?"

"Like most, you've partially accepted it. In that case, as time goes on, the forces of rejection usually get the upper hand, as they have in your civilization. Humans are headed down a tragic path.

"When an immature belligerent life form succeeds in unlocking the strong force that binds the atomic nucleus, its extinction is usually only a matter of time. Soon terrorists and dictators, even drug lords and gangsters will have chain reaction weapons. When 'eye-for-an-eye' or extortion become nuclear, the end is usually near."

"Can you people help us turn back from that path?"

"Jane feels we can. That's why she's sitting here with you. She's in daily contact with her mother, who is one of the most influential individuals in the universe. Some years ago, my wife was named to the Intergalactic Council and recently brought a request before them, to give humans another opportunity to turn away from violence and embrace the message."

"Everything I hear about your wife is amazing. Tell me, how do you defend yourselves without weapons?"

With a gleam in his eye, E.A. turned to Natasha's desk lamp. Suddenly it launched itself at the ceiling. The green glass cover and bulb smashed and sent a shower of glass fragments raining down on the wide-eyed president. The overhead light turned on and illumined the room.

In the next room, the agents grabbed their four-man ram and charged the door across the hall. They crashed through the door, rolled and came up with guns drawn.

Andrews stood quickly with his large hands extended and yelled, "STOP!"

The agents got to their feet and one asked, "You alright, Mr. President?"

Andrews' big laugh filled the room as, one by one, they saw the barrels of their small machine guns hanging limp. One swung his gun barrel around like a piece of pasta and laughed. By then, the doorway was crowded with agents.

Andrews looked back at the transponder. E.A. was gone. He

whispered to Liza Jane, "Did you do that?"

"No. That was father's doing."

"I see why people don't mess with you folks." He turned to the crowd of agents and said, "I'll be with you shortly. Get the door closed, I'm not quite through with my meeting."

The agents picked up their ram, holstered their ruined guns and filed out.

"I'm so sorry he's gone," Andrews whispered to Liza Jane, "I didn't get to ask him about his expeditions to Antarctica."

Liza Jane smiled, "You share his interest in exploration?"

"Yes. In a couple of days I'm embarking on a similar expedition. I've been planning my trip to the South Pole for years."

"You two can compare notes the next time you meet."

Andrews smiled at the thought of another meeting with one of his life-long heroes, "That would be great. Now, how can our government support you in your mission, Your Highness? I'll let people know before I leave."

"My mother is putting together a worldwide campaign for peace that starts October 15th."

Andrews interjected, "One of your first tasks, it seems to me, will be to turn the president-elect from his planned course. He intends to unleash a thermonuclear holocaust in a few days."

"I've asked my mother for her help in delaying that action until our campaign gets moving."

"When do I get to meet this lady?"

"Come back from your journey and join our Campaign for World Peace. She'll be front and center."

CHAPTER TWELVE

ANDREWS' FAREWELL SPEECH
SEPTEMBER 12, 2034

On the return trip to Washington, Andrews went through the important details of the meeting, but mostly he thought about the powerful attraction he felt for E.A.'s daughter. It was shocking to him. He hadn't had those feelings since Diane's passing and didn't think he would ever have them again. By the end of their meeting, he'd forgotten their age difference and wanted go someplace where they could be alone for a week and get to know each other.

The rhythmic thumping sound of the propeller blades of the presidential chopper was the only sound for the first twenty minutes. The information overload was acute. Andrews worked hard to sort out the priorities and re-considered the time schedule between now and his departure the following afternoon.

Finally, he turned and gave Holt a detailed account of the meeting. Between gasps, Holt outlined the points Andrews would need to cover in his farewell address to the nation scheduled for that evening. Holt and his staff had put together a farewell ceremony without precedent, being referred to inside the beltway as the un-nauguration. There would be three large banquets to allow hundreds in the administration to say their goodbyes. Andrews' farewell speech would be the keynote of the evening and would be broadcast around the world.

Staunch Andrews' supporters and leaders of the peace movement across the nation had organized their own farewell banquets with big screen televisions for the president's last speech. Millions were grieving his departure and dreading Vandenberg's inauguration the next morning.

Air Force One was bringing Vandenberg and his key people to Washington in the morning, then delivering Andrews to New Zealand in the afternoon. Andrews had decided to skip the Vandenberg inauguration, which he'd been told would be the largest show of military power in American history. The new president's first hours would send a clear statement to the world about the future. The wimps are gone. America has turned to its warriors to secure its future. On his first day in office, President Vandenberg planned to go before a joint session of Congress and get authorization to destroy Pakistan.

When the president was gone and the girls were alone, Natasha said, "With your people on our side, we're going to be able to make a difference, aren't we Liza Jane."

"Yes, I think so. What do you say we get Ary and go to dinner in Philadelphia? My father says it's a fine city."

"No thanks. The dining hall will do just fine for me. You two go ahead and have a good time."

"Come on, Natasha. It's important to me that we spend some time getting to know each other better. Have you ever been to Philadelphia?"

"No, I haven't," Natasha said, deciding it was time to address the gulf that existed between her and her two new friends. "You need to understand, Liza Jane, I have no money to spend. I'm only here because the university let me come for nothing. It was generous of them, but I sure feel out of place much of the time. Then, on top of everything, they put me in the same room with the richest girl in the school."

"When I look at you, Natasha, I see spiritual richness and a wealth of grace."

"That's wonderful, Roommate, but those qualities won't buy my dinner in Philadelphia."

"This will," Liza Jane said, handing her a plastic card.

Natasha took the card and looked at it, "A Visa card with my name on it."

"I got it for you. Feel free to use it."

"No. No. I could never use your money," she said, urging the card back on Liza Jane.

Liza Jane shook her head, "Keep it. It's a gift from the Calderan people, for helping me feel so at home in your world."

"I would never feel right using it."

"Try to understand this, Natasha, Calderans aren't concerned about money."

Natasha studied her eyes, trying to figure out what that meant, "You people have unlimited money?"

"The card has a high limit, the balance is automatically paid, and no one at home is counting."

Natasha hugged her, "Just like that, you can give me so much?"

"You've given me hope for my father's people. Your heart's as pure as any Calderan heart, Natasha. You have some fear and doubt issues to work out and wisdom to gain, but a pure heart is a priceless starting place. In fact, they put the two richest girls in the school in the same room; only one of us didn't realize it until now."

Getting into a cab at the Philadelphia train station, Liza Jane asked Ary, "Can you help her find some clothes, like you helped me?"

Ary told the driver, "Bloomingdales, please."

Forty minutes later, Natasha was standing in a three-way mirror in navy wool slacks and a beige linen blouse with a scoop neckline. Ary came up behind her with an emerald green blazer and helped her put it on. It fit perfectly. They all studied the image in the mirrors and agreed, the look was smashing.

Natasha looked at the price tag on the jacket sleeve and gasped.

"Don't count," Liza Jane whispered, "it's just a coat. Those numbers mean nothing to you anymore."

Ary said, "I saw some boots over there that work with that outfit."

"Oh, this is more than enough, Ary. Isn't this coat wonderful."

"Look Natasha," Ary responded, "we've got dinner reservations in two hours, we're in Bloomingdales, and you've got the magic card, let's shop! Miss!" he called to a passing sales lady who had been helping them, "My friend needs some help with her wardrobe and we've got two hours. How would you suggest we fix her up?"

"What's the budget?"

"No budget, just a time limit. We've got dinner reservations in two hours."

The sales lady smiled, "An interesting challenge."

Later, while Natasha signed a stack of charge slips, trying not to add them up as she signed. She leaned over and whispered to Liza Jane, "I'm not going to get an irate call from your dad, am I?"

"No. He'll never see the bills. I mentioned your card to him and he wired instructions to his bank in Boston to pay your charges automatically each month."

Their dinner reservations were at an elegant dinner club that the deputy ambassador in the Jordanian embassy had made for Ary near Bloomingdales.

After dinner, Natasha casually handed the waiter her card and whispered to Ary, "This feels illegal."

"Must be quite a feeling to suddenly become one of Princeton's richest students."

"I don't feel any different, but thanks to you I sure have some nice clothes. Your sisters are lucky to have you to shop with."

"They never listen to me. I was glad to be able to help."

Their waiter cleared the table and brought coffee.

Natasha picked up the plastic holder on the center of the table and read, "Hey, we have a dinner show. The Amazing Madison, hypnotist extraordinaire. Have you ever seen someone get hypnotized, Ary?"

"One of my security detail at home was cured of smoking by a hypnotist, but I've never seen one in person. Have you Liza Jane?"

"Never. Should be interesting. I'm surprised people are willing to be put under someone else's control, even for entertainment."

"Seems safe enough," Ary said.

The curtain parted and an attractive brunette in a dark blue sequined floor-length sheath walked onto the small stage carrying a hand-held mike, then she proceeded down several steps onto the restaurant floor.

"Good evening ladies and gentlemen. Tonight we're going on an adventure together to explore some deep dark secrets of the human mind.

"Do we have any adventurers here tonight willing to explore possibilities beyond your wildest imaginings? How about you, sir?" she asked a slightly built thirty-something accountant-type gentleman sitting at a table next to her.

He blushed and tried to beg off, but she put the mike under her arm and started clapping, and soon the whole room was clapping and urging him to try it. Finally, he reluctantly agreed and she kept clapping as he shyly stood next to her.

"What's your name, darling?" she asked and stuck the mike toward him.

"Walter Jones," he managed, fidgeting and adjusting his glasses.

"So what do you think, folks? Is Walter a dead ringer for Clark Kent, the man of steel, or what?"

The crowd agreed to loud cheering and applause.

At that, she turned and put her face close to Walter's, looked into his eyes, and whispered into the mike that when she snapped her fingers he would become a steel I-beam. Then, she snapped her fingers between his eyes.

Walter's bearing instantly changed. His posture became strong and erect. His expression changed to one of serious earnestness as he quickly arranged two chairs about six feet apart.

Then, to the astonishment of all in the room he lay down between the two chairs with his heels on one chair and the back of his head on the other. His body was perfectly straight without sagging or movement. It appeared easy for him, as though he could stay in that position for the rest of the evening.

Then The Amazing Madison asked his equally shy date to have a seat on Walter's chest. After some persuasion, she put a tiny bit of her weight on his chest. Walter's body remained absolutely rigid. A few minutes later the hypnotist held her hand as she stood on Walter's barely yielding body to a roomful of applause and cheers.

After lighting a cigarette, Madison woke Walter from his hypnotic trance and asked him to again stretch himself between the chairs. He couldn't, and the crowd laughed and clapped as he tried.

Next she hypnotized Walter's brother, Ned, and told him his hand was a glass ashtray. She put out her cigarette by grinding the lighted end in the palm of Ned's hand. After waking Ned and blowing the ashes from his hand, she showed the audience his completely uninjured palm.

For her next volunteers she turned to Natasha, Ary and Liza Jane and quickly hypnotized Natasha and Ary. Liza Jane felt her efforts to establish mental control, but refused to be hypnotized.

The Amazing Madison explained to the crowd that when Ary and Natasha awoke they would be extremely thirsty, but unable to lift the glasses on their table. They'd been told that the glasses had been attached to the table with powerful epoxy cement.

She snapped her fingers and both of her subjects immediately reached for their water glasses. To the crowd's amusement, they tried in vain to lift their glasses. Not only could they not lift them, they couldn't move them. Finally, Liza Jane picked up Natasha's glass and handed it to her. People at adjoining tables offered their water glasses and the two emptied them all.

On the way back to Princeton, they had the train car to themselves and rode along without speaking for much of the trip. Finally, Ary said, "I still can't believe I couldn't move that glass."

Natasha added, "Mine felt like it had become part of the table. Scary isn't it?"

Liza Jane said, "How about that cigarette she put out in that guy's hand?"

"Yeah!" Ary responded, "He let me see his hand after the show. It wasn't even red or blistered. Why? I don't get it."

"I thought those first two guys were part of the act, until she hypnotized us," Natasha said.

"Ned believed his hand was made of glass, so there was no injury," Liza Jane explained.

Ary wondered out loud, "Are you saying the atoms that make up his hand rearranged themselves to become glass? And the other guy became steel?"

The three spoke little until they pulled into Princeton. Natasha mumbled tiredly to herself, "What if she'd told me I was sick? What then?"

Liza Jane let it pass, surprised that neither of them was aware of the role hypnotism played in their world.

Andrews realized it would be the last time he put on his tux for a long time. Holt knocked and came in. The two old friends looked at each other for a moment, then embraced.

"A lot of great years, Mr. President."

"You can stop calling me that now, Hank."

"I don't know. The vote may not go according to predictions after your speech tonight. They're ready for us downstairs."

The security precautions were intense. All guests had to come through a single checkpoint a quarter mile from the White House as each person in each limo was checked against a list of approved guests and drivers. A hundred press passes had been issued to the White House banquet and were enormously coveted.

Andrews put in an upbeat relaxed appearance at the two outside banquets and said goodbye to the hundreds gathered at each. When he arrived at the White House it was time for his farewell speech to the nation, which was being transmitted around the world.

Andrews sat comfortably behind his desk in the Oval Office. The director counted down with his fingers, then pointed at the president, who spoke without notes or teleprompter. The largest audience in history, almost four billion, were watching or listening around the planet.

"Tonight, I wanted to say goodbye to the people of America. Your representatives in the Senate have indicated that they are going to vote to remove me from office tomorrow morning and I'm almost packed. My presidency was disappointing because it had to be so focused on international terrorists, and during the last few months nuclear terrorism cast its terrible pall across our country.

"A majority of Americans want retaliation in kind against

the homeland of the terrorists, and that standpoint is certainly understandable. A growing minority agrees with my stand to refuse to slaughter millions of innocent people in retaliation for the millions of Americans who have been murdered. When Vice President Vandenberg is sworn in, he plans to unleash our missiles and destroy much of Pakistan.

"The vice president is tired of hearing me talk about the importance of working for peace in spite of terrorism. I wanted to speak to you directly one more time before I go, because recently I've received some information that elevates world peace from a desirable goal to a definite possibility.

"To be perfectly candid with you, until a few days ago I had no idea how a lasting peace could be achieved. We all know how to wage war, but as we've discovered, waging peace is harder and we're not as good at it. That's why our citizens and allies have been urging nuclear retaliation. They feel that achieving peace is unrealistic. They argue that nuclear weapons exist, they've been used against our country, so we must use them in retaliation.

"What's changed that makes nuclear retaliation completely unacceptable? Fellow Americans and residents of planet earth listening tonight, everything has changed. I asked for this opportunity to speak to you because I needed to give you some important new information the incoming president has refused to hear from me.

"What I'm about to tell you, I've only known for twenty-four hours, and I'll warn you it's going to be as hard for you to believe as it was for me. But please bear in mind, what I'm about to tell you is the truth.

"Our government was recently contacted by a highly advanced species that has inhabited our planet for eons, but until now has been completely unknown to us."

The faces behind the cameras stared at him in breathless amazement.

"Their hidden country is called Caldera, and the Calderans have knowledge and capabilities that humans can barely imagine.

Recently they decided it was time to make themselves known to us, before we descend into the pit of nuclear holocaust. They want to give us one last chance to achieve permanent peace, instead.

"If our legislators vote to stop the incoming president from unleashing our nuclear missiles, the Calderan queen will arrive on October 15th to lead a six-month campaign for peace, that will go around the world. If they vote to authorize the nuclear holocaust, the Calderans will not help. I hope you'll participate in the campaign. Out of our terrible loss, it now seems possible that a lasting peace can be established on our planet.

"Tomorrow morning a new president will take the oath of office. He's a lifelong warrior, one of our greatest. His instincts are to fight, and those instincts have served our nation well for decades. But now you, through your elected representatives, must take firm control of the armed forces and order your new president to give this peace campaign a chance to succeed. I'm sure he'll insist that we deploy our nuclear missiles without delay, but he must be stopped. If we use those nuclear weapons we will forfeit the help of the Calderan people, and that would be the worst mistake we could make.

"Understandably, Vice President Vandenberg is having trouble believing that the Calderan people exist, or that an advanced secret species would be willing to help us. You need to prevail on him to stand down until the Calderans arrive and we must give their peace campaign a chance to succeed.

"Those in the new administration with itchy trigger fingers want nothing to do with such a campaign. So, it's up to you. If you want to get involved, log onto our website printed for you at the bottom of your screen. Thank you for listening and get ready to join the Campaign for World Peace."

The vote in the Senate on Wednesday the 13th was closer than many had predicted. Those voting for removal from office totaled 71—four more than the 67 required.

Boarding Air Force One for the last time was the most liberating feeling of David Andrews' life. He tried to hide his relief as he waved to his emotional staff, friends, and supporters on the tarmac, who had expressed repeatedly their amazement at his demeanor. It was he who was consoling them and wishing them well, as all their lives were about to change dramatically.

David's last minute telecast had astounded the media, the politicians, and the general populace. Some media outlets across the world suspected he'd become delusional and questioned his sanity.

His removal from office had been an excruciating ordeal for the nation. His appeal for non-violent action had gained traction over the weeks since the NYC bombing and millions protested vehemently outside the Capitol Building, but the senators sided with the majority of Americans and voted for removal.

David recalled what it felt like heading home for the summer after finals in college. This was that feeling of release times a hundred. Months of deep prayer had enabled him to survive, but it seemed, in hindsight, that two people were required for the job of president when the nation was dealing with international terrorism, one for domestic and another for foreign policy. He knew during his term in office how unavoidably the domestic front had suffered.

Up front in the main cabin there was no press corps, no crowd of aggressive men and women straining for access to power. For the first time in months he was actually looking forward to something.

The long first leg of the flight to Hawaii gave David the solitude he needed to begin his transition and were the most delicious hours he could remember. Twice he allowed interruptions by the steward to bring lunch and afternoon tea. Otherwise, he stared at the clouds or studied his Adventure Network binder.

He felt guilty, the hours were so sweet. He imagined the furious preparations going on in the Pentagon and the mass exodus from Pakistani cities, but stopped that thought process and demanded of himself that he let it all go. He decided to just say, I'm flying south for a few months, and I'm not going to think about world problems for a while.

As night fell, Air Force One began its descent for refueling at Kaneohe Marine Corp Base on the East Coast of Oahu. He deplaned to enjoy the sunset and talked casually with the ground crew. Looking south, he realized this balmy evening air was a taunting precursor of what awaited him below the horizon.

⸺⸺◈⸺⸺

"Good evening, Americans. This is Ted Kaufman reporting from the U.S. Capitol. Yesterday we experienced one of the most gripping events in our history. It was a day foreseen by the founders when a president tried to move the country in a direction counter to the wishes of a solid majority of its people. In a matter of weeks, David Andrews was removed from office and this morning Joseph Vandenberg became our forty-eighth president. The inauguration was preceded and followed by parades and fly-overs demonstrating America's military might and the new approach of this former Army general. Even the bands and orchestras at the inaugural balls last night were military.

"This historic change of presidents is taking place against a backdrop of unprecedented tumult. Millions of Americans strongly oppose the new president and even more millions strongly support him. I'm standing outside the House of Representatives in the Capitol Building this morning awaiting the arrival of the new president and his speech before the Joint Session in which he will request their support for his planned nuclear retaliation against Pakistan, the homeland of World Jihad."

Vandenberg waited while the sergeant-at-arms strode purposefully into the packed chambers and announced in a loud clear voice, "Mr. Speaker, the President of the United States!"

Vandenberg was struck by the realization that those words were announcing him. He walked forward into the House chamber to warm applause and felt the hundreds of eyes fastened on him. He shook hands with dozens that crowded toward the center aisle and glanced up at hundreds of rapt faces in the visitor's gallery. It was the fulfillment of a dream. The applause continued as he mounted the Speaker's platform and made his way to the podium, but he sensed the applause was more ceremonial than enthusiastic. He panned across the sea of faces and wondered. He'd expected voracious backing for the ideals he represented and this reception was not that.

When he began speaking, the audience immediately quieted and seated themselves, "Mr. Speaker, honorable members of the House of Representatives and the Senate, cabinet members, supreme court justices, members of the joint chiefs of staff, guests and friends, I'm honored to be your president and look forward to working closely with you as we take this country in a new direction.

"Since I gave up the command of America's counter-terrorism forces to become vice president, terrorists have successfully waged a nuclear war against us. They've destroyed three of our great cities and killed millions of innocent Americans. My predecessor allowed this destruction to continue without retaliation until you and the voters you represent decided to replace him with a soldier-president.

"Now it's time to show the world that America does not stand helplessly by when attacked. I've come to you this morning for your authorization to conduct the thermonuclear destruction of the six largest cities in Pakistan, a ratio of two cities for each of the American cities destroyed by their terrorists."

Scattered enthusiastic applause was soon overwhelmed by a noisy hubbub that filled the chamber, many voicing shock at the scale of his recommended retaliation. While the Speaker pounded his gavel for order, Vandenberg could read the sense of the voices and realized he'd overreached. Instead of quieting, the voices became more urgent.

He continued and the clamor subsided, "We must make the terrorists pay a heavy price and let the entire world know we will respond with enormous power, if attacked. That's the only way we can guarantee our future security. As well-meaning as President Andrews was in his efforts for peace, all he sent was a clear message to terrorists around the world that they can strike the United States with impunity. It's imperative that we immediately correct that gross miscommunication.

"If you decide in your deliberations that our retaliation should be scaled back from my proposed plan, we will alter our response accordingly."

The Speaker recognized the minority leader of the House, Winthrop Cunningham, a Democrat from Massachusetts who rose and spoke from his seat on the floor of the House chamber, "Many of us are surprised that you appear to be ignoring former President Andrews' revelations in his farewell address last night. Before launching a nuclear attack, it seems imperative that we fully investigate those revelations."

Vandenberg had listened to Andrews' ramblings the previous evening and felt sorry for the deluded fool who seemed to have cracked under the strain. Now, looking around the room he got the distinct impression that many of these people actually believed him. "Mr. Congressman, am I to understand that you believed those fantastic musings of the former president? Secret aliens who want to help us?"

The congressman responded, "Mr. President, how do you explain the amazing change President Andrews brought about in the lead terrorist? Those were not the musings of a fool, but a well-documented healing of the man's terrible hostility, in addition to his sight and hearing."

Vandenberg had learned through the years to control his facial expression and the tone of his voice, but he felt his temperature rising and knew his complexion was giving away his anger, "Ladies and gentlemen, we shouldn't allow ourselves to be sidetracked from the mission you inaugurated me to complete, or waste our time and energy investigating the fantasies of someone who has obviously become delusional. Secret species my . . . foot."

The debate continued for over an hour with dozens speaking emotionally for each side of the argument. Finally, the Speaker of the House accepted a motion that no retaliation be authorized, until former President Andrews' claims were fully investigated.

During the debate, Vandenberg took a seat and worked at keeping his anger in check. Through gritted teeth he managed a composed expression, but when the motion passed he walked stiffly from the chamber wondering how he or anyone could prove or disprove such mindless ramblings. He brushed past the press and felt devastated. The thought of resigning occurred to him, but climbing into his limo he decided to hold tight until people came around to his position.

———— ❈ ————

In the dawn light, David surveyed the scene beyond the wing as they approached Wellington, New Zealand. The cobalt South Pacific was matched in intensity by the dark green mountains. The twenty hours since his farewells at Andrews AFB seemed much longer ago.

He watched a downlink telecast of Vandenberg's speech and the debate on the floor of the House and wept from relief when Vandenberg's plan was rejected, at least temporarily. Watching

Vandenberg walk out of the chamber, David felt a kind of sympathy for the thwarted warrior. What else could Joe offer? How would he be able to find a way forward that didn't involve fighting?

After landing, he had an emotional farewell with the crew of Air Force One, then slept at the American Embassy before his afternoon meeting with Barclay Tullis of Adventure Network. During their meeting David confirmed the location of each cache on his map. The caches of food and supplies had been positioned at intervals along his 850-mile route from the Ice Shelf to the Pole and back.

The food had been chosen for simple nutritious meals, adequate to supply the 5,000 calories he would burn each day. They walked to the hanger and boarded the DC-10 ready for takeoff the next morning.

Under his dome tent and sleeping bag were provisions for the first three days travel across the Ross Ice Shelf to the first cache. They'd decided to make the first leg of the trip short, to give him a chance to settle into a routine with minimal weight. He repacked his backpack, set out his engineered clothing system, skis, poles and boots, and prepared to leave at five the next morning.

Twenty-five hundred miles south of New Zealand, the sea was dotted with bergs of all shapes and sizes. On the horizon, the Ross Ice Shelf loomed, glistening white in the cleanest air of the planet. After years of books, pictures, and videos he was finally here. He leaned back in his reclined seat, closed his eyes, and prepared himself to deal with this alien world. To grasp its size he envisioned the United States and Mexico combined, about 5 million square miles at an average elevation of more than 9,000 feet, the ice three miles thick near the pole.

He couldn't take his eyes off the Ice Shelf—two hundred thousand square miles of floating ice—the size of France. He envisioned glaciers skidding slowly off the interior of the continent to feed it and icebergs breaking off to trim it, the largest the size of Connecticut. On the Ice Shelf the sun would set about ten o'clock each night after eighteen hours of light. Then, after crossing the Ice Shelf and climbing up the Beardmore Glacier onto the interior plateau, the sun wouldn't set again until he left the continent. He overheard the temperature radioed from the American base at McMurdo Sound, minus twelve degrees Fahrenheit with twenty mile per hour winds.

His pilot came in low, approaching the 300-foot vertical face of the Ice Shelf. After testing the surface with his landing skis, he decreased the power and slid to a stop. With the engines idling and the plane motionless, the pilot turned and yelled over the engine noise, "Last stop, Mr. President. The end of the world."

David was transfixed by the view outside his oval window. A sparkling day with unlimited visibility. The immensity was shocking. The plane was a gnat on the endless whiteness under a gigantic blue dome. The pilot opened the door in the side of the plane and an icy blast gushed in. "Time for me to shove off, Mr. President!" he shouted, "I've got a date with a hot kiwi back in Wellington."

David climbed down the stairs and heard his first crunch of Antarctic ice. The pilot handed down his pack, skis and poles and then, in an ominous gesture, lifted the stairs, slammed the door, revved the engines, waved, and was gone in a blinding white flurry.

Instantly, David was attacked by the fear of sudden total isolation. He fought off those thoughts, fastened his ski bindings, and glided to the edge of the ice. Never had he seen anything like the scene below him. From the side pocket of his backpack he dug out his camera, but the viewfinder couldn't begin to capture the scene, so he took a dozen shots linking the panorama, then put it away. Hundreds of feet straight down, dark blue water lapped against the base of the ice. Birds wheeled slowly in the updrafts. In the distance, two tabular bergs, like white aircraft carriers, headed north. Then a humpback whale's broad back broke the surface.

CHAPTER THIRTEEN

ANTARCTICA
SEPTEMBER 14, 2034

When David had drunk his fill of these first impressions of Antarctica, he turned and headed south with a ground eating rhythm. After two hours he stopped for lunch, feeling tired from his long trip. A few hours later he decided to cut it short and set up camp. After driving the tent stakes into the ice, he packed snow on the ground flaps to anchor the tent walls. It seemed like ridiculous overkill. The air was dead calm. Using the vent system built into his tent, he lit his cook stove and made a meal of noodles and pemmican topped with dehydrated tomatoes and melted cheese. Deep in his down bag he envisioned the tent from high above and chuckled at the yellow speck on a world of white.

The first week was remarkably uneventful. The weather was calm and he made excellent progress toward the second cache.

When he awoke on the morning of the tenth day he made radio contact with Adventure Network's Scott Base station, plotted his location with his GPS navigation system, and adjusted his course. Headed south under windless clear conditions with his skis running fast he covered twenty-five miles in four hours.

After lunch the temperature plummeted to -43F. The wind

increased steadily out of the south, gusting to thirty miles per hour. His pace slowed dramatically in temperatures that reached -72F with wind chill. Heavy breathing made his mask ice up and his goggles kept fogging. The wind speed increased and strong gusts started ripping at him. An hour later his feet, hands, and face were in the first stages of frostbite and each breath was more painful than the last. Finally, he pulled up, too frozen to fight any longer. The katabatic winds flowing down off the polar plateau were too powerful to deal with.

Putting up the tent was tough. Despite the terrible cold, he took his time and used his weight to control it until the tie downs were secured. When he stood up, a powerful blast of wind caught him off balance and suddenly his mukluks were arcing upward. He landed hard on the wind slicked ice and lay there trying to get his breath. Getting up was excruciating. His right shoulder was injured.

Lying still in his tent the pain subsided, but with the slightest movement, sharp pain took the breath from him. Outside, the guy ropes whined, then screamed. The tent walls snapped like pistol shots. He forced himself to sit up and start dinner in spite of icepick-like stabs of pain.

A voice inside him kept saying, it's broken. The cook stove gradually penetrated his numbness. After a salmon dinner he realized his lunch hadn't been enough nourishment for the hard going and severe cold of the afternoon. The gale outside intensified. When he was sure it had peaked, a blast slammed his tent like nothing he'd ever experienced. He prayed the tent would hold, but thought it too much to expect. The sheet of nylon straining between him and disaster was being lashed by winds that shrieked and screamed like a crazed beast.

After an hour of prayer, he turned his thought from the storm to his shoulder. Sleep came in bits and snatches. When he dozed, Diane came to him sweet and warm. He lay on top of his bag, fully dressed, ready to battle the storm, if the tent failed.

By morning the wind was less violent, but the world outside was in whiteout. His remaining rations were next to nothing. After a small breakfast he turned off the stove to conserve fuel. Within minutes the cold was unbearable. It was -65F outside, -15F inside and falling. He relit the stove. The day was miserable and the storm continued into the night. He woke at five, exhausted from a fitful sleep, made coffee and looked out. The line between the air and the ground was invisible.

Suddenly, there was a titanic explosion that shook his whole world. He was knocked over against the tent wall and his stove and cooking gear tumbled against him. Besides the atomic shockwave, he'd never experienced such a powerful blast and couldn't think what it was for several minutes. Then he remembered reading about "snowquakes" common up on the polar plateau, when the overburden causes a four or six inch thick layer of lighter snow underneath to suddenly collapse or compress under the weight of a new layer of wetter snow. The snow from this storm had apparently caused a "snowquake" down here on the Ice Shelf.

His shoulder was now just a hard ache and he longed to get back on his skis. Life was miserable in his tiny yellow deepfreeze. He fixed some oatmeal, crawled in his bag and left the stove off as long as he could stand it.

To while away the frigid hours, he read the gospel of Mark. He focused his prayers on his shoulder. When he got too cold to concentrate, he relit the stove for a few minutes. The night dragged on, hour after endless hour of bitter cold punctuated by short respites of warmth. After a hot breakfast he opened the tent flap and looked into swirling ice. Visibility still zero! Cold, unbearable!

For the first time it hit him, he could freeze to death in the next twenty-four hours. He felt foolishly naive for putting himself in this situation. These storms weren't so terrible when you were reading about them. Living through them was horrific. Over and over he tried to raise Sam over at Scott, but only got crackling static. He transmitted his location and requested an air drop of white gas.

Thoroughly miserable he held off lighting the stove until frostbite began to turn his numb fingers gray, then he burned a few minutes of the precious heat source. Now, he was afraid to sleep. Death was muscling its way into his thought, laughing at him curled up in a pitiful shivering ball, buried in Antarctic snow.

He saw himself skiing happily across the Ross Ice Shelf with everything under control. "What was I thinking?" he muttered and shoved his gloved hands deeper between his legs, closed his eyes, and shook. Finally, the air quieted and he tried Scott Base again.

"Come in Mr. President, this is Sam at Scott Base."

He gave them his location and requested a canister of white gas. There was a moment of quiet, then Sam said, "Sorry sir, conditions won't allow a drop for at least twelve hours. We'll fly as soon as we can."

E.A. Appleton's toughness came to mind and he visualized him staggering away from his tent into that terrible storm. It struck him as a far better way to die than this. He started packing. When he unzipped the flap, the ice-filled air was still churning, but zero-visibility was less constant. By straining between the blasts, he could make out the surface. After an hour of painful work, he'd dug out the tent, talking to himself the whole time to steel his resolve.

At last he was on his skis making slow forward movements. When swirling winds enveloped him, he'd hunker down, covering his goggles with his arms. Movement helped. After a mile, his body began to give off some heat and the pain in his shoulder eased.

When he stopped for lunch he plotted his location, thirty more miles to go. That morning he'd gone two miles in an hour. With the improving light he could do better and set a goal to reach the cache in ten hours. Having a goal helped. After lunch he set out with renewed energy. Two hours later, however, fatigue from the sleep he'd lost began to weigh on him. He stopped, turned his back to the wind and ate some Power Bars, dried fruit and chicken broth, still warm in his thermos.

While he ate he realized, now was the time to dig down and get the payoff from his years of hard work. Back on the skis, he picked up the pace and talked to himself to keep his mind focused. Hour after hour he pushed himself. For dinner, he set up his tent without the tie downs, had a much-needed thirty-minute break and killed the last of his food and gas. Filled and warm, he pushed on. When the light began to fade he was delighted by one of the most fantastic light shows imaginable, Aurora Australis—the Southern Lights—pale green and pink wispy curtains, pillars and halos that seemed to float on the wind.

Then he saw it! What a sight that plywood box was! On the dim horizon, beneath the shimmering lights it looked like an eerie monument with a mast and flapping banner. These supply caches were the best things he'd found so far in Antarctica and also the only evidence that humans exist. An hour later he had his tent deliciously warm, drank some hot broth, and fell sound asleep.

The morning was almost clear with wispy, high, fast-moving clouds. After an hour of good progress, he came upon his first field of sastrugi, long parallel waves carved in the ice by prevailing winds. With ten days of provisions on his back, the two and three-foot obstacles made skiing precarious. His second fall slightly re-injured his shoulder, so he dug out his crampons and lashed his skis to his pack.

Three hard days later he came to an abrupt wall of ice six-feet high running as far as he could see to each side. He sat down with his map and his afternoon snack. Adventure Network had plotted the start of the pressure ridges several miles further south.

This wall was an obvious impediment, but also an important milestone. When the ice moves from the land onto the Ross Sea it gets broken by the tidal action of the ocean, which causes stress ridges like the one he was leaning against. He decided to stop and take on the pressure ridges the next morning. Then he heard it, a titanic unearthly groan from far below. He'd heard a sound like that once during a strong earthquake in California. The tide was moving and the ice was adjusting. He knew he was in for plenty of such noises from the bowels of the ice in this area.

The next morning, after a granola and coffee breakfast, he opened the tent flap and laughed. The huge ridge from the night before was now two feet high. Then he saw it. The whole sky was filled with ice crystals. Magical! He'd often read about "diamond dust" and hoped someday to see it. The air glistened and sparkled all around him.
Then, he saw high above him his first "sun halos" here and there, some double, some triple. It was the most wonderful atmospheric phenomenon he could imagine—like a prelude to the coming of the Messiah himself.

After two more days of hard going he reached the third cache of supplies and in the distance got his first look at the Beardmore Glacier, his route up through the Trans Antarctic Range onto the Polar Plateau. The easiest stage of his journey was drawing to a close.

The next day he was alternately in snowshoes and crampons climbing up through a mass of broken ice blocks and deep crevasses. He stopped for lunch after his first morning on the Beardmore and figured he'd covered three miles, tops. In front of him was the deepest crevasse he'd ever seen, at least a hundred and fifty feet deep.

After lunch, he worked his way slowly up the ridge to his left, skirted the giant crevasse and discovered an ice cave. He climbed up into the cave and dropped his pack. The walls darkened in color from amber near the entrance to aquamarine, then through deepening blues to cobalt.

In the silence he felt a churchlike essence and knelt in the center of the tall blue ice cathedral, closed his eyes, and prayed. He thanked God for his life and for the opportunity to glorify Him. He promised God he would make the most he could of his life and become a missionary for peace and love among men.

Then, he heard something further back in the cave. He drew a breath, sat back on his heels and assured himself it must be dripping melt water. The figure who walked around the ice outcrop at the back of the cavern was the most startling apparition of his life. A gray-haired man he'd seen once before in miniature approached him wearing a black bodysuit, black waist length jacket, and riding boots.

David felt dizzy and started to topple forward, but caught himself with both hands. He looked down waiting for his head to clear, wiped his eyes and looked up, sure the hallucination would have retreated back into the recesses of his imagination, where it came from.

"Sorry to startle you, David," the figure said, seated near him on a block of ice that jutted from the wall.

"Lord Appleton," he gasped. The cave walls swirled, the light dimmed and the ice floor slammed his face.

Grudgingly David awoke. A Tiffany lamp softly illumined the mahogany four-poster bed. The walls and ceiling were covered with light yellow fabric framed with dark Victorian molding. Squinting, he made out a foxhunting print in the fabric. Beyond the lamp a hand carved armoire looked old and hefty.

He didn't feel worried, just mystified. Where on earth am I? he wondered, and how did I get here? Wherever he was, this was the most comfortable bed he'd ever laid in, like a warm cloud. The crème-colored cotton sheets had the feel of heavy silk, an oversized down pillow, comforter and mattress enveloped him sumptuously.

He checked his watch. 10:25 AM. Tuesday, October 3. Fear made some moves on him that he fought off. He was hungry.

The ice cave! That's right, I blacked out in that cave! He was relieved to remember the ice cave, but still couldn't answer any of this. Wait . . . E.A. was there! Or, was that a dream? He called out, "Is anyone here?"

There were footsteps, then a voice, "How're you feeling, David?"

A cheerful life-sized E.A. Appleton walked into the room carrying a tray, "That was some sleep, I was beginning to wonder."

It couldn't be, David thought. He stared without breathing. The hologram-like image of Appleton in Liza Jane's room wasn't as implausible as this flesh and blood edition. This person resembled the famous explorer as he must've looked at a youthful seventy. The smile was the one in the photos he'd seen in books. For several minutes he stared at him; his hair was thick, complexion full of health. How could this possibly be Ernest Appleton at a hundred and fifty-eight?

"I don't get it," David said, blowing his nose in his napkin. "This is more dreamlike than the one I just woke up from."

"I have some explaining to do, don't I?"

"Where are we?"

"I brought you to my mountain retreat. This is Eagle's Mere."

"The one in Pennsylvania?"

"No, this one's in the Ellsworth Mountains of Antarctica."

David stared a while at the gathered fabric ceiling, then muttered, "That's about as plausible as any of the rest of this. There are no mountain homes in Antarctica and history books agree that you've been dead for a hundred and twenty-four years." As he spoke he was struck with the realization and muttered, "That's it! I'm dead . . . like you, aren't I? I must have fallen in that crevasse."

"We're both very much alive, David. Here, sit up and eat some lunch. I'll try to answer your questions."

David picked up a heavy silver soup spoon with an ornate "A" engraved on the handle and took a taste of the chowder, chunks of white fish in a heavy cream sauce. The dark tea was strong but delicious and the salad had an unfamiliar taste, rather bittersweet and mixed with sharp crumbled white cheese. He couldn't remember food tasting better.

"You're a tough man, David. I'm proud of you."

"E.A., level with me. What's going on here? The transponder image at Princeton I wrote off as some kind of Calderan trick. It's common knowledge that you froze to death at the beginning of the last century and it makes no sense that you should casually walk in here carrying a tray of food looking a youthful seventy."

"I've waited a long time for this moment, David."

"You have? For what . . . exactly?"

"Well it feels like I'm finally ready to finish building the bridge."

"I'm sure you know what you're talking about, but I absolutely have no clue."

"You're a genuinely good man, David, tough too. You have no idea how encouraging you've been to me and my wife over the past few months."

"I still want to finish my expedition, E.A. After we're done here, I'll get you to take me back to the Beardmore so I can make my way to the Pole."

"You've done enough for now."

David stared at him and considered giving him an argument, but said nothing.

"I watched you pray your way through nuclear terrorism, against enormous opposition, and am aware of what you went through out on the ice. I saw all I needed to see."

"What did you see, exactly?"

"A man who is learning to pray effectively, who doesn't run or give in to hardship. I know what it's like out there on the ice. You had a fractured shoulder you couldn't fully heal and kept re-injuring. You were in danger of freezing to death, out of fuel for your stove, attacked by hypothermia and frostbite and pinned down by a powerful storm."

"How do you know all that?"

"That was the moment I'd waited for, the test of your soul. You pulled yourself together, fought through the pain and showed me what beats in there," E.A. smiled, tapping David's chest, "The heart of a man!"

David closed his eyes, laid his head back against the pillows and thought for a while; I wonder if my mind snapped. I'm probably lying on the floor of that cave hallucinating, creating a fantasy to replace a reality I can't deal with anymore.

While David ate, E.A. told him about his life with Hamama and how she loved David from their first meeting after his crash in August.

"So your wife is the angel who healed me! Tell me about her. She's the most astounding part of this whole story. How does she do the things she does?"

"We'll get into all that soon enough. The Calderan people are in the business of transforming themselves."

"From . . ."

"From material beings to spiritual beings. That's their life work."

"Honestly, E.A., I can't believe you married an angel!"

"I assure you, David, there's nothing supernatural about Hamama. She's just an advanced individual, much more so now than when I first met her and fell in love with her."

"What a great story. Can't say I blame you. I fell in love with her myself."

"Everyone does. But let's leave her for the time being. I'll need some time to adequately explain my wife."

The chowder was getting cold, so David made himself eat.

When he was finished, E.A. said, "Let's go meet Hamani. He's been with me since my rescue and made your lunch."

David got up and E.A. handed him a brown robe and a pair of fleece boot slippers.

Hamani was standing at the end of the hall. His expression and features were similar to Hamama's, a black fur-covered face with feline features, large slanted eyes, erect ears, and drooping whiskers. He also wore a robe and boots, stood straight and smiled as David approached him. He bowed slightly and said, "You're the most welcome guest ever to come to Eagle's Mere, Mr. Andrews."

David offered his hand to the diminutive creature and Hamani accepted it gently with his small four-fingered hand. His lively eyes were completely at peace and joyful.

"This is all amazing to me, Hamani. I'm still trying to grasp it. The lunch was great."

"Glad you liked it."

Through the door, beyond Hamani, David could see a richly furnished nineteenth century living room with a fire burning vigorously in the stone corner fireplace.

E.A. walked by and said, "Come look at our view."

To the left of the fireplace was a large window looking out on a breathtaking alpine panorama. Across a steep valley was a wall of massive white mountains. As he looked, the sun broke through the overcast and he noticed the window instantly darken to cut the glare off the snow covered landscape.

E.A. said, "Hamani, I'd like to take Mr. Andrews with me to pick up my daughter a little later. Maybe you'd draw him a bath and lay out some clothes."

Hamani bowed and said, "First, I'll bring dessert and coffee."

"We're going to pick up Liza Jane?" David asked.

E.A. nodded and gestured toward two huge upholstered armchairs and answered, "Jane and the two friends you met are coming for a short visit."

David sank into the deep cushions and they both put their feet up on a shared ottoman, then asked, "Are we to the point yet where you tell me what's going on, E.A.?"

"Yes. This is the right time to explain why we reached out to you."

Hamani reappeared with a tray of pastries and steaming coffee in white mugs. As E.A. sipped the rich coffee, he took himself back to his first morning in Caldera. How dearly Hamama empathized with his stunned amazement. Then, he turned to the former president, "I consider my life a breakthrough, David. Hamama did a remarkable thing bringing me into Caldera."

"They hadn't had contact with humans?"

"None. What she did was almost unthinkable."

"Why'd she do it?"

"Hamama's the queen of Caldera and a great leader. She felt it was time to start building a bridge to the human world. Over time we fell deeply in love and became soul mates. Years later, I was appointed to the Calderan Council and when Hamama left to accept her new job on the Intergalactic Council, I became Lord of Caldera."

"Wow! That must have been a shocker. What's the Intergalactic Council?"

"Some still have a hard time with my role here. It's been one of the most controversial issues Calderans have had to deal with. The reason it works is that Hamama stands beside me. This probably isn't the right time to get into Hamama's new job on the I-Council."

"That's fine. So, you're the bridge."

"I'm just the first span. Hamama wanted to prove to her people that a human could fully grasp the Way."

"What's that?"

"Alignment with the messiah message. Hamama is an example of what's possible when you get fully aligned."

"And you've made a lot of progress toward alignment as well, haven't you," David said.

"It's the most exciting work I can imagine, David. It gives you access to the power Jesus used and taught to his students. As I said, Hamama loved you the moment she met you and suggested I invite you to follow in my footsteps."

"She wants me to come to Caldera?"

"We want to offer you our daughter's hand in marriage."

David stared at him in mid-expression and groped for a response. Nothing that came to mind seemed right, so he just stared. Out on the ice he'd had a chance to think through his strong attraction to E.A.'s daughter and realized how wrong it would be for her to get involved with a man his age. The thought of marrying her now seemed out of the question. An arranged marriage with a half-Calderan person young enough to be my daughter? Retreat from the human world and give up on it?

"You and your wife have done so much for me, this makes me feel ungrateful. I'm sorry, E.A., I'm a hundred-percent human and I've got a very different life in mind. I need to go back and dedicate my life to the peace movement. Bailing out and coming to live in Caldera wouldn't work for me."

"I understand," E.A. sensed the emotional reactions surging through him, "I made a mistake. Please pardon me."

"The human world's a terrible mess, but it's where I belong. Maybe there's a way I can work with you from there."

"Of course. Please excuse me. I've been away from human reasoning for a long time."

"What does your daughter think of the idea?"

"She's Calderan."

"What does that mean?"

"She doesn't live by feelings. It took me a long time to understand that part of the Calderan nature."

"Help me, then. I don't understand, either."

"The Calderan thought is so attuned to the Giver of Life, they hear His voice inside them. It's their conscience."

"Like Jesus," David mumbled, in awe of the idea.

E.A. continued, "They don't start from 'I want' or 'I don't want.' Liza Jane usually knows what she needs to do."

"I take it, if I was Calderan, I wouldn't feel any need to live out my own goals."

"You'd probably see things a bit differently."

"Are you saying your proposal is God's will?"

"We see it as part of a plan."

"I'm sorry to disappoint you, E.A., but it's not for me. On the ice, I decided to try to become an international leader of a movement to build the peace. I think I'll get a lot of support from around the world. I'm anxious to get back and get to work."

Let's go for a walk and I'll show you Eagle's Mere. First your bath has been drawn and you can get dressed. There are clothes in your room."

David opened the mirrored doors of the armoire, expecting to find some of E.A.'s clothes. Instead, it had a range of clothes that fit him perfectly. He walked through his bedroom into a bathroom with plastered walls that almost concealed the fact that it was chiseled out of stone. On the outside wall there was a deep stone bathtub filled with steaming water below a sheet of glass looking out at some of the earth's most spectacular mountains. It took a while for him to ease himself into the water and get used to the heat. But once in, he thoroughly relaxed and enjoyed the utterly opposite conditions on the other side of the glass.

E.A. was waiting in a black bodysuit and boots. David had never seen a man of fifty in better shape and he was over a hundred years past fifty. "How do you stay so fit?"

"I'll explain on our ride. When you learn to live the Way, you find yourself changing your thought about your body and dropping your belief in time."

They got into a cylindrical glass elevator overlooking a half-mile-long cavern. From the far end a brook flowed through a grove of birch trees, then under a stone bridge. A gravel road ran along the bank past a white gazebo with a Queen Anne shingle roof nestled in the birches. A pond in the distance was surrounded by grasses and wild flowers. Two mares with foals were feeding in the meadow.

"Looks like you brought some of Massachusetts with you."

"This place has been good for me. I love it here."

The elevator passed through a stone plaza into another underground cavern. Exiting the elevator onto soft dirt reminded David of the ball field on the bottom floor of Jadwin Gymnasium at Princeton. The ceiling and walls glowed with warm light. In the distance was another meadow, surrounded by a pine forest. A squirrel scurried away when the elevator opened and birds flew from the fence into nearby trees.

Hamani came around the rock formation to the left of the elevator leading two horses. The dark bay on his left whinnied and nodded an emphatic greeting to E.A.

"Hello Solomon!" E.A. called out. "Come meet a new friend of mine." The powerfully-built thoroughbred bumped him playfully with his head when E.A. tried to hug him. "This is Duke," E.A. introduced David to the second magnificent thoroughbred.

"I haven't ridden in years, E.A. I'll need to take it easy at first."

David and E.A. mounted and headed down a trail past a large pool, through an arch into another forested cavern. The trail crossed a natural bridge over a torrent that plunged through a jumble of boulders then out of sight.

For an hour E.A. explained what life is like in Caldera and

how hard he'd worked to change his thought. Through several more caverns they trotted and cantered stopping now and then to study mineral encrusted walls, clear pools and waterfalls. Entering one of the smaller caverns David reined in his mount and stared in amazement at the inside surface of the arch. It was covered with diamonds, sapphires, and rubies of all sizes interlaced with thick veins of gold.

"Beautiful, isn't it?" E.A. remarked. "When we blasted between these caverns we hit this jewel box. Hamani polished them."

"How do you keep people from taking them? That one diamond must be a hundred carats."

"It wouldn't occur to anyone to take them."

"Everyone is rich?"

"The Calderans have everything they need."

"How do they pay their bills?"

"There are no bills. It's different here. The needs are modest and there's enough to go around."

"Sounds like Eden."

E.A. laughed, "Does, doesn't it?"

Andrews was so deeply involved in their discussion, it was a while before he realized they'd re-entered the cavern with the elevator, but from the opposite side.

"Let's have a go at the course of fixed jumps I just built," E.A. said as he urged his big horse forward. They broke into a canter on the firm sand footing, jumped up a three-foot ledge, then down into a pond surrounded with cattails. Coming out of the water they picked up the pace and galloped a challenging two-mile course with David staying close behind.

Back at the stone-fenced paddocks, Hamani smiled as he watched them pull up, glowing from their enjoyment of the new course. They gave the horses to him, then headed for the elevator. Andrews noticed how much the steaming thoroughbreds liked

Hamani, who led them to the pool at the end of the paddocks to drink.

E.A. put his arm around David's shoulders and asked, "Will you give some more thought to our proposal?"

"I want to find a way to work with you, E.A., but I can't give up on my human life."

CHAPTER FOURTEEN

CALDERA
OCTOBER 3, 2034

"**D**o you think it's a good idea to fly on a day like this?" Natasha asked. The East Coast was socked in with un-seasonable sleet and fog. Newark International, JFK, and LaGuardia were all closed.

"We can fly in this," Liza Jane assured her.

Ary knocked at their partially open door then burst in, "Hey! Let's go to Caldera!"

Natasha gave him a worried look and said, "She says her dad can fly in ice and fog, but I just heard on the radio that all the local airports are closed."

"My father doesn't use airports. He's landing behind Jadwin Gymnasium in twenty minutes."

"This is so great!" Ary exclaimed. "What should we pack? What's the weather like in Caldera this time of year?"

"I have clothes for both of you to wear. Just put on jeans and a sweatshirt for the trip and take a backpack."

They threw their backpacks in the trunk of the Corvette and Natasha sat on Liza Jane's lap for the short drive to the parking lot behind Jadwin. At twelve, a silent silver object descended eerily out of the fog. Its broad circular base came to rest almost without impact between a Jeep and an SUV. It was steaming from the heat of re-entry.

Liza Jane urged her wide-eyed friends, "Come on, let's go," and headed for the ship.

"Do we really want to get in that thing?" Natasha muttered to Ary. The ship scared her, but she liked its quiet movement and the way it touched down so gently.

Ary said, "Come on, Tosh. Caldera is calling."

Natasha took a deep breath, picked up her backpack and they hustled to catch up. One of the oval windows facing them slid open and E.A. stood inside. Liza Jane waited at the edge of the ship and gave her reticent roommate a hand onto the seamless metallic skin. E.A. helped Natasha over the sill and shook her hand, "I'm so glad you could come, Natasha. I've been looking forward to getting to know you."

"This is an incredible treat, Lord Appleton. Thanks for inviting us."

As Liza Jane embraced her father, he said, "I've got a surprise for you, Jane." He turned and pointed at David standing in the doorway to the flight deck wearing a black bodysuit and high boots.

Liza Jane walked over, shook his hand and said, "What a fine surprise! I look forward to hearing about your trip and how you met up with my father."

"The trip was wonderful and terrible," David said, feeling uncharacteristically awkward, knowing she knew her parents' plan for them. "Your father has been very kind to me. I've enjoyed getting acquainted with him." She had an easy forthrightness and self-assurance that overshadowed her good looks. No guile. No games. She didn't use her looks to gain an impression and seemed sincerely interested in him. His uneasiness faded.

"David, you remember my friends, Natasha and Ary."

"Good to see you both again. Maybe later you can catch me up on what's been happening since I left. I've been totally out of contact since Vandenberg's plan was turned down by Congress."

Behind them, the window slid closed.

E.A. headed for the flight deck and said, "Prepare for departure."

They seated themselves in curved seats on the outside wall of the ship. The walls glowed with a soft opalescent light from inside and curved upward to become the ceiling.

Natasha became fearful as they lifted off and Liza Jane held her hands. "No seat belts?" she whispered with worried eyes.

"You won't need one, try to relax, Natasha."

"This is the first time I've ever flown."

Liza Jane touched the pad on the wall next to her and said, "This is Natasha's first flight, Father. Take it real easy, please."

"Will do, Jane."

Ary asked David, "How was your flight here?"

"Smoothest trip I've ever had."

"How does this thing work? It's so quiet."

"He says it interacts with the electromagnetic field and with the gravitational field. He controls it with his thinking."

At that, the ship elevated without vibration or noise, and slid easily southward over fog-shrouded hills.

Natasha sat with her eyes closed. Her clammy hands squeezed Liza Jane's. After a while, she forced herself to open her eyes and look out the window. They shot through the cloud cover and Ary wondered when they would level out, but they didn't. He asked David, "What do you think our cruising altitude will be?"

"We flew at about 50,000 feet on the way here, but we're obviously going higher on the way back."

The ship continued to climb. Above the cloud cover, sunlight caused some glare and the windows darkened instantly which caused the interior light levels to adjust automatically.

Liza Jane asked, "David and Ary, would you help me put some lunch together?" She led them to the galley between the parlor and the flight deck. When Natasha started to get up, Liza Jane said, "Why don't you sit still and get on top of your fear."

Ary asked, "What's for lunch?"

"Lunch is fish, salad, vegetables and fruit." She laughed and said, "Actually, that's most of what we eat in Caldera, along with eggs and bread."

Ary took lunch into the captain who said, "Thanks. Why don't you bring yours and join me."

Lord Appleton sat in one of two contoured high-backed chairs facing a semicircle of windows. In front of him, at an angle, was a three-foot-wide console, slightly higher than his chair arm, with a small blank screen.

Ary sat down and put his plate on the flat surface between their seats, "This is great."

"I love to fly. You know, you and Natasha have been a great encouragement to my daughter."

"I think it's been pretty much the other way around, sir."

"She didn't know what to expect. There's a lot of skepticism among our people toward humans."

"A lot of the time, I feel the same way."

"You helped her feel her mission made sense."

"David told me you run the ship with your mind. What if something happens to you?"

"Jane can fly it. Beyond that, it will return home by itself. I could have instructed it to go to Princeton, pick up the three of you and return home; but I would have missed out on this enjoyment."

"Would you mind if I ask you a personal question?"

"Not at all."

"Abigail and your son. I read up on your career and your family in the library the other night. Did they ever find out you were still alive?"

"Hardest chapter of my life, Ary. I was able to assure Abigail over the years, that I'd gone on to another experience and was doing important work. Through a trust I'd set up, her needs were taken care of. She was a brave woman doing important work, herself in addition to raising our son."

"Thanks for explaining. It must have been sweet and terribly hard at the same time."

"I missed my human life for many years."

Natasha forced herself to look out the window next to her. The earth was a beautiful blue curved surface swathed in clouds far below. She'd seen pictures from space like this in National Geographic and soon she could recognize features along the eastern coastline.

"How do you like Princeton, Natasha?" David asked.

"I love it! You were right to make me go there."

Liza Jane peered around the corner of the galley with a confused look, "Made you? How did that happen?"

Natasha told her about her visit with the president in Newark Hospital.

David added, "Her boyfriend, Troy, wanted her to go to Rutgers with him."

"What boyfriend, Tosh?" Liza Jane asked. "You've never mentioned him."

"Troy is actually one of my brother's friends. He saved my life the night I was knocked out in the burning bus I told you about, when New York was bombed."

"So, how did David make you go to Princeton?" Liza Jane asked.

"He told me he'd send the Army after me if I went to Rutgers. Presidents can be pretty convincing when they put their mind to it."

David chuckled, "Unfortunately, not quite convincing enough in other areas. What's been going on since I left?"

Ary was standing in the doorway listening and said, "Vandenberg couldn't believe the rejection. The whole world was watching. He turned several shades of red and looked like he was going to explode. He had no idea what to do or say. You could tell he felt like he'd finally gotten the top job, and these congressional idiots were trying to tell him what he could and couldn't do."

David laughed, "Poor Joe. He never could understand checks and balances. I'm sure he was tempted to threaten them. I know he was tempted many times with me."

Natasha asked, "What's it like out on the ice in Antarctica?"

"Toughest thing I've done, Natasha."

"I want to hear all about it. Liza Jane won't tell us, but I assume that's where we're headed. Is it beautiful?"

"Astoundingly so. And then suddenly it can turn ugly—deadly in fact. It's like no other place on earth. In spite of the scary powerful elements, I loved experiencing that amazing place."

Natasha smiled as she tried to imagine, "How do the Calderans deal with the ice and the storms?"

Raising his voice so he could be heard in the galley, he said, "I think we're all interested in the answer to that question, Natasha. Is it time to tell us, Liza Jane?"

They were quiet for a while. At length, Liza Jane brought lunch, sat down and said, "There are some things I can tell you in advance about my home. Long ago, when the climate turned cold on our continent, our ancestors domed over our caldera. Today humans call it Mount Erebus."

"Mount Erebus is an artificial mountain?" David asked.

"The upper third is a thick glassy material covered with snow and ice. One portion of the volcanic caldera is still active so they built a sort of chimney to release the gas and steam from the magma."

As Liza Jane spoke, Natasha looked south toward the ice cap. The Southern Ocean and most of Antarctica on the distant horizon were completely enshrouded in clouds. Liza Jane put her hand on the coffee table in front of her and a three-dimensional topographic map of Antarctica appeared with a blinking light showing their position, a thousand miles from the coast.

"Here's Mount Erebus," she said, pointing at the only mountain on Ross Island, "and this is the Ross Ice Shelf. It's floating ice that connects Ross Island to the mainland. There are two human settlements near Mt. Erebus, McMurdo Station is a U.S. base and Scott Base is a New Zealand settlement."

"How can Caldera be such a total secret, with those bases so close?" Ary asked.

"We're invisible to them. Our ships don't show up on radar screens and are at home underwater. So, miles from the edge of the Ice Sheet we'll dive and go to our transport bay under the ice. From there, we'll take a shuttle through the ice to Caldera."

Lord Appleton said, "Prepare for submersion. Please be seated everyone."

The ship slowed almost to a stop above frothy dark green wind-whipped twenty-foot waves; then, sliced cleanly into the water. The interior lights brightened, as the water outside got darker, then black underneath the ice shelf.

Soon, they emerged into a cavernous, brightly-lit bay, half water and half metallic landing base, all covered by a glowing dome of ice. They landed near two other glistening ships, both about three times larger than E.A.'s ship and gold in color.

The scene outside fascinated Natasha. The fuzzy video clips and blurry photographs of UFOs were obviously shots of these ships. The oval window across from her slid open. When she stepped out into the cold air, one of the gold ships was being lowered out of sight. She joined the others and they walked toward a pair of tall lighted doors at the end of an illuminated pathway across the metallic deck.

Liza Jane explained, "These Calderans are engineers and builders. They're dedicated to our ships and shuttles."

As she spoke, two short well-built male Calderans emerged from the oversized doors. They were less than five feet tall, but quite muscular. Their bodysuits were the same color as their black flat fur and emphasized their powerful bodies. They wore black fur caps that framed their feline faces and hung down to their shoulders.

Natasha was awestruck by the strange beings.

Liza Jane walked ahead and greeted them, "Hello General Landon and Colonel Ormani, let me introduce my friends."

Landon, the older of the two males, bowed crisply and said in a bass voice, "Welcome home, Your Highness. We trust your ship functioned adequately."

"Perfectly, as always. This is Natasha Cheatam and Ary Hussein, friends from my school. And this is David Andrews, my mother's friend you've heard about."

Landon bowed again and said, "Welcome honored guests. I hope your stay in Caldera will be a pleasant one. Your shuttle is waiting, Lord Appleton."

The shuttle moved out without sound, entered an ice tunnel that turned the windows white, and smoothly picked up speed. As they left the station, the lights inside the car came on and illumined the stainless steel and royal blue interior.

Natasha leaned into the acceleration and against Liza Jane, "Is it far to Caldera?"

"These trams go faster than you think. We'll be there shortly, Roommate."

"I can't wait."

Ary asked, "How does the shuttle work, Lord Appleton? It feels like a vacuum tube system."

"You're quite right, Ary." he answered, "Air is evacuated from in front and pumped in behind. Our shuttles run all over the continent."

"How do the tunnels handle the stress in the ice?" David asked.

"The engineers have crews working on them all the time. When stress builds up, they bore new routes. It's not difficult."

The air tram slowed and the door opened. Natasha walked out with Liza Jane and gasped at the beauty. The small station was made of polished black granite in soft flowing curves and was heavily landscaped with tropical plants.

Natasha whispered to Liza Jane, "It must be good to be home."

"It is, and having you with me makes it even better."

The two roommates led the way across a granite bridge that spanned a pond ringed with heavy foliage. A waterfall cascaded off the outcrop above and the bridge arched through a break in it. When they got beyond the waterfall they could see the vastness of Caldera.

Ary gasped, "Look at this place! It's huge!"

"Is your house far?" Natasha asked.

"About four miles."

"How do we get there?" David asked. "Walk?"

"No. We fly," she answered.

"We what?" Natasha asked.

"See those guys headed this way?" Liza Jane said, pointing at the gray cliffs in the distance. A half mile away, five enormous birds were coming toward them.

"You've got to be kidding!" Ary exclaimed, staring at the slow moving birds.

"I told you it was primitive. We've been flying pteros for ages. I think you'll like it."

Natasha stared breathlessly. Finally, she muttered, "I don't think I can do that. There must be some other way."

The pteros grew larger the nearer they got, powerful bodies with sixteen-foot wingspans. They landed in the clearing beyond and waddled toward them. The eight-foot-tall white birds glanced shyly at the humans and chattered among themselves, as they avoided the shocked stares of the strangers. Around their bodies and across their chests were golden girths and martingales to hold in place lightly made saddles. Thin gold hackamore bridles and reins dangled from their tall crested heads.

The closest one, with the most intelligent expression said, in a high-pitched voice, "Welcome home, Your Highness." He wasn't brave enough to look at the humans, who were staring in amazement at the talking bird.

"Thanks, Hardaway. It's good to be back." She walked over to him and said, "Watch me mount up, so you can see how the tack works."

Natasha said, "I have to walk. I'm not up to this."

"Ary, would you help her?" Liza Jane asked, "Relax, Natasha. Wantak will take good care of you." She called to a bird with sleepy eyes, standing at the back of the group, "Wantak, my friend Natasha has never flown on a ptero and thinks it might be unsafe. Would you come and take extra good care of her for me?"

Wantak made his way through the other birds, lowered his head to Natasha's eye-level and said, "Can we please be friends?"

Natasha drew back from the huge talking bird.

"Oh please, don't be afraid of me."

She took a deep breath and agreed, "Okay, Wantak, we can be friends if you'll be patient with me. I've never done any flying like this."

The ptero's expression brightened, "I'll take good care of you. Watch the princess and get on like she does."

In a minute, Liza Jane was mounted and said, "Follow me." Hardaway jogged toward the clearing, leaned forward and picked up speed. Hardaway unfolded his wings, pulled hard, tucked his legs up and was airborne. E.A. followed on Papadok.

David mounted Ganador, who quickly caught up with Hardaway. His face was beaming as he drank in the views on all sides, "This is one of the greatest moments of my life!" he yelled to Liza Jane, "I love this place!"

"I've looked forward to this, David, sharing my home with you. Flying makes me feel free."

After flying with them for a while, E.A. angled off toward the middle of the valley. At an unseen signal, Hardaway put his wings back and plummeted a hundred feet, opened his wings and banked hard to the right with Liza Jane gripping with her legs, and crouched forward.

Ganador said, "They're just showing off, David. This is too new for you to be doing any stunt flying, isn't it?"

"Hell no, Ganador! Let her rip!"

"Okay, I'll do what they do, so you'll know what's coming." At that, he dropped into a more gentle dive, then carefully banked right to catch up with the princess. David put his head back and let out a yell that echoed down the valley.

Ganador looked back in alarm, "Are you alright, David?"

He dropped the reins, extended his hands to each side letting his arms pump up and down with the rhythm of Ganador's wings and said, "Ganador, you have no idea how alright I am at this moment!"

Ganador was relieved and winked at the princess. At that, Hardaway dove again and barrel-rolled as he dove, with Liza Jane clamping his sides with vice-like legs.

Ganador said, "We can pass on that."

"No way! Let's go!"

The two pteros played follow-the-leader, climbing and diving, doing loop-the-loops, spinning and swooping down the valley, midst gales of laughter from both riders.

Back at the station Natasha readied herself to take off. "Thanks for waiting, Ary. I don't know why new things are so hard for me."

Wantak said, "Take all the time you want, Natasha. I'm afraid of new things, too."

"You are?"

"Yep. But, after I get up the nerve to try them, I usually wonder why I was so afraid."

"Me too. There, I guess I'm ready."

"Shyrok and I will be right behind you," Ary assured her.

"Okay, what do I do, Wantak?" she asked.

"Take a deep breath, relax and lean forward a bit."

"How's that?"

"That's good, but loosen the reins some. I've got to be able to use my neck."

"Guess I'm ready," she gulped.

Wantak started down the path. She leaned forward in her stirrups, caught herself tightening the reins, relaxed her hands and forced herself to breathe as they took off.

Shyrok pulled up beside Wantak after a moment and Ary asked, "How're you doing?"

"Scariest thing I've ever done in my life. Look how high we are!"

"Well, you're doing fine. Isn't she, Wantak?"

"Yes. She has good balance and strong legs."

"Before today, I'd never flown before. I haven't done as much of this kind of stuff as you people have."

Ary laughed, "Today you've flown in two ways no human has ever flown in history, except for Liza Jane's dad. Are you still feeling afraid?"

"Yeah. I've never been this high up."

Wantak glanced back, "Relax, Natasha, and try to enjoy yourself. I would never let you fall."

"I'll try. It is beautiful, isn't it?"

"Magical." Ary said looking all around, "Like pictures I've seen of Yosemite Valley, but tropical and indoors."

The valley was two miles across with small hills sticking up, here and there, above the dense foliage. Waterfalls dropped hundreds of feet from the thousand foot gray cliffs on their right, onto massive boulders.

Then, they saw three pteros approaching them, carrying small passengers in black bodysuits headed toward the tram station. One of the Calderan riders pointed at them and all three veered over for a closer look. As they passed, they smiled and waved.

"I've got to be dreaming," Natasha smiled, "I just waved to three Calderans flying on birds inside a mountain."

As they banked around a two-thousand-foot-tall cliff, the valley opened up and was four or five miles long ahead of them. Wantak and Shyrok stayed close to the right side of the valley. In the trees there were homes constructed of heavy natural timbers. In the distance, a lagoon came into view, bordered on the left by the thatched roofs of a village. On the right, a massive sixty-foot-tall gray rock extended out into the middle of the lagoon.

Wantak said, "That's the princess' home on the rock."

Ary pointed and said, "That's them, waving to us from the top of the rock."

Liza Jane stood waving in a short sarong, tied at her waist. David wore black shorts. Then, they walked to the edge of the deck, looked at each other, and launched out into space, arms spread, toes pointed, backs arched they plunged sixty feet to the lagoon below in matching swan dives.

Natasha gasped, "Oh, my God! Did you see that? Liza Jane's unbelievable, isn't she? That rock's like diving off a building!"

When the two surfaced, David threw his head back and gave another yell, slapped the water, piked and dove down out of sight.

Then, Hardaway and Ganador, perched on the rock beside the deck, put their wings back and dove like white-plumed projectiles into the lagoon. David and Liza Jane climbed into the saddles and the birds began running across the water pulling hard with their wings, until they had enough speed to lift off. Then, they flew up to meet Ary and Natasha.

"Welcome, you two. What happened to you guys?" Liza Jane called out.

"You get lost again, Wantak?" Hardaway smirked.

"I love Caldera," Natasha shouted to Liza Jane.

"I hoped you would, Roommate. When you land, put your shoulders forward and your weight in your stirrups."

Wantak approached the deck carefully and touched down almost at a standstill.

"Great landing, Wantak!" Natasha exclaimed. Standing still felt strange after moving with the motion for so long.

"I'm proud of you, Natasha, for being so brave," Wantak said.

"Bend down here, Big Bird." When he did, she kissed the side of his bony head. "Thanks for being so patient with me."

Wantak blushed and the other pteros gave him a hard time as they flew away.

CHAPTER FIFTEEN

AN EVENING IN CALDERA
OCTOBER 3, 2034

L iza Jane led the way across the bridge from the deck to the main house. It was furnished with chairs of natural fabric, hammocks of the same material, thick off-white rugs on wood flooring, and wood cases with what looked like gold trim. The roof was a thick thatch that swooped up to a high ridge.

At the entrance, a short beautifully made male creature stood in linen clothing and matching turban. His eyes were slanted and his small nose and mouth protruded slightly from his face. He had buff-colored fur and elegant drooping whiskers. He bowed and said, "Welcome Natasha and Ary. Your Highness, I laid out a dry tory for you and a sonanda for David in the afternoon pavilion." He handed towels to them.

"Thanks, Sammi, but remember, humans change only in private. I'll show Natasha to my suite and you take Ary and David to the guest house and give them their sonandas. We'll meet in the afternoon pavilion after we're changed."

David and Ary followed their host up to a small guest house with a view across the roof of the main house. He moved as though he weighed nothing and untied filmy draperies that fell across the open walls. "We made these for your visit. If you need anything, ask for me in your thought."

"You can hear what we're thinking?" Ary asked.

"Only if you need me. The afternoon pavilion is down these stairs. Instead of turning into the main house, continue on down." He took two black outfits from a drawer, laid them on top of the dresser, bowed, and left.

David smiled, "What a wonderfully gracious little being."

"A cat-like person," Ary said, picking up a black sonada outfit, obviously made especially for a human body. "Seems like a dream, doesn't it? All these marvelous little beings completely unknown to the rest of the world, living down here under the ice."

"I met a similarly wonderful Calderan gentleman at Lord Appleton's mountain retreat." David told him about Eagle's Mere while they changed.

The guest house was a miniature version of the main house with a thick thatched roof, open walls with great views, and wooden flooring. There were a few pieces of furniture and two hammocks.

Liza Jane led the way to her suite at the back of the main house. The furnishings were sparse but massive, made of cedar-like wood with gold fittings. On one inside wall, floor-to-ceiling bookcases were overflowing with books from the human world.

She opened a large hand-carved chest and pulled out two silk tories and handed one to Natasha. It was made up of a short sarong and a long matching overskirt that tied in front.

"It's heavenly, Liza Jane! Like woven air."

As Liza Jane and Natasha came down the last flight of stairs, Sammi gave them goblets of warm gatava, "Welcome to our evening sounds and prayers," he said with a bow.

Liza Jane's high-necked tory was a blend of burgundy, ocher and magenta. Natasha's was a blend of reds with straps that tied behind her neck, baring her back and shoulders.

She asked, "Does everyone pray together in the evening?" She was barefoot and smiled as she sampled the creamy nectar. "Umm delicious! What is this?"

"It's a drink we squeeze from a Calderan plant," Liza Jane replied, "similar to sugarcane. We often have it with our evening prayers."

"It's so rich!" Natasha exclaimed.

"Usually we pray in private, but we set aside this time at the end of the day to give thanks to the Giver of Life together."

David and Ary joined them wearing black silk pants gathered with ties at the ankles and black sleeveless silk tops tied at the waist. Sammi gave them goblets of gatava and explained the evening sounds and prayers.

From across the valley came a soft sustained breathy sound from a shell horn. Whoooouu. Joined, at length, by harmonizing notes, also sustained. Liza Jane lifted a large conch shell to her lips and added another layer of primeval resonance. From near and far came more sounds, then a simple turn of phrase together, whooo, whouu, who, whoouu.

The shell music continued to swell, filling the caldera. Neighboring households harmonized and improvised subtle phrases to enliven the simple chorus. As the light faded, the music diminished, as well. Liza Jane put the shell down and bowed her head.

Ary bowed his head too and opened his heart to Allah. Thank you for blessing your servant in this way, he prayed.

Natasha's heart could feel the sincerity of the sharing and she loved the soulfulness of the music. This was no empty ritual, but the unction of hearts touching each other like her church back home, hearts intertwined and thanking God for another day. She opened her eyes at the sound of bare feet and turned to see a small jet-black Calderan female in a long burnt-umber tory, lighting torches.

The Calderan girl went over to Ary, pulled a cylindrical drum from under the bench, and placed it at his knees, smiling shyly. Ary had never seen such exotic eyes. Then she placed drums of various sizes in front of the others and handed them carved drumsticks.

With the light now a rosy glow on the granite cliffs, the caldera was lit by more and more torches across the valley. From the distance came a deep drum refrain dom dom dom, dom dom da dom. Then again, with others joining in dom dom dom, dom dom da dom. David touched his drum softly and confirmed his largest drum was that tone and joined in softly on the third pass dom dom dom, dom dom da dom.

On top of the deep drums on the third pass, came a rhythmic trickling drum roll from the highest to lowest of their drum sounds di di di di di, da da da da da, do do do do do, dm dm dm dm dm, followed by the deep drums, dom dom da dom!

By the forth pass, Ary and Natasha could fit their parts in, behind Liza Jane's highest sounds. Across the caldera came this rippling roll from hundreds of drummers di di di di di, da da da da da, do do do do do, dm dm dm dm dm, dom dom da dom! Each time the deep drums finished the refrain, Natasha had to hold back tears, it was such a moving form of sharing.

After the twelfth pass, Liza Jane made no starting notes of the drum roll, but set her drum aside and listened. From all sides of the valley, master percussionists shared their music, answering and interacting in soaring flights of improvisation. Finally, the drum music dwindled.

Liza Jane got up and stood on the broad wood slab railing of the deck. From near and far, high voices sang in soft levels of harmony, "Let the reign," repeated over and over down the valley. Then, deeper voices joined in, "Let the reign of the Giver of Life, of the Giver of Life, of the Giver of Life," like chapel chimes. "Let the reign of the Giver of Life be established in me and rule out of me all evil. And may Thy word enrich the affections, of all living beings, and govern them. And may Thy word enrich the affections of all living beings and govern them, and govern them, and govern them."

Natasha had never experienced anything so embracing. It seemed as though a thousand bell-like voices were singing a prayer—to her. She was filled with a peace she'd never felt, completely satisfied to be who she was, to be doing what she was doing, where she was. Usually she felt others had richer experiences, other people had more solid lives. Tonight, it was perfect to be Natasha Cheatam. She opened her eyes and looked at Liza Jane and David. How beautiful Liza Jane was, golden skin glowing in the torchlight, soulful eyes glistening. She felt abashed. Tears came as she realized how seldom she'd ever been generous enough to genuinely admire another girl's beauty.

In the flickering torchlight, the colors in the tories came to life. The gold threads in Ary's sonanda also caught the torches and flickered reflections of the flames. Natasha closed her eyes and searched for thoughts she hoped would be acceptable to the Being they'd been singing to. She thanked Him for the richest evening of her life and said silently; help me become more like you want me to be.

The Calderan girl reappeared and said, "Our evening meal is set by the pool, Highness."

"Thank you. This is Sammi's soul mate, Halali. Ary and Natasha, my friends from school and David Andrews."

Halali bowed and said, "Welcome. Come and dine."

Liza Jane added, "Our evening meal is sometimes served while we swim and Calderans swim without clothing."

Natasha gulped.

"You and I can just remove our overskirt, Natasha. And Ary, Sammi made suits for you and David. I know bare bodies are difficult for humans."

"This is really hard for me," Natasha said.

"Why's that, Roommate?"

"I can't swim."

"Don't worry, I'll show you where the deep places are."

The pools were on the other side of the great rock from the afternoon pavilion. Three lighted freeform pools stepped down the rock below the main house. Warm water cascaded from one to the next, then down a smooth moss-covered rock to a lip about thirty feet above the lagoon. Around the upper pool were serving dishes of cold food and metal bowls held hot dishes over glowing coals.

Ary and Liza Jane swam in the upper pool with Sammi and Halali. Halali spoke so quietly, she was hard to hear at times. Everything about her was understated. Her body was petite with short shiny black fur. She had three tiny breasts, the highest just below her arms-the lowest near her waist.

Sammi swam so swiftly underwater, he shot out and landed sitting next to Halali. Their bodies were almost identical, except his coat was light gold and he was three or four inches taller at almost five feet, and his manner more assertive than his mate's.

"Your Highness," he asked, "are you enjoying life in your father's homeland?"

"It's better than I imagined, Sammi."

"Will you stay?"

"No. After mother's campaign for world peace, father wants me to find a mate and prepare to take his place. He's ready to retire and support Hamama's work with the I-Council."

Ary said with a wry smile, "I wonder who your father has in mind."

"David would be a fine soul mate," Halali said, smiling.

"I like the idea, if he's willing," Liza Jane said. "What do you think of him, Sammi?"

"He's not Lord Appleton."

"I think he'll mature like father has. Mother thinks he's perfect."

"Does your father live here with you?" Ary asked.

"No. He lives in the village."

"How did you end up with this fantastic place?"

"This is my mother's ancestral home."

"Why doesn't your father live here?" Ary asked.

"He likes being closer to the people. When my mother left to join the I-Council, he moved down to the village. The Calderans got to know him better and he felt in closer touch, so he stayed."

"I-Council?" Ary asked. "What's that?"

"That's a discussion for another night, Ary."

David and Natasha joined the group and he asked, "Natasha would like to go out on the ice, Liza Jane. Could we arrange an excursion outside?"

"I'll try to work that in tomorrow. After we tour Caldera, we'll go out on the ice if there's time, and then head back."

Natasha frowned, "Seems too soon."

Halali smiled, "You like it here?"

"It's like heaven, Halali. The human world is so screwed up. We could get blown to bits any minute."

"I thought it might be too quiet for you here."

"Just in these few hours I've felt some changes inside. Makes me wonder what would happen if I stayed."

Liza Jane interjected, "I need your help these next months, Natasha. You can come back after our campaign and stay as long as you want. If humans reject the message, you can come here to live."

"What can you tell us about the campaign?" Ary asked.

"It's coming together. You three were important to my mother's efforts."

"How were we important?" Natasha asked.

"She showed your thought profiles to the I-Council members, so they could see the goodness of your hearts."

"How'd she get them?" Natasha asked anxiously.

"I gave her the thought profiles I discerned in the two of you. And she developed her own assessment of David's thinking in their meetings. Your thought qualities were extremely encouraging to my mother. Your goodness shows through and overshadows your matter-based thinking."

Natasha's expression registered a rush of anger.

Liza Jane sensed her reaction and said, "I'm sorry to upset you, Natasha. That first day I didn't realize humans might want to keep their thoughts a secret. I should have asked."

She looked dazed and stammered, "I'm so ashamed to have you and your mother know my screwed up thinking."

"On the contrary, we were extremely pleased. Mother saw my father become powerful in the Way, Natasha, and the changes required of you are no greater."

"Your father told me it took him over fifty years to really begin living the message," Ary said.

"So?"

"That's an awfully long time."

"You've brought up one of the changes needed."

Ary laughed, "Okay, I'm impatient."

"No, you base life on time, which is part of the illusion."

Ary stared at her, "This is going to be some kind of campaign isn't it, Princess."

Natasha asked, "What do you mean, matter-based thinking?"

"Human's lives are based on their physical senses. Calderan lives aren't."

Natasha stared at her in confusion.

Ary asked, "What are you saying matter is, or isn't, Liza Jane?"

"It's a convincing illusion."

Ary rapped his knuckles on the pool deck, "Feels pretty solid to me."

"One illusion tapping another," Liza Jane remarked, "you might say we're dreaming all this and Jesus came to show you the difference between the dream and real life."

Sammi asked, "Who'd like to do some sliding?"

"Good idea," Liza Jane agreed, "Why don't you show Ary and David, I'll stay with Natasha."

Ary bounded up, "I'm ready for whatever you said, that's enough metaphysical jazz for one night."

"You coming, David?" he asked.

"No. I think I'll see if I can help Natasha with her swimming. Maybe she and I can join you later."

Sammi led Ary down to the bottom pool and showed him the water overflowing onto the moss covered sliding surface and falling to the lagoon below. "The easiest way," he explained, "is down the left side and off the bottom edge there."

"How about the right side?" Ary asked.

"You can see that side is steeper and more polished, the bottom edge curves up more, the further right you slide. That side takes quite a bit of practice, but you can do more in the air before you get to the water."

David gave Natasha a swimming lesson, while below Ary whooped and hollered as he learned to handle the sliding surface. Natasha gradually relaxed enough to take five or six strokes to the side. Her kick improved and she no longer minded putting her face in the water. Her arm strokes were stiff and she couldn't get the breathing, but it felt good to be overcoming her fear of water.

Liza Jane and Halali watched how patient and supportive David was with her. Natasha thanked him and climbed out. As she toweled off, she saw her sarong was nearly invisible. She instinctively started to wrap up in her towel, but Liza Jane was obviously at ease. Halali couldn't have been more discrete and she wore nothing. Caldera made bodies seem natural. She decided not to call attention to the issue, got her mind off her body and sat down next to Halali. "I'm supposed to be black, but next to you, I'm sort of medium brown."

Halali smiled, "We've heard of dark humans, but you're the first one we've seen."

"Do the Calderans care about color?"

"Not in the least. Humans do, though, don't they?"

Natasha laughed, "Yes, you could say that. We have a lot to learn from you people. Can you really see my heart?"

"Oh yes. Your heart will readily grasp the Way, Natasha."

"It thrills me to hear you say that."

"I see some snarls in Ary he'll have to unwind before he can make rapid progress, but you only lack the confidence that comes with understanding, much like swimming."

"I wish you could teach me."

"Come back after the queen's campaign and stay with us. I would be honored. Let's go see how Ary's doing on the slide. Would you two like to join us?"

"Sure. Let's go watch," David said.

They watched Ary jump from the edge and land standing sideways in the middle of the mossy slope, arms out, legs wide apart he accelerated. At the bottom, he gathered himself and launched into a couple of somersaults and a decent entry to loud cheers from above. Ary's strength and athleticism delighted Natasha.

Then Sammi flew down the right side. The curl at the bottom sent him into an intricate series of tumbling moves, ending with a sliver-like entry far below.

Ary applauded as he climbed back to the top. Near the bottom of the climb up the slope, Sammi knew Ary was about to leap out on the steep side of the rock and called out in an effort to stop him as he jumped. Gaining speed, Ary over-compensated and got his weight too far forward.

As soon as Ary got into trouble, Liza Jane launched herself across the slide in his direction. When Ary reached the steep curl at the bottom, he slammed into the polished granite surface at speed and his limp body flew off the curl, obviously unconscious. Seconds later, there was a loud slap on the water below.

David shoved off down the slide to help. As he worked to keep his balance, he saw that Sammi was in the water with Ary when Liza Jane reached him. David knew he would have seen him, if he'd used the slide to get back to the lagoon. Sammi had somehow moved instantly to Ary's side.

When he reached the curled edge, David dove, surfaced and swam over to them. Ary was floating face up, in Sammi's arms. The right side of his head above his ear was fractured and oozing dark blood. David could see bone fragments protruding above his ear and his body twitched and jerked convulsively. David stared without breathing. It appeared their wonderful young friend had been killed.

Liza Jane said quietly to him, "If you want to help, David, you need to wipe out any belief you have in what your eyes just reported to you."

"Thanks ... yes," he mumbled, still staring. He tore his eyes away and looked at Liza Jane, "What are you seeing?"

"I can't explain now, but if you want to support the work, mentally put him back on the slide and get him off perfectly."

"I can do that. What else?"

"Take him over to the stairs and carry him up to the pool deck. It's like resisting hypnosis, David. Don't give your consent to what you think you saw. It was an illusion. Sammi's taking care of him and I'm supporting his work."

As he towed Ary's body to the stairs, he prayed for all he was worth, then managed to climb out of the water with Ary's lifeless body on his back, arms hanging over his shoulders, blood running off his fingers. He couldn't sense any breathing.

Natasha had to sit down, she was sobbing so hard.

Halali's small hand was on her shoulder, comforting her, "You can't see through it, can you, Natasha?"

"I wish I could! He must be terribly hurt."

"Now I remember how hard it was for Lord Appleton at first. You humans are so utterly convinced by what your eyes tell you."

"You're trying to teach me, aren't you?"

"You need to see only what the Giver of Life sees."

"I'll try. Tell me what He sees."

"The spiritual Ary He made is intact; and can't be harmed by a collision inside an illusion."

"So, in His eyes nothing happened to Ary. He's alright."

"Correct. He doesn't see energy forms."

David approached them, staggering slightly with labored breathing, carrying Ary up the steps.

Halali asked, "Can you make it to the main house, David?" He nodded, breathing hard. She turned and hurried ahead.

Natasha asked, "How are you doing, David?"

Through heavy breathing he said, "I've got him back on the slide going off under control."

"Is that what I should try to do?"

"Not 'try,' Natasha." When he paused to get his breath on the top pool deck, he felt Ary's body stir.

Halali had made up a bed next to the fire pit and she washed the blood from Ary's hair and from David's back and arms.

While he was being cleaned up, Ary regained consciousness, looked at Halali and mumbled, "Hell of a wipeout wasn't it?"

Halali smiled, "You should stay in the middle of the slide for a while."

"Oh man! My head and shoulder are killing me. And my wrist," he moaned and closed his eyes hard, grimacing.

Liza Jane and Sammi joined them. Sammi stirred the fire enough to get it going, and then added some logs.

"I can still see that granite curl coming at me," Ary said, closing his eyes and massaging his shoulder.

"Don't argue against us," Liza Jane said.

"Amazing!" Ary exclaimed. "Right now the pain in my shoulder is draining out! Like someone pulled the plug in the tub," he said, still massaging his shoulder.

"You're letting go of it," Halali said softly, still cleaning his hair with a damp cloth.

"What are you crying about, Natasha?" Ary asked.

"Don't mind me," she said, wiping her eyes, "I'm just so grateful you're okay."

"How'd I get up here?"

"David carried you," Halali answered.

"Wow! That's impressive. I'm a load to climb those steps with."

"Actually, I was concentrating so hard on getting you off the sliding rock safely; it took my mind off the climb. I barely remember it."

"Is that how you do it?" Ary asked.

"Like we were saying after dinner," Liza Jane said, picking up and dropping his leg, "this body of yours is made of energy. Remember the dinner show in Philadelphia? A hypnotic suggestion of an accident in an energy dream can be corrected, if you aren't fooled by what your senses try to tell you."

Ary's eyes glazed, "I'm sorry, I don't get any of this."

David said, "Liza Jane's dad helped me by comparing it to railroad tracks that appear to meet in the distance. We've trained ourselves to see through that illusion. Your fall was like the converging tracks. Sammi knew the truth about your real being, the same way we know the tracks don't meet."

Sammi had his back to Ary, stoking the fire. Ary tapped him on the shoulder. When he turned, Ary looked deep into his eyes and said, "Thanks, Sammi. I'll never forget what you did for me tonight."

Sammi just smiled and nodded.

From deep thought David asked, "When he was falling, Sammi, you were instantly back in the lagoon to help him, weren't you?"

"I can be where I'm needed, that's natural."

"Natural for you, maybe, for me it seems impossible. How do you move through space like that . . . instantly?"

After a period of quiet Sammi answered, "Someday, David, your movement will become a function of your thought, independent of your body."

"You promise?"

Sammi smiled and nodded, "The same way Lord Appleton met you in that ice cave."

"I wondered how he managed to meet me in that obscure cave. I just happened onto it in my climb up the glacier."

Halali finished cleaning Ary, and Natasha walked with her to the service area carrying a pail of reddish-brown water, "Do you and Sammi have children?"

"Our little girl is in the village tonight."

"What's she doing?"

"There's a shadow play, I think. Maybe dancing, too."

"I'd love to see it. Would we be too much of a distraction?"

"I don't think so."

When they returned to the sunken fireplace, Halali whispered in Liza Jane's ear.

She nodded, "Good idea. Father asked us to come for dessert and we could see the puppets, too. Would you guys like to go down to the village? You up to it, Ary?"

"Sure, I'd love to see the village."

This time Natasha mounted her ptero without trepidation. The six took off from the deck. At night, Caldera was even more beautiful to Natasha. The rock cliffs had an opalescent glow and the lagoon glistened far below them. They landed on the beach and walked toward the firelight. In a crowded clearing, a sheet was stretched between two palms and a fire danced behind it.

The shadow puppets on the sheet entranced the children in the clearing. They were lost in the story of how Fracnoy, one of the great pteros of all time, saved Issacan, the prince of the sea birds, when the ancestors of the Calderans first journeyed to Caldera. In return, the sea birds promised to provide the Calderans with fresh fish for all time. Through the eons the sea birds worked so hard fishing for themselves and for their friends that they turned into penguins, birds that "fly" only in water.

When Issacan made his famous speech extolling Fracnoy's strength and courage, it made Wantak cry. When the puppeteers took their bow, the children cheered as though it was the first time they'd ever heard the story.

Dozens of Calderan parents beyond the torches started playing soft drum music. Two of the older children, a male and a female, barefoot in black and white bodysuits, walked hand in hand to the center of the clearing, where they suddenly took on the movement of penguins.

Natasha was amazed how closely they could imitate the emperor penguin's body language. After much dignified waddling, the two dove into an imaginary sea and became birds of fabulous "flight." They swooped and spun with leaps that shocked the human onlookers. Natasha estimated they were eight feet off the ground in their highest leaps, while doing complicated dance sequences with relaxed ease.

Then, some smaller children joined the dance portraying a school of frightened fish, turning as one to escape the penguins. Finally, Issacan captured a small fish, picked it up with the help of his partner and laid it in front of Lord Appleton, seated on a raised dais of flowers.

The two penguins bowed to him. He stood and bowed back, with solemnity, and said in a voice all could hear, "Thank you, Prince Issacan and Princess Mariana, and all our great penguin friends, for feeding us through the centuries. We will ever be your brothers and sisters."

Issacan and Mariana bowed to him again, then to the crowd and "swam" leaping and pirouetting out of the circle to cheering and applause.

Slowly the crowd dispersed. Many of the children came over to Lord Appleton and said goodnight. He knew each by name. Some saw Liza Jane and ran over to welcome her home. They were shy toward the humans, but beautiful with flashing grins and eyes. A two-foot-tall bounding delight jumped into Sammi's arms and asked if she could stay with the grandparents and the other children.

Sammi said, "Of course," then introduced Savana to Liza Jane's human friends. Throughout the introductions, she looked at Natasha, then whispered something in Sammi's ear, still grinning at her.

He said, "Natasha, Savana wonders if you would hold her for a moment. She has a question to ask you."

Natasha took the little black child and held her close.

"What's your favorite story, Natasha?"

"I love the story about Issacan and Fracnoy."

"Me too," she said in a small firm voice. "Tonight, that's my favorite."

"What are you and your friends going to do tonight?"

"We'll fish and swim in the lagoon, then sing and tell stories around the fire until we fall asleep."

"Do you do that often?"

"Yes. Would you tell me a human story sometime?"

"I would love to," she said and kissed her cheek.

Savana giggled and rubbed her cheek, "Bye, Natasha, maybe I'll see you tomorrow." She hit the ground bounding after the others.

"What a precious child," Natasha said.

Halali beamed, "She's a blessing to us."

Natasha watched her run through the trees toward a distant bonfire, "Wow! What a way to grow up."

They all headed toward E.A.'s pavilion. On the way Halali said, "Sometime, Natasha, I'd like to hear of your childhood. We know so little of the human world."

"Frankly," Natasha chuckled, "I'll take your way, anytime. I can imagine how happy Savana will be all her life, with a childhood like this."

"Yours wasn't so happy?" Halali asked.

"It had its good moments, but there was a lot of unhappiness mixed in."

CHAPTER SIXTEEN

NATASHA'S HOUSE
OCTOBER 3, 2034

Lord Appleton's pavilion was small with intricately colored hand-carving on the posts, eaves and ceilings. It was set out thirty feet into a pond, with flat irregularly shaped stones leading out to it. He welcomed his guests warmly and invited them to sit on cushions around the fire pit.

"Hamani made gentosi pudding," E.A. said. "Here, Ary, help me dish it up."

Lord Appleton pulled a heavy black pot from over the coals and tasted the contents, "Umm. I think you'll like this. Ary, spoon that heavy cream on as I fill these bowls, would you?"

Hamani appeared with coffee and E.A. continued, "This drink hasn't caught on in Caldera, but Hamani and I like it. The plants thrive here."

Liza Jane introduced Hamani to Natasha and Ary.

The dark hot pudding was tart under the sweet cream. The coffee was stronger than most Americans drink it, but small sips tasted good with the pudding. Natasha got Ary to put some cream in hers.

As they got comfortable in the big soft cushions around the fire, E.A. said, "I have news from your mother, Jane."

"I was just thinking about her, how she would enjoy being here for my friends' visit."

E.A. continued, "After you mentioned Natasha's pastor and her prayerfulness, Hamama looked in on her church. She feels it's the right place to start the campaign, if they're willing."

"Oh my goodness!" Natasha exclaimed, "That would be wonderful! But St. Johns is small and plain, Lord Appleton, nothing special."

"On the contrary, Natasha, Hamama feels it's perfect."

Natasha teared up, "Why wouldn't they be willing? I have no idea what's involved, but surely they'll want to do something so important."

E.A. stirred the glowing coals, then said, "I think you need to go back in the morning, Jane, so you and Natasha can run our plans by Reverend Pettis and the deacons tomorrow. Then, hopefully, he can get the membership's approval on Sunday. There's a lot to do before the 15th. You'll need to commune with your mother to find out what she has in mind. I know the engineers are working on plans."

"You're right, Father. You'll have to explain to the overseers at the mine and the fishery. We'll visit them on another trip. We should get some rest now. Are you coming with us tomorrow?"

"No. I need to stay here. Just send the ship back."

They said goodnight, then, from the porch Liza Jane whistled a signal pattern and the pteros came soaring over the trees and landed on the shore of the lagoon.

David and Ary were asleep before their hammocks stopped swaying.

Natasha lay in her gently moving hammock and looked across the valley at a scene of such otherworldliness, it seemed she was already dreaming. In the distance she could hear the laughter of the children and their sweet singing.

Memories of her abusive alcoholic father came back. She swore silently, as she had many times before, she would be loving and patient every moment, if she married and had a child.

To end the best day of her life, she reached out again in her thought to the Giver of Life. I want to make You some promises, she said inside herself. From now on, I'm going to be more courageous. I can see now that fear and timidity are a waste of life. How did that prayer go today? Let the reign of the Giver of Life be established in me and rule out of me all evil. And may Thy word enrich the affections of all living beings, and govern them. Goodnight. Oh! And thank you for putting Ary back together after his crash tonight.

The next morning the valley was clouded over and a light rain dripped from the eaves. Natasha carefully exited her hammock, put on her bodysuit and slipped into the riding boots left by the door. Liza Jane's hammock was empty.

She made her way through the main house and found that Sammi and Halali had set breakfast on the hearth of the fire pit. The fire felt good in the damp air. Sitting across from Liza Jane, she enjoyed a breakfast of omelettes, fruit, pastries and hot chocolate. As they ate, the rain let up. Liza Jane explained that Calderans reserve time after breakfast for prayer and invited David to join her in the living room. Natasha retired to her bedroom.

Ary used a rug in the guest pavilion to say his morning prayers. He'd admired the intimate closeness the Calderans felt to the Giver of Life and the practicality of their prayer in solving problems. He knew his relationship with Allah was more distant and his faith less closely connected than theirs. He spent the time relating to Allah as a very present help and in thanks for his remarkable recovery the night before.

Liza Jane said, "David, tell me how you're thinking of matter."

"I've always liked physics. One of my favorite high school teachers drew a childlike diagram of a drop of water magnified a billion times. Expanded from a quarter-inch in diameter to fifteen miles, the drop became a mass of jiggling atoms, held together by electromagnetic attraction, two hydrogen atoms clinging to each oxygen.

"Then he drew a diagram next to it that showed a hydrogen atom with the orbit of its single electron expanded to a half-mile in diameter. He surprised the class by drawing the nucleus of this enormous atom the size of a pebble. Then came the real shocker, he said if we removed all the space between the particles in your body, what was left would fit easily on the point of a pin.

"I'm trying to understand what Sammi did last night to erase Ary's injuries. It was obviously beyond physics."

Liza Jane said, "Human physicists now define that pinpoint of stuff as energy."

David thought about that for a while before he said, "I'm beginning to get what Dr. Kramer tried to explain to me, energy and mass are different forms of the same thing! That concentrated energy . . . can have mass."

"Almost right," she explained. "Energy appears to have mass when it's concentrated. Your energy body is the result of millions of years of mental evolution inside an electromagnetic illusion."

David fought the defensive flack his mind began throwing up and demanded of himself, Listen! Don't argue. Give these new ideas a chance!

Liza Jane continued, "Now we come to the surprising part. Your real identity is the result of your unique expression of consciousness, not mentally arranged energy particles."

"So, I'm made of ideas."

"Yes. The Giver of Life thinks you. You're an expression of His qualities blended in a unique way. You're one of a kind."

"What about this two hundred and forty pounds I pack around, that hurts if I fall."

"Have you ever fallen in a dream?"

"Yes, actually I have. When I was little, I used to intentionally wake up to escape a dream I was falling."

"That falling body in your dream was a creation of your consciousness, right?"

Suddenly, he could see it. She was saying this whole material deal could be virtual reality. If he could save himself from falling in an extremely life-like dream by waking up, what if something like that were possible in this energy illusion? "Is that what Sammi did?"

"You're getting it, David. We need to leave soon. I'll meet you on the deck in front."

Then, he remembered Liza Jane's explanation by the pool, '. . . you might say we're dreaming all this and Jesus came to show you the difference between the dream and real life.'

David wondered why the Giver of Life gave a damn about a male energy-being crashing in an illusion. Then he realized, He doesn't think Ary as an energy being. The Ary He thinks is a spiritual being that didn't crash. Sammi somehow wiped out the seeming accident by correcting the dream from an awakened standpoint. Sammi set aside physics and used . . . what? That, he realized, was what Lord Appleton had been working his way through since his arrival in Caldera.

From the deck, they heard Natasha calling. The group was getting ready to leave.

Suddenly, the bitterness he'd always felt toward his father drained away, like the pain in Ary's shoulder the night before. It no longer mattered that his father had never known how to love him.

Liza Jane didn't ask Hardaway for any stunts this morning. The four of them flew together down the far side of the valley. They flew over more villages and lakes along the floor of the caldera, then landed at the black granite tram terminal and walked through the opening in the waterfall to the waiting tram.

A cold rain was falling as Natasha and Liza Jane caught the 11:10AM train from Princeton to Newark. Settled into an almost empty car headed northeast, Natasha studied the backyards outside the window and thought about how best to prepare her friend for what awaited them at the other end of this train ride. How could there be a greater contrast between their homes and living environments?

At length she turned to her roommate and began, "I'm glad you've been to Newark and know it's a tough place with some good people—like Reverend Pettis and my mama. My younger brother will be with her and he's deeply good like her. His name is Charles, but we call him Cooksey."

Liza Jane asked, "What about your sister?"

"Lisa's usually in trouble. She's in jail now, I think."

"I saw her picture on your dresser, great looking."

"That's part of the problem. She's heavy into drugs, turns tricks to buy 'em."

"Turns tricks?"

"She sells sex to men."

Natasha was quiet while Liza Jane turned to the window. She let that shocking thought sink in before she said, "Hard to believe, isn't it?"

Without turning from the window, Liza Jane answered, "It's terribly sad, but understandable."

"Tell me what you think about my sister. I've worried about her my whole life."

Liza Jane turned back to Natasha, "I'm beginning to be able to see a little through human eyes. She knows nothing of the law and lives as though it doesn't exist."

"What law is that?" Natasha asked, glad at the thought of having someone so wise shed some light on the great sadness of her life.

"Some humans feel so bad about themselves, they think they have nothing more to lose. It no longer matters what they think or do."

"But what's the law you referred to?"

"Progress to perfection. It's one of God's laws."

"Lisa?"

Liza Jane smiled and nodded, "It may not be on this plane of experience, but Lisa will turn eventually . . . inevitably. It's the law."

Natasha suddenly felt a sense of hope for her sister she'd never felt. Tears welled up and rolled down her cheeks. "She's not damned to hell?"

"That's where she is now. It's shocking, how far off the track people can get. My father tried to tell me."

"Too far off for your mother's campaign to turn us around?"

"No. People at the level of spiritual development my mother has attained can reach anyone."

"My older brother's named Julian. He's worse."

"Oh great!" Liza Jane exclaimed.

"He's twenty-two and big trouble. Five of the last ten years in prison and probably going back, if he's not killed first."

"I'm starting to see what your mother's been up against."

Natasha smiled and waved as the girls emerged from the Newark station. Her little brother looked taller than the last time she saw him. Her mother had a healthier glow than usual. She didn't look tired.

Natasha said, "Liza Jane, this is my younger brother, who we call Cooksey."

The broad-shouldered young boy with calm round eyes stood next to Mrs. Cheatam at the Newark station. He grinned, stuck out his hand to Liza Jane, and said, "Pleased to meet you. Been wanting to thank you for helping my mama."

"You're welcome. I love her like I love your sister."

Cooksey took the small suitcases each girl was carrying and they got in a big Buick. Margaret drove and the two girls got in the back seat. The engine ran rough. The interior had once been fancy, but had become tattered.

Mrs. Cheatam chatted happily, glancing at Natasha in the rear view mirror. Cooksey was quiet and sat with his back against the door, smiling at the girls in the back.

"You guys hungry?" he asked, widening his eyes. "Mama baked a surprise for you."

"Sweet potato pie?" Natasha asked.

"You'll have to wait and see," Margaret said, raising up to see her in the mirror.

"Tell us about your trip, Sis," Cooksey said.

Natasha smiled and said, "We had a good time, but it was pretty boring."

Liza Jane chuckled.

Cooksey said, "I always know when she's lying. It wasn't boring at all, was it Miss Appleton?"

"It was a number of new experiences for your sister."

"Where do you live, Miss Appleton?" Cooksey asked.

"Call me Liza Jane. I'm from a small country near Australia."

"You went all the way down there?" he exclaimed.

While he asked, they made a sweeping turn into the driveway of a small yellow house. A carport was all you could see from the street. Next door a small trucking company was surrounded by a chain link fence with coiled razor wire along the top. Hanging from the side of the carport, a basketball backstop had no net and a bent rim. The dirt under it was packed from heavy use. The fascia around the eaves was partially repainted and most of the paint had been scraped from the carport posts long ago.

Cooksey walked ahead and unlocked the barred screen door and both locks of the brown paneled front door. Bars covered the windows. The air inside was overheated and fragrant from Margaret's pie in the oven. Cooksey took their suitcases into Natasha's bedroom. Twin beds and a small dresser almost filled the room. The frame of the mirror over her dresser was lined with photos.

"Tell me about these," Liza Jane said pulling out one of her standing in front of a large handsome boy with his arms around her waist. He was wearing a light blue tux and the background was a dark blue sky with a moon, some stars, white flowers and four Grecian columns.

"That's my senior prom photo," Natasha said. "Mama made the dress, isn't it pretty?" The dress was red, short, tight, and sequined with a low neckline and tiny straps.

"Ary and I looked at dresses like that. They looked too hard to make at home."

"It took weeks. Cooksey and I helped. My date was shocked. He'd only seen me at school and church."

Liza Jane started to ask about a picture of her in a long gown, holding roses and wearing a tiara on her upswept hair, when Margaret called them to lunch.

Cooksey said grace, then Margaret set a tray of pulled-pork sandwiches and a large bowl of cold slaw on the table. Each plate had a small bowl of her special barbeque sauce for dipping.

"Mama, Liza Jane and I have a meeting with Reverend Pettis and the deacons this afternoon that will go through dinner. We'll be home for dessert. Can we borrow the car?"

"Of course you can. Can I get a hint of what the meeting's about?"

"No. Its top secret, I'm afraid. We'll see you later."

The meeting was in the Fellowship Hall that adjoined the church. Reverend Pettis was dressed in suit slacks and a dress shirt open at the collar. Some of the deacons were dressed in work clothes, a few in slacks and dress shirts. All the deacons had workingmen's hands and faces that told stories of tough lives. They were dignified and serious about their duties to their church.

They had set up two six-foot-long folding tables with fourteen stackable chairs. Everything in the room showed years of use. At one end was a kitchen and at the other there were small class areas set up for Sunday School with plywood dividers on rollers.

Reverend Pettis began, "I think you know Natasha Cheatam. Her Princeton roommate's name is Liza Jane Appleton and she has a proposal for us to consider that Natasha related to me briefly this morning by telephone. Why don't you let us know what you and your mother have in mind, Miss Appleton?"

For the next several hours Liza Jane explained her mother's plan for the creation of St. Johns Park, the part their church would play in her mother's campaign, and the endowment that would be established to cover the perpetual maintenance of the park and their church.

The girls returned home at nine o'clock. Natasha hugged her mother for making her favorite dessert. "Liza Jane, you don't need to eat it. It's a taste you probably have to grow up with to appreciate, I think."

Then, there was loud pounding on the front door.

Margaret's expression hardened as she got up and walked through the living room to the door. She opened it the few inches allowed by the security chain and screamed, "Julian!" The door swung open and a large man in dark clothing walked in carrying another over his shoulder. Natasha went to Margaret, who was shaking and crying.

"What happened, Jabal?" Margaret asked.

"It's real bad, Mama Cheatam. Where can I put him?"

She looked at the blood running off Julian's hand and said, "Put him in my car. Let's get him to the hospital."

Jabal laid him on the vinyl-covered sofa that had the look of leather. "He said he was hit too bad to mess with hospitals. He wanted to come home."

Margaret kneeled beside her son. Tears fell off her cheeks as she stroked his head.

"What happened, Jabal?" Natasha asked.

"Latinos jumped us behind the mall and Moe started shooting. They had an assault gun. Killed Moe and hit Sonny. I don't know about Bobby. Somehow they missed me. I picked up Sonny and drove him straight here."

"We're supposed to sit here and watch him die?" Margaret asked, her eyes now angry, "You boys get shot up and drag yourselves home to die like animals?" she said, staring at her son, soaked with blood above the waist.

Natasha looked at Liza Jane, who nodded. Natasha burst into tears and threw her arms around her mother, burying her face as her mother embraced her back, both sobbing heavily. Finally, Natasha regained enough composure to say, "Liza Jane can help him."

Margaret stared at her daughter, not comprehending.

"Like she helped you. We don't need a hospital."

Margaret put her hands together and bowed her head, "Thank you God, for sending your angel to save my boy!"

Natasha dried her face on her sleeve and asked, "Can you do it, Liza Jane?"

"Fixing his body wasn't so difficult."

"What's she talking about?" Jabal asked. "She the one healed your mama?"

"Yes, you did right bringing him home," Natasha said.

"Can she save Sonny?"

"Yes."

Jabal sank to his knees in front of Liza Jane and said, "I swear . . . if you can save him, Miss, I'll give the rest of my sorry-assed life to the Lord Jesus Christ . . . tonight."

"Careful what you say, Jabal." Margaret said.

He lowered his face to the carpet, sobs racking his broad back, "I swear it. I swear it."

"Can you feel His power, Miss Appleton?" Margaret asked, "Is it happening?"

"His body's okay, but his thinking's so scarred, I can't mend it. I could ask my father to help him."

"He would help my brother?" Natasha asked.

"I'll ask."

Natasha embraced her. "You're saving my whole family."

"We should cut these clothes off and clean him up," Margaret said.

"Let's put him in my room," Cooksey said, "I've got some of his old jammies. Jabal can help me."

Together, they cleaned him up. As they pulled his soaked undershirt from underneath him, a flattened lead slug fell off the sofa and wobbled on edge across the carpet.

Jabal muttered, "The hole was right there," gently touching Julian's abdomen below his heart. "I got a look at the Latino's face and swore I'd kill him. Now, the little son-of-a-bitch can live 'cause I'm coming to Jesus."

Julian slept peacefully in Cooksey's bed. Margaret and Natasha stood at the door and looked at him. Natasha said, "I don't see the anger."

Jabal was sitting in the living room, staring out the window with a faraway look, "We just had us a genuine miracle on your sofa, Mama Cheatam. Like Jesus walked in here and gave him back to us."

Liza Jane was sitting in the dining room with Cooksey and said, "That's actually what happened, Jabal."

He turned away from the window with a troubled look, "You Jesus, come back to save us?"

"No. But I do the healing he taught."

"You mean someone could learn to do what you just did?" he asked.

"Yes. Many have."

"Oh man," he said and turned back to the window.

Natasha brought a pot of hot water with a sponge and worked on the sofa and carpet. The water in the pot quickly turned reddish-brown and got darker as she worked.

Cooksey said, "I didn't get my pie, Mama."

Margaret smiled at him from the kitchen and brought him a big piece. "You want to try some, Miss Appleton?"

"Sure. The coffee's delicious."

"Come on Jabal, Cooksey implored, you can't resist sweet potato pie."

"Can I borrow a shirt, Cooksey. This one's ruined."

He and Cooksey came to the table, after they'd cleaned up. Jabal had on a Chicago Bulls sweatshirt that was tight in the shoulders and short in the sleeves. He was strikingly handsome with kind eyes and a boyish grin.

"Jabal," Natasha said, "let me introduce my roommate, Liza Jane Appleton. Liza Jane, I'd like you to meet our old friend, Ed Berry, who we call Jabal."

Jabal stuck out his large hand and smiled, "Pleased to meet you, Miss Appleton. You've sure made your mark on this family. Everyone's grateful to you."

Margaret asked, "Can you tell us how you do your healing?"

"Is there any way I could learn?" Jabal asked.

Liza Jane started to explain, but could tell her words weren't registering and didn't pursue it.

"So, it's not a special gift?" Margaret asked. "My Auntie Harriet did some laying on of hands."

"Jesus taught a bunch of fishermen to heal and they taught others. It was part of his message," Liza Jane explained.

"Why do you think it was lost?" Margaret asked.

"The Roman Empire was converted to Christianity and the message got buried in the paganism of ancient Rome."

"So, we had it and lost it," Jabal said. "I want to learn, but right now I'd better go home and get some rest. Can I come for breakfast, Mama Cheatam?"

"We'll expect you at eight."

"See y'all in the morning. Thanks again, Miss Appleton. I'll never forget what you done for Sonny tonight."

The next morning Margaret was humming along with a devotional program on the radio when the girls came out, wearing robes over their nighties. Cooksey was still sleeping on the sofa.

"Jabal called earlier," she said. "He asked about Julien and if he could come with us to church. Said he'd been up praying and thanking God most of the night."

"He's like a third brother to you, isn't he, Natasha?" Liza Jane said.

"His mother drinks and lives with a man who beats her up. He's with us more than them, wouldn't you say, Mama?"

"In another land, Jabal would be a prince. I know he's done some bad things, but that's not his nature."

Margaret called Cooksey, "Wake up, Charles Lewis and come to breakfast."

He woke easily and asked, "No sign of Sonny?"

"Not a peep," Natasha answered.

Margaret brought a platter of pancakes, eggs and sausage, sat down and said, "Let's pray. Then, we can say the 23rd Psalm, whoever wants to."

A knock came at the door. Cooksey opened it and grinned, "Jabal looks like some big preacher gone bad."

He was wearing a black suit with a pinstripe, a black string tie with a pearl tie ornament, and a white dress shirt. His walk was turned-in and he moved with the ambling grace of a wide receiver.

"Sit down Ed, we were just going to pray."

Jabal whispered, "Good morning," and smiled at each one around the small table, then sat down at a place set on the corner with a folding chair.

"You know this Psalm, Miss Appleton?" she asked.

"No. I'll just listen."

Margaret reached over to the windowsill and picked up a worn Bible, opened it to one of the ribbon markers and set it in front of her. Halfway through, everyone became aware of Julian standing in the living room in Cooksey's red robe.

Margaret said, "Come have some breakfast, Sonny."

Julian opened another folding chair and they made room.

"This is Liza Jane, my roommate from school."

"You the one healed mama?"

"Yes."

"That ain't all she done," Jabal added. "What do you remember of last night?"

"I got hit. That's all I remember."

"I thought you were gone, so I brought you home."

"I remember I told you to. Knew I was done."

"Miss Appleton saved you, like she saved your mama."

"Where was I hit? I don't feel anything."

"Catch," Jabal said, and tossed the flattened slug across the table. Julian caught it and looked at it as Jabal continued, "Just below your heart, big hole."

"That's what I thought. I don't get it."

"You were healed, like in the Bible," Margaret said, "Now everyone eat, your breakfast is getting cold."

Julian sat staring at the chunk of lead in his hand, a sour look on his face.

"You might at least thank her," Jabal said, "for saving your ugly butt."

"I've seen those guys before. We'll get'm tonight."

"Not me. I've given my life to Jesus."

"What?"

"Cause he saved you through Miss Appleton's prayers."

"Then, I'll go by myself. What about Moe and Bobby?"

"Moe's dead. I don't know about Bobby."

"Bobby'll go. You losin it, eh Jabal?"

"Nope. Actually, I think I'm finding it."

"Can I get a ride, Mama?" Cooksey interrupted, "I've got to be there by nine for choir rehearsal."

"Sure. I've given up letting you make my heart ache, Julian," Margaret said, looking at him calmly. "Miss Appleton explained last night, your mind's been damaged."

"My mind ain't damaged."

"Not expressing no thanks, for one thing," she glared disapprovingly.

"Hell, I'm thankful."

"Going back out to kill someone or get yourself killed, that comes from a damaged mind. You can't think right."

"You want me to run and hide?"

Natasha added, "Liza Jane says your thinking could be healed like the bullet hole."

"So I'd think like you? No thanks, Sis."

"No, Sonny," Liza Jane said, "so you'd think like you."

"Who do you figure I'm thinking like?"

"You're not thinking really, just reacting."

"I think you're full of bull is what I think," Sonny gave her a sour look with his shaved head tilted.

"Shame on you, Sonny." Jabal said, shaking his head, "Shame on you."

"Look who's talking. You done turned yourself into one of these ninnies." He walked into the living room. "Where'd you put my clothes?"

"They're all ruined," Cooksey said, "take some of mine. I need to go, Mama."

"Would you give him a ride, Sis?" she asked.

"Come with me, Liza Jane."

Walking out to the car, Liza Jane said, "You can sure see what a son like that could do to his mother."

"I was proud of her. In the past she would have exploded and they'd still be going at it at the top of their lungs. Here she was, calm and cool as you please."

Cooksey came jogging out half-dressed. St. Johns was only five blocks away. Two dozen cars were in the parking lot an hour before the service. Cooksey got out and hurried toward the door, looked back and waved.

"Sing good," Natasha called to him.

On the way back to the house Natasha asked, "What can we do about Julian?"

"My Father told me he'd see what he could do."

"You reached him! Oh, I would be so grateful."

When they got back to the house, Jabal was sitting in the living room staring out the window.

"We just got the word on Bobby," he said to Natasha.

"Dead?"

"They had to take his leg off. Couldn't mend it. Four years ago he won the long jump at the state meet, twenty-three feet six inches. My friend since kindergarten."

"Mine too," Natasha said.

"I feel so bad," he said wiping his eyes. A tear escaped the corner of his right eye.

Margaret walked out looking splendid, her black outfit was topped off by a large white hat with black and white feather trim.

Natasha made a "catcall" whistle and said to Liza Jane, "We'd best hustle, young lady.

CHAPTER SEVENTEEN

ST. JOHNS
OCTOBER 5, 2034

J abal drove with the two girls in back. Natasha wore a navy wool suit and Liza Jane a burgundy skirt, emerald green blouse, and a tan blazer.

"I feel like I'm escortin beauty queens," Jabal said.

"You don't look so bad yourself, Darlin," Margaret said looking sideways at him.

"Wish Sonny was with us," he said, looking away from her.

"The rest is up to him," Margaret sighed sadly.

"I'm proud of you, Jabal," Natasha said.

"I'm ready to drop that name, if you're willin, Sio."

"I'm proud of you, Ed Berry," she said, smiling to his eyes in the rear view mirror.

——————◦((◦))◦——————

The lady ushers wore white blouses with purple epaulets and moved with friendly, but formal bearing. The upper half of the wall between the auditorium and the foyer was glass and Liza Jane could see the church was full. An usher walked over to Margaret, whispered something to her, then turned and marched toward the double glass doors of the center aisle. Ushers at the doors opened them in unison, and they were led to the front of the congregation where seats had been reserved.

The choir was sitting behind the platform in white satin robes. The music director played quietly on a large console organ to the left and the choir director sat at the piano to the right of the platform.

Behind the podium, three relaxed ministers in red upholstered built-in seats waited as the last people found places in the balcony over the foyer. Above the balcony was a stained glass window with a large Jesus carrying a lamb. Next to the piano, in pews arranged at a right angle to the congregation were a dozen deacons and opposite them a group of senior women, the "mothers" of the church.

Liza Jane could feel the earnestness of the hearts crowded into the small church. The choir sang a medley of hymns. People of modest ability were given solo parts and rose to the occasion. Cooksey and another boy were given an important passage and paid close attention to their director, a vibrant young woman who played a driving engine of a piano that moved the choir with spirit and feeling.

Two ministers offered greetings and prayers and set the stage for Reverend Pettis' sermon on Jesus' parable of the prodigal son. As he told the old story, he moved about, using his voice to lift his listeners, "How will you welcome your son back from his riotous living? Will you run to him and embrace him?" Many cried out, "Yes, preacher! We hear ya!" He would call back, "Are you listening?" and "Can I get a witness?"

A tall older woman became overwrought with the power of the message in her heart and lost control. She stood and shouted, flinging her arms, then fell sideways and was caught by those sitting by her. Three ushers came quickly and helped her up the aisle, tenderly dealing with her thrashing and shouts of "Yes Lord! Thank you, Jesus."

At the end of his sermon Reverend Pettis said, "Recently I was to make a call downtown, to visit one of our church family, who seemed ready to go on to the Lord.

"I was introduced to Dr. Whitcomb and we went in to see Sister Cheatam. What happened earlier that evening has been on my mind from then until now. Would you mind standing, Sister Cheatam?"

Margaret stood, turned, waved sweetly to the congregation, then started to sit down.

"Please, just stand there a moment. I ask you now, does this look like a woman with a heart struggling to beat its last?"

"No!" many voices responded.

"Something happened in that hospital room earlier that night that Dr. Whitcomb, Sister Cheatam and I will never forget. You had some visitors, didn't you?"

"My daughter, Natasha, and her roommate from school."

"Before you take your seat, would you introduce that beauty sitting next to you." She made the introduction and sat down as applause poured over Natasha.

"Natasha, were you praying for your Mother?"

"Yes. I was praying my best."

"Can you describe what happened?"

"Dr. Whitcomb left us alone with mama, then my roommate said she could help her."

"What did she do?"

"Nothing that I could see. But, when I looked at mama's face she was relaxed and sleeping. So, I kissed her and she woke up, well."

The crowd called out, "Praise God! Thank you, Jesus!" Some held out their hands, palm open to better receive the power of her words.

"Thank you, Natasha," Reverend Pettis smiled. "When I got there, the girls had gone back to school and Sister Cheatam was chatting happily with the nurses. Dr. Whitcomb told Mrs. Cheatam and me that her heart was joyously doing its job, like the heart of a young girl."

Many in the crowd murmured their gratitude.

"We have a wonderful privilege this morning, friends. She's made me take a fresh look at the healing in the gospels and the Acts of the Apostles. Before I introduce Natasha's guest, let me tell you a short story she made me remember. When I first came to be your pastor, I was dressing to make my rounds of the sick and shut-in. As I dressed, a voice told me I was to heal someone that morning.

"Several deacons were with me and as we approached the first house, I was told by the voice that this was where I was to heal.

"What was my reaction? Joy? Eagerness? No. I was afraid! I said 'No' to the voice. I answered, 'I'm just a young preacher. What if I fail in front of the deacons?' I thought about it all the way up the stairs and decided it wouldn't be wise to try such a thing.

"I walked into the lady's bedroom, where she'd been in bed for most of a year. As I shook her hand, she said, 'I was told in my prayer last night you would heal me, Preacher.'

"I said, 'Yes, I know.' And I knew at that point, I wasn't personally responsible. This was something she had worked out with God. I didn't even know what her problem was, but I could feel the healing taking place.

"I'd forgotten about that morning, until I was sitting with Dr. Whitcomb and Sister Margaret. Miss Cheatam, would you introduce your guest to us, please?"

Natasha stood and said, "Reverend Pettis, ministers, deacons, members and friends of St. Johns, let me introduce my Princeton roommate, Liza Jane Appleton."

As Liza Jane stood, the congregation stood with her and began a long standing-ovation, calling out their thanks and appreciation for healing their friend. The deacons stood, as did the ministers behind Reverend Pettis, applauding.

Reverend Pettis motioned for quiet and said, "This as a historic day for our church, Miss Appleton. Would you say a few words?" He moved aside and motioned to the podium.

Ed gently nudged her, gave her his arm and escorted her to the podium. The congregation seated themselves.

Reverend Pettis leaned back to the mic and said, "Let me introduce Natasha's other important guest, Mr. Ed Berry."

Ed said self-consciously into the microphone, "God bless St. Johns."

The crowd greeted him back.

"I'm not much of one for public speaking, but this is a big day for me, too. Last night I gave my life to the Lord Jesus Christ and it was Miss Appleton, here, who turned me around."

The voices of the crowd were strong and instant in support of his news.

"Last night, my friend and Natasha's brother, Julian, was shot and dying. You could drop a fifty-cent piece in the bullet hole under his heart. I knew I'd lost him as I carried him home.

"Within a few minutes, after she saw my dying friend, Miss Appleton healed him. None of us could even find any sign of the wound. We cleaned him up and put him in bed.

"I'll never be the same man I was, before I saw God repair that hole in my friend's chest through the prayers of Miss Appleton. I'm thankful to her for saving my friend, and to you people for building this church for me to come home to."

The applause broke out again and many stood and called out their support for Ed Berry. A minister motioned to a deacon who ushered him to a seat in the front pew with them.

Liza Jane stepped to the microphone and said, "Like Ed, I too love St. Johns."

The applause erupted again.

"You've helped raise Natasha, my roommate, who's one of the best humans on planet earth."

A wave of supportive voices acknowledged that fact.

"I'm a disciple of the Christ from a distant land. In our culture his healing is our only form of healing. I won't be able to attend your church, but I would be pleased if you would consider me an honorary member of St. Johns."

The crowd reacted vigorously in approval, the ministers applauding and nodding in agreement.

Liza Jane spoke briefly into Reverend Pettis' ear and made him smile, then she leaned back toward the mike and said, "God bless St. Johns!"

The preacher motioned to the choir director to come to the podium and said a few words that made her nod and smile. The choir director turned and said something softly to the choir and then returned to the piano.

Reverend Pettis walked over to the podium and said, "Miss Appleton has made a request of us. Can we refuse her?"

He cupped his hand to his ear and the crowd as one voice said, "No!"

"I didn't think so. Natasha, would you sing for us?"

The choir director raised her right hand and the choir stood together. The organ and piano started softly, the sweet strains of Amazing Grace.

Natasha mounted the steps of the platform and one of the ministers handed her a microphone. She turned with moist eyes to the crowd and sang. The choir joined in behind, humming, then singing in support of her rich voice.

When they walked in the front door, Ed called, "You still here, Sonny?"

"Yes," came the subdued reply from the bedroom.

Ed looked in, "You alright?" His friend was dressed, lying on the bed staring at the ceiling.

"Come in and shut the door."

"What's up, Man?"

"Strange things been goin on in here, Jabal."

"What now?"

"See that black box on the dresser?"

"Yeah."

"When I woke up, after y'all was gone, a little white dude was standing on it."

"You musta still been dreaming."

"That's what I thought. So I sat up and said, 'Who're you?' to the little guy."

"And?"

"He just smiled this cool smile and said with a big ole voice, 'Mornin, Julian.' I swear to God, I liketa peed the bed, Jabal."

"He knew your name?"

"He knew everything. Said I'd be dead by summer. Said Jesus sent him to talk me inta livin."

"My God! You think he really did send him?"

"Hell, I don't know. He said Jesus wants me to live."

"What else?"

"He knew all about respect, how I been fighting for it, but never really had none. He asked me to cross over and find my respect on the other side."

"The other side?"

"Of life, dipstick."

"Oh."

"I told him about you and how lame you was, bailing on me. He said, 'Nah, Ed's on the road. He's gonna live and get his respect.'"

"He said that?"

"We talked about fighting. He ast if it'd ever done me a licka good. Said 'Jesus was no chicken, even though he didn't fight.' I said, 'Romans hung him out to dry, didn't they?' He said, 'No, actually Jesus hung them out to dry, Julien. Everyone knows that score, Jesus one, Romans nothin.' Then, it happened."

"What?"

"This is the part . . ." he looked at Jabal, smiling a smile Jabal hadn't seen from him since they were kids. "This is what really got me."

"What!"

"An angel, Man."

"No!"

"All of a sudden there was all this light and she was sitting there on the dresser, shining up the whole room."

"This is fantastic! What did you say?"

"I didn't know what to say. I just stared at her like a rummy."

"What'd she do?"

"She said, 'I need your help, Sonny.'"

"No!"

"Swear to God! Man, I lost it. That hit me hard, Man. An angel asking help from me!"

"Go on!"

"Finally, I got it together and asked her what kind of help she needed."

"What'd she say?"

"She said she needed help with her Campaign for Peace."

"You gonna help?"

"Hell, Man! If an angel asked you for help, what would you do?"

"I'll help with you."

"Damn right you will, Jabal."

"What do we have to do?"

"I don't know. What do you know about a Campaign for Peace?"

"We'll have to ask Sis and Miss Appleton. They know."

"The angel said she'd be there, looking for me, Jabal."

"Jesus Lord, Sonny! What I wouldn't give to meet a real honestagod angel."

"It's more than you can even handle. I'm tellin ya, Jabal, you won't believe it."

After a knock on the door Natasha asked through the door, "You guys ready for dinner?"

"Come on in, Sis," Julian said.

Natasha opened the door and smiled at Julian's peaceful face.

"What's this bouta Campaign for Peace?" he asked.

"Starts on the 15th. Yesterday, Liza Jane and I got Reverend Pettis' permission to use St. Johns. Why?"

"Sonny had some visitors while we were at church," Ed said pointing at the box on the dresser.

"I see. What do you know about the campaign, Sonny?"

"Nothing, 'cept I promised to help. You have to set this up for me, Natasha. I promised."

"This is Liza Jane's mother's campaign. You can ask Liza Jane about it."

Natasha came into the dining room with her arm around Julian's waist, "I found a new Julian in Cooksey's bedroom. He wants to help with the peace campaign."

Margaret stood staring at him, holding a bowl of baked apples, "Merciful heavens, the prodigal son," she mumbled.

"We're going to need your help, Sonny and yours too Ed," Liza Jane said.

"What can we do to help?" Julian asked.

"To start with, we need to buy a whole bunch of houses."

"We do?" he replied with wide eyes.

"Yes. And I need you to get Duke Sims and his friends to help, too."

Ed and Sonny looked at each other, then back at her. Finally, Julian said, "I don't think you really want the Duke involved, Miss."

"Yes we do, Julian. Mr. Sims promised to help. Just mention my name, he'll remember."

<hr />

Larry Bianchi and Ian Caldwell turned into the campus at 9AM, as they had every day for a week in their stolen red plumbing van.

"Wake up, Junior!" Larry's big voice jarred Ian awake.

"Do we gotta go through it all again? I'm so sick of it."

"Don't start whining. Today could be the payoff."

"We go over and over every damned detail. What d'ya say we back off a just a bit? We've got it down by now."

"Don't rile me, Ian."

"Is this how you built your company, Uncle Larry?"

"You don't make it, if you can't focus."

Larry Bianchi glared at the road ahead. His nephew had no idea what he'd been through. It had taken all the fortitude he could muster to make it through the last year. His company was in shambles, a casualty of the prolonged construction recession. Next week the IRS had notified him that they would start levying his accounts and impounding his equipment. His attorney was drafting a Chapter 7 bankruptcy for the company and another for him and his wife personally. Twenty years of work and everything he had left was about to go down the drain.

When things got tough, he'd reacted as he always had, by working harder, but hard work wasn't enough to solve this problem. As the losses continued to mount he'd grown bitter, the kind of anger he hadn't felt since the Iraq War.

Over lunch one day, his banker explained to him who was to blame for the year long recession. Who else? Congress!

His banker explained that for decades they've overspent their budgets, let the trade imbalance get out of control, piled one entitlement program on another, until the problems became too big to solve without costing them an election. So, instead of working for solutions, they decided to let the problems persist and that's why the economy started tanking last spring. And now the bombings have shut down everything. There was no way his construction company could survive. When his wife told him about the filthy rich Princeton student, he went into action. Larry Bianchi wasn't going down without a fight.

⸺ ((●)) ⸺

Liza Jane listened from the back of the graduate seminar on quantum physics. Human physicists were attempting with ever more powerful machines to understand the basic building blocks of matter. It seemed ironic that bigger and bigger machines were required to study smaller and smaller particles. Some day they would get to the logical extension of Dr. Kramer's discovery: the basic building block of the universe is consciousness.

She'd read Einstein's work and marveled at his clear glimpses and mostly deft conclusions, all from intuitive mathematical analysis. It seemed right that one of his protégés was leading the way out of the matter illusion.

The professor, Dr. Lyons, led a lively discussion. Liza Jane smiled at the directness and incisiveness of the students, not intimidated by the lecturer or his reputation. It was like watching a group with a bogus map, heading energetically in the wrong direction. She wanted to raise her hand and tell them, but instead just listened.

After the seminar, Dr. Lyons looked up with a stern expression as Liza Jane walked by his lectern and said, "Miss Appleton, can I have a word with you?"

"Yes sir."

His eyes joked with her over his specs as he said, "Dan Kramer warned me about you. I was expecting some tough questions from back there."

"I'm just auditing the class and didn't feel I should get involved in the discussion."

"I'm only interested in what you think, young lady, not your enrollment status."

"Seems strange, the way you divide life into these disconnected studies."

"Hell, I'm over my head half the time in physics."

"To me, all your sciences are interrelated."

"Science has become too complicated for anyone to work in more than one discipline in any depth."

"Perhaps you're making it too complicated."

"You are a troublemaker aren't you," he laughed. "Let me walk you out."

They chatted for the block and a half to his VW van. As he said goodbye, Liza Jane opened her notepad, jotted something and handed him an equation. $E = M$.

"What about the c-squared?"

"My equation actually stands on its own. C-squared is just the amount of energy required to produce the illusion of mass."

"I can see you've been hanging around Kramer too much."

"He's right. You should hang around him more yourself."

He was stunned by her confident tone. As she headed up the walk, he looked back from her to the equation.

The evening his wife told him about Princeton's richest coed,

Larry had plunged into action. Months of impasse were broken. Now, after many hours of planning, he was ready. The tall rich blond walking toward the arch was going to put him back in business. She was alone on her way back from the seminar. There was no one between her and the van and the kids behind her would lose sight of her when she turned the corner.

As Liza Jane approached the arch she picked up a source of malicious thought and stopped, looked around and listened. Anger was so common in the human world. Her father had warned her to be on guard and she was, but none of it had been directed at her, so she turned the corner and walked through the arch.

Larry stepped from behind a column, hit her with a leather sap and caught her with his left arm as she fell. He carried her quickly to the side door of the van, climbed in and shut the door. The van started slowly down the access road, turned left into the street and eased into traffic.

In a hushed voice Ian asked, "Anyone see?"

"No. Drive slowly."

"Didn't hit her too hard, did ya?"

"No." Larry put a headband over her eyes, then taped it in place with duct tape.

Larry emailed a ransom note to Natasha Cheatam from a stolen laptop, demanding a $10 million ransom, while Ian drove down to the Arontack River. They turned into a vacant farm four miles from town and backed up to a dilapidated barn adjacent to a large pond. He opened the doors of the barn and connected the helicopter they'd stolen from Larry's largest rival on Long Island to the trailer hitch on the van. After pulling it out of the barn, he removed the blond, opened the windows and both roof vents of the red van and rolled it down the bank. It floated for a few moments, then slowly sank out of sight in the brackish water.

Larry stuffed Liza Jane behind the seats and squeezed handcuffs on her wrists and ankles. Then the stolen Bell cargo chopper headed for an abandoned farmhouse on a remote stretch of the Jersey shore. His Army flight training was rusty, but it was coming back. Above the noise Ian said, "Gotta hand it to ya, Uncle Larry, clockwork. Everything, like clockwork."

"This is the easiest part. Stay focused, Ian."

They both felt movement and Ian watched their captive regain consciousness.

Liza Jane came to with a start and jerked against the cuffs and slammed her head against a seat support. Her head throbbed against the tightly wound duct tape. The shackles and the pulsating machine sickened her. She caught herself and didn't scream, gritted her teeth and fought for control. Breathing dirt that danced against her face off the metal floor made her cough and through the coughing she tried to think clearly. The pounding in her head worsened. She hated this noisy vibrating contraption. The nerve of these fools!

As she got control of her thinking and removed herself mentally from the nightmare-like experience, the pain subsided and she focused on the handcuffs. Nothing. She didn't have the power to open them. How pleased she'd become with her progress in the Way. Now, here she was, needing the power of certainty and realization, but her thought was so full of fury she was powerless.

She sensed two males. One full of bitterness, the other, she couldn't get much of anything, unthinking. She tried to deal with her anger. Then, a wave of nausea gripped her and her stomach cramped. Her mind was spinning and she couldn't stop it.

By the time the shuddering craft touched down and the engine quieted, she was more at peace. Through the unshackling and re-shackling, she felt the big one's strength. Her father had always seemed physically strong to her, but this man had enormous strength.

Ian stowed the chopper in the barn and Larry deposited the girl in the room prepared for her. Her cuffs were attached to a chain belt. Boards had been nailed over the windows and the furniture removed except for a bed frame with a mattress.

Without sight, she slowly explored her prison. No matter how hard she tried to focus, her smoldering anger defeated her efforts to align herself with power from the Giver of Life.

Natasha couldn't make out Liza Jane's telepathic message inside her thought. Her voice wasn't clear enough, but she could sense distress. She hurried back to the room, but there was no roommate and no note. They'd agreed to meet at eleven and work through lunch and the afternoon, organizing the tasks remaining to start the campaign. She knocked on Ary's door.

"Have you seen Liza Jane?"

"No."

"We'd planned to work all afternoon. There's so much to do. She's twenty minutes late and left no note. I'm worried, this isn't at all like her."

"She must've forgotten."

"Not a chance." Her voice tailed off as she imagined an attack on her roommate. The thought sickened her. Suddenly, she felt so dizzy she had to grab the doorjamb to keep from falling.

Ary steadied her, picked her up, carried her into her room, laid her on her bed, and asked, "Why so upset, Tosh? You're trembling."

She described the distress in Liza Jane's telepathic message.

"That's wild. She's started talking to you like she does her mom. I remember now, she mentioned a physics seminar. How about the cell phone I gave you? Any messages?"

"No. She doesn't use phones or the internet.

"Check anyway."

She scrolled down her messages and read the ransom demand.

At the third or fourth word she screamed and burst into tears. He took it from her and read the note.

"This is the worst thing conceivable, Ary! If anything has happened to her it would wipe out the peace campaign."

"Let's try to reach her father. Maybe we can transpond with him."

She got up, still wobbly, located the two transponders and opened them on the floor. They sat on her bed and stared at them. Nothing happened. Ary found her hand on the bed and said quietly, "We'll find her, Natasha, and she'll be fine."

She looked into his eyes, took a deep breath, interlaced her fingers in his and said, "Let's reach out to Lord Appleton in our thought. These things work mentally, somehow."

"What should we think?"

"Let him know we need him. Ask him to come to us."

After a few moments, they saw a faint glow in the box.

The light stayed dim, then dwindled. Natasha closed her eyes, tightened her grip on Ary's hand and said, "Lord Appleton, please come to us. We need to talk with you."

"Whoa! You did it!" Ary exclaimed. A blurred image above the box quickly came into focus.

When the figure evolved into a small image of Lord Appleton, Natasha said, "Thank you for answering our call."

"I've just got a minute, Natasha. I'm communing with the Calderan Council right now."

"I'm so worried, Liza Jane called to me for help and I just got a ransom demand."

"The Council is deciding our response right now. There's strong feeling among the members to bring her home. Some Council members feel she isn't strong enough for this mission."

"This is awful! We have to find her," Natasha said.

"Her mother's not in favor of ending her mission and has agreed to help."

"Is she with Liza Jane now?" Natasha asked.

"Let's make contact with Jane and ask her."

A moment later, Liza Jane's light image glowed above the second lighted box, blindfolded and shackled.

Natasha sobbed softly against Ary's shoulder.

"You alright, Daughter?" her father asked quietly.

"My head's not pounding quite so badly."

"Is your mother coming, Jane?"

"Yes. Ary and Tosh, would you contact David?"

"What should we tell him?" Ary asked.

"My mother will intervene, but tell David he needs to contact the government police. Humans need to make the capture, without violence. Ask David to send help."

"How does he find you?"

E.A. interrupted, "I'm in my ship above the house where she's being held captive, right now. I'll guide the rescuers."

Andrews answered the phone in his Springfield home, "Yes, Ary. What's up?"

"Liza Jane's been kidnapped."

"Damn! I should have known she could be a target."

"She's not badly hurt, but her people are understandably upset. Some want to bring her home and terminate her mission."

"She should have been given federal protection. We've got to rescue her immediately and keep her mother's campaign on track."

"This is Natasha, Mr. President. We've got Liza Jane on the transponder. She asks if you can get the FBI to make the rescue. Her father's ship is right above the farmhouse where she's being held and he will guide the rescuers. Her mother is with her and wants you to deal with her daughter's captors, hopefully without violence."

"I can have some Army Rangers there within the hour. Ask Lord

Appleton to pick me up here in Springfield, Illinois. I'd like to be there when she's released."

"Of course, David," E.A. responded. "I'll be there in fifteen minutes."

Liza Jane could see her mother's face as she spoke, "It's important that we fully understand Mr. Bianchi's thinking and motivation, Liza Jane," Hamama said as she opened the handcuffs with her thought. As Liza Jane unwound the tape caught in her hair, her mother explained, "I've learned a great deal from working with the Iraqi general, and Natasha's brother. We have to completely understand how to deal with anger-based thinking in order to make our campaign a success."

"I have work to do in that area myself, Mother."

"This experience has been good for you, Jane. I knew this mission would show you some of the progress you have yet to make."

"Who're you talking to in there?" Ida Mae Bianchi demanded from the other side of the door.

"Just myself, Mrs. Bianchi."

"How'd you know my name?"

Ida Mae unbolted the door and opened it. To her amazement, the prisoner was free of her bonds, sitting on the bed next to a small radiant light figure.

Hamama suggested, "Why don't you invite your husband to join us and we'll discuss your predicament, Mrs. Bianchi."

"Our predicament?"

"Yes," Hamama said kindly. "You and your husband will soon be on your way to prison with Ian."

They heard Mrs. Bianchi groan and collapse in the hall.

Larry was lying on the sofa when he heard her fall. He sat up and opened his eyes, but could see nothing. He called out to her and to Ian. His wife didn't answer and he could hear Ian snoring at the kitchen table. He found his gun on the table next to him and yelled, "Ida Mae! Ian!"

He got no answer from either and buried his face in his hands in terror. Slowly he opened his fingers, but there was just blackness. Then, suddenly, there was a glowing female inside his thinking.

"Hello, Larry."

"What is this? Who are you?"

"You'll regain your sight when you can see clearly that nothing good comes from terrorism."

CHAPTER EIGHTEEN

DAVID AND LIZA JANE
OCTOBER 8, 2014

When it ascended from the blighted New Jersey farm, E.A.'s ship left behind the Apache gunships. Above them, six gold ships hovered then moved southward. Suddenly, one of them broke ranks and swooped close, waggling a parting gesture. Liza Jane waved to General Landon, who banked toward the southern horizon and accelerated instantly to ten thousand miles per hour.

David exclaimed breathlessly, "MY GOD! Look at that thing go!"

Hamama shook her head and said, "General Landon always had a streak of showoff in him."

David heard her in his mind, rather than with his ears. She was sitting on the other side of Liza Jane. He grinned at the sight of her.

Liza Jane said, "Hard for the general to stand off and not go into action, I'll bet."

"He was beside himself!" her mother responded, "The idea of someone stealing his godchild!"

"Thank goodness he didn't blast them."

"I had to convince him for the thousandth time, the Calderan Way would resolve the problem. Makes him grind his teeth," she chuckled.

David was enjoying the give and take between mother and daughter when Hamama looked at him. He sensed the depth of her affection and surprised himself by saying, "E.A. says my being here was your idea in the first place, Your Majesty."

"I've come to love you, David. You're a lot like Ernest. You have a heart like his and I know you will make an important difference to your world."

"I've given a lot of thought to E.A.'s proposal and feel honored that you want to make me part of the bridge between your people and mine." He turned and took both of Liza Jane's hands and looked into her eyes, "So, if Liza Jane's willing, I would like to marry your daughter and join your family."

Liza Jane smiled, "I'll make you glad of that decision, David Andrews."

E.A. walked in from the bridge and embraced him, "Welcome to our family, David." Then, with his hands on their shoulders, he closed his eyes and said, "With gratitude for the good that will flow from this union, I acknowledge before the Giver of Life, the joining of these two soul mates, David and Jane."

Hamama slipped her arm around E.A.'s waist and said, "You should give them the rest of your news."

"The Calderan Council has agreed that if you made this decision, David, I could pass my title to my daughter and retire. Are you ready to take that step, Jane?"

"Yes, I'm ready, Father."

"Let's pray together."

The four joined hands and E.A. said, "Giver of Life, bless the Calderan people and their new leader. Give her the wisdom to fully grasp your Way. Bless our son, David, as he walks at her side, and works to strengthen our bridge to the human world. Hold these two in the palm of your hands, forever."

Strong emotions surged through David. Suddenly, for the first time in a very long time, he felt part of a family.

E.A. continued, "David, are you willing to be consort to the Calderan queen and share her burdens?"

"I am."

"I'll stay and support you both as long as I'm needed."

They drank several toasts of warm gatava. Finally, David asked his bride, "Can I kiss the queen?"

She nodded hesitantly, "This is not our custom, David. I don't know how."

David took her in his arms, looked into her pale yellow eyes and kissed her. Her lips quivered at his touch. Then, she closed her arms around his neck with the fingers of one hand in his hair and kissed him back, soft and sweet.

Finally, they eased their embrace and she drew a long breath, glanced over her shoulder at her mother and said, "Oh my! I see what you mean. I'm trembling all over."

Hamama smiled, "I promise, you'll never get used to those feelings. My heart pounds every time."

"Umm. That was nice," she said, smiling at her new husband. "How about the rest of the human marriage customs? We need a honey . . . what is it called, David?"

"A honeymoon for our first date?" he asked with a wry smile.

Liza Jane blushed, "That's not right, is it."

E.A. said, "I'll stay with Reverend Pettis in Newark tonight and you two can slip back to Caldera. Your people have been planning a celebration, in hopes this day would come. Tomorrow afternoon, we'll meet in Newark. After the campaign, you'll have lots of time to be together. This ship is yours now."

Hamama interrupted, "I need to go. This is one of the great moments of my life." At that, she levitated to kiss her husband, then her daughter. Lastly, she kissed David on the cheek, which he felt inside him, like her voice. Then she left, smiling happily.

"Where's she off to?" David asked Liza Jane.

"She's still making arrangements."

"Can you tell me more about the campaign?"

She shook her head, "No, let's let it be a surprise for you. Oh Father, we need to pick up Tosh and Ary."

David sat down, pulled Liza Jane onto his lap, and wrapped his arms around her, "I know I'm going to love you."

"I have the same feelings. I've always known I would marry a human man and I've dreamed he would be someone deeply good like my father. And you are."

"I need to tell you, I'm feeling a bit awkward right now. We barely know each other. I'm old enough to be your father. And it's been a very long time since I've been intimate with a woman, or even been with a woman."

Liza Jane slipped off his lap, "I don't want to rush things. Human ways are more physically intimate than ours. I've been concerned I might seem cool to you."

"You're fine. This is just going to take a little time to get used to. I don't have an arranged marriage every day."

Her father's voice interrupted, "I reached Natasha on Ary's cell phone. She's on the intercom, but a bit fuzzy."

A crackly voice came from the speaker behind David's head, "Can you hear me, Liza Jane?"

"Yes, Tosh. Meet us behind Jadwin. You're both invited to our wedding reception in Caldera."

Ary's Corvette was waiting. Liza Jane noticed how happy her roommate looked and how beautiful. Ary put the top up and they held hands as they walked toward the ship, laughing at something she said.

When Natasha saw her roommate, she burst into tears and embraced her. Ary embraced them both and when they untangled he had tears, as well. Natasha said, "I was so worried, just prayed and prayed you were okay. Thank God you are. Ary kept me together. I couldn't have gotten through it without him."

She and Liza Jane rocked back and forth with the taller one stroking her hair gently, "I'm glad to be back together. Now, we need to sit down, so Father can take off."

━━➤ ◄((◉))► ◄━━

Ted Kaufman looked into the camera lens and spoke quietly to the millions anxiously awaiting his report about the mysterious happenings in Newark. "I'll begin this morning by introducing my two guests. First, Henry Holt, former President Andrews' chief of staff and second, Reverend Robert Pettis, the pastor of St. Johns Missionary Baptist Church in Newark.

"During my daily updates I've tried to describe the remarkable developments taking place in Newark during the past week. If you've missed some, I'll quickly recap for you. Liza Jane Appleton, the Calderan princess, showed up last week with hundreds of checks for $500,000 each, made out to the owners of all the homes within a mile of St. Johns. What's going on, Reverend Pettis?"

"Many have asked, Mr. Kaufman, why St. Johns? Why did the princess choose our small church in one of the older neighborhoods of Newark as the place to start the Campaign for World Peace? The answer is that she visited our church as a guest of her college roommate. She loved our church and has decided to honor us in this way."

"Mr. Holt, doesn't this seem like a strange way for the people of Caldera to introduce themselves to the human world, through a small obscure church in a black neighborhood of Newark?"

"I asked former President Andrews about that and he said, 'Reminds me of the approach Jesus took in his homeland. He chose to start by teaching working class people around the Sea of Galilee. This makes perfect sense to me'."

"Reverend Pettis, tell us about the homes they've purchased around your church."

"These are small older homes worth between $100,000 and $150,000. It's been a wonderful windfall for those homeowners. Also, people haven't been told this, but where the homes were rented, the tenants have been given checks for $50,000 to generously cover their relocation expenses and in some cases to purchase homes of their own. Owners and tenants had until noon today to remove whatever they wanted from the homes."

"Mr. Holt, tell us about your old boss. What role is he playing in all this?"

"President Andrews called me this morning to announce his marriage to Liza Jane Appleton, the newly-crowned queen of the Calderan people."

"Our former president is married to their new queen. That's big news, isn't it, Mr. Holt?"

"It is. In fact, I haven't heard any news that was more encouraging than this in years, Mr. Kaufman. Also, you may have heard, Ted, they gave the City of Newark a check for $500 million to purchase the rights-of-way and city improvements in that area of town."

"So what's it all for, Mr. Holt? What are they planning to do with all this real estate?"

"I asked President Andrews."

"And what did he say?"

"He said, 'You'll have to wait and see, Hank'."

* * *

The trip south went quickly. David focused on getting better acquainted with his new bride. Liza Jane flew the ship and David sat next to her.

"How are you feeling about marrying an older man who is pretty much a complete stranger, Liza Jane?"

Liza Jane was quiet for a while before answering, "I know you better than you might imagine, David. I love your kind nature and your deep goodness."

"You didn't mention the age difference."

Again there was a silence before she responded, "I've always known I would marry a younger man."

David chuckled and said, "But instead you married a much older one."

She turned to him and smiled, "I hope you can soon get over your fixation with the number of times the earth circles the sun. That's not a good measurement of anything."

"I've made sixty-one trips since my birth in 1973. Just for the record, Your Majesty, how many times have you circled the sun?"

"I haven't wanted to tell you because I know how bound humans are by the laws you've made up regarding time measurements."

"Tell me anyway."

"I was born in your year 1914."

David stared at her in shocked disbelief.

Finally, Liza Jane broke the awkward silence, "It's not too late for you to get out of our marriage, David. I know what you're thinking."

"No. Please pardon my astonishment. You seem so . . . so young. How can you . . . look . . . and act like a twenty-year-old?"

"Let's let this go for now, David. And please don't tell my human friends. They might not understand. I hope you will soon be able to see through the illusion of time and especially years. All they do is make you old."

"When I'm a hundred and fifty-eight do you think I'll look as good as your father?"

She smiled and winked, "Better."

———◦((◦))◦———

"Ted Kaufman, ladies and gentlemen. It's my pleasure to be sitting across from President Vandenberg in his private office in the White House. Good morning, Mr. President."

"Morning, Ted. It's great to be with you and your audience."

"First, if you would, please tell us about your recent obvious change of heart, Mr. President. We hear no more from you about nuking Pakistan."

"Well, Ted, I must admit I was fit to be tied after Congress turned me down flat. I went back to the White House in a fit of rage and thought seriously about resigning, as I lay in bed staring at the ceiling all night."

"Then what?"

"Ted, do you remember how absolutely loony I thought President Andrews sounded talking about a secret alien species and angels and all?"

"Yes sir."

"Well, in the middle of that night, I got mine."

"Excuse me, Mr. President, you got your what?"

"President Andrews' angel was suddenly sitting on my dresser glowing softly in the dark."

"Oh my goodness! What'd she say?"

"She said, 'Good morning, Joseph.' No one's called me that since my mother passed."

"Then what?"

"She confirmed everything President Andrews had tried to tell me as being the God's truth. I thanked her for forgiving my pigheadedness and asked her why she'd allowed someone like me to become president."

Ted laughed and asked, "What was her answer?"

"She said she wanted David to marry her daughter and become a bridge between Caldera and the human world. She said she needed my organizational skills to support her campaign."

"Did you agree to support it?"

"Hells bells, Ted! What do you think? What would you do if you had an angel sitting on your dresser?"

"So, how are you going to help her?"

"No. No. Ted. The 'how' is between me and her. But she did say I could send Colonel Braxton to your show tomorrow with satellite photos of what they're doing. You know we had to set up a 'no fly' zone over that part of Newark last week because too many newshounds and their choppers were hovering overhead."

"Have you spoken with former President Andrews since you took office?"

"Yeah. I'll tell you, that was one tough call to make. I basically spent ten or fifteen minutes apologizing and telling him how totally wrong I was and how absolutely right he was about everything. I told him I had no business taking over his job and if he hadn't moved on to an even bigger job, I'd step down and welcome him back immediately. Then, I assured him I was ready 24/7 to do anything he asks and provide everything he needs. I'm putting the entire federal government at his disposal during this crucially important Campaign for World Peace."

"All this because an angel called you, Joseph?"

President Vandenberg laughed and said, "All I'll say is that President Andrews sure can pick mothers-in-law. If we can learn half of what she's going to try to teach us, we'll see permanent peace come to this troubled planet."

"Thank you, Mr. President. There you have it, ladies and gentlemen. Everyone President Andrews' new mother-in-law calls on seems to have a complete transformation. Will she be able to transform you and me, as well? Tune in tomorrow morning for satellite photos of what's happening in Newark."

David relaxed on the flight deck enjoying the view from 100,000 feet and contemplated his new life. Glancing at his amazing new wife he asked, "What's our speed, Your Majesty?"

"The trip takes about ninety minutes and it's about 9,000 miles, so that's about a 100 miles a minute, Prince Andrews."

"What's the top end on this thing?"

"No idea. It automatically calculates the speed and altitude for a comfortable flight to your destination. We should take it up in orbit sometime and see what it'll do."

"Have you been to other planets?"

"I haven't been anyplace. This ship's just designed for local use. Father's been all over the planet."

"And your mother?"

"Lots of star systems in many galaxies."

David watched the distant edge of the earth darken and contemplated the possibility of traveling to the Andromeda Galaxy, the Milky Way's nearest neighbor, 2.4 million light years away. How could she travel such distances he wondered? Worm holes?

Liza Jane interrupted his thought, "Let's focus on each other, David. I've been praying that you could feel at home with me and with our people."

"There's so much I have to learn."

"Just relax. Let the Calderan people love you and cherish our marriage. They know what you've been through and they're all praying you can be happy in your new life."

David watched a storm vortex turning far below, "You think it's realistic to expect humans to give up violence?"

"They must."

"I grew up in a home full of anger. Sometimes I'd beg my parents to try being kind to each other."

"How did they respond?"

"They'd glare at me then go on fighting. It was their only form of communication."

"My father feels the same skepticism. When we found out that terrorists were using chain reaction weapons, my mother and I decided to try to help humans survive."

They were both quiet for a time, then David said, "I wonder, if my parents had been given the choice, 'Either change the wiring of your hearts, or die.' Could they have?"

"That's the question. What do you think?"

"I don't know. When I was small, I'd lie in bed listening to them screaming at each other downstairs, crying my heart out."

"That's so sad. Natasha's my inspiration in all this. She grew up good and kind, no matter how much hatred and violence was going on around her. And now I hear how you grew up, so I know it's possible for humans to be good and kind, no matter what."

"Can you fit in here with me?" he asked.

Jane stepped from her chair and squeezed her hips in with his. They wrapped their arms around each other and he turned to her slightly illumined face and touched her lips with his, "We'll never be like my parents, will we?"

"It'll only get better."

"He sang with a Hank William's twang, "It'll only get better, from now to forever, from now to forever, amen."

"I promise," she whispered and kissed him back.

"Every time we fight, I'm going to remind you."

"No fights, ever," she whispered and kissed him again.

"How does your mother travel?"

She looked at him a moment before saying, "She doesn't."

He studied her eyes and waited, smiling.

"When your expression of life is only what the Giver of Life is thinking, you can be wherever He thinks you or needs you."

David thought about that, "And since He fills the entire universe . . ."

"She is wherever she's needed, instantly."

"Can you do that?"

"Not yet. But we will."

"We?" he smiled. "What kind of progress does it take?"

"You get right down to it, don't you? We're comprised of thoughts, what we think of ourselves, what others think of us, and what the Giver of Life thinks of us."

"I can see the possibility of bringing my own thought into line with His, but what can you do about other peoples' thoughts about you?"

"Calderans only recognize each other's true identity. In your world you have to build an impregnable defense against false thoughts about you. I didn't do a good enough job of that and got into trouble."

"Tough for your dad. His wife's made the breakthrough and he's still stuck here with us."

"He'll soon be traveling with her. He's already traveled."

"That's right, he traveled to meet me out on the ice. Seems amazing."

"Not to us. There are many more of us working out in the galaxies, than live in Caldera."

"What are they doing out there?"

"They serve the messenger. When he's born to a life form ready for the message, some of us are assigned to support him while he grows up."

"You're his guardian angels!" he exclaimed. "Protecting the Christ child!"

She laughed, "That's what humans call us."

He imagined an exotic alien virgin listening to a Calderan angel explaining the wondrous origin of the child in her womb. "Perhaps on a planet ten billion light years from here, a virgin is having a baby tonight."

"There are marvelous stories of the Christ child's birth told across the universe," she said. "A pure-hearted couple in humble circumstances, fulfilling centuries of prophecy by their spiritual seers."

"How long do you think it'll take me to get my first assignment?"

"That's entirely up to you, my prince."

"Ted Kaufman here, ladies and gentlemen. This morning my guest is Colonel Jim Braxton, who brought some satellite photos of what's happening around St. Johns Missionary Baptist Church in Newark.

"Colonel, before we look at your photos, what's your take on all this? Who's making the decisions? Who's the real leader of this campaign?"

"I get the feeling the daughter, Liza Jane Appleton, is calling the shots and her Princeton roommate must have a lot of influence on her. May be ironic, Ted, but Miss Cheatam seems as much an ambassador to the Calderan queen as former President Andrews."

"I've met Miss Cheatam, Colonel, and believe me we could do a lot worse. What about all the construction?"

"A large area around the church was sealed off on Monday by a high opaque fence. General Landon's guys in the gold ships have been coming and going constantly."

"What are they doing with all the houses they bought?"

"Here, let's take a look at some photos. The houses, the streets, everything is gone. The colonel showed him two slightly murky photos, "These satellite images will give you an idea."

Ted brought the first photo up on TV screens around the world, "What do you make of it, Colonel? Looks like they're making a big park."

"Yes, that's the look of it. The houses and streets are gone and they've built that huge grandstand and a stair structure. They all dwarf the church, which is now the centerpiece of the whole development."

"What's the stair thing for do you think?"

"I couldn't make it out, so I had the guys over at the CIA take a look with their equipment. They think it's a stairway up to a big landing pad. Looks like they're going to make their entrance in their big gold ships onto that pad."

Ted got excited, "They've painted the stairs and the grandstand gold to match their ships."

"Paint? Come on Ted. That's not their style. I had the CIA guys run a spectrogram from one of their satellites. Look at the way it reflects the light. That's gold, Ted, it's all solid gold!"

Ted looked again, "Doesn't seem possible. Those grandstands are huge! And look, the stairs are too." Ted leaned back smiling, "I like these people, Colonel Braxton. Bring thousands of tons of gold to a rundown part of Newark and build a grandstand and stairs with it in a park around Natasha's church. If it looks like this on a blurry digital image from a hundred miles up, imagine what it looks like up close. These people are fantastic. What kind of help have they asked for so far, Colonel?"

"The first need has already been met. The Air Force brought in their children's choir from all over the country."

Ted smiled, "I got that word this morning. They've flown in boys and girls from every state in the union. Over two thousand, I'm told."

"That's right, the colonel confirmed. We're still finding housing for them. I can't wait to hear them sing."

"Reverend Pettis told me about their rehearsals. He said none of us will ever forget hearing them sing. He said his choir director weeps while they rehearse accompanied by the New York Philharmonic Orchestra. I hear the administration is going to help with transportation for the campaign."

"Right. We're going to provide bus transportation for the people that don't have their own."

"Buses for how many people. Any idea?"

"We don't know yet, but I'm sure it'll take as many as we can come up with. I know we've gathered over thirty thousand, so far."

"Thirty thousand buses!"

"And we know that won't be nearly enough for the crowds they're expecting. We may need a half million before we're done."

"Buses?"

"The colonel smiled and nodded. "This is no small-time campaign these people are cooking up, Ted."

"How are they handling the publicity? I haven't seen any ads on the major media."

"I asked the former president. He said his mother-in-law has put out a special invitation."

"What kind of invitation? Can we broadcast it?"

"Ted, you're probably not aware, but all forms of transport are booked solid into Newark this week. My adjutant said most of the charter planes and buses in existence are en route to Newark. All the hotels from Boston to Phily are booked."

Ted beamed, "How could I doubt the mother-in-law's effectiveness? Reverend Pettis mentioned that members of his congregation are putting up hundreds that have already come. They each heard a voice in their prayer, asking them to come to Newark. An elderly lady staying at the pastor's own home told him on Saturday she walked out of her house in Cleveland and started hitchhiking. She had almost nothing to eat on the way."

"Colonel Braxton said, "So the invitation was sent to people who could hear it in their prayers."

"Yes. They obviously wanted to start with people who pray effectively."

"Sounds like they've got hundreds of thousands here and more on the way," Ted said. "I'm disappointed in myself for not hearing her invitation. Did you get yours, Colonel?"

"No, I'm afraid not. When I asked about food, water, toilets, and emergency facilities the former president explained that the guys in the gold ships have all that under control."

———————

Sailing across the sky at 6,000 miles per hour Natasha realized she'd had no fear on this trip. Ary had fallen asleep holding her hand. His head was nestled against her head and shoulder. She studied their two hands with fingers intertwined on the sofa cushion, some dark brown fingers and some light tan. She'd resisted the temptation to pray to God for Ary's love. She knew that was wrong. But she did pray to be worthy of his love if he should come to love her. Now his breath was on her skin between her shoulder and her right breast. It felt warm and sweet. She closed her eyes and thought about Caldera. Going back to heaven with her best friend and the man she loves. What could be better?

As the air tram left the terminal, Natasha asked Ary, "What thoughts fill your head on your return to Caldera, Prince Hussein? Like many of the nice places your folks have sent you off to?"

He laughed, "You sure know how to put a worldly punk in his place, don't you? Caldera is in a league by itself. It beats the hell out of anyplace I've ever been. How about your return trip, Your Natajesty?"

"Peaceful. Real peaceful," she said with her head laid back on the top of the seat and her eyes closed.

When the air tram door opened, David felt a curious mixture of apprehension as the stranger-husband of their beloved queen, and a deep sense of joy at being part of this fantastic culture. David and Liza Jane exited last, but were first to see the procession coming toward them. Ary and Natasha were captivated anew by the domed immensity of Caldera. In the distance, conch shell horns echoed down the valley.

Natasha said, "Well, there goes the element of surprise." She glanced back at Liza Jane and exclaimed, "Look what's coming!"

Ary turned and saw eight white pteros in gold harness waddling in unison toward them surrounding an open white carriage.

CHAPTER NINETEEN

RETURN TO CALDERA
OCTOBER 8, 2034

David and Ary looked at each other and exclaimed with their eyes, what on earth?

Natasha called, "Hello, Wantak!"

One of the two leading pteros raised his wing in greeting and responded, "Welcome back, Natasha!"

The other leading ptero said, "Welcome home Queen Appleton and Prince Andrews!"

"Thanks, Hardaway," Liza Jane answered. "Can you guys handle four of us?"

"We've been practicing," Hardaway assured her. "After you've put on your robes and hats, climb in and we'll show you."

Liza Jane pulled a pile of floral robes from the carriage. Flowers had been woven into floor-length sleeveless garments. There were also hats for the men and headdresses for the women, all of woven flowers. Fragrances billowed around them as they tried to separate the robes.

Natasha delighted in her robe and headdress, she thought no garment could make people look more joyful. The broad-brimmed flower hats, if made of black felt, would have given the men the look of Dutch merchants in a Rembrandt painting. The headdresses were closed on top, tapered outward and leaned back, shaped a bit like Nefertiti's famous Egyptian headdress.

Ary marveled at Natasha's radiance. He was becoming keenly aware of the powerful feelings developing in his heart for this soulful, guileless, beautiful woman. He was looking for the right moment to tell her of these feelings, but knew this wasn't the time. He just smiled at her and helped her up into the carriage. It was made of metal filigree and rolled on tall white wire wheels, everything covered with flowers and flowing white feather decorations. When they were set, the pteros trotted down the granite path leading out of the station with a rhythmic stride that quickened until Hardaway and Wantak opened their wings and pulled hard followed by the other six. When the long harnesses grew taut the carriage left the path and soared slightly below the surrounding pteros.

Natasha clapped and realized her complete lack of fear, "Bravo Wantak! Bravo you guys!"

The others joined in the applause as the pteros climbed up into the vast interior of Mt. Erebus. They flew in formation, two in front, back, and on each side of the carriage, their powerful wings stroking the air in unison.

Liza Jane whispered, "Welcome home, David."

David laughed, "I don't even dream stuff this good."

Liza Jane smiled and hugged his arm.

Natasha put her head on Ary's shoulder and had feelings for him stronger than those she had for Caldera. He put his arm around her shoulders and embraced her. She loved having him caress her. She'd never done anything but role playing, when guys came onto her. She'd never shared real intimacy with a man and had long wondered if she could. Her father had soured her on the motives of male affections.

Liza Jane sensed what was going on and gave her support to the love flowing from Natasha's heart for her wonderful man, like the melting of a frozen stream.

She got David's attention and pointed to pteros coming toward them. As they neared the carriage, the Calderan riders reached into cloth saddlebags and threw handfuls of flowers and called out, "Welcome Home, Queen Appleton and Prince Andrews! Welcome honored guests!"

Liza Jane thanked each by name. Soon, there were ten, then twenty, then thirty pteros with riders jockeying for position to honor their new queen and her soul mate. By the time the lagoon came into view, the carriage was filled, yet the Calderans kept throwing flowers.

Then, the drums started. Dom dom dom, dom dom da dom. Dom dom dom, dom dom da dom. And the conch shell horns. Whooo whouu who whoouu. Whooo whouu who whoouu. The vast caldera resounded. Di di di di di, da da da da da, do do do do do, dm dm dm dm dm. Dom dom da dom. The bumbulating music went on and on with layers of intricate, rolling, tumbling drum solos, like water freshets woven over, around and through the basic melody. Di di di di di, da da da da da, do do do do do, dm dm dm dm dm. Dom dom da dom.

Ary felt tears on his shoulder, put his finger under Natasha's chin, lifted her face and kissed her.

Her heart melted and she wanted to curl up with him someplace warm and dark and private. Then, she sat up, wiped her eyes and drank in the tumultuous celebration with a luminous smile, waving to the wellwishers.

It suddenly dawned on Ary as they approached the village that the earth's truly advanced people didn't use electric technology. In fact, they'd never bothered with electricity at all, except for some form of generated power for supplying light and fresh air inside their mountain home. Instead, in their private lives they focused solely on plugging into the power flowing from the Giver of Life.

The eight pteros delivered the carriage to the village. Complicated drum rhythms continued and pteros were landing everywhere. Snaking conga lines formed with a human leading each line of dancers. Finally, the drum music subsided and the mayor invited everyone to enjoy a feast on the grassy common where a ten-foot-tall smoking construction of palm fronds was being disassembled. Inside, between layers of coals and leaves, were fillets of fish that had been cooking all day. Large glazed vessels were full of soups and vegetables.

Liza Jane and David were seated with their friends on colorful rugs of woven flowers, covered with plates piled with fruit, bread and pastries. The aromatic rugs were spread on the edge of the pond by Lord Appleton's home. Platters were brought from the tall smoking construction, piled high with salad and fish and shellfish.

After dinner came a time of sharing. The Calderans sang to their new queen and prince, gave them dances and heartfelt words. Savana listened from Natasha's lap, then stood and said things everyone enjoyed. Natasha stood with Savana on her hip and said, "My little friend, here, gives me the courage to say a few things to you. My name is Natasha and I join you in wishing Queen Appleton and Prince Andrews great happiness here in Caldera. In two days we start a campaign for peace that we pray will turn the human world away from violence.

"You are the example we need. It's important for us to know that it's possible for people to live in peace. The Lord Jesus, gave us the message; but, as you know, we didn't embrace it like you did. He spoke of being a city on a hill that can't be hid, a candle on a candlestick that gives light to all. You are those things to us, a bright shining example. I thank you from my heart. I'm going into the Queen Mother's campaign carrying a vision of a human world living in peace, like you do here in Caldera. God bless the Calderan people."

The whole assemblage stood as one, cheering and applauding. When they were seated, Liza Jane remained standing and said, "You remember how unsure I was, when I left. I had no idea if my plan had any chance of success. Guess who the first person was that I met in the human world."

"Natasha!" came the answer from hundreds.

"When I woke up that first morning, I found I was living with this being of transcendent goodness and purity. I knew immediately, there was hope for my mission."

Another ovation and loud cheering. Ary applauded too, and as the ovation diminished he kissed Natasha.

Natasha gave him a look of mock astonishment.

"The second human I met was Ary Hussein."

Ary came over and put his arm around Liza Jane to more cheers. "This one, too, was a surprise to me. A lionhearted man like my father who followed his effective prayers from a distant land to find a way to become a leader in our campaign for world peace."

"Through my mother and father you've followed my new soulmate's life," she smiled and extended her hand to David. As he stood the drums started anew, with spontaneous dancing. The celebration went on with Liza Jane and David standing together, their arms around each other.

When the noise died down, she continued, "My father has told you how David stood fast against the forces of violence and revenge, and of his decision to come to Caldera to join me in the Way."

Again, the warm feeling in the gathering was softly voiced around them.

"You know my mother's insight and how she loves this man." That truth was acknowledged all around. "Let's embrace him and support him. I've prayed all my life for a soulmate to love, like my mother loves my father, and I've found him."

More enthusiastic cheers and applause.

At length she continued, "Tonight is our first married night as soulmates and we look forward to being alone together. Thank you for this wonderful wedding party. As we leave, let me teach you a tune and get you to hum it with me."

She went once through the tune of Amazing Grace, then the rich voices of the Calderans took it from there.

Liza Jane whispered in David's ear and they held hands as they made their way across the stepping stones to her father's house. They stood on the porch as the humming turned to Calderan favorites, then they waved goodnight to the village.

The pteros began landing to pick up the guests, while the villagers hummed their old favorites. Natasha and Ary joined Sammi and Halali, with Savana holding on behind Sammi, and they flew across the lagoon and landed on the deck of Liza Jane's home on the rock.

In E.A.'s oversized feather bed, David and Jane gave each other the sweetest gifts of loving their hearts could conjure. At first it felt a bit awkward to both. But soon her shy novice gave way to exquisite touching and kissing, then shuddering warm embraces led to rapturously deep joining. The dawn found them in and out of dozing and loving each other, deeply enjoying the pleasure given and received.

At Halali's suggestion, Sammi set up several mattresses in the main house next to the fire pit, so they could all sleep together. The music and dancing continued into the night in the village.

Savana snuggled next to Natasha who told her a story she loved about Br'er Rabbit, Br'er Bear, Br'er Fox and the Laughing Place. Ary told her one of his favorites from his homeland, How Princess Najika Saved the Lion Prince.

Sammi and Halali curled up together and fell fast asleep.

Natasha's fingers traced the hollows and ridges of Ary's muscular body as they snuggled quietly. His muscles quivered when the touching got too soft, but he enjoyed the sweet caressing. At length, Natasha turned her back and he enveloped her in his arms. They spoke softly and watched the fire go down.

Ary watched the fire dance to the distant drum music. It made Natasha's hair flicker. Tradition marched back and forth in his mind, decrying his feelings for this beautiful dark-skinned Christian woman. He'd never felt the weight of his heritage working so powerfully against him.

After a long silence, she asked, "What are you thinking, Prince Hussein?"

"About the campaign," he lied. "Imagine telling the tribes of the Middle East they have to get along from now on, or else."

"What makes it so hard for them?"

"History and tradition."

"Love is surely more powerful than tradition," mon petite prince.

"I know it is, Natasha."

She turned to him and traced his lips and nose with her finger, until he kissed her. Along with tears and silent revelations, pentup longings were shared by both.

"Will you marry me, Natasha?"

"Are you sure that's what you want?"

"Positive. You're the woman I've been looking for all my life and wondered if I'd ever find."

"I love you with all my heart, Ary. But what about the traditions and your family?"

"I'll love you forever, Natasha. The traditions and my family will never come between us. I promise."

"I'm yours, Ary."

The crowd around St. Johns Park had gotten used to the gold ships coming and going. The smaller silver ship was different enough to attract attention.

Around the five-hundred acre park, over a million people waited. The talk among the huge crowd covered a wide range of speculation. What was going on inside the fence? What kind of campaign were the Calderans planning? What would their role be in the future? Could a peace campaign actually eliminate hatred and terrorism?

Friendships developed as hundreds of thousands arrived on Sunday and Monday. A few shared the invitation they'd received and soon it spread through the tents, their prayers had brought them to Newark. The devout of all religions and denominations had been called. Racial and religious differences fell away as they prayed together and taught each other favorite prayers and hymns around campfires in the night.

Sound trucks lined the curbs with RV's and trailers connected by miles of wire. Nightly news updates showed the spirit of unity developing in the campgrounds around the park. St. Johns Park was the talk of the planet. The gold ships, stairs, and grandstand visible above the fencing became familiar TV images. Reporters told and retold the story of this obscure church in a poor black part of Newark, chosen by the Calderans for the start of the campaign.

Reverend Pettis had installed an automated telephone information service. It welcomed the arriving campaigners and invited them to St. Johns Park on Sunday October 15th at 4PM. Reverend Pettis stayed in his office and prayed nonstop. Whatever was coming, he was determined to be ready.

Liza Jane watched as David brought the ship down on the lawn behind the church, "The ship responds as though you've been flying for years."

David chuckled, "I grew up riding dressage. It thinks a bit like a horse. Look at this place, Jane!" They embraced while they admired General Landon's handiwork. "You can probably tell I'm feeling more comfortable as we go along here."

She kissed him and said, "I love you more each hour."

Ary and Natasha were standing at the windows when they walked in from the bridge. Natasha turned with a teary smile and exclaimed, "Look what they've done, Liza Jane!"

Liza Jane put her arm around Natasha's shoulders, "Give the Calderan engineers a construction project, then, get out of the way. Creating environments like this is their specialty."

They had excavated a tiered bowl several hundred feet deep forming an enormous grass amphitheater. Brooks flowed to a lagoon that surrounded a small stage of gold at the base of the stairs Colonel Braxton had pointed out on the satellite photo. The church had been moved next to the lagoon and refurbished with a coat of white paint and a new black roof. It was dwarfed by the stairway and the curved choir grandstand.

Natasha said to Ary, "A few days ago this was busted streets and funky old houses."

"When do things get started?" Ary asked.

"The gates open at four sharp," Liza Jane answered. "Let's go see how Reverend Pettis is doing. He and General Landon have become great friends."

Inside the church, Natasha called to Reverend Pettis, but got no answer. Then, she heard his big laugh outside the back door of his office and looked through the sidelight, "Come here, Liza Jane," she whispered.

Reverend Pettis and E.A. were out on the lawn sitting in folding chairs. The reverend was dressed in dark slacks, white shirt, red tie and suspenders. General Landon sat on the grass. The three were sharing a long submarine sandwich.

Natasha opened the door and embraced her pastor for a long

moment. Finally, an emotional Robert Pettis removed his glasses and wiped his eyes with a big handkerchief. "The Lord sure works in mysterious ways, doesn't He Natasha?"

"He sure does. Who would have thought St. Johns would be the starting place for a world peace campaign?"

"I've always thought of our church in those terms, but I'm thrilled to have the world thinking that way. Miss Appleton, General Landon tells me this afternoon I get to meet Queen Hamama."

"I can't wait to introduce you to my mother," Liza Jane responded standing in the doorway with David.

"Reverend Pettis," Liza Jane said, "I've been feeling the depth of your prayer. Would you tell us some of the ideas you've been working with to support our campaign?"

"I've been praying with all my might to support the idea that we can drop violence, to know it's possible. If we could ask Jesus what to focus on, I know he'd tell us to take a look at Matthew 5, 6 and 7, his Sermon on the Mount."

Liza Jane nodded, "Ary do you know that sermon?"

He shook his head slightly, "Only of it."

Reverend Pettis smiled at him, "I know it's not part of your religion, Prince Hussein. Most people that call themselves Christians don't really know it either." He chuckled, "And those that think they know it, mostly don't. I've always seen it as God's plan, how he wants us to live. The map to eternal life."

"I'm thrilled to have you involved in our campaign, Reverend," Liza Jane said. "How would you paraphrase that sermon?"

He paused then said, "Love your enemies, love them that hurt you, love people that kidnap you, and love terrorists that blow up cities."

"We've got a tough job on our hands, don't we?" Ary said.

Reverend Pettis' big laugh agreed, "Humans sure haven't bought it, have we, Natasha. I've been teaching it for thirty years and get along fine, until I get to the 'turn the other cheek' part. Then, come the blank stares. People are sure that's the dumbest strategy ever."

"But Reverend," Liza Jane asked, "wasn't Jesus able to prove the power of his message?"

"Of course he did! He let his enemies murder him; then, walked out of his tomb to prove what he'd been teaching. Then he left."

"How does a miracle like that relate to us, though?" Ary asked earnestly.

"That's quite a question, Ary, coming from you," Liza Jane responded.

Ary stared at her, taken aback, "I thought so," he said quietly. "I died the other night, didn't I? Sammi brought me back to life."

"Yes. Sammi brought you back to us."

"Wow! You lead quite a life, Miss Appleton," Reverend Pettis exclaimed, "but like Ary said, the way Jesus worked seems miraculous to most people, almost irrelevant. They don't see that what he did could work for them. After a nuclear attack, for instance, to love those who did such a thing and turn the other cheek. It seems ridiculous. Just ask that man standing next to you. People can't see how such a message could give them power."

"Is that what we have to do to make this campaign work?" Ary asked.

"We need to show people how to align themselves with the Giver of Life's power," E.A. responded. "That's all it takes. When the power of Love is brought to bear, there are no more nuclear explosions, in the same way that darkness vanishes in the presence of light."

General Landon stood and said, "Your Majesty, it's time."

Liza Jane smiled broadly, "Open the park, Godfather."

The general marched back up the aisle to his command post in the front of the church. At precisely four o'clock the gates slowly started opening and revealed the world's largest amphitheater. The campaigners saw, beyond the lagoon, the hundred-foot-tall golden stairway and a choir of two thousand children in their places on the grandstand. Next to the stage was the small white church across a golden bridge spanning the lagoon.

Above the expanse of undulating grass were ten gold ships, stationary at two hundred feet above the sloping ground. At an unseen signal they turned, as one, to show their round bases to the oncoming crowd. The bases were a hundred feet in diameter. When they stopped, the New York Philharmonic began playing Handel's Messiah. Then, the children's choir joined in singing the words to Handel's music. As the campaigners had promised, there was no rushing, no discourtesy, no jostling for position. Hundreds with physical problems, blind, elderly and disabled were helped to their places. All the thousands walked calmly to the farthest extremity available and squeezed together to make sure everyone got a seat.

E.A., David, Liza Jane, Reverend Pettis, Natasha and Ary stood at the front windows of the church, watching the campaigners arrive.

"One of the largest crowds ever assembled, Reverend," David said quietly.

"How many watching on TV do you figure, Mr. President?"

"Probably close to five billion around the world."

"Just think," the reverend said. "What's the program, Your Majesty? Is this when we meet your mother?"

"Not yet. You need to go out there and welcome your guests."

Robert Pettis stared incredulously at her and after a long pause asked, "Me?"

"This is your church, Reverend," she smiled.

A tear started making its way down his face. Then, like a thrown switch, his big smile broke through, "What should I say? How will they hear?"

Liza Jane said, "Reverend Robert, there's no human more

prepared for this moment than you. Just welcome them. They've come to St. Johns. They'll hear."

The Reverend looked up at David as he found his handkerchief, "You sure this isn't your job, Mr. President?"

Andrews smiled and shook his head, "We've all come to your church, Reverend."

Liza Jane added, "After the reverend's welcome, Natasha, would you sing our hymn?"

"I had a feeling," Natasha said, "Sure. I'd love to."

"Okay then, let's get started," the reverend said. He tightened his red tie, put on his suit coat, and walked out the front door with a big white handkerchief in his hand.

When the crowd saw the lone figure approaching the stage, a hush started down front and worked its way through the crowd. Everyone got seated and strained to hear if he was saying anything.

Natasha nudged Liza Jane and pointed to the front row at the edge of the lagoon, across from the stage. There, rocking back and forth to the music was her beaming mother, with Julian and Ed. Behind them was Duke Sims and his crew.

Liza Jane smiled and whispered, "A just reward for all their work. Julian and Ed have hardly stopped working for ten days and nights."

Then, Natasha pointed out Cooksey on the end of the bottom row of the golden grandstand.

Suddenly, the bases of the ten ships lit up into gigantic high resolution screens, showing Reverend Pettis step onto the stage. With his thousand-watt smile and warm manner he said, "Welcome peace campaigners!" The ten ships transmitted his tone, inflection and volume perfectly to the three million.

The most applause ever heard on earth tumbled down across the lagoon and wrapped around the reverend and those in the church.

He introduced himself and continued, "Welcome to St. Johns Park and the start of the Campaign for World Peace."

The distant backdrop, beyond the golden stairway was a mass of towering thunderheads, churning up to forty thousand feet. Distant rumblings of thunder and flashes of lightning in the dark clouds shot here and there.

Reverend Pettis took notice, "Looks like our future, doesn't it? Storms on the horizon. I've come to tell you the purpose of this campaign is to prove that we have the power to dispel storms."

More waves of applause and shouts of agreement poured down to the stage.

"Let's start with a prayer. Let's turn our hearts to God, our power. Our Father." Millions of voices joined in with the reverend and huge lighted words appeared on the ten ship bases, "Which art in heaven. Hallowed be thy name." The words of the millions at prayer were so massive, they moved billions to join in, as they watched on TV around the world. The reverend wiped his eyes, breathed deeply, and continued, "Thy kingdom come. Thy will be done on earth, as it is in heaven." At that, a flash lit up the dark clouds and a huge bolt sent fingers snaking to the ground. Then, an enormous clap of thunder rolled across the crowd from the clouds moving closer to St. Johns. When he could, the reverend continued, "Give us this day our daily bread. And forgive us our trespasses, as we forgive those who trespass against us. And lead us not into temptation, but deliver us from evil. For Thine is the kingdom, and the power, and the glory, forever. Amen."

At that, dozens of multi-legged lightning bolts slashed down the sky with booming blasts of thunder.

"Whoee!" The reverend exclaimed, "Do you think we're working alone out here in this campaign?"

"No!" came the enormous response.

"Do you think this is some kind of small-time campaign?"

"No, Preacher!"

"I don't think so, either. We're being called on to do something important. What is it we're being called on to do? What's the key word of this campaign?"

"Change!" was the massive response as the word appeared on all the screens.

"A long time ago, an English ship captain was called on to change. You may have heard of him. He'd spent his career hauling captured, shackled black slaves crammed down in the hold of his ship from Africa to the New World. One day he saw the light. He saw the evil of what he'd been doing and devoted the rest of his life to serving God.

"John Newton was his name and he wrote the hymn that will be one of the themes of our campaign. Let's give a big hand to Natasha Cheatam and our children's choir, and ask them to sing John Newton's hymn about changing. Natasha Cheatam, singing Amazing Grace."

Natasha turned to Ary who embraced and kissed her, then whispered, "Knock'em dead, Darling."

Natasha could feel the applause inside her as she crossed the bridge onto the stage. Robert Pettis embraced her, waved to the people and headed back to the church.

"How about a big 'thank you' for Reverend Pettis!" Natasha said and pointed at the retreating figure.

Robert turned back and acknowledged the ovation, waving his handkerchief, then shaking his head and wiping his eyes, walked back to the church midst the thunderous applause.

Natasha's smile lit up the screens, "God bless our Campaign for World Peace!" she exclaimed, "and God bless St. Johns."

The clouds had stopped moving. The sun was coloring the massive clouds as they churned, creating a breathtaking forty-thousand-foot backdrop behind St. Johns Park.

She said softly, but was heard by all, "This is a big moment for me . . . for all of us . . . isn't it?"

"Yes!" came the enormous response.

"I want you to meet the people, besides Reverend Pettis, responsible for me standing here. Would you thank, with me my mother, Margaret Cheatam, down here in front." The applause started and Margaret shook her head and her right hand emphatically at her daughter. "She's a little shy, you'll have to work on her a bit." Finally, Margaret stood, smiled shyly, and waved to the crowd. Her beautiful face lit up the screens and the applause poured down for her.

Natasha continued, "Those two young men with her are my brothers Julian and Ed, who many of you have gotten to know these past ten days." The applause continued as the screens went from one to the other. Ed looked at her and tried to get her to correct her mistake, but she just smiled at him and applauded. "And my little brother, Cooksey," she turned and pointed at him in the choir.

Cooksey waved and smiled.

"Also, my best friend and the person, along with her mother, responsible for this campaign, Her Majesty, Queen Liza Jane Appleton of Caldera and her new husband, former President David Andrews." Liza Jane and David stepped from the front door of the church, smiled and waved. "The queen's father, Lord Ernest Appleton of Caldera, formerly of Boston, Massachusetts. And last, but certainly not least, my fiancé, Crown Prince Ary Hussein of Jordan."

Ary gulped, stepped out and waved. His parents and grandmother in a palace far away, looked at each other and shared tears of joy for their son whose prayers had landed him in the middle of the Campaign for World Peace. At the same time their eyes acknowledged the jolt of Natasha's color and religion.

Through a sudden break in the clouds, burst a dazzling display of golden rays, surrounded by breathtaking color.

"The first time through, I'll ask our choir to hum my accompaniment, then I'll get you to help me out. You feel like doing some singing?"

"Yes, Natasha!" said the millions.

"I thought you would," she smiled and motioned to the choir director and sang.

Amazing grace, how sweet the sound
That saved a wretch like me.
I once was lost, but now am found
Was blind, but now I see.

T'was grace that taught my heart to fear
And grace my fears relieved.
How precious did that grace appear
The hour I first believed.

Through many dangers, toils and snares
I have already come.
Tis grace hath brought me safe thus far
And grace will lead me home.

"Thank you," she turned to the choir and applauded and was joined by a flood of appreciation.

She motioned for quiet, then said, "Now it's your turn. Let me accompany you. Choir would you lead our audience?"

The choir began and the audience joined in singing the words on the screens. Over the millions of voices, the ships picked up Natasha's soaring humming accompaniment. Her harmonies danced with the music and thrilled hearts around the world.

In the third verse, the volume began to dwindle, as more and more of the singers saw what was happening beyond the golden stairs. The light of the sun's rays coming through the opening in the sunset had formed a long pathway of light.

CHAPTER TWENTY

THE CAMPAIGN FOR WORLD PEACE
OCTOBER 15, 2034

N atasha saw the crowd staring into the distance and turned. By squinting, she could see tiny figures coming down a glistening light path. She smiled, turned back to the crowd and said, "Let's hum our hymn as we wait to welcome our new friends. The Calderan people are coming to St. Johns Park to begin our Campaign for World Peace."

No one could take their eyes from the spiritual beings walking down the long pathway of light coming out of the sunset. David trembled as he squinted into the light, his left arm around Liza Jane's waist he whispered to her, "I love your mother for doing this."

"It's her gift to your world, David."

With his right hand on Robert Pettis' left shoulder, David whispered to him, "What an entrance! Do these people know how to get our attention, or what?"

Reverend Pettis took a big shuddering breath and let it out, "They must be full of love, is all I can figure."

Distant music became audible. They were walking in cadence holding hands and swinging their arms to joyful distant drum music. The music increased in volume, as the oncoming figures got closer, riffs that sparkled with percussion virtuosity.

Natasha walked back across the bridge to the church and stood encircled in Ary's arms, watching with her friends out on the lawn.

Ary said softly, "You were terrific! I've wondered all along, if we were kidding ourselves with this campaign, but I'm through doubting."

Natasha shook her head slowly without looking away from the magical procession, "No more doubting."

When the light walkers reached the pad at the top of the golden staircase they stopped. Then, two of the radiant beings continued down the stairs holding hands, a small female and a tall well-built bearded human man with long hair to his shoulders wearing a loose fitting robe. Both of them seemed to be made of light.

Without diverting his eyes, David told the preacher, "That's her, Robert. That's Liza Jane's mother. Who's that with her?"

Liza Jane glanced up at him and smiled.

The hundred, or so, small radiant male and female beings on the landing looked around at St. Johns Park, enjoying the scene below. They spoke and laughed among themselves; then, one pointed at Liza Jane and waved. Liza Jane got her father's attention and they waved back.

When the couple reached the bottom of the stairs, they walked across the water onto the stage. Liza Jane panned across thousands of faces staring breathlessly. Many wept. Some embraced joyously. A few had fainted and were being attended by those around them. Most, calmly let the realization sink in of what was unfolding before them.

Natasha glanced at Margaret. The warm light of the sunset made her tear streaked face glow. She had a calm happy expression. Julian was pointing at Hamama and whispering behind his hand to Ed Berry.

Reverend Pettis mumbled, "Could it possibly be?"

The thunderheads, now pressing the park, let loose with hundreds of dazzling lightning bolts. Thunder blasts shook the park. At length, the bearded light figure turned to the thunderheads and raised his hands. The lightning stopped and the thunder rolled away into the distance.

One of the TV cameramen on an elevated platform trembled at the images he was capturing in his camera. His chest seized up, intense pain shot through him, up and down his arms. Then he collapsed, falling with a resounding crash onto the audio equipment piled below the scaffolding.

The man at center stage heard the crash and the ten screens zoomed in on his expression. His eyes showed deep concern for the fallen cameraman. He pointed at the empty platform and said, "The man who fell, bring him down front here, to me."

Members of the television crew picked up their unconscious comrade and started making their way down to the front. People moved right and left to let them pass.

The man on stage smiled, opened his arms, and said to the crowd, "It's good to be back. I hear you've had a good look at the end of the eye-for-an-eye road, and need a refresher course in my Father's message about loving one another."

The screens beamed his generous smile and twinkling eyes to the astounded millions.

"Nice crowd, Hamama."

The silence was total. Natasha wept against Ary's shoulder, watching. David smiled his broadest and put his long arm around the reverend's trembling shoulders. Silent sobs racked Robert Pettis' thick chest.

"You've probably figured out who I am," the man said. "Let me introduce this person standing next to me. Do these people know who you are, Hamama?"

The screens panned to her small glowing countenance. She replied softly, "No, my Lord."

"She calls me that, because she works for me," the man said, grinning. "You can call me, Jesus, my human name. This is Her Majesty, Hamama, Queen Mother of the Calderan people, your neighbors and my close friends and working associates through the ages."

Tentative applause was heard here and there.

"Come now!" the man said. "This Campaign for World Peace and my return to your planet for this campaign were her idea. She's done all this for you."

At that, the roar of applause eclipsed any sound ever made by human hands.

"These people," he turned toward the group on the landing, "are some of the Calderans that have been my support group through the ages. They help me bring God's message to planets like yours throughout the universe." He turned back toward the people watching from the stair landing and asked, "Which of you said you were part of my support group, when I brought the message to earth?"

Two of the male shining figures raised their hands, stepped forward and waved, a gesture met with warm applause.

Jesus continued, "Unfortunately, they've got to get back to their assignments, but they wanted to come with me and wish you well on your campaign for peace on earth."

He said to the small figures, "I'll see you in a few earth months. If I need your help, I'll call."

At that, the small creatures slowly disappeared, smiling and waving to the campaigners. The crowd waved goodbye. The hole in the sunset had closed and the light pathway was gone, but the fading sunset was still monumental shades of reds, pinks and golds in towering cumulonimbus clouds. Ten more gold ships suddenly appeared, providing lighting from their bases as the sun went down.

Jesus looked around and said, "Didn't the Calderan engineers do a great job here?"

As the applause rolled in, Jesus applauded, as well, "Hamama, have they met General Landon?"

"No, Lordship," Hamama replied, "I thought he might confuse them. The only Calderans the humans have seen so far have been human-looking, like my husband and daughter, or non-material ones like me and your support group."

"The general probably will confuse people," Jesus chuckled, "but after all, he and his people built this place and we ought to thank him. Lord Appleton, would you ask the general to take a bow."

The applause was heavy until General Landon emerged from the double doors at the front of the church, then it dwindled considerably. The light figures were surprising to the humans, but this flesh and bones Calderan male was even more so.

Jesus said, "This is the commander of the corps of engineers that built this park. His people are providing the large screens, the sound production and lighting; so, let's hear it for General Landon and his troops."

The ovation was modest as the humans stared at the small well-built cat-like person pictured on the ten screens.

Jesus interrupted and said, "Come on people. You need to do better than that. We're counting on the general for the success of our campaign." At that, the applause grew. General Landon came to attention and bowed to the campaigners.

"Over the next three months you'll get accustomed to the Calderan engineers and their marvels. General, what's the next stop for our campaign?"

Landon's voice boomed at first. The ten screens zoomed in on his head and shoulders and the crowd studied him in amazement as he answered, "Last night, Lord Jesus, we got the go-ahead from President Vandenberg to build Peace Park #2 in what was downtown Houston."

Jesus turned back to the millions, "Can you come with us to Houston?"

"Yes!" came the unanimous booming reply.

"What about the radiation contamination, General?"

"We're building an amphitheater for ten million there that will be ready in two weeks. The radiation has been eliminated."

"How will we get there?" he asked.

"President Vandenberg is providing fifty thousand buses. My people will furnish the food, shelter and fuel and we're planning rallies in each town along the three routes we'll take, through the North, Midwest, and the Southeast. Thousands of additional buses are being gathered along the route."

"Where to from there, General?"

"We also got approval to build a Peace Park in Kansas City for twenty-five million, that we'll have ready in four weeks and another on the central coast of California for fifty million, that'll be completed in six weeks."

At that point the four men carrying the unconscious cameraman stood holding him next to Margaret and the boys.

Jesus said, "Would you people make some room, so they can lay him on the grass?" When they'd laid their comrade down, Jesus thanked them and they went back to work.

"Our cameraman's had a heart attack, some broken bones and internal injuries. Is there a healer in the house?"

After an uncomfortable silence, midst embarrassed laughter, someone called out, "You heal him."

"Thank you, I may have to. No healers, out of these millions?"

There was another long awkward silence. Finally, he turned and said, "I see what you mean, Hamama. No one?" Again, he waited. At length, several down front pointed toward the church. Jesus turned and saw Robert Pettis walking toward the bridge.

"Are you a healer, sir?" Jesus asked.

"A modest one, Your Lordship."

"He calls me that, because he works for me, too," Jesus said smiling. "Come here, Robert. Have you folks met Reverend Pettis?" The ovation was instant. "This is your church, isn't it, Robert?"

He nodded and said, "Yes Lord, I'm the preacher here."

As Robert walked onto the stage, Jesus opened his arms and embraced the stocky black preacher and patted his back as Robert struggled to keep from breaking down. They stood together embracing. "Robert's a little touched, finally meeting his boss in person," Jesus told the crowd, "I'm touched too, finally meeting you, my good and trusted worker."

As Robert got his emotions under control, Jesus went on, "You folks should take note of this man. By the end of the campaign, when I ask for a healer you need to stand up and come to my aid, like he just did. We're going to need millions of healers and each of you needs to be one of them."

"Can you walk over there and heal that man, Robert?"

"Across the water?"

"Yes."

"No, sir, I can't."

"Okay, you walk around and I'll meet you over there. But, before this campaign's over, Robert, that answer needs to be, 'Yes sir, I can.'"

While he waited for Robert, Jesus knelt by the unconscious man and wiped the grass and blood from his forehead. Margaret was three feet away and feeling lightheaded, but fought through her dizziness. He obviously wasn't made of flesh and bones, but she could see the scar tissue on his hands. A tear made its way around her plump cheek. It struck her, how kind it was for God to send his message in the form of this spiritualized man kneeling next to her. She could feel his tender love for the injured man as Reverend Pettis joined him, kneeling on the other side of the unconscious cameraman.

Jesus looked at Robert's serious face, "Heal him, Reverend. I'll support you."

"It helps me to put my hand on him."

"That's fine."

Robert put his dark hand on the man's forehead, bowed his head and closed his eyes. His thought went back to his experience with the deacons, healing that sick woman years ago. He knew God would heal His beloved child, lying here on the grass and he felt the strong support of God's son kneeling next to him. His prayer engaged naturally, like strong gears, from forty years of practice.

Inside his eyes there was a sudden radiance and he could sense the healing taking place in the cameraman. When he opened his eyes, Jesus was smiling at him and the cameraman was regaining consciousness. The crowd watched on the screens and a great cheer went up as Robert helped the cameraman to his feet.

Sensing what had taken place, the man smiled and waved to the millions who responded with applause.

Jesus said at length, "Do you feel up to going back to work?" he asked the man.

"Yes, sir. Thanks for fixing me up."

"Thank the preacher here," Jesus said, putting his arm around Robert's shoulders.

The cameraman nodded and shook Robert's hand, then began making his way through the crowd, shaking hands, giving high fives, and putting his hand on shoulders along the way.

Jesus continued, all the while beaming at Robert, "See what happens when a pure heart makes contact with God? Our Father does the work. He's the power that runs the universe and He will answer a pure-hearted prayer.

"During the next weeks I'll re-teach you my message. It's simple. I know you'll get it this time. While we're at it, I'll teach you to heal. When we get your thought aligned with your Father's, you'll be able to access His power and these problems you're facing, that seem so difficult, will yield. What time is it, Robert?"

"Six o'clock, my Lord."

"General Landon, what have we got for dinner?"

"Pizza, your Lordship, the trucks are here."

"Let's eat," Jesus said, "We need to clear the road around the outside of the amphitheater and we need a thousand volunteers or so, to unload the trucks, please."

A hundred delivery trucks entered the park and alternately turned left and right to make their way slowly around the perimeter of the crowd.

Jesus inquired, "Where did the food come from?"

"Pizza Hut, Lordship. In covered baskets as Hamama requested."

"Help yourselves," Jesus said. "Reach under the cloth cover into the basket and take a piece, but don't look under the cover."

As the trucks were unloaded, the large wicker picnic baskets were passed toward the middle. Thousands of pieces were taken from each basket along the way, but they never got lighter. When a basket reached the front, Jesus took a slice and handed one to Robert. "When they meet, pass them back to the outside and take another slice. Then, we'll load them back in the trucks. The drinks have been donated by the Coca Cola Company and they'll follow the baskets.

"Hamama, her family, and I will join you in your prayers and hymns tonight after we have a planning meeting. In the morning we'll start the teaching. We've got six weeks to turn you into healers and teachers. When we leave Central California, the Calderans will take you to every corner of the planet to teach the message to the rest of the world."

While the campaigners ate, Jesus asked the general, "What else do we need to tell them about tomorrow and about our departure next week?"

"These twenty ships will stay with us and we'll communicate through them. Our breakfast meal will be served here from 7 AM until 9 AM. McDonalds has donated ten thousand baskets of Egg McMuffins plus coffee, orange juice, and hot chocolate. Next week we'll split up into three caravans. The Queen Mother will head up the first, Lord Appleton the second, and Queen Liza Jane Appleton and Prince Andrews will lead the third."

"Thank you. Can you give us a report on the terrorists and the bombs?"

"Yes, Lordship. The terrorists are either deceased or captured. The five bombs they purchased have all been detonated and the source of their bombs destroyed. Their threat has ended."

A tremendous cheer erupted and a standing ovation that went on and on.

When he could, Jesus said, "I've invited General Samir al Hammabi, the reformed leader of the terrorists, to join our campaign and help the people of the Middle East countries to understand what he's learned about the survival of your species.

"I must tell you that I have no other message than the one I gave your forefathers. The metaphors will change, I'll probably use cars and software, instead of wheat and sheep, but there's only one message. Pure love connects you with the power that runs the universe. When you're filled with God's love, you have access to the power you need to solve any problem. You only need an absolute faith that all things are possible to God, a spiritual understanding of Him, and an unselfed love. Doesn't sound so hard, does it?

"Your neighbors, the Calderan people, got the same message, thoroughly embraced it, and have become some of the most powerful people in the universe. Hamama's husband, Lord Appleton, proved that a modern human could align his consciousness with the Father and access His power. That's what we're going to concentrate on for the next ninety days. Are you willing to change?" he asked.

An enormous "Yes!" resounded and echoed into the distance.

"Are you ready to learn to live the power of Love?"

Another massive "Yes!" thundered down to the stage.

Jesus' smile lit up the screens and he turned to the small group at the front of the church and motioned for them to join him on the stage, "Okay. In the morning we'll get started learning to live the power of God's love and I'll see you later this evening."

Liza Jane took hold of David's and Natasha's hands and Natasha grabbed Ary's and E.A.'s as they walked across the golden bridge to join Jesus, Hamama, Reverend Pettis, and General Landon. The children's choir began the Hallelujah Chorus from Handel's Messiah accompanied by the orchestra, as the millions began making their way out of the great amphitheater.

Jesus turned to Landon and asked, "General, can you make room for this group in your ship tonight? We need to get to know each other and start planning our campaign."

"It would be my honor, Lord Jesus. Come with me."

E.A. joined Hamama, Reverend Pettis, and Jesus walking behind the general toward his ship parked on the grass behind the church. David, Liza Jane, Ary, and Natasha put their arms around each other and the four of them looked up at their beaming faces projected on the bases of the golden ships as they headed for their first planning meeting of the campaign.

David looked at his wife and said, "Can it get any better than this? Seems like life can only go downhill from here."

Liza Jane answered, "Do you really believe that?"

"No," he chuckled, "I just wanted to hear you say that. This campaign is actually going to work, isn't it?"

She smiled and nodded, "I think so."

He stopped, took her in his arms, and kissed her long and sweet, to massive applause from those still exiting the park and watching their kiss on the big screens.

Finally, David and Liza Jane turned to the millions and waved while they applauded.

"Better than this?" he whispered as he waved.

"Darling," she whispered, "we're just getting warmed up."

The End